STALE TALES

STALE TALES

Amador Amado

ISBN: 979-8-9876421-6-0

Thank you, Alicia Cole, for creating the stunning book covers!

TABLE OF CONTENTS

Chapter 1	Camp-Down.	1
Chapter 2	Trick or Retreat.	20
Chapter 3	Last- Stop.	35
Chapter 4	Consuelo.	50
Chapter 5	A Taste for Waste.	66
Chapter 6	Cold Adam.	83
Chapter 7	Chuckles.	97
Chapter 8	Baiting Site.	114
Chapter 9	Demonic Fertility.	133
Chapter 10	Upon Evil Soil.	145
Chapter 11	The Gila Killa.	165
Chapter 12	Anna's Karma.	188
Chapter 13	The Hunt.	208
Chapter 14	The Cenotaph.	224
Chapter 15	Writer's Block.	243
Chapter 16	Deadly Delivery.	264
Chapter 17	The Cursed Treasure.	285
Chapter 18	The Kilt.	299
Chapter 19	The End of the World.	316

CHAPTER 1
CAMP-DOWN.

The plan was in motion, Charles was to pick up his pal Derick first. He pulled up to the front of his home and honked. Derrick had lost track of time and wasn't completely ready. He received a phone call from Charles reminding him of the agenda. Derrick replied, "Shit! My bad bro. Let me finish getting my stuff and I'll be out in a jiff."

Charles told him, "Damn, well try to hurry up because I don't want to get there when it's dark bro."

Derrick answered, "Don't worry, we'll get there with enough sunlight to set up.

I'm almost done, I just need to pack a few more things."

Charles responded, "I'll be outside then. Don't take too long," and hung up.

As Derrick was occupied with his task, Charles was texting his girlfriend, Desiree. She was concerned as to why he was late to retrieve her from her residence. Charles informed her of the reason behind his delay. She texted, "Why did you even invite him if you know I don't like him? I told you it should just be us two getting away for the weekend. Anyhow, I'm already packed and ready to go. I'll see you when you get here."

Charles wrote back, "I'm sorry baby. I promise I'll make it up to you. We're going to have so much fun out there, you'll see. See you in a bit. I'm going to hurry him up." To which she didn't reply.

Charles then opened up one of his social media applications and entertained himself with some comedy videos. He was preoccupied laughing at a guy who was an aspiring singer but sang like shit. Charles was chuckling when he heard a thud on the roof of his SUV. He dropped his phone which fell to the ground- right next to his foot. Derrick had tossed his canoe over the roof rails and began securing it with ratchet strap tie downs. Charles bent down to grab his phone without being able to see. He swerved his hand blindly on the floor mat feeling for his device. Derrick was laughing at him since he knew he had gotten startled. He finished tying his canoe and stepped inside the vehicle. Charles told him, "You fucking asshole. You almost made me shard my trousers. Desiree is fucking pissed at me because you're making me run fucking late." As he checked the time on his cell phone.

Derrick uttered, "Ha, ha, ha. I didn't know you scared easily buddy. And about your girl, I was the one with the idea to go out there in the first place. Maybe you should stop letting her control you so much and grab your balls back from her grasp."

Charles commented, "Shut up fuck face and buckle up."

"Stop by Renee's first before you pick up your slave master." Commented Derrick. Charles replied, "Slave master? You're the one who told me to hook up with her." "Hook up, not keep her." Stated Derrick.

A few minutes later, they arrived at Renee's dwelling. She was standing outside waiting for them, packed and ready to head out. She walked up to the vehicle as Derrick got out and grabbed her things after giving her a kiss on her lips. She got in the back seat and Derrick opened the rear tailgate. He tossed her things inside as she yelled, "Be careful with my bag! I have some fragile stuff in there." She was somewhat upset.

Derrick shut the tailgate and hopped back in the passenger seat. He uttered, "I bet they're not as fragile as Charles' heart." As Charles drove off.

Charles punched him on the shoulder and replied, "Fuck you D. I'm not as sensitive as you. Remember that time you cried for days because your ex broke up with you?"

Derrick mentioned, "I cried because she kept my fucking game console bro not because of her. Bitch never returned it either. I had to work overtime just to buy myself a replacement." They both laughed.

Renee inquired, "So that story was true? I always thought you had made it up just to make me laugh and earn some points to get in my pants."

Charles informed her, "Yeah, he's not lying about that. It really did happen."

It took them about ten minutes to get to Desirre's house. She was inside saying bye to her parents. They told her to be safe out there and if she needed anything to call them. She hugged them both and grabbed her bag- which was bigger than the others.

She walked out of her house looking like she was headed to a job interview. Weaning some black slacks, black high heel shoes and a white long sleeve button up shirt. Derrick uttered, "Where the fuck does she think she's going? Hasn't she ever gone camping before?" As she walked up to the SUV while Renee giggled.

Charles got out and ran to get her bag. He also waved at her parents who were standing by the front door. He put her stuff in the back of his ride and then had to open the door for her since she stood next to it without getting in herself. After he opened the door for her and she got in; he jumped back in the driver's seat and darted out of town. Renee had greeted Desiree and they began discussing their trip. Derrick didn't even turn around to acknowledge her. Renee told Desiree, "I like your outfit but don't you think you're a little bit overdressed for the occasion?"

Desiree replied, "Girl, a woman could never be overdressed for any occasion. By the way, have you been there before? Charles tells me there's a water hole and a waterfall. It's supposed to be very romantic or something."

Renee answered, "No, I've never been there but Derrick says someone told him about this hidden oasis. He googled it and showed me pictures which looked very pleasant."

"Oh." Responded Desiree.

The trip had an average of seven hours driving time before getting to their intended destination. During the drive, the girls chatted about multiple subjects as Charles listened to music and Derrick took a nap. When they had approximately thirty minutes left, Charles pulled over to fill up his SUV. Derrick woke up and went inside the store to grab some alcohol and rolling papers. The clerk seemed odd, weird and unfriendly. He didn't greet Derrick as he walked in or up to the register. He just scanned the merchandise and gave him his total. Derrick paid and left as the clerk stared at him. Derrick got back in the vehicle after placing a thirty pack in the cooler as Charles asked him, "What you buy, some extra small condoms?"

Derrick replied, "Ha, ha, very funny. If I did, they'd be for you buddy not for me.

I'm a deep penetrator and not just a surface flesh wound inflicter like you."

Charles smiled and walked back to the pump to remove the nozzle. He looked over at the clerk inside and observed his eerie gaze, looking directly at him. He got back inside the SUV and asked Derrick, "Did you do something to the employee inside D? He looks fucking disturbed."

Derrick responded, "Nah, that fucking guy didn't even say a word to me other than, it'll be twenty with sixty-four cents. Dude's just a small-town fried brain." They drove away staring back at the awkward guy while Derrick flipped him off.

Moments later they had arrived at their destination. Good thing Charles SUV had off road capability since the dirt road leading to the campground was rugged and muddy. Desiree jumped out and began filming herself with the waterfall in the background. She was obsessed with social media validation. Too bad for her, they had no signal to post anything at the spot.

Derrick ran out, removing his clothes as he got to the water hole. He jumped in and shouted after entering, "It's pretty cold! But I like it." He swam towards the waterfall and saw a steady stream on the side which formed another waterfall heading down into a river.

Charles began taking out all their things and assembled his large tent. Renne walked over to the edge of the water hole to look at her boyfriend having fun. He told her, "Take off your clothes and get in here baby."

Renee uttered, "Let me grab my goggles. I want to see if I find any shells at the bottom."

He stated, "Can you bring me a beer while you're at it?"

Renee ran over to the SUV and got her bag. She took off her clothes and grabbed her goggles. She wore her bathing suit under her casual wear. She then put her linens on top of her bag and walked to the back of the ride to get a beer from the cooler. After-wards, she went to take a dip in the water. Desiree was filming them inside the waterhole- enjoying the moment. She then walked back to where Charles was and asked, "Can you cover me while I change into my bathing suit?"

Charles had finished setting up the tent and was about to set up the grill but paused to attend his girl. He let her inside the tent and covered her as she changed. He tried getting some sexual healing but she pushed him away. She then strolled out and sat at the edge of the water. Charles began cooking up some steaks and baking potatoes for them to eat after the dip. Derrick was drinking his beer and holding his woman in his arms. Desiree was jealous her man wasn't in there with her too and looked back at him. He smiled at her, she just smirked and turned back to look at Derrick and Renne. She got in the pool and screamed, "It's way too cold!"

Derrick laughed at her and followed Renee as she snorkelled on the surface hunting shells. He poked her butt and she jumped up, gasping for air. They both laughed as Derrick swam away and allowed her to continue her underwater search. Derrick spotted something shiny on the other side of the water hole. He exited the pool and walked over to investigate. He stumbled upon an abandoned campsite. The shiny object reflecting in the sun was an unopened beer can. "Great." He uttered as he began to locate more unopened cans. Derrick gathered the beer and shouted, "I found a treasure over here guys, come take a look!"

Renee and Desiree got out of the pool and headed over to his location. They began to search around and found more unused items left behind. Desiree picked up a bottle of wine and Renee a wine opener. Countless objects were dispersed surrounding a burned-out flame. Renee questioned, "Who do you guys think left this behind and why?"

Derrick replied, "Who cares honey, free booze is free booze."

Desiree commented, "What if something bad happened and they left this here while running for their lives?"

Derrick stated, "Clearly you've seen way too many horror films to contemplate such a hypothesis."

Renee responded, "What if she's right? I mean no one in their right mind would bring these things out here to leave them behind."

"What if it was a couple who got in a fight and they just took off or they had an emergency where they had to depart in a hurry? There can be countless possibilities other than the worst-case scenario. Anyhow, y'all can stay here playing detective while I take these bad boys to the cooler for later." Commented Derrick as he walked over to their campsite and the girls followed.

Charles saw them heading his way and figured Derick was going to take over the grill so he could take a dip in the pool. As

Derrick came closer, he shared the news with him. Charles was curious as to who and why did someone abandon their brew. The ladies came right after with the bottle of wine and wine opener. They explained their theory to Charles but he too didn't buy it. He instead grabbed a beer and flipped over the steaks he was grilling. He then asked Derrick, "Would you mind taking over so I can take a dip to cool off?"

Derrick answered, "Sure, what else are you cooking?"

Charles replied, "There's a couple more steaks in the cooler and the potatoes are baking near the flame. The seasoning is right here just don't add too much of it. I don't like it tasting too salty."

Derrick took over the grill as he grabbed himself a chair to sit down in and drink another beer. Charles took off his clothes and bolted straight into the water hole. He jumped inside and swam over to the waterfall. Desiree had grabbed her phone again and resumed her recordings. Renee stayed behind with Derrick and rolled him a joint to smoke. When the food was ready, they ate and gathered around the grill which was just a grill top sitting above some stones that were already there. So inevitably it served as a campfire as its second function. The sun began to set as they all drank some booze and chattered about their lives. They passed a joint around and drank, laughing and having a good time. Renee asked Charles, "Did you bring stuff to make smores by any chance?"

He answered, "I sure did. Let me go get them from the SUV."

He returned momentarily and handed each of them a metal stick with a rubber grip at one end and two prongs at the other. He then passed out some marshmallows and displayed the chocolate bars so they'd know where to find them. They began making smores and continued congregating joyfully. Life in the city had been forgotten and they attuned to nature. Desiree yelled, "Ah!" As she viewed a skunk nearby. "Get it away from here." She ordered Charles.

Charles shooed the creature away. He tried to console her but she shoved him away, complaining of the wildlife around them.

Renee and Derick looked at each other, smooching and giggling. Renee asked Derrick, "Have you heard any creepy stories about this place?"

Derrick answered, "As a matter of fact I have. There's a legend the locals call The Carnivore. They say he is a wild living man who dwells through the woods nearby. He stalks and hunts humans and when you least expect it, he ambushes you. He then slices your throat with a primitive knife made out of stone. Then carries your lifeless corpse to his cave to eat without even cooking you. He enjoys his meat rare and bloody. He also makes tools out of your bones so they won't go to waste."

"Shut up Derick!" Stated Desiree.

Charles was laughing as Renee inquired, "How come nobody has caught him if he's out there killing people?"

Derrick responded, "You can't catch a man who knows the lands better than anyone else. Plus, he doesn't kill often. A human body lasts him about a year or so to consume. His prey make it to the town's missing person list but don't raise an alarming concern like a serial murderer would." The females were in shock, unable to determine whether he was pulling their legs or not.

Charles uttered, "Alright, alright. It's my turn to tell a tale."

Desiree interrupted him saying, "No, I don't want to hear any-more scary stories.

Besides, you don't even have the proper imagination to pull a good one off."

Derrick butted in stating, "Nonsense, let the man speak his mind. Stop cutting him off and go to bed if you don't want to participate. Or you can volunteer in sharing your own fable since you're criticizing him for not being competent enough to do so." She rolled her eyes and shut her mouth.

Charles continued, "The folks around this neck of the woods warn tourists and visitors to look out for The Decapitated Chiqala-or little one. A small native american girl who was brutally murdered by conquistadors who charged into her village. Back when the natives roamed these hills foraging, before settlers dismissed their established lifestyles and practices. In the days when they trekked the grounds barefoot."

Desiree disrupted the story complaining, "Get to the excitement already. This is the longest, most monotonous introduction ever." Derrick and Renee shook their heads in disagreement and told her, "Shut the fuck up already!" Which she did.

Charles resumed, "So when the foreign intruders stumbled into her village. They began killing all the men and raping the women. They burned down their homes as well. The Chiqala witnessed her mother being sexually assaulted and tried defending her. One of the men in the combating unit smacked her as he released her mother's hands in assisting his partner to hold her down. The little girl then grabbed a knife and stabbed the man in the jugular, killing him. The man raping her mom took out his axe and swung it back at her. This caused her to lose her head which plummet to the ground and burned in the fire. He then finished sexually assaulting the mother and killed her too. The Chiqala suffered such a gruesome death that kept her wraith alive-searching for her head and mother. She wonders about the campgrounds tracking down women. When females come into contact with her, she rips their heads off to try them on herself. So far she hasn't found the right fit. So, I suggest y'all go to sleep with your heads covered tonight, for she might sever your heads off to see if any of them will allow her to have a visual of the land to search for her mother." Derrick clapped as the laddies huddled together, frightened by the tale.

Desiree uttered, "Ok, enough now. Seriously, I'm not going to be able to sleep if y'all continue to tell horror stories." As she chugged on the wine bottle she found earlier.

Renee embraced Derrick and snuggled her head into his chest. He grasped her in his arms and told her, "It's alright baby, I won't let the Chiqala take your head." Chuckling afterwards as she fussed for him to spoil her with protection and safety.

Charles got up from his chair and grabbed more wood to place in the fire since the night's temperatures dropped a bit. Desiree finished the wine bottle and tossed it in the fire as he filled it up with logs. There was a small flicker of blaze that trickled towards Charles. He quickly veered his body away from it and shook his head, while looking at his careless selfish girl. She on the other hand refused to apologize and instead got up and headed into the tent to get ready to fall asleep. Derrick and Renee got up as well but they wandered into the woods to have some adult fun and tlc.

Charles began gathering their trash and placing it inside plastic bags. He then entered the tent and tried cuddling with Desiree but she told him, "Not now, I'm sleepy and they could catch us nude in here."

Charles replied, "They're probably out there doing the same baby. Derrick takes forever with his foreplay so we'll have sufficient time to start and finish before they're back."

Desiree stated, "I said no Charles. Let me go to sleep now. I don't want to have sex out here like some wild woman without morals." Charles shrugged it off and exited the tent to sit back down near the flames.

He was sipping on a beer and watching the stars up above when he heard some branches cracking behind him. He jumped out of his chair and turned his flashlight on.

He shined the light around but couldn't make out where the sound had come from. He grabbed his pocket knife and walked into the woods in search of the culprit.

The following morning, Derrick and Renne woke up in the middle of the woods where they had crashed out after having drunk sex. Derrick was the first to open his eyes as he heard some birds chirping over them. Renee laid her head over his chest and felt him moving around. She arose from her sleep and smiled at him. She then said, "Good morning handsome. I guess the little Indian girl didn't come to rip my head off after all."

Derrick chuckled and replied, "Good morning to you too, babe. Guess she didn't. Maybe she figured you didn't have enough brains for her to utilize your head and left upset." Laughing out loud.

Renee commented, "She probably came by but saw this big hunk next to me and felt threatened to even try it." They kissed and began having morning sex.

Just as Derrick had nutted and Renee had orgasm, they heard Desiree shouting, "Charles! Where are you? This isn't funny!" They both got up and put their clothes back on.

Derrick and Renne walked over to the campground and saw Desiree panting frantically- searching for Charles. She got scared when they came out of the woods and held a rock up in the air about to release it at them. "Whoa," Uttered Derrick, "Put it down now and tell me what happened?"

Desiree had tears in her eyes as she said, "I fell asleep after you two left. Charles wanted to have intercourse but I refused so he walked back out here. I don't know if he ever came back or not? Whether he fell asleep in the tent or if he stayed outside. I woke up and couldn't find him anywhere. I'm scared that something happened to him."

Derrick replied, "He probably fell asleep and woke up before you did and decided to take a hike. He's an active early bird, you should know by now."

Desiree pointed at some small footprints near their campsite and asked, "What about that? How do you explain those?"

Derrick took a closer observation and answered, "Maybe they were here before we set up from a previous family who camped here, we just didn't notice them yesterday. There's no need to worry about Charles, he's a strong grown man who can fend for himself."

Desiree uttered, "What if the Chiqala came by and mistook him for a female, ripped his head off and left his lifeless body somewhere out there in the woods for us to find?"

"Come on, are you serious? It was just a made-up story he told us just like mine.

All for entertainment, for shits and giggles," mentioned Derrick.

Renee told them, "I don't know but I'm sure he's fine just like Derrick said. No reason to panic. I'm starving, do you know if he brought anything else to eat?"

Derrick and Renee strolled over to the ice chest and searched for edibles. Desiree scattered her worried gaze out into the woods. Derrick and Renee went over to the back of the SUV to check if he had packed some goodies. Desiree shouted out Charles' name once more but had no success locating him. She then saw Derrick and his girlfriend munching on some granola bars and drinking out of water bottles. Derrick grabbed a handful of pecans from a bag and put them in his mouth. Renee looked over at Desiree and told Derrick, "She's been mean to him all night and now she's worried about him? I mean I do hope he's alright but if not, I'd rather it be her gone instead." Derrick agreed by nodding his head as he continued to scarf down grains, oats and nuts.

Desiree strolled over to the back of the SUV and told Derrick, "Would you kindly whistle for him or go look for your friend please?" Derrick swallowed his food and tried whistling but was unable to until after he took a sip of some H2O to clear his pipes.

There wasn't a whistle calling back to Derrick's. He shrugged and uttered, "He must be jogging pretty far with his headphones on or something." Desiree scrunched her teeth and went over to have a seat in one of the chairs around the fire which was about to go out.

Renee followed her and handed her a granola bar to eat meanwhile Charles returned safely. Desiree took it and opened it, then took a bite since she was hungry.

Derrick rolled a joint and turned it on saying, "Nothing like the first puff of the day to relax away." He then began taking down his canoe from the roof rack.

When the canoe was on the ground, he walked it over to the water and hopped in. Renee jumped inside with him and they oared around the water hole smoking. Desiree took a seat in one of the chairs as the others were in the water. She pondered to look inside the tent for clues left behind and got up. She walked into the tent and looked around. She found his car keys but his vehicle was still parked outside to consider it suspicious. After all, it's not like he'd take them and jeopardize losing them out in the woods. She then spotted his wallet under the blanket. That also didn't prove a point other than he didn't want to lose it maybe. Nothing else stuck out in the tent to raise a concern. She walked back out and took a seat in the chair, looking around to see if she would see Charles heading her way. Derrick and Renee were floating in the raft over the water and Derrick uttered, "Whoa! Did you see that?"

"See what?" Questioned Renee.

Derrick answered, "I swear I just watched a small statured hobbit peeking out from behind the waterfall." As he maneuvered the canoe towards that direction.

"You're stoned out of your mind, aren't you?" Stated Renne as she giggled.

When they were right under the waterfall, it was too high for them to see behind it. They weren't about to go under it and run the risk of tipping over. Derrick commented, "I might be tripping bad huh? Damn, this is some potent weed."

Renee responded, "Yups, you sure are. Fabricating you witnessed a hobbit and he flipped you off." She chuckled and he laughed at her joke since he hadn't specifically said that.

They finished their doobie and continued to float over the water for a bit longer until Derrick rolled over and toppled the canoe upside down. They both submerged in the water and came up gasping for air. Renne inquired, "Why'd you flip it over? I was enjoying the experience and you ruined it."

Derrick stated, "I thought you wanted to look for more shells and figured we'd learn what to do in this type of situation at the same time. I guess I allowed my intrusive thoughts to win." As he laughed at her and splashed water in her face.

Renee splashed water back at him and uttered, "The only shell I found out here was your penis." As she tightened her hand under water- around it.

Derrick swam away and pulled his raft with him by the bow line. Renee had dived under to swim away from him, under the impression he was going to retaliate. When she surfaced, she saw him almost at the edge and starting to walk out. She quickly swam over to him and helped him take his canoe out of the water. They set it down on the soil and walked back towards the campground. When they got there, Derrick asked Desiree, "Has he come back yet?"

Desiree answered, "No, let's go look for him. It's already been about two hours since I woke up and didn't find him. Maybe he got injured while jogging and needs our help to carry him back here?"

Derrick replied, "Alright, let me just dry up and change." He went to the back of the vehicle to gather some clean dry linens and so did Renee.

Derrick and Renee had swapped out into some unwet attire and walked over to Desiree's location. Derrick said, "Ok, well let's get going. I think it would be a good idea if we split up our search since we don't know which way he headed."

Renee uttered, "Hell no, I'm not going out there alone to look for him. What if a bear attacks me or something?"

Desiree stated, "Yeah me neither. Why don't we just walk in several directions for about fifteen minutes or so and head back if we don't encounter him?"

Derrick said, "Fine, you two scary cats. Let's start over here first then." They strolled into the woods heading south.

As they searched for Charles, they yelled out his name and Derrick whistled as loud as he could. They had reached their twenty-minute deadline with no positive response. They now walked back towards the camp to try another direction. When they got to the camp, Desiree had to pee. She hid behind the SUV and squatted. Meanwhile, Derrick looked around to see if he noticed anything missing or any signs he may have returned and didn't find them but nothing stuck out. He then decided to leave a note as Desiree cleaned herself and pulled up her shorts. From there, they headed north.

They were strolling for about five minutes when they came across the road they had used to drive in through. They crossed it and continued trekking. Along their way they encountered a deer, a six-point buck to be exact- about two hundred yards away. Desiree took out her phone and took pictures. They had come to the twenty-minute time frame and headed back to their camp. Charles was nowhere to be found or heard of yet. They eventually got back to the camp and saw the note was still present and untouched- indicating he hadn't gotten back. They were a little hungry and decided to make themselves some sandwiches with items taken by Charles. Derrick grabbed the bread from the SUV and the mayo, bologna, cheese and ham from the cooler. All three of them prepared themselves one with chips to compliment their meal. When they finished feasting, they headed east to continue their search.

Desiree was whimpering and panting frantically, hoping she'd find Charles. She had even begun speaking to God and promising him she'd be a better woman to him if he'd be found. They trekked for about twenty minutes and once again, failed to locate him anywhere. They headed back to the camp as it started precipitating lightly. By the time they made it back, the storm had moved in closer and was pouring over them.

They took shelter in the tent and heard the water trickling outside. Derrick said, "It's been too long for him to be out there without coming back. Are you sure you didn't murder him Desiree?"

Desiree wept and refuted, "How dare you accuse me of such atrocity! I care about him even though I don't show it! Besides, do you really think me weighing around a hundred ten pounds can carry a two hundred twenty-pound man and discard his body in an attempt to hide my crime? Use your head, Derrick."

Derrick replied, "Yeah, you're right. I'm sorry for bringing that up. I'm just getting worried about my bro Charles. He's not the kind to disappear just like that. He's very routine-like to the point you could call his next move ahead of time if you watch his patterns."

Renee hugged Desiree and told her, "It's ok, don't cry. We'll find him before you know it and he'll be here back with us enjoying this trip." The questionable hope made Desiree sob uncontrollably.

They decided to put on some panchos Charles had in his vehicle and continue looking for him in the rain. They couldn't hear three feet away from their presence with the pounding water from up above but they followed Derrick as he led them west bound through the thick trees and brush. Their feet were wet from the puddles forming all around them. They couldn't even see where they placed their step-in front. Suddenly, Desiree fell after stepping in a hole in the ground. She shouted in pain.

Derrick picked her up and checked her foot. Her ankle was sprained. She couldn't put weight on it anymore without causing discomfort and agony. She told them to leave her there and go back for her after they kept looking for Charles. Derrick placed her under some bushes which provided shelter from the rain since the ground was dry under them. He and Renee resumed their search. Derrick grabbed her hand and walked, whistling as she yelled out his name. They got quite farther this time, five minutes longer speculating the rain was slowing them down but it hadn't. They then waited and shouted out his name several times. Renee noticed a worried look in Derrick as he desperately hoped he'd find his pal alive and well. Not a trace or lead had caught their eyes or ears. They walked back to where they had dropped off Desiree. When they got there, she was gone. Derrick uttered, "What the hell is going on? She was here not long ago and now she's gone. Fuck! Whoever is fucking with us, know I'm not going to tolerate this bullshit and fight back!!!"

He then heard his name being called. He ran towards the sound of the voice and found Desiree hidden under another set of bushes. It wasn't Charles which sucked but he had found her. She claimed to have crawled after the water had begun to cover her. Derrick helped her up and he and Renne provided support for her to walk on one foot all the way back to camp. Desiree was exhausted by the time they got back- panting with dismay. She could not believe they hadn't found Charles and that she had injured herself in the process. There was nothing else to do but wait around and see if he'd return by the end of the slowly approaching night. Derrick left Desiree in the tent and made her a makeshift ankle brace with twigs and some clothes he found in Charles' bag. He walked outside to grab a beer as Renne consoled her and kept her company- feeling empathy for her. The dark sky crept in on them and they had already decided to wait for Charles to come back before anything else was suggested.

They eventually slept in as the rain continued dripping over the tent. Renee handed Desiree some painkillers and she fell asleep. Renee ended up closing her eyes soon after as Derrick stayed up wondering where his buddy was at. The beer had finished, even the one he had found nearby. He closed his eyes and dreamed away seeing his pal sound and safe back at the campsite. There was movement outside the tent in the middle of the night which woke up Renee. She heard light chatter in an unfamiliar language and shook Derrick awake. Derrick got up and ran outside with a knife in hand to defend the girls at all cost. Desiree rose from her sleep terrified her and Renee were all alone in the tent as Derrick checked what was out there. The girls held hands and Desiree asked, "Do you think he's ok? I hope he comes back with Charles."

"He should be alright. He's a tough man to be taken down easily if there's danger outside knocking."

Desiree screamed, "Derrick, did you find him?" No one answered as they both looked into each other's fearful eyes.

Renee shouted, "Babe, are you alright? We're getting scared now! Stop playing if you are, please!" But Derrick didn't respond.

Desiree asked, "You think maybe the gas station attendant is responsible for Charles' disappearance and now Derricks too?"

Renee answered, "He better not. I'll beat the living shit out of that awkward fuck."

Renee got up and walked to the entrance of the tent. She peeked out to observe if she saw anyone out there but it was too dark for her to see. The rain had concluded by this time. Desiree handed her an extra flashlight she found lying around. Renee exited the tent and went looking for Derrick- hoping he and Charels were both well outside somewhere pranking them.

Ten minutes had passed by and Desiree was now in distress all alone and unable to get up on her feet. She crawled out to the entrance and shouted all their names. She couldn't even see anything outside so she crawled back towards the car keys and hit the unlock button. As the lights flickered twice, she caught something small running around a few feet away from the tent into the woods. She couldn't make out who or what it was but she crawled back into the sheets cringing and holding the blankets with both hands together right under her chin.

Charles nor Derrick or even Renne ever came back. She couldn't sleep with the anxiety she felt inside as she heard light chatter in a distinctive language outside. She yelled out, "Leave me alone motherfuckers! I have a gun on me!" Whimpering and panting.

Desiree suddenly heard the tent open up and saw a small shadowy figure creeping her way. She thought it was the headless

Chiqala who was there to decapitate her. She felt some small hands grab her feet and she screamed, "I had nothing to do with your death, baby. I'm sorry they did that to you and your family. Killing me won't bring them back!" She was dragged out of the tent in total darkness and taken away just as the rest of her group. Her roaring horrific scream could be heard from miles away but it didn't reach a human ear.

A couple of days later, there was a wrecker at their campground loading up Charles' SUV. The man Grabbed their stuff and took down the tent. He folded it back up and tossed it in the back of the vehicle. He grabbed the folding chairs and placed them in the SUV as well. He also picked up the canoe and tied it on top of the SUV. When he was finished hooking up the ride, the man drove off to take it to the wrecker yard just as the other vehicles left unattended in that particular location.

The locals knew better than to be out there at night when the Floresiensis came out to hunt for their community. These hobbits stood no taller than three feet while on their tippy toes. They were known to eat human flesh amongst other wild species in the area. No one knew exactly where they lived since, they had heard a statement about a little boy who got out alive and shared the information years ago. These hobbits lived behind the waterfall just where Derrick had thought he'd seen them. There they had all four of the campers tied down and chopped them up alive with their jagged sharp teeth. In order to feed themselves and continue to strive in their natural habitat away from civilization which had rejected their kind many centuries ago.

They made clothing out of their victim's skin and wore no shoes. That's how the small footprints were left behind when Charles went missing, allowing the Chiqala story to sound plausible. Their society averaged approximately thirty strong who lived deep inside the rock formation behind the waterfall within a complex cave system with tunnels and chambers.

CHAPTER 2
TRICK OR RETREAT.

Victor was a young man who had run out of options in life, following his high school graduation ceremony. Living with his mother was becoming complicated since she had begun to ask for his cooperation with the cost of living. He had attempted to enlist in the service but didn't pass his ASVAB. He was about to be twenty years of age and couldn't find a job in his hometown. He also didn't qualify for government assistance to enroll in school and he surely didn't have the means to do so either. So, he had applied at a drilling company just as the rest of his pals in his similar position. Today was his first day at work and he had arrived a day before to the bunkhouse. He'd have to share half a single wide trailer with another floor hand who had already been there a few months. His bunkmate woke him up on his way out. Victor was running late, unaccustomed to rising before the sun. He jumped out of bed and got dressed then grabbed his gear. He got in his car and sped over to the drilling location.

When he got there, the crew had finished their relief safety meeting and began unloading their equipment from the trucking company who moved their rig to their new site- all hands-on deck. Frank, the driller who was in charge of the crew told Victor,

"You must be the new hand. Go help that other floor hand rig up. And tomorrow, I want you to get here in time to listen to our meeting. If not, I don't want you on my crew and will have you removed."

Victor stuck his hand out but Frank turned away as Victor said, "I'm sorry."

Victor ran over to where Rick and the other crew members were at and assisted them in unloading the equipment. When they had concluded retrieving the material, they began connecting electrical lines, mud lines, hooking up pumps and hydraulic lines. This process was to take them all day. Every part needed to be assembled like a puzzle. Victor wasn't used to being out in the sun and began sweating his ass off. By mid-day, his body began to cramp up and it didn't matter how much water he drank- it wasn't sufficient. The company man had shown up to the location to speak to the driller. He told him, "This is going to be a tricky one. You might not like the sound of it but that's what they want. Twenty-five thousand feet, horizontal well."

Frank replied, "What? Are they serious? Damn, well I can't contest their decision. Alright, my crew will get to it."

The company man uttered, "Good." As he walked away.

The crew began to rig up as the company man's truck picked up dust heading out of there. Victor felt like quitting since his body wasn't used to the hard work. He felt he needed the slightest excuse to take off but at the same time he needed to make momma happy or move out. So, he summoned his courage to exceed his labor capacities- pushing his body to the limit.

The night shift took over and finished rigging up. They penetrated the surface within a couple of hours after Victor and his crew departed the location. Drilling through the surface, the derrick hand kept his eyes on all the fluid in the pits. The motor man monitored the gauges for the top drive. He knew his motor was running properly since his torque gauges were good. They tripped out the hole. The driller started pulling out the pipe. The floor hands set the slips and broke the pipe off with the tongs.

Victor had made it back in one piece to the bunkhouse. He was hungry, drained of energy, and filthy but he jumped into bed and called it a day instead of attending to anything else. He experienced nightmares throughout the night that he was still out there doing everything all alone.

The next morning, his alarm woke him up and he quickly jumped in the shower to wash up. He brushed his teeth and grabbed some premade peanut butter and jelly sandwiches his mother had made him. He got dressed and headed out to the briefing while eating one of his sandwiches.

When he got there, Frank had just spoken to the night's driller and received the pass down. The rest of the crew arrived and they began their muster. Everything was on schedule. The casing crew showed up and they started running casing with their power tongs. They ran casing all the way to the bottom of the hole to pump cement down inside. The drilling crew had rigged down the casing crew. Then the cement crew came in as the drilling crew rigged them up for them to pump the cement. Victor was once again perspiring profusely, unable to maintain his bodily fluids in line. He drank and drank water and his bunkmate- Rick, handed him some Pedialyte packs to pour into his water bottles. Rick told him, "You'll get used to it eventually and it'll all become routine. Just make sure to not dehydrate out here because it'll take long before the emergency services remove you from here to check you out."

Victor responded, "Thanks man, I really appreciate you looking out for me. I'll get you a box to replace these packs you gave me when I get my first check."

Rick uttered, "Don't worry about replacing the packs. Just make sure you keep up and don't slack off or I'll have to meet another bunkmate before this rig is down."

Victor replied, "Alright, I'll just follow your lead and not slack it."

Frank shouted, "Rick! You and the worm get back to work and stop goofing off! Y'all live together and can cuddle all night in each other's loving arms!" The crew laughed. (Worm is oilfield jargon intended for the rookie.)

They got back to work as the tool pusher began his inspections and filing out work orders. They required new hydraulic pumps and motors to raise the rig. He was also fixing some lines on the rig and was about the busiest one out there so far. The driller was watching the screens observing the pump pressure, hook load and weight on bit. They then took a quick lunch break after a man pulled into their location to sell them home made food from his van. Victor had a few bucks and bought himself the most expensive burrito he had ever purchased. It was a philly cheese steak wrapped inside a store-bought flour tortilla. He drank some of his sports drink after the first bite since he almost choked due to having a dry mouth. Frank told him, "Easy there worm. Ain't nobody going to perform CPR on you out here. Bet you're a gagger and spewer aren't you?" The guys in the crew all chuckled.

When the cement hardened- almost at the end of their shift- a third-party nipple crew went to install the Blow Out Prevention. This was a safety measurement in case they had a blow out- the section could be sealed to prevent unwanted fluid shooting up the rig floor. The BOP diverts the unwanted fluids. Victor's body was adjusting to the temperatures and he had managed to hydrate himself. He and the crew continued to work their butts off until the end of their shift. They passed down the information on their drilling process over to the second crew who had shown up to take over.

Victor got in his car and drove to the bunkhouse. When he entered, he removed all of his clothes and jumped in the shower again after eating another PBJ. When he finished, Rick was cooking himself some chicken and rice. He offered Vic some and he accepted. He also volunteered to help him cook. They both spoke about their lives in order to get acquainted better. Just as they sat down to eat, they heard knocking at their door. Rick got up and it was Frank who went over to tell him, "Your pal Angel is out here fighting with Oliver. Go settle him down before he gets in trouble."

Oliver was the tool pusher and Angel was another floor hand. When Rick got to where they were- Angel swung his hand and connected Oliver. The physical scuffle had been initiated and everyone there jumped in to separate them. They were ripped apart from each other as Angel made it clear he was angered because Oliver hadn't paid him some money, he had loaned him. Angel then got in his car and drove off. Victor was in shock this had all gone down in his presence since he wasn't the kind to engage in combat. He and Rick then headed back inside to finish their meals. When they cleaned their plates, they saw some movie and called it a day.

On the third day, they were all at the drill site after a successful meeting. Angel and Oliver hadn't made peace and were avoiding each other. The crew got back in the hole and continued drilling. The derrick hand went to the board and latched up the stands of drill pipe. The floor hands made up the drill pipe and pulled up the slips. All hands-on deck were tripping the hole. When they got back to the bottom, the driller hooked up the top drive to continue drilling. The operation was running smoothly and they had some time on their hands to relax after the past two strenuous days. Frank told Victor, "Hey worm, I need you to jump inside the reserve pit and pull the plug at the bottom to let it all out."

Victor replied, "How deep is it located at?"

Frank uttered, "The floor is probably about ten to fifteen feet deep."

Victor jumped inside and swam downward. He surfaced up and yelled, "I can't locate it, Frank!"

Frank stated, "Then get back in there to find it, worm. I need this done now so we won't force the pipes. I also don't want to stay here all night. I've got plans to go buy candy for tomorrow to hand out to the kids in my neighborhood." He lived in the nearby town with his family.

Victor dove back in and was down there for some time. Rick had gotten a bit worried he might have drowned but he came out of the top of the water informing he failed once more. The whole crew began to laugh at him. That's when he realized they were playing a joke which he fell for. He got out and was informed there wasn't a plug at the bottom. They were all messing around when all of a sudden, the safety man arrived unannounced. He was there to give them shit just as always. He began nitpicking about the safety cables and high-pressure lines not being installed. Rick got to it right after hearing him. The safety man checked their paperwork and found some missing information to which Oliver got on it. He ended up reprimanding the whole crew for the infractions before he took off. Frank was fortunate he didn't observe Victor all wet and missing his eyewear but then again it really wouldn't make a difference. He told Victor to put his glasses on though, as they continued with their functions. Frank had the drill bit at around twenty-seven hundred feet when their hydrogen sulfide monitors began whaling danger. The crew didn't stand a chance to evacuate in time. They all dropped to the ground and were gone. There was something different about this pocket they had struck open. The chamber had a mixture of H2S with another unknown gas which no man on earth had ever discovered, came across accidentally, evaluated or studied scientifically. The nearby towns began to smell the bad odor released in the air. It wreaked fowl with a hint of rotten flesh.

The night crew members had arrived at an empty rig. The day shift wasn't presently working on site. Their bodies had been raised from the dead in search of brains to eat. The night shift driller ran to the deck to check the gauges and began controlling the abnormalities from it being neglected for a few hours. The H2S had dissipated along with the unknown gas which caused the day crew to turn into zombies. Out of nowhere, the day crew began attacking the night shift. The driller was the last one to be victimized. He shouted, "Frank! What the fuck are you doing? I don't want you to kiss my neck! Get the fuck away from me you queer!" Frank had superhuman strength and didn't lose this one.

When they had all transformed, they strolled towards the lights of the town. It was the perfect plan to expand their kind. They'd go undetected as what they had become with the current event taking place the following day when they'd make it to their destination. They began ambushing people they'd come across in their path. Their first prey was an older man working outside in his farm land right in the outskirts of town. They also took his entire family at their home.

From there, they all walked closer to their mark and attacked some security guard who was watching over a rig which was placed on hold. The police department headquarters was broken into and all the officers were turned into dead walkers. There was no way they'd contact the other nearby towns to inform them of the situation which took them by surprise. Little by little the whole town was sabotaged. Their numbers grew and they spread to the other towns around.

Halloween had arrived and the neighboring town's kids were out walking the streets in their costumes- hunting for candy. Some kid in a superman suit pointed at the crowd of zombies and shouted, "Look! They look so cool. Like the television shows and movies."

His friend replied, "I want to take a picture with them, here take my cell phone as I get in position." He handed his pal his phone and ran towards the crowd of brain munchers.

His friend was trying to get his phone to work and didn't notice the crowd had eaten his buddy. When he looked up, Victor grabbed him and began to rip his head open. They both joined the gang of dead walkers unwillingly. One by one all the kids out collecting candies in their bags and baskets were nabbed. Their parents who accompanied them too were taken along for the ride. From there they got closer in proximity to a nearby city with more residents than the two towns combined.

When they arrived at the city, the residents were under the impression it was a big show, some type of parade. They became victims and learned the hard way it was all real and no actors were hired to entertain.

City by city, state by state the chemical infused disease spread until the government became aware. The president ordered the military to take charge of the situation at hand. He made it clear deadly force was necessary and allowed. The troops started getting prepared to head out and combat the domestic threat. As they began to load up their aircrafts to be transported, they all were attacked. The first line of defense was compromised and the fort that housed them became a hunting ground to the brain munchers. Those who attempted to repel the attack were confused as to why they weren't dying from the bullet impacts their weapons dispersed. One of the commanding officers yelled, "Aim for their heads! Shoot these sons of bitches!"

A soldier commented, "Sir, it's not working! They keep charging in our direction! It seems to only work in the film industry and not in real life!"

The officer questioned, "Private! What the fuck do you mean it's not working? You shoot them right between the eyes and take them down!" The other soldiers agreed his orders weren't effective just before they all were taken out.

The whole country was in chaos by this time and the word had just begun to air on the local news but it was too late. The reports stated, "Our country is in a crisis as zombies have invaded most of the cities and towns. If you spot a limbering human headed your way, don't eliminate the fact it's not trick or treating. The military has issued a warning that shooting them in the head is ineffective." Suddenly the reporter was attacked by a group of dead walkers ending the transmission.

Those viewing the information found themselves preyed upon during, after or right before the broadcast. A man sitting in front of his television set was watching the report when he heard his windows break and witnessed the brain munchers enter his home to attack him. He shouted, "No! Get out of my house and go get my ex-mother- in-law! She's the one with the brains!" The group of zombies paused at the sound of their favorite dish.

The large group of migrating dead walkers had left their footprint behind. All cities and towns looked like they had been bombed and abandoned by the population residing in them. Every single military installation was wiped out. All law enforcement facilities were overruled by the dead walkers. No one was left in the country alive by the end of sundown. From there, the zombies navigated into the next countries spreading in large groups expanding like a blast of force to not be reckoned with. Country by country they gained territory along their destructive stampede.

Mexico was the only one doing a great job at exterminating them. Just as anywhere around the world the power in a mexican to get the task done was being fulfilled. The cartels, soldiers and all law enforcement got together to fight back. It made sense why in the states when someone needed a job well done, they'd look for a mexican. The group of fighters gathered along the borders to their country and fought aggressively. They had concluded the only way to take out the threat was to inflict damage to the heart which was still pumping blood to the body. Bleeding out the brain munchers was the only remedy to stop them in their tracks. They had set barricades and trenches along the borders and shot the hearts or carotid arteries of the zombies. Those who came in close contact with the country's defense were chopped up and mutilated until their blood fully drained from their bodies. This battle lasted approximately two weeks.

In November- the first through the second- the day of the dead was celebrated by killing more brain munchers. The Mexican population had joined in the effort to suppress the invasion along the separating perimeters. Women, children and men fired rounds at the crowds of zombies heading their direction. Victor and his crew had made their way across after finding a breach in the division and Angel was recognized by his uncle in Mexico. He somehow remembered where he lived and how to get there. His uncle was walking down the street from his house headed to get some corn tortillas when he spotted his relative lumbering his way. He said, "Angel, is that really you? I haven't seen you in several years. How's your mother doing? Did you come to seek refuge from the invasion? Come here mijo and give your uncle a hug."

Angel didn't reply to his inquiries and continued lumbering towards him. His uncle felt something was off and took out his machete. Angel was well in his reach when he displayed infected signs. His uncle swung his machete and decapitated him. His headless corpse still charged forward. The uncle then punctured his heart with his machete and stopped him dead in his tracks. That was the end for Angel.

One of the cartel leaders had captured a dead walker and kept him as a pet. He fed Victor animal cerebral matter and experimented by giving him beer. He didn't exactly like beer but he drank it when the drug lord mixed it up with brain fragments. He'd start dancing to any kind of music the leader would play on a radio he had in the shed where he kept the zombie captive. He would use this brain muncher to entertain his men, family and visitors. Everyone would come to see Victor's act.

One day, the cartel boss gave him zombie brains and the dead walker consumed them. Within the days to come, the brain muncher displayed signs of cognitive behavior. He thought he had found a cure to the outbreak. He shared the news around the town and it spread like a wildfire.

There were rumors that a large crowd of them had penetrated Mexicali but wasn't confirmed concrete. From that group the people detained another and had similar results with experimental trials. There was a video circulating of one getting eaten by a great white shark out at sea. The shark had to be shot down due to the possibility of it becoming contaminated.

The president of Mexico filmed a presentation to the masses watching. He stated, "Dear fellow countrymen. I address you cordially with the utmost sincere appreciation for the counter attack on this invasion of brain munchers attempting to enter our borders. As you all are aware, the best and most effective measure to utilize is by bleeding them out. Shooting them in their hearts or slicing their carotid arteries and of course dismembering and mutilating them. Keep up the hard work and have faith we will succeed where other countries have not. I stand with you and we stand together, Viva Mexico cabrones!" The broadcast ended.

All those who saw the televised speech cheered and chanted retorting the president. Mexico had become a safe haven for any known survivors and small groups who traversed the lands headed towards the safe zone.

Frank was gunned down in a shopping center where he tried attacking a police officer's child. Oliver was chopped up soon after crossing foreign land. He was caught by a local defense group along with a few others of his kind. Rick had been run over by a modified and fortified truck which was patrolling the town. Most of the night shift oil field workers were mutilated before they got anywhere near Mexico. The last surviving brain muncher from the original group was Victor and he was enslaved, shackled at the mercy of the drug lord. The cartel boss heard about the president's speech and went over to the metal shed he housed Victor in. He walked inside after removing several security locks from the door. He gave Victor some dog brains and teased him a bit. He placed some brain matter at the end of a shovel and was poking Victor as he ate off the tool. Some of his men were with him at the time and were laughing since Victor was unable to pick up the pieces which fell on the ground as he looked at them with a desperate gaze. He tried moving around but wasn't capable of bending over to pick the fallen remains. The boss then picked them up with the shovel along with some dirt and fed them to him. One of his men asked the boss, "How come you just don't execute this fucking mind eater?"

The boss explained, "I want to keep him around like a trophy. I've been studying him and have seen how he was demonstrating healing properties after ingesting zombie brains. Then I started feeding him animal cerebral matter and he's gone back to his normal state. So, I'm not going to get rid of him just yet."

The security detail questioned, "So is this your scientific experiment or something?"

The jefe replied, "You can call it that. I'm also going to feed any of my enemies to it. So, he has several functions for his existence. I might just send him off to combat our nemesis." Chuckling afterwards.

The guy uttered, "You're crazy, man, keeping him alive right in your property some yards away from where you lay to rest at night."

"He doesn't scare me one bit. If he were to escape and attack me, that'll be the end of him." Said the boss as he looked deep into Victor's eyes as if he understood the warning.

The men left the shed after locking it down. They boarded their SUV's and headed towards the border to continue repelling intruders. When they arrived at the frontline, the cartel leader criticized an old man who was being squeamish about shooting a mother and her two children who were making their way towards them. The boss told him, "Shoot them, they're brain munchers! Shoot them or I'll shoot you after I take them out!"

The old man replied, "They're just kids. I don't have the heart to kill them."

The boss commented, "You coward." He raised his rifle and took aim then shot all three. He then had his men beat up the old man for not following his orders and putting everyone at risk.

A few days had gone by and there were rumors of a large group of zombies penetrating the perimeter during night watch. All the people on the border were on high alert. They weren't allowed to walk alone anywhere in town for safety purposes. The armed numbers took turns to patrol the town. They had also received news of an outbreak in the opposite border sector of the country. They didn't want to become the next town to be invaded. A convoy of trucks came across a straggler near a farm land. They overkilled the brain muncher and reported their success back to base. The cartel boss was in charge and ordered them to look for the rest of the zombies who may be close by. The group searched the farm land. The property in question belonged to the drug lord himself. Some of the men in the convoy hopped off and marched on foot. They trekked a few hundred feet when they observed approximately fifteen dead walkers gathering around the shed where Victor was isolated. The men on the ground dispatched the trucks over to shine their lights on the brain munchers. Briskly, the vehicles made it over to the area where the threat was and shined their lights over the shed. All the dead walkers were annihilated. The group then radioed over their accomplishment and left back to the border.

That night when the cartel boss returned to his home, he walked in and found his family missing. His house looked like it had been ransacked by thieves. He called out his wife's name and then his son's but there was no answer. He checked every room and was unable to locate his family. He then went outside to search for them. He ran to the shed where he held Victor and found the locks had been shot apart. He turned on the light inside and discovered Victor wasn't chained up anymore. When he turned around to continue looking- his wife bit him. He ran from her as she persisted behind him. He realized she had turned. His son came out of nowhere and bit him as well. He was distressed with unbelief regarding his loved ones having become brain munchers. He wept in agony as he sprinted back inside his house. He shut the door behind him and heard his wife and son scratching at it trying to gain entrance. He thought about what he had to do. He was faced with a tough choice whether to kill his wife and son then himself. Or allow his wounds to transform him into one of them and face the masses together who'd eventually exterminate them three. As he stood by the front door listening to his significant other and child growling- Victor came up from behind and ate his brain. Within a few minutes he became a dead walker. The townsmen and women were unaware of this situation.

The sun came up the next day and the people were worried about the boss who hadn't arrived or checked in. They went to his residence to look for him. There, they encountered his son and he was destroyed immediately. They gained entry to his dwelling and shot Victor who was hanging around waiting for his prey to come to him. They proceeded forward, room by room and came across his wife. She was eliminated with a sword jammed straight through her heart. When they got to the back of the house, they witnessed the drug lord eating his dogs brains. He was fired upon until neutralized. From there, they reported back to the second in command who was the chief of police about the occurrence. He wasn't happy to hear the bad news but the perel had been addressed and contained. He puffed on his cigarette and told the group to double check that property and make sure no other dead walker was present before returning to the border.

Days had gone by and small fractions of survivors had begun to arrive. The town grew in numbers and deterred any zombies from crossing their boundaries. All services had become manual labored. Water had to be brought up from a well in order to avoid contamination.

Electricity was provided only by the generators they had scavenged during the first wave of attacks. The internet ceased to exist. The only form of communication was through radio air waves and frequencies. Food was running scarce with all the newcomers. So, every now and then, small groups of armed men would travel outside of safety to scavenge edibles. Mexico had survived so far though and that was fascinating. Within the weeks to come, less and less brain munchers were encountered. Eventually all of them had died off on their own without being able to suppress their hunger. The people in the safe haven reconstructed the world one step at a time. What once was, had vanished and the new lifestyles were adopted. The cartel for one took a huge blow since there weren't many consumers of their products. Life for humans continued but not without worries the dead walkers might come back to strike again.

CHAPTER 3
LAST- STOP.

The missing person report filed by the El Paso County Sheriff's department added to the other seven within a month's span. All the victims had vanished along the rest stops IH-10 westbound, mile marker 51 and IH-10 eastbound, mile marker 50- outside of Fabens, Tx. Law enforcement presumed it was the violent acts of a deranged serial murderer out on the loose. Another speculation was human trafficking groups operating in the area for the resale of human organs. Whatever was going on, it needed to be halted in order to return safety to the millions of travelers who'd utilize the public restrooms in their vicinity and the residents in the area. During their seventh investigation, no hard evidence was recovered at the scene. Only a baseball cap was left behind on the ground from the second missing person whose location was abroad. Another clue was a purse from the fifth victim whose whereabouts were astray. Including her wallet and cell phone which had a dropped call from her boyfriend in Washington. No blood, signs of violence, signs of forcible abduction or entry nor any forensic evidence was collected at the scenes so far. Which puzzled the sheriff's department and other local authorities collaborating in the cases.

None of the missing persons bodies had been recovered. Word had begun to spread via local news channels which only made the detective's occupation hazardous. News reporters and chismosos gathered outside the rest stops confronting the authorities leading the investigation for answers. The red tape separating the crowd and the investigators breached several instances with family members of the missing people demanding closure. The Sheriff's office spokesperson was on site about to have his speech aired. News channel nine's field reporter started the interview as her cameraman filmed the live coverage, "Are there any leads your office has accumulated after this being the seventh person missing in the area?"

The spokesperson answered, "Our office has conducted investigations for all seven cases which remain open and unsolved. We have no leads indicating foul play or the presence of a serial killer on the loose. We are well aware rumors have surfaced and are circulating on the matter, confusing and alarming the population in the area. Our office has not gone public with any misleading information and therefore we encourage those who're afraid to leave their homes to not let this situation compel them. We're diligently working twenty-four seven around the clock searching for any evidence leading us to a suspect or suspects. We also encourage the public to come forward with any information which may help us. We're asking for the public's cooperation at this time. We'll be more than glad to hear whatever anyone has to say regarding this situation. Your statements will remain anonymous. We thank everyone for their patience and will continue to provide our cities and towns with peace of mind, thank you." He then headed off towards his unmarked unit.

The news reporter stated, "Well there you have it, directly from the sheriff's office. Stay tuned for we will bring you the latest news and updates following the seventh person gone astray here at these public restrooms right behind me. Reporting to you live from news channel nine, Maria Morales."

As the spokesperson departed the area in his vehicle, the crowds bombarded the unit with trash. He was on his cell phone talking with his boss about the interview. His boss told him, "That was very good you involved the public that way they feel the pressure we're faced with. How long will it take you to get back to the office? Can you stop by the gas station and grab me a pastry? You still owe me one for that bet you lost by the way."

The spokesperson- Mr. Ballesteros replied, "Yeah, I hadn't forgotten about the bet and I'll be at the office in maybe twenty to thirty mics."

His supervisor uttered, "Alright, thanks for remembering and you know which kind I like. See you then." They hung up as Ballesteros drove into a service station to grab the pastry and get himself a fountain drink.

While in the store, he was interrogated by some of the locals about the incidents unraveled. The clerk also wanted to know what was going on. They all were terrified to leave the comforts of their homes other than for necessary purposes. He didn't answer any direct questions regarding the cases. He only told them to not be afraid and continue to live their normal lives. He paid for the products and got out of there right before the customers became irate and attacked him. When he got back to the department office, he handed his boss his request and said, "Paid in full, I'm debt free now."

His boss uttered, "About time you paid up. I was beginning to consider placing your balance in collections." Chuckling as he opened up the plastic wrap protecting his sweet bread.

Ballesteros walked out of his boss' office and headed towards his, to continue with his work at hand. On his way there, he ran into one of the detectives in charge of the cases. Ballesteros inquired, "Any luck yet? Wish it was you whose unit got trash tossed at instead of mine from the crowds at the scene who you've been avoiding."

The detective replied, "They took me off the case and assigned it to Martinez. So go ask him for the update. As far as facing the angry mob at the scene, I won't have too anymore. And about you getting trash thrown at you, well that's your job to represent the department with any questions or concerns." He strolled away with a smirk on his face.

Ballesteros confided in Martinez's abilities to solve these cases. Martinez had been with the department for about thirty plus years and was a senior detective whose reputation stood firm on his experience and success. He knew the cases were now in good hands and soon there'd be an arrest made and a criminal in custody. He then walked into his office listening to his phone ring. He picked it up and heard, "Officer Ballesteros, this is Beatriz Collins with news channel fourteen. Would you happen to have a moment to answer a few questions regarding the missing people's cases?" He hung up on her after informing her she could see his interview on channel nine.

Ballesteros sighed with relief from being back in his office and not out there giving statements on things out of his hands. The disappearances had to have a reason behind them he thought, right before he cleared his head and resumed his reports. As he finished his paperwork, Detective Martinez entered his office. He greeted Ballesteros and told him, "Did you see anything suspicious while you were out there at the rest stops? Maybe someone who stuck out? I have reason to believe this kidnapper might have been in the crowd looking with egotism at us, unable to capture him."

Ballesteros questioned, "So you're telling me this might be the work of a serial kidnapper or killer?"

Martinez answered, "Not necessarily, it's just a theory of mine. It would make sense otherwise had it only been one person's disappearance but we've got seven reports now. I'm attempting to narrow my search and come to a determination on who might be responsible for the crimes."

Ballesteros uttered, "I wasn't really focused on the crowd itself to have noticed anyone strange. I will mention though, the group was agitated and threw trash at my car as I drove away."

Martinez said, "I understand the people seek justice and feel we've come short of it so far. We can only deal with the obvious until we apprehend a suspect and question them. No one apparently observed anything out of the ordinary and we have zero witnesses come forth with information. I'm heading over there right now myself and hopefully the spectators won't make it hard on me to do my job. In case you hear anything, please contact me immediately." Martinez then walked out and headed to the parking lot to get in his unit.

Ballesteros submitted his paperwork to his boss for inspection and then got on the internet to see if he could find any other similar cases in the world. He came across the countless missing persons in Ciudad Juárez, Chihuahua. He wondered if they were related. If somehow the person on the other side of the border responsible for the acts ingresses into the states and is now continuing his atrocities in the sector. But it couldn't have been the same person since across the border only women had gone astray and one individual was caught. They had four men and three women disappear in the area, so that possibility was eliminated. He continued searching and came in view of a posting on a website about ten creepy unsolved rest stop mysteries. He read through them but found nothing compiling in resemblance to these particular cases.

He then began reading about Donald Leroy Evans "The Rest Area Killer" and was curious to know if it may be a copycat murderer. There was also a Wikipedia link about the Highway of Tears but once again it was strictly female victims. He found nothing crucial regarding any rest stops in Texas. Only a website which stated there were seventy-six stops throughout the state which had been ranked some of the safest. Then he came up with the idea it could be a truck driver who may frequent the area and is familiar with the surroundings. He texted Martinez with his presumption and then turned off his monitor to head home for the day.

Martinez advised him he had thought of that already and asked DOT to send him over logs of drivers traveling through the interstate where the possible crimes were committed. His boss stopped him as he exited and told him, "Hey Ballesteros, did you hear that Martinez is on the case now? I bet this will be solved in less than a week, want to bet on it?"

Ballesteros replied, "Yeah, he came into my office earlier and made it clear to me he was leading the investigation. I wouldn't bet against him. But I'll bet you, there will be another victim before the investigation is resolved." They shook hands on that and parted ways.

Ballesteros arrived at his home and found his girlfriend cooking supper. He went straight to his restroom to shower. She followed him and asked, "I saw you on the news today. You looked so confident in your choice of words. Also, very handsome honey. Have you all gotten any leads already after your interview?"

Ballesteros responded, "Thanks baby. Nothing yet to be exact. It seems like these people were abducted by aliens or something. They left no trace behind stating otherwise."

His girlfriend uttered, "Oh, well I hope you all capture whoever it is. I'll be in the kitchen if you need anything."

"Ok baby," replied Ballesteros.

When he got out of the shower, he sat down to eat with his girlfriend and they talked about her day.

They finished their meals and headed out to a bar to have some drinks. It was around ten at night when Ballesteros' phone rang. His boss shared the news, "So I owe you. I just got a call informing me another disappearance took place at sun drop. This time it was an employee who was cleaning the restrooms. He was heard yelping by a truck driver who observed him enter the men's room. When the truck driver returned to check his status, he saw the man wasn't present or anyone else for that matter. As if he disappeared into thin air. Sorry if I woke you up or interrupted your activities. I just wanted to notify you as soon as possible."

Ballesteros commented, "Damn, this is getting out of control and I don't know if I'm ready to face the reporters and calm the worried residents so soon. I'll just see you tomorrow since I'm about to lay in bed." They terminated their call as Ballesteros re- laid the info to his girlfriend.

She had begun to cry and get worried something might happen to one of her loved ones. She had some relatives and friends in the trucking industry. Ballesteros calmed her down and they both laid in bed. Before crashing out, he did double check the doors and windows to his house. Even though the possible crimes were secluded to the rest areas, he wasn't about to exclude the possibility of a serial murderer in the area. He also didn't reside near the zones in question but, "Better to be safe than sorrow." he whispered while securing his dwelling.

When Ballesteros arrived at his office the next day, his boss informed him more details of last night's disappearance. He stated, "This last victim who vanished in the public restrooms left about two feet of scratch marks leading into the toilet bowl. The responding officers mentioned his uniform shirt was floating in the bowl and they're in the process of dismantling the entire shitter to check the drain for more evidence. The trucker was brought for questioning but he stuck to his initial story and was released. I'm afraid you're going to have to go live again and calm the locals some."

Ballesteros replied, "Damn it! First, I need to have my coffee then write a speech before I head on out there to speak to the reporters. FUCK!" He slammed his office door behind him and took a seat at his desk.

He got up and headed to the break room to make himself a cup of caffeinated beverage after staring into the ceiling. Martinez bumped into him in the break room and asked him, "Were you already informed of the latest update on last night's eight victims?"

Ballesteros responded, "Yeah, I'm going to have to go out there and have a public conference once more."

Martinez stated, "I'll be headed over there myself so I'll see you at the scene." Ballesteros gave him a thumb up as he took his first sip of coffee.

Ballesteros rushed to his office and began gathering some of the information from the reports so he could jot down a speech. He glanced through his last one and pondered something distinctive. He began to write down the words floating in his mind. His boss walked in and handed him a pastry telling him, "Here's my payment. I hope you give a good speech so we can keep the public off our backs."

Ballesteros uttered, "Thanks and I hope so too." As he resumed his soon to be verbal statement.

He proofread his essay when he finished. He left his office and traveled to the rest stops. Upon his arrival, he observed Martinez handing over an evidence bag to the forensic team on site and walking back into the restroom. Ballesteros got out of his unit and strolled towards Martinez's location, just in case he needed to add something to his declaration. He avoided the crowd and reporters at all cost. Martinez was in there poking at the drain as the toilet bowl sat on the side next to the wall. Detective Martinez was flashing his light down in the hole. He wasn't able to retrieve any further evidence. He turned around, greeted Ballesteros and updated him with, "We were able to recover a sock which may belong to our latest victim. It was stuck approximately a foot inside. I have reason to believe whoever committed this attempted to get rid of the evidence by flushing it down the toilet before he left. We still have no suspect available and I'm placing an officer at this site twenty-four seven to ensure the perpetrator doesn't commit another offense."

Ballesteros commented, "I knew you'd get the job done. Glad to hear you've found more evidence and hopefully this is over soon. By the way, are these the scratch marks on the floor I heard about?" As he looked at a trail of scratches, broken nails and blood.

Martinez replied, "Yes, it is. I've gathered some DNA samples and sent them to the lab in hopes they're not from our victim but from our subject in question. I also took some photos and attached them to my report. That's all we have for now, hopefully any of these details will help you address the reporters."

Ballesteros responded, "Thanks, I'll add a little more to my speech before making it." He then wrote down some of the information Martinez shared.

Ballesteros walked out of the active crime scene to face the masses congregating outside. The reporters rushed him to get his statement and the onlookers booed him. Ballesteros had about ten microphones in front of him waiting for his speech. He cleared his throat and said, "The sheriff's department offers its deepest condolences to the victims and their families. It is very unfortunate we had another person go astray last night but we have stepped up our security measures. This is no longer a secluded incident. We will continue to work around the clock and place a deputy at these locations twenty-four seven. Our street patrol units also have been advised to be on high alert while out in the field and we've boosted their numbers to assure the public's safety. Our latest victim was an employee who was working at the site. We were able to recover DNA samples amongst other evidence and all have been sent to our laboratories for review. We've also obtained DOT logs in order to track down the commute of truck drivers and possibly question some regarding the events they may have witnessed. We will not stop our efforts in apprehending the responsible parties of these disappearances. We will find those liable wherever they're hiding and bring them to justice. I hope everyone here has a great day." He then marched out of there and headed into his unit as the reporters followed him with questions.

Ballesteros jumped inside his vehicle and turned it on, ignoring the reporters who stood by the driver side window. He then sped away as the crowd tossed objects aimed for his unit. Ballesteros drove back to the station and was congratulated by his superior on his public appearance. He went to his office and continued writing his reports to be submitted. The sheriff himself went over to thank him personally for his speech and told him to keep up the hard work. Ballesteros replied, "Thank you sheriff but I'd rather be out in the field searching for the person responsible for these acts than be congratulated for a press conference. I feel as if I'm not making a difference and yet held accountable for the unsolved crimes."

The sheriff uttered, "Nonsense, your line of duty is necessary to our objective in ensuring the public of their safety. Without you confronting the reporters, they wouldn't understand the behind the scenes of these investigations. Don't belittle your position by the guilt the residents are trying to inflict on you. I personally know you've been laboring with extreme pressure but you've managed to obtain a positive outcome so far. You'll see when Martinez nabs the perpetrator, you'll enjoy your job again. Hang in there in the meantime and bear with us all." Ballesteros nodded his head as he observed the sheriff exit his office.

Soon after, one of the sheriffs training academy instructors for new recruits walked in with a group of cadets. He introduced them to Ballesteros and told them, "After successfully completing the academy and working at the county jails, you guys can apply for deputy and then move your way up the ladder to detective and then one day even become our spokesperson. I'm sure Ballesteros here can share some stories of his ventures within the department."

Ballesteros uttered, "The academy should have you all prepared for the line of duty. When you've achieved the minimum dedicated time as correctional officers, I encourage you to apply for deputies.

Being out on patrol is exciting and eventually when you get bored of it you can ask to transfer to the detective side. From there you can move up just about any direction you desire. It takes time but it's well worth it. I once stood in y'all's shoes and look at me now in my very own office." The trainer thanked him and they all walked away to continue their tour.

Ballesteros' boss barge through his office and told him, "We have a suspect in custody and he'll be interrogated shortly to see if he confesses to the crimes. He has a promising record trailing back to 1993 with multiple arrests and one convicted murder charge. Two attempts which he was found not guilty for. Including a dozen other violations which he's served time for. He was released from the state a few weeks ago right around the first abduction."

Ballesteros' eyes widened with excitement and relief as he replied, "Hell yeah, hopefully he confesses and we seal these cases. I'll be over to the interrogation room shortly to see for myself." He handed his boss a breath mint headed towards the location of the subject in question.

Once he got to the questioning room, he stood outside to monitor Martinez's performance. The man began telling Martinez he wasn't responsible for the acts. He gave an alibi for each of the time frames when the disappearances took place. Martinez hammered him with lies about having witnesses and evidence pointing otherwise to see if he'd crack and admit. The man in their custody continued pleading innocence. Martinez presented him with pictures collected at the scenes. The man requested legal counsel and refused to speak any further. Martinez went outside and talked to his team of detectives and inquired with Ballesteros for his opinion. Ballesteros replied, "I want to believe his story of non- involvement but why did he ask for an attorney? He's probably hiding something from us. I say you leave him in there for a bit and then go back in and try deescalating the dialogue to lure him in for a confession."

Martinez said, "I was thinking the same. Well, guess I'm taking my lunch break and will be back to burp in front of the subject so he can get hungry then want to cooperate in order to eat." The detectives and Ballesteros laughed and walked away, leaving the guy by himself in the room.

About thirty minutes later, Martinez came back to the interviewing room and took a seat across from the suspect. He burped and mentioned, "That was a good burrito. Have you eaten already?"

The subject replied, "I can smell it all the way over here man, excuse you. I haven't eaten anything since last night. I was about to, when I got picked up." His stomach was growling.

Martinez uttered, "Well sucks for you. If you'd cooperate, I'd be willing to bring you something." He then took out a chocolate bar from his pocket and began to enjoy it slowly, enticing the subject.

The guy said, "Man, that's fucked up how you're eating in front of me after I told you I was hungry."

Martinez uttered, "You want some? Here, have a piece so you won't accuse me of being arrogant." The man thanked him and put the piece in his mouth then requested a glass of water.

Martinez told him, "With ice or no ice?" Being sarcastic.

One of the other investigators went to grab the man a glass of water. He then brought it back to him and handed it over. The suspect questioned, "Has my lawyer been informed I'm here already? Because you guys haven't allowed me to contact him."

Martinez commented, "Why sure, he has been notified. Even the president has been informed by this time." The man answered, "You really are some asshole, aren't you? I'll play your waiting game then and not speak anymore till then."

"Suit yourself, I'm getting paid for every minute and second unlike you." Stated Martinez as he finished his chocolate bar and continued staring down the subject.

Eventually the suspect was released without probable cause, evidence or admittance. The department was back to square one.

Ballesteros left for the day as well as his boss and Martinez. A deputy stood guard at the rest stop deterring and hindering anyone from committing criminal activities in his presence. He had been relieved from duty by another deputy who was going to remain at the site overnight. Within his first hour he reported over the radio, "Unit 915 to dispatch."

"Go ahead, unit 915." Responded dispatch.

"Dispatch, I'm hearing noise coming from inside the restroom. I'll be going in to check. Standby for confirmation." Radioed the deputy.

"10-4." replied dispatch.

Seconds later the deputy's radio aired. There was shouting coming from the deputy himself who was being attacked. He appeared to be in distress to the point he fired one shot from his service weapon. Dispatch notified all units and they rushed to the scene. The transmission stopped on the deputy's frequency approximately six minutes before the first officer arrived on scene. When he radioed back to dispatch, his voice was muffled in shock- frantically stuttering- relaying what he was witnessing. The macabre finding the deputy described was inconceivable. Most of whom hearkened the details believed the deputy was fabricating them. Multiple units surrounded the restroom and everyone on the case was called and woken up. This crime scene was gruesome and it hit home. The sheriffs set a perimeter and began combing through it expecting to catch someone. The responding deputy was transported to the hospital since he had become mute and was unable to communicate any further. They placed a blanket over him due to the fact he was shivering out of frightening dismay.

Within minutes the sheriff's office had apprehended an unhoused man in his thirties who was located about half a mile from the crime scene. In his possession he had a ten-inch bladed knife with fresh blood on it and a wallet which belonged to the employee who was the eight victim. Martinez arrived and he too was baffled about the findings as he began filming everything in still pictures. There was blood on the walls along with scratch marks. The deputy's service weapon laid on the ground a few feet from the toilet bowl in the women's restroom. Some of the deputy's hair strains were scattered along the ground yanked from the roots with flesh attached to them. His left eye floated in the toilet's water, looking directly at Martinez when he peeked inside. The empty shell casing had landed near the sinks to wash one's hands. The deputy's badge had flown upward with enough pressure to stab into the ceiling and remain adhered. Blood was dripping from it.

The vagrant individual was questioned about the instance. He refused to cooperate with local authorities. He did mention he had found the wallet in the restroom the day before and took it with him. This had happened after the custodian's disappearance. As far as the blood on his knife, he swore he had defended himself from a coyote out in the open field where he was pinpointed at. The sheriffs took the knife to the lab as well as the wallet. The man continued to deny any involvement. He was booked but released once the results from the blood on the knife came back negative unmatching any of the victims. Ballesteros made another announcement after the arrest of the homeless man. The responding deputy made a full recovery. The deceased deputy's family received his pension and life insurance. The disappearances abruptly ceased afterwards. Law enforcement wasn't unable to say why but they truly believed it was the work of a serial killer who was only taking a break from his evil deeds and would soon recommence his atrocities.

They never expected the culprit to be a slime monster who hunted humans for its survival. It had been part of an experimental test conducted by the armed forces in Ft. Bliss. It managed to escape and flushed itself into the drainage system. Ending up in the Rio Grande where it roamed freely and preyed upon the wild life- till it grew bigger and hungrier. Then it began hunting and devouring humans after traveling back up the drain system and ending up near the public restrooms. It would enter the person's body through the anus as they'd sit down to utilize the toilet. Then it would eat the intestines, suck them down whole and consume the rest of the body within seconds. Taking the soul down the drain to never be seen or heard from again. It was able to travel through the drain system back and forth from the women's toilets to the men's undetected. Even after all the missing person reports were removed, nobody considered it to not have been a serial murder who committed the crimes.

Law enforcement officials were sure it was a serial killer on the loose and he'd eventually immerse once more. After the monster grew in size, its appetite got bigger and it had begun to catch those not using the toilet as well. When the deputy shot it, it fled the area and hasn't surfaced back up to prey yet. At least nothing has been reported so far. The military never had the chance to even take responsibility for it either. It was at large in the water systems and might still be alive right now, stalking its next victim. A few people have since vanished into thin air after using the restroom. Whether it be in public restrooms, workplaces and even in their own homes. All cases remain unsolved and the mystery became a legend in the making.

CHAPTER 4
CONSUELO.

Martin and his best friend Ben had a hobby of exploring and treasure hunting since they were in their youth. They would always look for lost treasures or relics. In their teens, they began metal detecting with an old Garret Grand Master CX lll. From there they started magnet fishing through canals, rivers, creeks and streams. They also scuba dived and snorkeled in search of valuables. They had managed to collect a ton of artifacts from the American Civil war as well as native goods. They also gathered several gold and silver coins. Jewelry and valuable metal made dishware too, added to their collection. Some of their findings they'd sell online and others they kept for themselves. A few ended up in museums. They resided in Albuquerque and were presently together pulling back their ropes to see what their magnets grabbed from the Rio Grande. Martin had something heavy on the end of his. He pulled with sure strength and began yanking something up the bridge. When the item was closer to him, he shouted, "What the heck! I caught the rim of a car with no tire!"

Ben started cracking up and replied, "That's a sign you need new rims for your car Martin. You've been traveling with that bent rim for almost a year. Luckily you haven't gotten into an accident."

Martin uttered, "It probably is a sign. I've been having to refill it with air more often. You think this rim will fit my ride?" Chuckling afterwards.

Ben replied, "I wouldn't place that on it if I was you. It's rusted and deteriorating away. I think the one you have on there already is a safer bet than that one." They both were laughing.

Ben felt something stuck to his magnet and said, "I might just have the car that rim belongs to on my end. Feels kinda heavy. Hopefully it's something cool or we're going to have to move to the other side of this bridge." He started reeling his rope in.

When he was able to see down at what the object on his magnet was, he observed it looked like a treasure chest. He got excited and so did Martin. Once the wooden box was up with them, they tried opening it but it was not only old and filthy but locked as well. They rinsed it off some, with their water bottles and flipped it over wondering how to open it. It had a keyhole but they had no key. Martin told Ben, "It's got to have something valuable inside to be locked right?" I can't wait to open it and see what's in there. It's pretty heavy too."

Ben answered, "I bet it's got some gold that'll help us retire young. Do you see a big rock or something we can break it open with? Or how about something to pry it?"

Martin commented, "No, don't break it. The box itself might be worth something. Let me go to my car and grab something to open it with." He ran towards his parked ride some feet away.

Moments after, Martin returned with a crowbar. He jammed it in the edge of the case, between the top and bottom. He lifted the crowbar as Ben held the case down to the ground. Pop! It opened up. They flipped it over to remove the water from inside. A bunch of old clothes fell from within. Ben said, "Is this a joke? Who would lock their clothes up in a wooden case as if it were worth anything?"

Martin replied, "Someone who only had their clothes and treasured it maybe?" As he shrugged his shoulders.

They quickly went through it and grabbed some trash bags to place the ancient linens inside to discard afterwards. Ben was a bit upset since he projected the case would be filled with gold or something valuable. Martin told him, "It's alright bud. We've found plenty of treasures before and even though this isn't one, it was funny to have come across it and will be one of those weird hilarious stories to share." Ben picked up the case and threw it on the ground, causing it to break into pieces.

Martin said, "Now look at the mess you made. We're going to have to pick it up and throw it away otherwise we might be subject to a fine." They collected the fragmented pieces of wood and then Ben spotted something on the ground.

Ben stated, "Holly shit, look at this." He lifted a necklace from the floor, dirty and rusty but he believed it may be worth something- so he pocketed it after Martin glanced at it.

Both then gathered their trash and dumped it. They got in Martin's ride and headed towards Filiberto's to grab a bite. Martin got himself a carne asada burrito and

Ben grabbed a chicken bowl. They took a seat in the dining area to enjoy their food. They first talked about their many adventures. Then Ben began telling Martin how his girlfriend had broken up with him. He said, "She told me she needed space and I agree, so do I. She wants to control my every move and gets mad because I don't tell her where I'm at all the time. I've never even questioned her location ever."

Martin replied, "That's good you cut her off then. There are types of women who don't want to submit and most of the time they're paranoid you're cheating on them since they're the ones doing it. Besides, you're still young and will find someone better. She'll be back once she's done with her hoe phase, if that's the case. I suggest you don't even bother paying her any attention when she does."

Ben uttered, "I couldn't agree with you any less. Her friend Jennifer has been hitting me up and I think I'm going to take her on a date or something. She seems interested in leading elsewhere rather than friends."

Martin said, "You go bud. You take her out and hopefully she's serious so Julie gets jealous and wants you back even sooner. Just don't leave a diamond for a pile of dirt or it'll be like the case we just found. All full of worthless materials and not worth the effort." They giggled as they wrapped up their meals.

From there, Martin dropped off Ben at his house. Ben went straight to his game station to play. Jennifer facetimed him and he began to chat with her. She asked him, "What're you doing? Did you have fun magnet fishing today with your friend? Did y'all catch anything good?"

Ben answered, "I'm playing online. Yeah, we had fun. Didn't get anything worth bragging about but I lured this wooden case full of old women's clothes. Then this necklace fell out of it, which was about the only valuable article I came across."

Jennifer replied, "Oh that's nice. Let me see it." He pulled it out of his pocket and showed it to her.

Jennifer uttered, "That's cool, it looks old. Are you going to clean it up or anything?"

Ben responded, "Yeah, later. I'll scrub some toothpaste over it and hopefully it shines back up again."

Jenny said, "So have you spoken to Julie?"

Ben commented, "Nah, and I don't want too either. She's just a waste of time. A lost cause unlike you. By the way, do you have any plans for later?"

Jennifer uttered, "Ha, ha, yeah, she's pretty immature, I'll admit that. Thanks for comparing me highly against her. I've got nothing planned. Why are you going to ask me out on a date?"

Ben told her, "Actually I'd really like to hang out with you. Do you want to go watch a film with me?"

Jenny stated, "Oh wow, sure. I'd love to."

Ben replied, "Alright, then I'll pick you up around seven, sounds good?"

"Yes, I'll be ready by then. I'll see you later Ben." Jenny said as they ended their facetime and he continued gaming.

Later that evening, Ben went to pick up Jennifer. He saw her exiting her house and thought she looked so femininely beautiful. He got out to get the door for her and then got back in. They drove to the cinemas and paid for their tickets. They walked into the theater room and up the stairs to the second to top row. They took a seat near the middle and observed how they were the only ones there. Ben told Jennifer, "You know, sometimes I wish I had met you first instead of Julie."

She smiled and blushed. She replied, "Well it doesn't matter to me because her loss could be my gain." She leaned in for a smooch. The movie previews came on and some people walked in to view the film.

Jennifer put her head into his chest. He began caressing her head and running his fingers through her hair. It seemed like they were meant to be all along. During the movie, Jennifer got scared and dug her face into his chest. He held her tight, letting her know she was safe with him. She hugged him firmly and planted a kiss on his lips. Ben was fascinated by the way she carried herself. She was a sweet gal and that turned him into being chivalrous. At the end of the flick, he drove her home and they kissed goodbye. As she was exiting his vehicle, he said, "Oh wait. I had almost forgotten to give you this." He took out the necklace he found in the river and handed it to her.

Jennifer questioned, "Is this the one you found earlier today? You cleaned it, awe, thank you Ben." She then French kissed him and walked inside her house.

The next morning as Ben slept in comfortably, he got a call from Julie. He rejected it and went back to sleep a bit longer. He thought she wanted to argue about dating Jennifer or something.

When he eventually woke up, he noticed she had left a voicemail. He was about to erase it but instead listened to what she had to say. Julie was with no doubt in distress. She said while sobbing, "Jenny is dead. Her mother called me this morning to let me know. She told me she found her in her bed with a silver necklace in her hands and a frozen gaze of fright in her eyes. She suffered a heart attack and is now at the county morgue."

Ben jumped out of bed with disbelief. He called Jennifer but her phone was off. So, he called Julie back and spoke to her. She was inconsolable and so was he. He eventually hung up on her and drove over to Jennifer's home to speak to her brother.

When he got there, several of their family members were present, supporting them through their hardship. He rang the doorbell and was let inside by Leon- Jennifer's older brother. They knew each other from school and he shared the news to Ben. Leon repeated what Julie had informed him. He did mention the necklace he had given her left with her body since they weren't able to remove it from her grasp. He also said it was a picture locket which Ben had no clue that it wasn't just some oval shaped charm. She had passed away with her eyebrows raised in a state of anxiety having her mouth locked shut with so much pressure she cracked several teeth. He told her brother that if they'd be able to recover the necklace, he'd like to have it back to have something to remember her by. Ben gave his condolences to him and his family and departed back to his home.

As soon as he walked into his bedroom, he began crying loudly in the first stages of desperation. Martin called him on his cell phone and he picked up. Martin said, "What's up bud? How'd it go last night on your date?"

Ben answered while whimpering, "She's gone."

Martin inquired, "Why're you crying, and what do you mean she's gone, gone where?" Ben informed him, "She was found dead this morning in her bedroom."

Martin felt empathy and replied, "Damn, I'm sorry to hear that, bro. I see why you're sad right now. How'd it happen though?"

Ben stated, "Her mom found her dead in her bed with her eyes wide open and tightly grasping the necklace I found yesterday in her hands. She died from heart failure."

Martin replied, "What the hell? Are you serious? She wasn't even out of shape or old enough to have passed from heart complications."

Ben uttered, "I know she wasn't, but that's what really happened, whether it sounds fishy or not."

Martin told him, "You want me to go keep you company, bud? I understand it might not be an adequate moment, but I'd like to accompany you through this tough time."

Ben commented, "I appreciate your support, Martin, but I'd like to be alone right now to gather my thoughts. I'll contact you tomorrow if you don't mind?"

Martin said. "Alright, well, my phone and door will be available for you if you need anything, bro. Just ask, and it shall be done. Talk to tomorrow, and once again, I'm very sorry about what happened."

Ben responded, "Thanks," and they hung up.

Later that night, Ben had some horrifying nightmares and woke up with night sweats-gasping for oxygen. He saw an old woman with only half her body and one arm, crawling his way as he snorkeled in the water. She crept into the water, and all went silent besides some patterning sound. She then swam over to him and got a hold of his hand. She stared deep into his gaze, and that's when he woke up. He was running late for work. So, he jumped out of bed and took a quick shower before heading out of his apartment.

From there, he headed to his job. He was employed by a small business shop downtown that targeted tourists with local goods and souvenirs. He worked for an older man who had been born and raised in Burque. The man told Ben, "Come help me unload some merchandise from my truck." As Ben arrived and followed him.

They grabbed some new souvenirs and took them inside the store. The owner took them in the back to inventory and price tag before putting them out on display.

Ben went back to the front of the store while the owner organized the merchandise. He observed some man in the entrance speaking to someone on his cell phone before entering. The man was talking about some morgue worker who died in her sleep. He described the employee's death as coincidentally similar to Jennifer's. When the man hung up and went inside, Ben asked him, "I'm sorry to be nosey, but the person who you were speaking of, did she by any chance have a necklace locket in her hands when she was found?

The man looked at him confused but answered, "Yes, how'd you know that if no one has been informed of such detail?"

"My friend Jennifer was found the same way yesterday morning. Her body was taken to the morgue, and I have reason to believe the necklace has something to do with the strange deaths."

The man was a detective who was there to shop for a gift for one of his friends who was visiting him from out of town. He had reason to suspect Ben knew more than he stated and took him to the precinct for questioning. Ben told them all he knew in comparison to both cases. He explained to them where he had found the necklace and how Jennifer obtained it. He had an alibi and was released from their custody after nothing was implemented; he was guilty in either of the cases since they were both treated as natural causes. His boss had been worried about him, and as soon as Ben got the chance to call him, he did so.

It turned out the lady from the morgue thought it would be a good idea to take the necklace from Jennifer's body and keep it for herself. Another detail from when her body was located was that she had bitten the tip of her tongue off and chipped some teeth from clenching her mouth shut. Ben was more suspiciously concerned about the necklace and had advised the detectives to try and locate it. He also called the morgue to talk to someone about his hunch. He received confirmation that the necklace wasn't located anymore and was missing.

Martin called him and told him he had experienced a similar dream about a woman missing half her body, crawling towards him. Ben explained, "I have a feeling that the necklace we came across in the wooden case is cursed. It may appear wild but two people in its possession have died in their sleep and both were found clinching it in their hands."

Martin uttered, "So what do you propose we do?"

Ben stated, "We need to locate the necklace and get rid of it before anyone else dies." Martin questioned, "How exactly are we going to be able to track the necklace?"

Ben mentioned, "I was given the name of the lady who worked at the morgue, and I was able to find her address. I plan on breaking into her home at night and searching for it there. Her coworker said she didn't have it when her body was taken in. So, I'm guessing she dropped it at her house or someone else took it."

Martin replied, "Alright, I'm down to help out in whatever you feel necessary." They agreed to meet up at dawn.

Ben and Martin met up as planned and drove over to the lady's address. When they got there, they quietly exited Ben's vehicle and tippy-toed to the back of the dwelling. Once in the backyard, they checked to see if any of the windows were unlocked. Martin located one that wasn't secured; they pushed it open and made entry. Once inside the residence, they turned on their flashlights and ventured through the rooms. They located the woman's bedroom and searched for the necklace. They were about to give up when Martin found it under the bed. He picked it up and showed it to Ben. Then all of a sudden, the room went silent, and they heard the same water- dripping sound as in their dreams. They looked at each other, and Ben spotted something moving on the ground. He turned his light towards the location of the movement and witnessed the old woman crawling their way while grunting. They both ran out of the house and jumped over the fence, heading towards Ben's ride. As they jumped over and tried proceeding towards the vehicle, they unwillingly weren't able to direct themselves properly. They were running in place and couldn't move from the same spot they were in, no matter how hard they attempted to sprint. They looked back and saw the woman pulling herself forward with her right arm; the left one was missing as well as her lower extremities. They both were petrified, and Martin decided to toss the necklace, which broke their pause and allowed them to run and jump in the car. They then got the hell out of dodge as Martin looked back at the old woman who had vanished from where she last was.

When they arrived at Martin's residence, they consulted with each other about what had just occurred. They were in shock and couldn't make sense of what they both had witnessed. Martin got out of Ben's car and headed inside his house. Ben drove towards his apartment and both weren't able to get a good night's sleep with the nightmares that followed.

The following day when Ben was at work, he came across some more bad news. He learned from a radio station he was listening to that some man was found dead this morning in the same fashion as Jennifer and the lady from the morgue. The man was walking by the deceased morgue lady's house and found the necklace on the ground. He took it with him and the woman with no legs got him. Ben decided to contact the detective in order to inform him of the possibilities of him dying from the same cause. When the detective picked up his cell phone he said, "How dare you call me to tell me how to do my job. Just who do you think you are?"

Ben answered, "I'm not telling you how to go about your business sir. I'm only trying to help you solve these cases and prevent anymore from happening. I don't want anyone else to suffer like my friend Jenny."

The detective replied, "Well your suspicions are inconceivable. There's no way what you've described to me is a possibility. You should stop watching horror movies because they're affecting your thoughts. By the way, the neighbors from the lady who worked at the morgue called in some suspicious activity at the deceased women's residence. When the officers responded, they said they found one of the back windows open and things were moved around inside the house. If I find out you're responsible for the intrusion, I'm going to arrest you for tampering with evidence." He then hung up the call.

As soon as Ben put his phone down, the lady from next door walked into the souvenir shop. She ran a small pawn shop next door. The woman walked up to Ben and asked, "By any chance do you know a thing or two about plumbing?"

Ben answered, "I sure do Miss. Lola. Do you have an issue at your shop?"

Lola replied, "Since I opened up this morning, I've been hearing some water dripping and I can't figure out where it's coming from. Can you help me out please?"

Ben uttered, "Yes, let me just inform my boss I'll be stepping out for a minute or so to assist you." He went to the back of the shop to notify the store owner.

Ben and Lola went next door to her pawn shop. Ben heard the water patterning and began searching for the probable cause. He looked around for some time and wasn't able to locate the leak. He found it awkward there was no leak present nor a puddle visibly left behind. Lola asked him, "Did you find it?"

Ben responded, "No mam, I find it weird though. I can hear it too but I don't see anything to pinpoint where it's at."

Lola uttered, "Well don't worry about it then. I'll just contact a plumber to come have a look. I don't want to take any more of your time and have your boss dock your pay."

Ben stated, "Alright mam, well I apologize I wasn't able to assist you but I do hope you find and fix the issue." He began making his way out of her store.

Something caught Ben's attention before he got to the entrance which caused him to turn around to view the jewelry display. There he spotted the necklace in the center of all the jewelry. He questioned Lola, "Where did you get this?" Pointing at the necklace.

Lola stated, "Some man came by first thing this morning and sold it to me. It looks old and it's really nice, isn't it? Maybe you should get it for your girlfriend, I'll even give you a discount on it if you'd like?" She opened the display and grabbed it.

Ben looked at her and said, "You need to get rid of it and not touch it."

Lola stated, "Nonsense, this was made in Mexico around the seventeenth century. It's missing the photo from the locket but it's made of high-quality silver. Here take a look at it, feel it in your hands."

Ben retorted, "You need to get rid of it or you're going to die!" And ran out of the shop.

Ben ran back next door and called the detective. After informing the investigator of the necklace's current location, the detective told him, "You seriously need to stop fantasizing about your conspiracy theory. I'd also recommend you get off any drugs you might be consuming." He then ended the call.

Within the following hour or so, Ben observed police units heading next door. He went outside to check what was going on and he viewed them putting red tape at the entrance to Lola's shop. He inquired with one of the officers at the scene about what had happened but the officer told him to mind his own business. Then the detective he had warned, strolled through the shop's entrance to investigate Lola's death. She too had the necklace in her hands and her teeth broken from the pressure of tightly closing her mouth in fear. The detective found out from a witness that Ben was the last one inside Lola's shop before she was found deceased. He went next door and cuffed him. Ben was taken into custody for questioning.

The detective had run prints at the dead morgue's employee's house and they matched Ben's. He couldn't justify when he actually left them there since Martin denied they had broken into the woman's home after she was found dead. Martin's fingerprints were not discovered at the home, only Ben's. He was also charged with the possible murder of Jennifer and Lola. The detective couldn't place him at the scene of the crime of the man who was found lifeless on the streets after he found the necklace in the front of the lady's house.

Ben was booked and facing capital murder. He was sent to a correctional facility while he awaited trial. One day, as he woke up in his cell, an officer placed a manila envelope through his tray slot. Ben grabbed it and opened it, believing it was good news. As he ripped the side open, a silver necklace fell onto his bunk. He froze stiff not knowing what to do with it or who had sent it to him. The envelope didn't contain a return address. Suddenly he began hearing water trickling inside his cell. He immediately tossed it down the toilet but before he was able to flush it, the woman with no lower extremities crawled under his cell door. Ben froze as he saw her making her way towards him and no one was there to help. She climbed up towards his neck and he began to seal his mouth shut with pressure. He heard his teeth crack as she groaned near his mouth. The woman gazed into his soul and he began to have convulsions. He suddenly broke free from her and flushed the necklace down the drain which caused her to disappear from his presence. His neighboring cell mates described him screaming hysterically in need of assistance. Ben was found inside his cell swearing distorted dialogue as he attempted to puzzle the story while speaking to himself. He was taken to a psych ward where he remained unaware of life in general. He was found guilty by insanity and never saw freedom again.

His friend Martin, and some of his relatives visited him at the ward but they weren't able to hold a conversation with him since he kept speaking to himself trying to figure out the mystery behind the necklace. Martin also tried fighting in his defense but never admitted he took part in the break in. He refused to implicate himself involved in the crimes Ben was being charged with. The woman continued to torment him in his dreams until one day he could no longer bear it and hung himself. Even on his last breath, Ben argued out loud what went through his mind but he died unable to gather his thoughts and solve the reasons for the woman's existence. The woman's name was Consuelo and her life's summary is as follows.

New Spain had collapsed in the seventeenth century. There were various diseases which hit the numbers of the indigenous people. The Spanish rulers who had invaded their territories not only robbed them of their resources but also infected them with their illnesses. The native population plummeted in a major decline. The Spanish government had sent explorers, missionaries and settlers to Mission Dolores in San Francisco. Illustrations of the miraculous apparition of the brown Virgin of Guadalupe brought comfort and acceptance to both Indians and criollos. Estafado was taught along with maiolica ware in Puebla.

Consuelo was of mestizo descendancy. Her father was Spaniard and her mother was indigenous. She had been brought up with both cultural backgrounds. When she was fourteen years of age, her father made her marry a prominent Spanish businessman who was twenty-seven years old. She got pregnant soon after and gave birth to a girl who they named Yolanda. Her husband had a dark side no one ever knew though. He was a drunk, liar, thief and cheater. He ended up abandoning Consuelo and their daughter. Some say he moved out and started another family with his mistress and others claimed he went back to Spain. Yolanda- his daughter- was about to turn three when this occurred. Consuelo moved from Puebla to go live with her grandmother in what is now New Mexico. She and Yolanda settled right in after a long journey. Consuelo began making pottery she had learned to create in her home town and sold it at a local public market. She was beginning to make it on her own when a group of bad men came into town causing panic. They would gang up on the men and beat them. They'd steal and trick the people in town. Asking for money in return for peace in order to not hurt them. This gang of men one day kidnaped Yolanda after they attempted to collect a payment from Consuelo's sales. She searched for her daughter and when she found her, the men tied her up to watch them rape and kill her in her presence. They left Consuelo in the same room her child laid deceased in. She managed to free herself and grabbed her lifeless child's body in her arms. She was in deep sorrow, sobbing until some of the men in the town found her. They helped her give Yolanda a proper burial and she vowed revenge on the gang who took her kid.

She eventually stumbled on the gang as they terrorized another female victim. She began swinging a machete at the men, slicing several and distracting them long enough for their prey to run away. She wasn't strong enough to defeat them on her own though. The group of men disarmed and grabbed her, tying her up. They beat her mercilessly and took turns in raping her. One of the men observed a silver necklace around her neck and snatched it off of her. She pleaded for him to return it to her. It had a picture pendent of Yolanda, the only photo memory she owned of her. She offered to cooperate with them and do as they please with her as long as they gave her her necklace back. The men didn't comply and continued raping and torturing her. When they had enough, they took her down to a water well and began mutilating her body with machetes as she remained alive. They severed her waist and burned her legs and left arm. Her right arm remained attached to her torso when they tossed it into the rock well. She was carrying her belongings in a wooden case since her plan was to skip town after venging her daughter's death. The men threw her case in the well with her, along with the necklace and pendant she begged for. Over the years to come, the well was covered over and a dwelling structure was built on top. The weight of the home made the rock well break and it eventually sent its stagnant water towards a canal along with Consuelo's wooden case and silver necklace. Before she passed, people swore she was infected with evil. They claimed she had made a pact with the devil himself.

This explains how she was able to return to earth and hunt those in possession of her beloved necklace with the picture of Yolanda in it.

CHAPTER 5
A TASTE FOR WASTE.

Mrs. Crumply was watching the news as her friend Noah fixed her uncooperative toilet flange. In their small town, there had been multiple suspicious deaths trailing some years back. The local police department hadn't apprehended any suspects. They had dozens of interviews with potential leads but nothing solid yet. Mrs. Crumply enjoyed obtaining her information from the news and she sat on her living room couch in the present moment doing so. They had reported another possible murder. A female in her early thirties was located in a riverbend hiding behind some brush- disemboweled. Her breasts had been sawed off and were missing along with her buttocks just as the rest. Mrs. Crumply worried for herself and other town residents. Everyone in town feared to be next to die.

Noah walked out of the restroom and over to where Mrs. Crumply sat. He told her, "I was able to fix the flange. It was a little loose and I tightened it some after replacing a broken screw. It shouldn't give you any more trouble."

Mrs. Crumply replied, "Thank you Noah... How much do I owe you?"

Noah answered, "You don't owe me anything Mrs. Crumply. Consider it a gift or small token for all the meals you've shared with me, plus the good friendship you've offered over the years."

Mrs. Crumply uttered, "You're such a blessing Noah. Ever since I met you, you've been nothing but an honest, kind and generous young man. Let me get up and serve you something to eat then. It's the least I'll accept in return." They both walked over to her kitchen.

Mrs. Crumply began heating up some leftover meatloaf and mashed potatoes she had cooked the previous day. Noah took a seat and watched her as she spoke to him.

She said, "Have you heard they found the body of a woman over by the riverbend? I hope whoever is killing people is caught and it stops. I'm actually scared to go out even to the store to buy needed goods once the sun goes down. I've been locking my doors and paying attention to any strange noise I hear as I watch television before going to bed. I'm pretty paranoid and since my husband passed away, I have no one here to defend me if such an event arises. How about you Noah, are you taking any precautions?"

Noah commented, "I don't watch the news, so I didn't know they found another person dead in town. As far as taking my precautions, I also lock my doors and sleep with a baseball bat next to my bed. You at least have a dog as the first line of defense. I need to get one also to keep me company at my mother's house. If ever you feel in danger, give me a call and I'll come running down here."

Mrs. Crumply responded, "Thank you Noah. You know, my friend from down the road has some puppies for sale if you're interested? I think she might even be giving them away since they're not full breed and are keeping her up at night disturbing her sleep."

Noah answered, "Yeah, let her know I'm in search of a furry buddy please." Mrs. Crumply said, "I'll call her right now. Here's some food for you to eat, meanwhile I give her a ring." She handed him a plate and strolled over to her landline.

Mrs. Crumply engaged in a conversation with her friend and informed her Noah wanted a pup. Mrs. Crumply hung up and walked over to her kitchen. She told Noah, "She says you can go pick one out right now or even take them all from her hands since she's fed up with them. When you're done eating, I can drive you over there and then to your home so you won't have to walk."

Noah swallowed his food and replied, "Thanks Mrs. Crumply. I sure appreciate your fast connections and hospitality. Sometimes I wish you were my mother."

Mrs. crumply uttered, "No problem and I too wouldn't have mind raising such a fine young man like you. Since I wasn't able to give birth to my own. I'll never get to experience motherhood other than having you around which brings me comfort." They both had a moment of coincidence filling their voids. Where she always wanted children and he wanted a mother after his had passed away some years back.

Noah concluded indulging in his delectable meal and Mrs. Crumply grabbed her car keys. They walked outside her home as she locked her front door. Both entered her vehicle and drove down to see the puppies. When they got there- Flower was waiting for them. Her and Mrs. Crumply were in their seventies and had grown up in town together. Flower greeted them both and welcomed them inside her dwelling as Mrs. Crumply introduced Noah to her. She offered them water which they both rejected politely. Noah began looking at the puppies which were in a clothed cardboard box with their mother located in the living area. He picked a male up in his hands. He fell in love with this particular pup. The puppy licked his face as he pulled him in for a closer observation. Noah said, "I'll take this one if you don't mind, Flower?"

Flower replied, "That one is the least nagging and most independent. That's a great choice Noah. You sure you don't want to take them all with you? Maybe you can sell them or something? I'm too old to be taking care of these puppies when momma wants a break or doesn't feed them promptly before they cry loud enough to disturb my rest."

Noah answered, "Thank you Flower but I wouldn't be able to care for all of them either. Let alone feed them, I can barely sustain myself."

Flower inquired, "How old are you and what do you do for a living? I don't think I've seen you around town before. Have you been living here for a while?"

Noah responded, "I'm nineteen years old and I do odd jobs to provide for myself. If I don't make enough off of the jobs, I resort to hunting for food which helps. I haven't seen you around either. I suppose we've eluded each other long enough." He chuckled and continued, "I hardly go out other than when someone calls me because they need something fixed. I stay home most of the time reading books. I was brought here by my mother when I was under a year old and have been here since."

Flower uttered, "Oh, you're very young. About the same age as my granddaughter who lives out in the city. That's good you keep yourself busy working, hunting and reading. You think you have a chance to look at my truck? It doesn't want to start and I haven't been able to head to town to get some stuff done?"

Noah told her, "Sure, I can check it out for you." They all walked outside as Mrs. Crumply spoke highly of Noah's experience.

Flower handed him the keys to her truck. He opened the door and took a seat at the driver's side. He inserted the key in the ignition and tried cranking it up. The engine didn't even sputter a bit. He got out and walked towards the front of the truck. He opened the hood and saw her battery terminals were dirty and corroded. He requested some boiling water which Flower stated, "Just my luck. I was boiling some to make myself tea. Let me go grab it." She walked back into her home.

Moments later, Flower came out with a pot of boiling hot water. She handed it to Noah and he poured some over the battery terminals to clean them. He had no tools in hand to remove them in order to properly clean them up but he wanted to check if that was the issue first. He then cranked the truck but it died on him. He turned the headlights on and noticed they weren't operating at normal power. Noah told Flower,

"I think your battery is either bad or it may just need to charge up. I have a battery charger at my house and it can check the voltage as well. If Mrs. Crumply doesn't mind taking me to my house to check and bring me back, I can have this issue resolved in about twenty minutes or so."

Mrs. Crumply said, "I don't mind one bit. It's not like I have anything better to do anyhow."

Just as they were getting into Mrs. Crumply's vehicle- Sergeant Tobias was passing by in his unit. He greeted them, then informed them to keep their doors locked and to not be out late at night alone due to the possibility of a serial killer on the prowl. He then drove off to continue warning the residents in town after the latest body was found. Mrs. Crumply drove Noah back to his house. He got out and ran inside to grab his tool bag and his battery charger. He sprinted back to the car and they headed back to Flower's dwelling.

When they arrived, Flower had finished making her tea and offered them a glass which they accepted this time. Noah got back under the hood and removed the battery terminals. He cleaned them up and connected his battery jumper/ charger to the power source. He then saw it wasn't completely drained so he jump started the truck within the timeframe he had mentioned. Flower was pleased and told him, "Oh, thank you very much Noah. I don't know what I would have done without you. How much do I owe you for your service?"

Noah answered, "Don't worry about it. The pup will do in return for this small favor. Just tell anyone you know that I can help with things around their house or cars please."

Flower grabbed a twenty-dollar bill from her pocket and stuck it inside Noah's pants stating, "Here, take this. I will be offended if you don't. I sure will let people know you're an honest humble worker of all trades." Noah kept the twenty and they said goodbye.

Mrs. Crumply dropped him off at his house with his new puppy. She said bye to him and drove back to her residence. Noah walked inside his home and put the pup down. He grabbed a bowl and gave it some water to drink. He sat down in the living room watching the dog scoop a drink. He told the puppy, "What should I name you boy? What name would you like and will respond to, hm?" He paused to ponder and then uttered, "Pot! Flower gave me you and your name will be Pot. Sounds good buddy?" As he nudged the pup on its head.

Later that day Noah made Pot a collar and chain and they walked into town to get him some food with the twenty Flower had paid him. When he got to the store, he greeted Gus- the owner. He then walked over to the dog food section and grabbed some loose pebbles and placed them in a bag to be weighed. He walked up to the register and Gus told him, "I see you got yourself a new friend there. Just take the bag with you and make sure he'll actually eat before I sell you some more."

Noah replied, "You sure Gus? I've got money to pay." "Positive Noah, you go on now," retorted Gus."

Noah thanked him and walked out with Pot. They were walking down a road less traveled but it was the fastest route back home. As they trekked along, Pot jumped up and started barking at something behind some bushes which caught his attention. Noah pulled his leash and told him, "Come on Pot, it's probably just some raccoon or skunk." Pot followed his new owner as something in the bushes gazed at them.

When they safely managed to return to Noah's home, Pot was fed some of the dog food as Noah observed whether he liked it or not. Pot devoured all of the food as if he had never eaten before and was starving. Noah chuckled and said, "Damn Pot, you're a beast aren't you? First you barked at something that scared you with bravery and now you're scarfing down this food like you're going to war and might never eat again." Pot looked at him wiggling his tail.

Noah played with Pot a bit. Made him bite down a towel and try ripping it out of his hands to strengthen his jaw. Afterwards, they laid in bed and closed their eyes. During this process, a sound woke them up. Noah grabbed his bat as Pot barked. Noah peeked through the window and searched for a possible intruder. He was unable to see correctly so he got up and headed outside with his Louisville slugger in hand. Pot followed him as they both exited the front door to check. Pot took off running and Noah pursued right behind. An adult size raccoon took off once it heard them both approaching. Noah was relieved and picked up Pot off the ground because he was going to continue chasing the trash panda who was scavenging for food into the woods. Noah laughed and told Pot, "You're such a brave little doggy, aren't you? Good boy! I'm proud of you Pot." As he rubbed his nose over his.

They both went back inside and back to bed. Noah placed his bat nearby and laid Pot next to him. Pot snuggled with Noah looking for body heat. Noah hugged him and they both dreamed away.

The next morning when they woke up, Pot had peed on the bed. Noah woke up with the side of his body cold and wet. He was a little upset but got up and cleaned the mess. He also showered Pot right before he fed him. As he was finishing up, he got a call from a woman who told him Flower had recommended and directed her towards his services. She needed him to fix her kitchen sink which was clogged up and spilling over the floor. Noah told her, "Let me have your address and I'll be over there in a few. I just need to finish some things I've got going on and I'll be right over there."

He took his bed sheets and comforter out of the washer and placed them in the dryer. He then took a quick shower after scrubbing his mattress. When he got out, he got dressed, put Pot outside, chained him up and grabbed his tools. He took his bike and peddled over to the lady's residence traveling right by Mrs. Crumpleys who lived a short walking distance from him. When he got there, he rang the doorbell. The woman opened the door and let him in. She showed him where her issue was and let him get to work. He first plunged the sink which didn't help alleviate the clog. He then began removing the water out of the sink with a pitcher and threw it outside in her garden to not let it go to waste. Once the overfill was addressed, he began unscrewing the plumbing pipes under the sink. When he disassembled the pipes, he discovered there was a dish cloth in there which was the problem. He removed it and put everything back together. Once he was done, he turned the sink on and observed it functioning properly. Noah then told the woman, "All done mam. Found this cloth in there which was not allowing the water to go down."

The woman replied, "Oh my, I've been looking for that for about a week now. I didn't realize it had fallen inside the sink drain. Thank you, Noah, for fixing my issue. How much are you going to charge me for the job?"

Noah told her, "Well it didn't take me long but it was a plumbing issue. Let me see here." As he thought of a decent price to charge.

"It'll be thirty dollars mam. Does that sound alright to you? Stated Noah. The woman uttered, "Wow, that's a fair price. Normally the plumbers charge one hundred just to come take a look. Sure, let me go grab my purse. I'll be right back." Noah waited for her in the kitchen looking at the pictures she had on her refrigerator.

When the woman came back, she handed Noah two twenties and said, "Here you go Noah. I don't have change to break one."

Noah went through his pocket looking for change but the woman told him, "Keep the forty. Don't give me back the difference. I think forty is fair enough since I believe you under charged me for your work. I'll spread the word out with my contacts to promote your services."

Noah replied, "No mam, I can't accept forty when I charged you thirty. I do appreciate you telling others about my work but I'm an honest person."

"Nonsense Noah, accept the extra ten as a bonus or tip of gratitude," Answered the woman.

Noah kindly took the forty after she refused to receive it back. He then left her house and got back on his bike. He peddled his way back to his home. Halfway there, Sergeant Tobias pulled him over and told him, "Hey Noah, have you seen anything strange around town? Any new comers or visitors that may be looking for trouble perhaps?"

Noah answered, "How's it going Sergeant? Nope I can't say I have. You know I keep to myself when not busy. I will keep my eye open though now that you've mentioned it."

Tobias inquired, "Where are you coming from with that tool bag on you?"

Noah responded, "I'm coming from this lady's house down the street. She called me to fix her clogged sink. Now I'm headed back home to check on my dog?"

"Alright, when do you think you'll have a chance to check out my home? I've got a broken window I'd like replaced," said the sergeant.

Noah commented, "I can go right now if you'd like me to? I'd need to take measurements of it and see if they have one in town."

Tobias uttered, "It measures twenty-four by twenty-four and I already ordered it."

Noah said, "How'd you break your bathroom window?"

"How'd you know it's the bathroom window I'm trying to fix?" Questioned the sergeant. Noah stated, "That's a common size for bathroom windows sir."

Tobias replied, "Oh, I see you know your stuff. Had this bird fly into it and shattered it leaving a mess behind. I'll give you a call when it comes in, sounds good?" "Yeah, let me know when it does so, I can go replace it for you," responded Noah.

"Great, in the meantime keep your eyes open for anything suspicious. We might have a serial killer on our hands. A carnivore to be exact, we keep finding bodies with missing flesh."

Noah asked, "Should I be alarmed about this killer? You're making me worry now."

Tobias told him, "You're a big boy who can handle himself, so don't be scared. This person targets women only. Anyhow, I'll keep you posted. You have yourself a good day now and stay out of trouble."

As he drove off. Later that day, Tobias was called to a suspicious person walking down one of the roads in town. He drove over there and found a woman's corpse hidden behind a tree. He radioed the activity in. He then heard a branch crack and turned his flashlight on, directing it towards the sound. He spotted a person running away and gave chase after. The subject took off and Tobias lost sight. As Tobias heard sirens heading his way, he searched with his flashlight and gun drawn for the suspect. Then something knocked his light from his hands. Tobias fired a round and hit a tree in the woods where they both were. He was unable to see clearly since it was dark. Then he felt a blow on the back of his head and fell to the ground.

When he regained consciousness, his partners were out looking for him. He made his way towards them and informed them of the occurrence. They set up a perimeter on the roads surrounding the woods. By the end of the night, they had recovered the dead body but failed to apprehend the suspect who evaded their perimeter.

The local news sent a reporter out on the field to cover the story. Tobais's head- ached so he took some pills to help him out. He had managed to not get murdered but also to not catch the killer and he was upset about it. He was medically cleared by the paramedics on scene. When all was said and done, he went back home and threw some things around in anger. He poured some whiskey in a cup and chugged it. After a few drinks, he fell asleep.

During his rest, Tobais woke up and checked who had rung his doorbell. There was a package outside in his door steps. The window had arrived. He grabbed it and took it inside, then called Noah to let him know so he could fix it as soon as he had a chance. Noah replied, "Yes sir, I can go over right now if you're available?"

Tobias uttered, "If you're not gonna make too much noise it'll work. Otherwise, I'll call you after I wake up. Had a long night at work and got out a few hours ago."

Noah told him, "I won't make much noise. Matter of fact, just tell me where you left the window, leave the door open and I'll wake you up when I'm finished."

Tobias answered, "Ok, I'll leave the window in the restroom. The back door will be unlocked and I'll be asleep in my room till you're done. Thanks Noah, see you later." They hung up and Tobias placed the new window on the bathroom floor and unlocked his back door before he locked himself back in his room and closed his eyes.

Noah tied up Pot and grabbed his tool bag. He then rode his bicycle over to Tobias's. When he got there, he quietly set his bike against the exterior wall and entered through the back. He walked over to the restroom and found the new window there. He took the new one out and took measurements of the old one and compared them both to make sure before he started. He began removing the old window which was halfway broken out already. He shoved a pry bar between the side and pulled out the frame almost with ease, after slicing through the old caulking. He then gently placed it on the floor. He grabbed the new window and began fitting it in the window sill using his level as a guide. Tobias had also purchased some foam insulation spray so Noah grabbed it and began spraying it around the window as he screwed it in place. When he finished, he let the foam set a bit before cutting off the excess. Once he removed the excess and cleaned up a little, he began cocking up the edges. He had been there for about three hours now and he had concluded the installation. He put all his tools away inside his bag and cleaned up all the mess. He then went over to Tobias's bedroom and knocked.

Tobias got up out of bed and walked over to the door to open it. Once he swung it open, he saw Noah standing on the other side. Noah told him, "Sorry to wake you up but I'm done now."

Tobias responded, "That was fast, let me go see how it looks." He walked out of his room and over to the restroom then continued, "Wow, you did a great job Noah. I'm very pleased with your work. Tell me now, how much are you going to want to get paid for it?"

Noah answered, "I'm glad you're pleased with the way it looks. It took me about three hours to do so, how does sixty bucks sound to you?"

Tobias uttered, "That's too cheap Noah. Come follow me back to my room so I can get my wallet." They both strolled over to his bedroom and he got his wallet and said, "Here's eighty for doing excellent work."

Noah took the money and commented, "Thank you sergeant. This is really going to help me out a lot."

Tobias noticed Noah's hand was cut up and asked, "How'd that happen to you?

Did you cut yourself with the old glass?"

Noah hid his hand and replied, "No, I cut it up last night while opening up a can of food to feed my dog Pot. Anyhow, I'll get out of your way so you can continue sleeping" Tobias walked him out and locked the door as he observed Noah hop on his bike and take off.

Noah peddled to Gus's store to buy some food for him and Pot. When he got there, Gus was sweeping the front. Noah greeted him and walked inside. Noah went through the freezers looking for some chicken. He found a bag of breasts and then got himself some corn tortillas, bell peppers, onions and tomatoes. He was planning on cooking some fajitas. By the time he took his items to the counter, Gus was back from sweeping. Gus began to charge him and asked, "Did your dog eat the food after all?"

Noah answered, "He did and thanks for reminding me I need to get more." He ran to get a small bag and took it to Gus.

When Gus rang all his items up, Noah paid him and departed the store. He got on his bike and peddled towards his home. Upon arrival at his residence, he noticed Pot wasn't where he had left him. His chain had been broken and he was missing. Noah began shouting his name out but didn't hear him bark back to him. Noah opened his door and walked inside to drop off the food. He then ran outside shouting and whistling for Pot.

He searched relentlessly for his pup but didn't find him. When he finally had given up, he walked back inside his home sad and wondering what had happened to Pot. He began cooking, placing some food in Pot's bowl and sat it outside hoping he would sniff it and return to eat. His house smelled delicious as his stove top helped him prepare the fajitas. When he finished, he served himself a plate and warmed up some tortillas. He then took a seat outside on his front porch looking to see if Pot smelled his food and wanted some but Pot was nowhere to be seen. Noah finished eating and took his dirty dish to the sink to wash. He then exited his home, once more shouting Pot's name and whistling. He had no luck again so he went inside his dwelling and turned on his television.

He began watching a movie and looking at his door wishing he'd see Pot standing outside as he continued to read a book he was on. Noah began closing his eyes while reading. Next thing he knew, he had fallen asleep with his door unlocked. During the middle of the night, he woke up to something clawing his spring door. Noah got up thinking it was Pot but it was actually a coyote eating the food he had left outside for Pot. Noah scared him away as he yelled at it and walked to the front door. Noah went outside and observed the coyote running away but still no sign of Pot. It was around midnight and he decided to take a stroll in search of his pup. He locked his front door and took off.

He was walking down the street whistling. He ended up all the way by a creek about half a mile from his home. There was a promiscuous female sitting down on a wooden bench looking at the flow of water. She looked up and saw Noah headed her way. Noah walked over to her and asked, "Excuse me, have you seen a little brown puppy around by any chance?"

She replied, "No, sorry but why don't you come take a seat next to me?"

Noah answered, "I can't, I'm looking for my dog." She played with her hair, running her fingers through it and lifted up her skirt to reveal more skin.

Noah was walking away from there when she shouted, "Come back here! Come talk to me, I want to get to know you!"

Noah felt his blood boil and told her, "I said no!"

The female responded, "Are you a queer or something?"

He then ran back towards her and began attacking her. The woman tried yelling for help but he covered her mouth with his hands and began strangling her by the neck. Suddenly, sergeant Tobias and his men rushed over. They had set up a trap to catch the female predator. Noah had killed the woman and once he saw the police, he took off running. They chased him and eventually caught up to him. He was taken down to the ground and handcuffed. When they picked him up to see who he was, they were all surprised to see him. One of the officers had radioed that the woman was dead. Tobais looked at Noah and asked, "What have you done Noah? I can't believe this. Are you the one responsible for the other deaths?" Noah remained silent but there was a distinctive predatory look in his eyes they had never seen before.

He was eventually booked into the town's small jail. Word spread fast around town and no one believed it was Noah. Some even defended him saying he was innocent. He was processed and Mrs. Crumpley went over to see if she could talk to him. Tobias denied anyone coming into contact with Noah. When they finally interviewed him, he confessed to the other murders and said he didn't intend on killing that girl while searching for Pot. Everyone was in shock. He began to tell his side of the story and the reason he had done such gruesome things. No one expected to hear what followed.

The saddest thing a child can live in life is to be raised without love, without peace- restrained from the proper guidance to become a warm-hearted person. Noah was like a dog who didn't know any better than that he had experienced. The miserable treatment his own baring mother offered without impunity. Since the day he was born, Noah was raised in a world of chaos. His mom refused to breastfeed him at the hospital or care for him. She requested the nursery assume full responsibility as she healed from her cesarean delivery and withdrawals from her substance abuse.

As he matured, she would neglect him to sleep with men or binge drink. He grew up figuring life out of fabricating his own concept of it. His biological father wasn't in the picture since he was a product of a one-night stand. His mother would mistreat him by physically, emotionally and mentally abusing him. She would employ manipulative tactics and introduced the slaughtering of animals for consumption at an early age. Giving him his first taste for blood, unable to buy groceries. She was such a bitch that he felt resentment for her. Matter of fact, he developed hate for women-exercising misogyny. His mother was self-employed, she would sell her body to whatever man paid the price. She even intended on introducing him to the sex industry but he rebelled and murdered a male would be customer at the age of eight. He was also not enrolled in school because he would get into so much trouble and she wouldn't prioritize his education over her selfishness. It wasn't a mystery he'd turn out to be a psychopath. What other positive outlet could be fundamental for him to engage in other than eliminating those he viewed as evil? Those he construed a resemblance of his mother in.

A trigger initiated from fear which would promote a reaction of violence. Only to satisfy his taste for human flesh in order to associate his actions with the comforts of his upbringings, as a hunter, butcher and carnivore. He was never questioned or arrested for the death of his momma. It had been ruled accidental but it wasn't quite so.

Noah had observed his mother in the bathtub drinking alcohol after one of her John's had departed. He then took the opportunity to toss her hair curling iron inside the water and electrocute her till her heart came to a permanent stop when he was ten years of age.

He was eventually transferred to a maximum-security facility due to the reputation he gained from the televised trials of all his atrocious acts. He was presently found in the special housing unit where he could be safe from the general population or vice versa. The medical department prescribed him heavy doses of Seroquel. He remained heavily sedated in his cell under the medication up until one day when he was out in the yard for his hour of recreational time and another inmate stabbed him to death. He left this earth without being charged for his mom's death. Karma states, "You can run, you can hide but if not, tomorrow I'll strike tonight." The inmate who killed Noah was related to one of his first female victims.

Mrs. Crumpley assumed responsibility for Noah's corpse and arranged the burial proceedings. He was put to rest in the town's cemetery where not too many showed up to take part in. Those who did, witnessed a broken mother in Mrs. Crumpley as she argued he was innocent. She contested till her last breath Noah wasn't capable of what he was charged for.

As for Pot- while Noah was out working, the coyote who had gone over late at night to eat the dog food- took him. It saw an easy meal and consumed Pot with minimal effort due to its size. It later returned to where he had prayed upon Pot in search of more to eat. Noah missed his pup till his eyes permanently shut closed to never reopen once more.

CHAPTER 6
COLD ADAM.

It was a nice day out in the Sun City. Parents gathered at neighborhood parks with their children, enjoying the fall weather. The summer days had kept them mostly inside due to the excessive heat. Sports games were being practiced and played by adults and teens. The recreational centers were flooded with activity. An ideal circumstance for ice cream trucks and food vendors to make some dough. Lines gathered around the trucks offering goodies to the people. An elotero man shook his cart bell as he walked around Memorial Park. Customers waved him down to purchase elotes en vaso and enteros. He'd smother them in mayo mixed with butter, granulated cheese, red chili powder and lime. The price for a cup was two bucks fifty and the corn on the cob was three fifty. This product sold regularly without issue. A delicious snack for all and highly recommended to those who'd never had it. Some children surrounded the elotero who was parked behind the ice cream trucks. The parents engaged in verbal communication feeling their children were safe. The community was recognized for their ability to come together and live in peace.

As the sun began to fall behind the Franklin Mountains, the vendors had sold enough to call it a day and head out. The crowds had dissipated and only a few remained at the park. Once the vendors had departed from the location, a mother yelled out her son's name, "Paco! Paco!"

There was no response. She began to panic as she searched for her child who was four years old. Shouting and yelling out his name, along with a quick threat as to what she was going to do once she'd find him- she traveled through the park. The street lights had turned on and just about everyone had gone home except for this worried mother who couldn't find her kid after three rounds around the location. She called the police and a unit drove over to her distress. She informed the officer of her troubled situation and gave a detailed description of her son including what he wore. The officer annotated the information, especially the shoes the kid had as a code Adam protocol law enforcement utilized in such a case. Another unit arrived and they drove around the park with their spot lights- brightening up the unlight areas. They did a quick drive by and got out to search on foot. Moments later, they had searched throughout the whole location without any success. One of the officers approached the mother and asked her, "Do you have any friends or relatives who live nearby who your son might have visited?"

The woman answered while sobbing, "No, we don't live around here. We live in the north east but I wanted to bring my little Paco to this park since he likes it so much," in a broken tone.

The officer felt her pain and uttered, "When did you last say you had a visual of him before you noticed he wasn't around?"

The woman replied, "He was with a group of kids who he met here. They were buying snacks from the ice cream trucks and playing as they stood in line to be served. God, please help me find Paco! I'm begging you!" Her agonizing whale could be heard from afar as she broke down in a desperate rage.

The officer stated, "Don't worry, try to calm down. We will find him soon. He probably left with one of the kids he was playing with to their house nearby. As soon as their parents realize he's there, they'll come looking for you with him by their side. Have faith that everything will be alright." He then radioed the other unit to drive around the residential area surrounding the park.

A few hours later, other units had merged in search but returned empty handed. They had cruised around the neighborhood and extended their perimeter outward without a positive outcome. The woman was interviewed by a detective on the scene and an investigation was initiated. Her family had to go get her and take her home because she didn't want to leave without her son.

In the following days, the news aired her story and requested anyone in the public with information on the missing child should come forth to assist in locating the boy. Flyers were dispersed throughout the city by friends and relatives as well as strangers who joined their efforts to find Paco. Social media flooded pictures of the missing boy and people were becoming alarmed by the situation.

A week had gone by and Paco was still astray. The residents from El Paso remained positive and resumed their normal activities, once again filling up the city parks with their families. There were multiple children enjoying the playground at Ascarate Park. It wasn't unusual to see ice cream trucks and food vendors present on a good day there either. The murky pond water was an attractive fishing spot for some but only to catch and release. The ducks who called the park their home were being fed by visitors. Everyone was having a splendid moment. Families came together creating fond memories just as those the parents recalled as children. Parents remembered the tall rocket which was replaced with a modern playground. For some it was a nostalgic moment to take their kids to the same place they visited to play when younger.

Out of nowhere, there was commotion over by the lake. Some kid had fallen into the water while chasing the ducks. Men jumped inside the water to retrieve the young boy. A crowd had gathered and cheered the heroes who saved the kid from drowning. He was returned to his mother, who disciplined him immediately. As the group of spectators dispersed, a woman began shouting her daughter's name, "Lily! Lily!"

With the recent case of the missing boy, the mother panicked and ran around searching for her daughter. The people at the park helped out as word spread quickly that a little girl was missing. The mother was escorted in a vehicle around the park to look for Lily. Some random man offered to drive her around since her head wasn't right to do so on her own. The ice cream trucks and eloteros also complied but there was no sign of the little girl. The police department was dispatched to the scene and they too combed through the area without any luck. Law enforcement conducted several interviews with witnesses in order to establish the last time she had been seen. No one recalled the little girl though, not even the kids at the park. She had been playing by herself due to the fact she only spoke Spanish and was unable to establish a friendship with the other kids who conversed in English. Her mother had an accent as she was learning the common language after relocating from Juarez a few years back.

The search was concluded and she was handed a case number by a detective who promised her he'd find her daughter. She drove home all alone with the worst case of impunity unable to do anything about Lily's disappearance. The exact story occurred with this woman as with Paco's mother. The news interviewed her and shared the footage. Social media went berserk and flyers were scattered around. The city residents had their worst fear construe danger in belief of a kidnapper on the loose. Everyone became highly vigilant of their surroundings and the safety of the children around them.

In the weeks that followed, there were more reports of missing children under the age of seven. These events were pinpointed to parks. People gathered outside the police main headquarters and rallied for justice. They felt the department was responsible for the rapture of kids taking place throughout the city. There were currently five cases being investigated without even one being solved. Halloween was right around the corner and the residents feared it would not be safe taking their kids trick or treating. The crowd got agitated and began attacking officers who left and entered the building at shift change. The riot team was called out to take control of the angry protestors. News reporters on scene were interviewing the demonstrators who chanted, "Find our kids and keep them safe! Find our kids and keep them safe!"

One of the members of the protest spoke to a reporter who asked him, "What possible outcome are you all expecting with this demonstration?"

The man answered, "Your answer is in our plea. Find our kids and keep them safe!" He retorted.

The reporter inquired, "How do you feel the police department is handling these situations and what can they do to prevent more raptures?"

The man replied, "The police aren't fulfilling their duties to serve and protect. Our tax dollars are going to waste as they upgrade their equipment but not their work ethics. They should be hiring more personnel to secure the city and its residents from any danger or harm."

The reporter uttered, "You don't think the police is diligently working in the cases and attempting to recruit new officers though?"

The man responded, "I can't speak for the police, they have their own spokesperson who hasn't responded with a public statement. I can only talk about what we hear and see. We hear our kids aren't safe to play at the parks. We see they're vulnerable to kidnap and the only one this falls on is this department who's incapable of living up to their profession."

The reporter commented, "You can't assume full responsibility for the safety of the children reflects on the police department alone, do you? I mean, we as parents, as a community should establish preventive safety measures to facilitate security amongst us all, wouldn't you agree?" The man went mute without a rebuttal as the riot team began spraying water from tankers at the mob.

The large group of protesters fled the scene leaving a trail of trash behind with their picket signs left over the ground. The police department made a formal public announcement that same day to address the propaganda that they were the only ones responsible in the matter. Things seemed to quiet down following the speech. The heat had cooled off and without new reports of nabbed children, the public celebrated halloween.

The children were accompanied to pick treats from houses. Although the unsolved situations worried the population, they maintained perseverance and a positive attitude towards moving forward. It wasn't the first time they had come together to do so. They had overcome a tragedy some years back where the slogan, "We are El Paso Strong," surfaced. Children ran up and down the streets picking up candy from the generous people handing them out. They dressed in costumes where most assumed the character of their wardrobe. A car full of teens drove past a crowd of kids walking around the neighborhoods in the north hills. The teens tossed eggs at the crowd of kids, hitting a few. The victimized children yelled for their parents' rescue. The situation caught the eye of all those nearby. As the people returned to their activities, a man hollered his daughter's name, "Esme! Esme!"

The girl had left his side to get candy from one of the houses. The father had turned his attention towards the crowd of kids who were vandalized by the teens. It had only taken him around fifteen seconds to return his gaze towards his daughter but she had vanished by then. The man searched for Esme, grabbing kids who wore similar costumes by their shoulders to turn them around. Again and again, he apologized to the parents and informed them he had lost his own. Barbie costumes had become a thing after the release of the film earlier that year. So, you can only imagine just how difficult it had become for him to find one barbie out of a hundred nearby. The man continued combing through the trick or treaters without a positive outcome. He placed a call to the police department who took a while to arrive since they had received thousands of calls about other incidents. This marked the sixth case of raptured children in the city. When the officers attended the scene, the people booed them. They took the fathers story and began searching for the little girl.

After several hours of intense search and rescue efforts, the officers regrouped with no clue as to the whereabouts of Esmeralda. Her father was desperate and enraged. There was a crowd of spectators who helped look for her and also one who antagonized the officials. Her father left heartbroken after receiving a case number which was filed for her disappearance. When the area cleared up from kids trick or treating and the heavy presence of marked units- the residents gossiped about the occurrence.

The following day, the police spokesperson addressed the public during a live media coverage. He stated, "The El Paso Police Department along with other multiple agencies has been investigating the abductions occurring in our community. We will continue to enforce zero tolerance for child predatory individuals and or organizations. Anyone found in violation will be penalized with the hardest of convictions possible. We're aware the community has criticized us recently and would like to refrain from the negative feedback. We are not solemnly responsible for these disappearances. The citizens of El Paso must also accept accountability for their negligence in providing safety for our children. We advise everyone to be extremely watchful of their surroundings. If a child is left unattended, contact us immediately while monitoring the child's activity and location. If anyone or anything suspicious attracts one's attention, contact us without hesitation. To parents who engage in outdoor activities, keep a close view of your kids and don't be misled by distractions. If possible, gather with other parents and work together in observing the children's security. Do not leave your kids unattended for any reason while out in public. We first believed these cases were only restricted to parks but as we all know; the strategy has been altered. We still don't have any leads but we are working consistently around the clock to eliminate any threats to our city residents. Either way, we must all do our part in protecting tomorrow's future by starting today. Our children's safety is our priority. Thank you and you all be safe." He then walked back into the main headquarters.

El Pasoans had become terrified to leave their kids alone. The parents who held jobs left their children at school and worried all day long for their wellbeing. The scenario somewhat resembled the covid 19 lockdowns where the streets were empty without those who had no essential purpose- staying indoors. The police department had just released new cadets into the field who complied with the requirements of the academy. More black and whites patrolled the streets in an attempt to deter criminal activity. This went on for approximately two weeks. In which there weren't any new raptures. During said time, no arrests were made.

Slowly, the people began going out with their kids again. This time, they followed directions to gather in groups and collaborate in watching over the Children. Things began taking shape and it had been almost a month since Esmeralda's disappearance. The parents with missing children formed an alliance banning together and began patrolling the recreational centers around town. They had recruited a large team of enthusiastic volunteers who'd assist them in their rounds. Safety being a priority within the city, the residents put their part as well. Life seemed to have regenerated itself along the border city. Parents fought their worries and began taking their kids out to the parks, movies, amusement parks and other facilities offering fun for the children. Thanksgiving was coming up within days.

Over at Tobin Park, there were many people enjoying an evening with a cool breeze as the kids played. Complacency started
trickling back into the minds of the residents since there had been
no more abductions reported. It all came to a screeching halt
when an older woman began yelping her grandson's name, "Hector! Hector! Come on, let's go home now!" Where could this boy
have gone? She wondered.

Frantically she began looking for him and the people present helped her. They searched relentlessly for Hector but he had
become the seventh victim. Police units surrounded the park and
began searching for the kid. All nearby areas were closed off to
vehicular access before being cleared from the road blocks the
department established. They had a suspenseful feeling they
would find the boy before it was too late. Car after car, one by
one, they were all eliminated as the one being used to facilitate a
crime. The grandmother was devastated with the news the officers
passed down to her. They had come up empty handed without
Hector.

Then as they were about to head out, a group of people ran
up to one of the roadblocks with Hector in their arms. He had
been saved by the witnesses who claimed to have seen the person who nabbed him out of the park. Several units who obtained
the description of the subject darted in search of him. They drove
through alleys and streets all around the neighborhood but were
unable to apprehend the perpetrator. The witnesses were questioned on the situation they had experienced. They all described
a dark hispanic man weighing about two hundred pounds and
standing at approximately five feet two inches with a medium to
heavy build. He was wearing a blue Dallas Cowboys shirt, dark blue
jeans and white sneakers. They were inconclusive to his age but
ranged between twenty-seven to thirty-seven. He had been seen
walking with Hector up Hondo Pass. Until someone noticed the
boy attempting to get away from him which is when the witnesses

took action and the suspect took off on foot. No other potential leads surfaced on the direction of travel the criminal fled towards.

Hector was questioned and he and his grandmother were taken to the north east regional command center to view some line up photos of past criminals who fit the description given. They also called in a sketch artist to compile a drawing from the boy's narrative. The police spokesperson addressed the news the following day. He presented the sketch and asked the residents, "Please contact the emergency service number if anyone knows the whereabouts of this subject in question. The sketch was derived from witnesses and the victim who was rescued from harm yesterday. This man was last seen running away near Hondo Pass. He was described as a male hispanic between twenty-seven and thirty-seven years of age. Weighing approximately two hundred pounds and standing at around five feet two inches with a medium to heavy build. He was last seen wearing a blue Dallas Cowboys t-shirt, dark blue jeans and white sneakers. We're thankful this time his intentions failed and the boy was recovered. This was all because of people following our protocol and coming together for the safety of our children. Rest assured our department has not forgotten and continues laboring hectically around the clock to find and put those responsible behind bars. Thank you and you all be safe out there."

Calls began flooding the emergency dispatch office with people claiming they knew the person in the drawing. Some were investigated and others were disregarded as phonies. No arrests were made from the leads which flocked in. The residents did however feel a sense of pride due to their resistance and heroic act of saving a kid. Some potential suspects were taken into the police station for questioning. They were hammered during interrogation but all had an alibi which excluded them from being the one in question. Eventually all the men who generally fit the description and were not found probable to be charged were released from custody.

Thanksgiving rolled along and people forgot about the threat. Once again, they began visiting and utilizing public recreational centers and other forms of entertainment. Masses gathered at Veterans Park as kids played in the playground and engaged in sports. A police unit rode by slowly keeping an eye out for any suspicious activities. The officer hit the brakes as he almost stuck a teen riding his bicycle carelessly in front of the patrol unit. The officer shouted, "Watch where you're riding! You need to be more aware of vehicles circulating on the street!"

The young man replied, "Sorry officer, I didn't see you." The officer shook his head as the boy peddled away.

The officer drove over to the convenience store located across from the park to use the restroom and grab himself a drink. When the officer exited the store and was about to enter his unit- a man directed him towards a woman who was relentlessly searching for her son at the park. The officer drove over to where the mother was located and was informed of the issue. He immediately radioed in the emergency and other patrolling officers arrived. They began looking for the boy and making roadblocks. The other people at the park assisted in the hunt to find the kid. Everyone there was worried for the child's safety. Then all of a sudden people began beating up a man who drove his elote cart around the park. Some other kid had witnessed him nabbing the missing boy. The crowd turned on the man with violence as they began going through his cart. Someone located a secret compartment within the man's cart and opened it. There sat the kid inside shivering with fear and shock. His name was Adam and he had been saved. The man was brutally beaten by residents and the police had to intervene before they'd manage to kill him. He was taken into custody.

The man fit the previous description given from the last boy who was rescued. He was a dark hispanic male weighing around two hundred pounds. He stood at approximately five feet two inches with a medium to heavy build. The news reporters drove over to the park to take statements as they went live. The man who approached the officer outside the convenience store said, "I was headed towards the store when I heard a woman yelling out her son's name. She looked terrified and I knew then she had lost her child. I then ran over to the store since I had seen a police vehicle driving around and was now parked at the store. When I got to the front, the officer was coming out and I let him know there was a woman who needed his help. The officer then drove over to where the lady was at and everyone began searching for the boy. Some kid mentioned he had witnessed the elotero placing the kid inside his cart and that's when we approached the man. He seemed guilty while being questioned about what the kid had seen and tried to run away. Some of the people there beat him up and the police had to save him. While this was going on, some man opened up his cart and found a secret chamber inside where the missing kid was found. I'm just glad the kid was rescued and that the man was arrested. Hopefully if he's the one who took the other kids, he confesses to doing so and where they are now."

The man in custody did admit to nabbing the other children from parks. He began telling his side of the story. He was booked into the El Paso County Jail without bail. He was also separated from the general population who had a hit on him. None of the previous kidnapped children were recovered but the man opened his mouth and had shared the following summary with the detectives handling the case. His name was Jorge and he was from Guatemala. He had traveled a long stretch from his home towards Mexico in order to ingress into the United States. He took part in the first wave of immigrants who made illegal entry in 2019. He had no family or friends in the states. His sole purpose was to run from his past and leave it all behind. A dark past which found him as he attempted to rehabilitate himself. A human trafficking organization who he was previously employed by to be exact. They somehow tracked him and pressured him to continue laboring for them. His American dream had been shattered by then. Realizing just how difficult it was to actually acquire it. He had a hard time allocating a job and so he bought himself a food cart to sell corn. He would travel the city parks making small profits from his product sales. That's how he would come into contact with children, who were his main consumers. During a strenuous phase, he had no one to reach out to for support and that's when the criminal organization enticed him to rejoin their purpose. He began luring kids with free elotes and then he'd nab them. Jorge had built a sophisticated metal chamber which was also sound proof in the middle of his cart. A door swung open to display the hiding spot. Something he easily maneuvered while pretending to retrieve new cups from under. There he'd place the kids and make his way to a specific location afterwards. At the drop off point, he would hand over the minors in return for currency. These children were never to be seen or heard of once in the hands of the organization. Some would be used for their organs and the others would be sexually exploited for profit. Jorge detested his occupation, which is why he had tried to flee. He alone wouldn't be able to take down the organization. He couldn't fight them because they were extremely powerful and his family's lives were at stake. He had become a coward, stuck between good and bad- unable to choose wisely.

Therefore, after his capture, he worked with law enforcement to take down the organization as a confidential informant and gained protective custody for it. His family was granted immunity after seeking asylum from the organization which pursued them.

The stash house was busted but no kids were recovered from the warrant. The ring came down one by one all over the world.

Involved individuals were turning on each other. From organized crime to politicians to celebrities and even religious cardinals all tumbled down the ladder. The hit was so intense that Jorge was given leniency on his sentencing for his cooperation. He was now even viewed as a hero. The elite didn't let him continue though.

They had power even within the strictest lines of law enforcement. He was assassinated as he headed to take the stand on this high-profile case.

From there on, the court system failed the citizens as loop holes were allowing the would be condemned to walk free. The whole thing was washed away eventually and continued to operate under the scrutiny of the victims. The city of El Paso was taken off the list of potential locations to operate since they stood strong against being easy hunting grounds.

Jorge's family started a new life somewhere secret with a new identity. His kids missed him after mourning his death. His youngest, who was five years old, had to pay the price eventually though. The organization found their location and kidnapped the kid. He was never returned to his mother.

CHAPTER 7
CHUCKLES.

Damian was sent off to bed by his mother whose boyfriend was enroute to play adult games as he slept. Damian didn't want to go to sleep though, he had been having horrific dreams that would wake him up in the middle of the night. He kept seeing a clown in a multi-colored suit, big orange shoes and a red bow tie. This clown would harass him to the point Damian would wake up over a puddle of urine on his bed from the freight. This had been reported to his mother for a few days now. So, Damian told his mother, "Can I go to sleep with you? I'm scared to sleep alone in my room."

His mother answered, "You're a big boy now and big boys don't sleep with their mothers. It's best if you sleep in your own bed because you toss and turn too much at night and don't allow me to rest properly." Or so was her excuse.

Damian replied, "Please mom, let me sleep with you!" By then the melatonin drink she had prepared for him had started taking effect.

She said, "There you go honey. Follow your dreams now and sleep tight." As he nagged but closed his eyes, she kissed his forehead.

Her boyfriend texted her, "I'm outside now. Did he go to bed so I can come in?" She replied, "He's asleep, come inside baby."

The man walked up to their house and saw Monique- Damian's mother- standing by the door in a white laced gown. The guy approached the door as Monique opened it to allow him in. He grabbed her by the waist and kissed her ever so passionately. He then grasped her ass and squeezed his present to come. She closed the door behind them and told him to have a seat on the couch. The man took a seat as he observed Monique jogging towards the back of her home to have one last glance at Damian to make sure he was out. Moments later, Monique went back to her living room and hopped on top of her boyfriend's lap. She placed her breasts in his face and asked, "So what was it you said you wanted to do to me?" As she felt him kissing and sucking on her.

She moaned as he stated, "I said I'm going to make you mine and allow you to relive all the stress life has left inside of you." As he held her but cheeks in his palms and placed her nipples into his mouth.

Monique was turned on and she felt her boyfriend's strength push her down on the couch. He then made his way to her vagina and teased her a bit. He kissed her private, over her underwear. Then he suddenly removed her underwear and began kissing her skin beginning with her ankles. He slowly made his way to her sexual organ and began smooching it too. He licked her clitoris a few times as he watched her jump up with desperation. He then began swabbing his tongue over her spot and she moaned uncontrollably, clenching her hands on the couch pillows. Monique stopped him and uttered, "Wait baby, let's go to my bedroom so we can lock ourselves inside without me worrying Damian might wake up and catch us." Her man agreed and they went to her room.

Monique locked her door as her guy laid on her bed. She then walked over to her bed and got on. He used his force and maneuvered her to sit on his face. She didn't resist because she knew what was to come. He got back to eating her out so good she was cuming within seconds. He performed oral sex on her for about ten minutes before he decided it was time for him to be pleased. Monique grabbed his crotch and began rubbing her hands over his pants, feeling his erected penis. She then pulled down his shorts and sat up as comfortably as she could. She jerked his shaft up and down and then inserted it inside her mouth. Her boyfriend was aroused and allowed her to act freely upon him. He got excited since he had been dwelling on this moment all day and ejaculated in her mouth. Monique slowed down and swallowed his semen. She then continued to suck on his dick till he took her off and laid her flat on her back. He mounted her and inserted his cock inside her pussy, then began pounding the shit out of her- tossing her legs up in the air. Monique was in heaven while her man fucked her hard and adequately enough to make her orgasm multiple times. As she was cuming, she heard Damian laughing out loud. At first, she thought she was hallucinating but he was really bursting with laughter. She moved her boyfriend off of her, got dressed and ran towards his room.

As she got closer, she heard a distinctive song murmuring, similar to the ones played at the circuses during the clown performance. When she opened his door, it stopped and she witnessed him with a huge smile on his face but with a sour look of distress over his eyes. She quietly walked up to his bed and noticed his chest wasn't rising from him breathing properly. She moved him around but he was unresponsive. She yelled for her boyfriend to rush over which he did. The guy took the kids' pulse but there wasn't one. Immediately he began CPR on him with chest compressions and breaths. He had ordered Monique to dial 911. The man continued performing CPR on Damian but there was no sign of life in him. When the paramedics arrived, they too began CPR- taking over from the boyfriend's efforts. They hooked up the AED but it signaled," Shock not advised," due to there not being the slightest pulse to indicate it should administer a charge.

Damian was transported to the hospital where he was pronounced dead upon arrival. Monique wept in anguish unable to cease her pain. Her boyfriend attempted to comfort and console her but losing her son was too much for her to bear. The doctors tried to remove his smile manually but his mouth would move back uncooperatively. They found it strange but had no medical explanation to describe it. Monique received her family's support after she informed them of the bad news. Her parents and siblings rushed to the hospital to mourn with her. No one could believe Damian had passed away at only five years of age. His body was eventually transferred to the morgue and Monique along with her family had to go home.

She was unable to rest for the days to come. She had to make funeral arrangements which she couldn't afford. Good thing her family and friends started a go fund me account for her and when the time came, she had enough to pay for everything. She never recovered from her loss even after her boyfriend married her and they conceived a child together. She did love her new daughter but it wasn't Damian. She recalled his last words the night she put him to rest. Eventually she too dreamed the same clown and was found unresponsive the next morning with a untraceable smile on her face.

There had been numerous cases of adults and children dying in their sleep. Not all had been reported to have a smirk on their visage after detection of their corpses. There was a detective who began noticing similarities in some of the cases. In particular those found with the unerasable grin. He began putting pieces together on the deceased and went around asking their loved one's questions. He was at the moment over with Dwaine- Monique's widowed husband. The detective inquired- as the door opened, "Hello, may I speak with Dwaine please?"

Dwaine replied, "Who are you and why do you want to talk to me?"

Detective Jones answered- as he presented his bandage for view, "My name is detective Jones from the homicide department. I'd like to have a word with you about your deceased wife and step son."

Dwaine let him inside and said, "What is it you'd like to discuss about them? It's been over a year since they left?"

Jones took a seat after being instructed and responded, "Well, I've been assigned several other suspicious deaths which all the deceased have been located with a smile on their face. I have reason to believe there's much more to a natural cause of death and I'm going around speaking to their families to paint a better picture."

Dwaine commented, "I did find it awkward myself that they both had a grin on their face after passing. So, tell me detective, how can I help you in your search?"

Jones uttered, "I'd like to know if by any chance they shared anything with you prior to their deaths? Any information of lucid dreams or suspicious activity you may recall?"

Dwaine told him, "Actually now that you mentioned it, Damian had been having nightmares about a clown chasing him before he was found dead. Monique didn't tell me anything about her having nightmares, seeing strange things or people though."

Jones began annotating the information as he replied, "Would you happen to have a description of this clown?"

Dwaine answered, "Nope, I sure don't. I didn't think much of it at the time. I also wasn't married to Monique during that moment so I didn't get to know Damian well enough to ask. After his departure we got married and had our daughter. Monique had somewhat moved on after time. She began working and getting back to do what she loved, which was makeup tutorials on line. She seemed fine right before I found her dead lying next to me. I will say that night I somewhat woke up in the middle of my sleep hearing clown music. I thought I was dreaming and just went back to bed."

Jones replied, "Clown music, eh? Sounds strange but I'll write that down on my notes. Is there anything else you might remember about them which you might find relevant to my investigation?"

Dwaine mentioned, "Not that I could remember to be honest."

"Alright, well thank you for conversing with me. I'm going to leave my business card with you in case you recall something else. Give me a ring if you have any more information or questions, please. You have a great day sir," said Jones as he exited the home and walked to his car.

Detective Jones then went over to another family member of the deceased he was investigating. There too he was informed of a possible clown in their nightmares. As well as a clown song being heard playing the night they died. Jones went to approximately eight residences and in every single one they mentioned the same story about the music and lucid dreams. Jones was skeptical about it at first since he didn't believe in supernatural occurrences yet within time of hearing the similarities, he began to question the possibilities while sitting at his office.

He started looking up clowns offering services in the city and came across almost one hundred of them. He had to narrow his searches so he started placing calls and talking to each one personally. One by one he began eliminating suspects. Most had already quit their characters and others had been out of town doing shows during the time of death in his cases. Jones left for the day and headed home after a long day at work putting the pieces to a puzzle and unable to see a clear picture. He had begun to take interest in clowns so when he arrived at his house, he saw videos of some during their acts. He made himself dinner and watched clowns all evening long until he fell asleep.

The following day, as he arrived at his office- he was informed there was another suspicious death where the victim had a smirk on their face. Jones rushed over to the coroner's office to see the body. When he showed up and observed the corpse of a woman in her mid-twenties he witnessed first-hand the untraceable smile. He began studying her alongside the medical examiner who was doing the autopsy. He took notes and asked questions which the examiner told him, "I don't have an explanation to why or how this body is still smiling and the tissue will not cooperate. This is the third one I've encountered already though. They all presented no signs of struggle or assault. Their eyes do appear to have seen something horrific yet the rest of their anatomy states otherwise. Other than their heart which stopped functioning and caused their deaths."

Jones jotted down the info and asked, "Have you seen or heard anything else out of the ordinary while working on the corpses?"

The medical examiner stated, "No not at all. I mean other than the usual weird noises that spooked me before when I first started working here."

Jones questioned, "What type of noises are you referring to?"

The examiner uttered, "You know, the noises structures make when contracting and expanding. The noises one hears of water pressure running through the drain pipes and stuff like that."

"Oh, yes I see what you mean," Responded detective Jones.

Shortly after, Jones departed from the coroner's office and headed to the home of the deceased woman to speak to her family members. Upon arrival, he heard someone sobbing out loud since this case had just taken place less than 24 hours ago. He knocked on the door and stood there for about two minutes, listening to a woman whimpering. The door swung open and the father of the deceased asked him, "Yes, how may I help you sir?"

Jones introduced himself and was allowed inside as he stated, "Thank you for allowing me to speak to you during such a tragic moment. I express my most sincere apology and share my condolences with you and your family. The reason behind my visit is because I've been investigating several deaths where the persons were found with a grin on their face. Your daughter, may she rest in peace, is the latest one."

The victim's dad replied, "Yes, she was found with a smile on her face and we don't know how it happened. It was and still is a mysterious shock to us. She was healthy and didn't consume drugs or alcohol. She resided on her own in the guest house behind our home. I apologize for my wife crying in the back."

Jones commented, "No need to apologize mister. After all, it's reasonable and would not be if y'all wouldn't weep or mourn your daughter's departure… Around the time of her death, do you recall listening to clown music or heard her say anything about having lucid dreams?"

The father uttered, "No, I can't hear well and wouldn't have heard anything inside my room coming from hers. She also didn't share any details of her dreams with me. My wife had a better, deeper connection with her and might have some answers to your questions if you'd like for me to ask?"

Jones responded, "Don't trouble her with my inquiries. Instead, if you wouldn't mind, may I see where she lived?" The dad answered, "Sure, let me grab my set of keys and I'll take you over there right now." Jones waited as the man grabbed the keys.

When the man returned, he had a set of keys in hand and they walked over to the guest house in the backyard. The man opened the door and allowed Jones to enter. Jones began searching around and went room by room looking for any possible clues. Nothing stuck out though besides a clown nose under her bed. Jones asked the father, "Did this belong to your daughter?" As he retrieved the nose off the ground.

The father asked, "What is it? I don't remember seeing her with that red ball. I couldn't tell you if it belonged to her or not."

Jones told him, "It's not a ball. It's a clown's nose. Did she like clowns or have clown costumes by any chance?"

The dad commented, "No she didn't. She actually was terrified of clowns. That's weird you found a clown nose under her bed."

Jones placed the nose inside an evidence bag and thanked the father for his time and cooperation. He then departed from the residence and drove back to his office.

When he arrived, he turned the nose to the laboratory hoping they could recover DNA off of it. He wrote a report on his interactions with family members and then continued watching clown videos on his computer. While doing so, Jones caught a glimpse of a clown outside his office window. He rose from his seat and darted outside. When he swung around the front door to the police headquarters, he saw the clown turning a corner. Jones gave chase and went around the corner himself but by then, the clown had vanished. The sidewalk was empty and he found it disturbingly odd. He continued strolling through the street hoping he'd come across the clown. He searched through the alley dumpsters and under the vehicles parked along the side of the road. Under one of the cars, he located a red bowtie similar to the one described by some of the relatives of the deceased. He picked it up and headed back to the office with it after glancing through the vehicle above for signs of the clown.

As he got to the entrance, he heard clown music. He turned around to try and locate it but he wasn't able to, due in part that the music stopped. Jones felt goosebumps running up the back of his neck. He went inside the building and headed to the forensic department to turn the bowtie to them. Afterwards he went back to his office and began watching an evil clown movie.

He began falling asleep at his desk so he turned the film off on his screen and walked out to grab a coffee. When he got back to his office with his cup of energizing beverage, he discovered a plastic flower laying over his desk. The flower was a novelty item used by jokesters where it would be filled with water and have a push button to squirt fluid from the middle of the flower to an unsuspecting person. Jones placed his cup next to the flower and picked up the foreign item. The flower splashed a light stream of water at his face. Jones turned his face away and got up from his chair. He went around asking everyone in the building if they had left it on his desk. No one admitted to pranking him or leaving the flower there. He began to question his sanity. He then went back to his office with the flower in hand. He had inquired with the detective next door to his office if he had seen anyone going into his while he had gone to get some coffee. The other detective stated, "No Jones, I saw you headed to the break room but no one else other than you returned from there afterwards."

Jones uttered, "Well someone left this flower at my desk. I'd like to know who and why?" The other detective told him, "I was on the phone the whole time and didn't see anyone else going inside your office Jones. Maybe it was there the whole time and you hadn't noticed it?"

"I know I might be exhausted from work but not to the point I'm hallucinating and losing my mind. This wasn't in my office before. Someone left it while I grabbed a coffee." The other detective remained mute as Jones exited his office and headed back to his.

Jones tossed the flower in the trash and took a seat back in his chair to continue watching the film he was almost done with. He took a long sip of his coffee and was observing the motion screen video. Jones' eyes felt heavy even after consuming most of his cup of coffee. He began shutting them until he fell asleep. During his nap, he saw the clown in his dreams. It was telling bad jokes but Jones couldn't stop laughing at them. No matter how hard he tried, he cracked up in laughter. Jones suddenly woke up and he realized he was chuckling. The detective next door stood by the doorway and asked, "Are you alright bro? You fell asleep and were laughing pretty loud. You were also playing some circus music which stopped before I got here as you woke up."

Jones replied, "Yeah, I'm fine. I just had a funny dream that's all. Sorry about my phone playing unusual music on it. I must have fallen asleep while playing a video or something."

The detective commented, "Alright, well I'll be heading out for lunch now. I just wanted to make sure you were ok. See you later." As he left the area headed towards the front entrance.

Jones was mesmerized; he had dreamed about the clown which had been described to him. He began writing down a description of the clown he observed in his dormant visions. He then began searching for one similar to it online. Eventually after a few hours, he gave up and decided to call some shops who made custom clothes and others which sold common clown suits. Jones took off to speak to some people at the shops in order to find out if they had the one the clown in his dream wore. The first one he dropped by had a massive selection of commercial costumes which had been mass produced in China. Jones glimpsed through them but didn't find the exact one the clown in his dreams whore.

He took off and went to another store which sold new and used ones. The store manager helped him go through the ones which were similar to the one he described to her but the exact one wasn't located. From there, he visited a custom shop and described the suit in his dream. The woman there informed him she had never made that particular type of suit but she had a picture of one her father had created for a customer about sixty years ago. She then grabbed a picture album and began going through it. Jones glanced at the photos but patiently waited for the one she had mentioned to him. As she turned the pages slowly, the next one in line gave Jones goosebumps as soon as he saw it. Not only was it a photo of the suit but of the clown in his dreams wearing it. Jones asked, "Do you know who this clown is? Or if he's still alive by any chance?"

The woman answered, "No, I'm sorry but these pictures are of my father's work and customers and he's no longer with us to even ask him."

Jones inquired, "How about receipts dating back to those days in the picture?

Would you happen to have them around still?"

The woman stated, "Not even, my father worked at another building before it burned down in a blaze. All of his suits, receipts and contacts were lost in the fire. These pictures got saved because the day before, he took this book home with him so he could swap out the actual book since the other one was deteriorating."

"Chucks, is there any way I could take this picture with me or snap one of it?" Asked Jones.

The woman responded, "This picture has sentimental value to me to not be able to hand it to you but you're more than welcome to take one of it with your phone." Jones snapped a few still shots of the clown who was the number one suspect in his cases.

He then left the shop wishing one of the victims was still alive to confirm the clown from the picture was the one they dreamed of. He returned to his office and began going through the case files he was investigating. As he was reading through the paperwork, he decided to check the files uploaded to the computer system to see if anyone had experienced and reported dreams of this clown and survived. He came across a report dating back a few months where a young man had survived the nightmares. He had reported a possible attack which was investigated but nothing was solved since there wasn't an actual person committing the infractions which occurred in a dream. Jones grabbed his keys and drove over to the man's home.

When he arrived at the man's house, Jones exited his vehicle and proceeded up to the front door. He knocked then rang the doorbell which was hiding behind a mailbox full of correspondence untouched for weeks. Jones stood at the door for several minutes before someone eventually opened it. Jones said, "Hi, I'm detective Jones with the homicide unit. Are you Mr. Sanders?"

The man answered, "Yes, that's me, how may I help you detective?"

Jones replied, "I have a few questions regarding a report you filed some months back. Do you have time to speak to me right now?"

Mr. Sanders stated, "Yes, come on in. Thank you for coming by in reference to that report which no one helped me with." He allowed Jones access to his living area where he granted him a seat.

Jones began asking him, "The report says you had several nightmares about a clown. Do you remember what the clown looked like?"

Mr. Sanders responded, "Yes that's correct and yes I still remember the clown."

Jones inquired, "May I ask how you stopped having those dreams if you have by any chance?"

Mr. Sanders uttered, "I continued having those dreams over and over and still do from time to time. What I did was, I set an alarm clock to wake me up every twenty minutes so that I could escape the torment. I've been doing that since and it's been working for me. As soon as I fall back to sleep and see him, my alarm sounds and wakes me up. I've also been praying, studying the bible and asking God to help me."

Detective Jones took out his phone and questioned, "Is this the clown in your dreams, The same one you described at the police station?" Showing him the snaps, he took on his phone. Mr. Sanders viewed the pictures and shouted, "That's him alright!

Where'd you get the pictures from? I don't want to see them anymore, put them away! Is he real and still alive?"

Jones quickly turned off his cell phone screen and put his phone back in his pocket saying, "I'm sorry about that. I didn't mean to trouble you with the picture. I just want to make sure he is the same one you've reported. I don't know if he's still alive and

I got the picture from a custom suit making shop I just visited. See there have been several people dying as they sleep after having visions of this clown. I'm investigating why people are having nightmares of him."

Mr. Sanders told him, "Oh, I'd like to know myself why? So, you mean to tell me others have seen this clown in their sleep as well? It kinda makes me feel better that I'm not the only one. Although it sucks, some have died from it."

Jones commented, "Yes, there are others and I'm one of them now. It happened after I began investigating these cases. I'm going to try your method of setting my alarm to wake me up. Hopefully I can beat it just as you have and find out who this clown is."

Mr. Sanders mentioned, "You too have been seeing him in your dreams? I'm sorry to hear that but I do feel better that I'm not crazy as those I've shared my story with have made me seem."

Jones responded, "Unfortunately yes, I've seen him myself. You're not insane to believe your own story is true. I'm going to take off now but I'm leaving you my business card in case something pops up or you find out anything. I'd also appreciate getting your number so I can keep you updated on this."

Mr. Sanders wrote down his number and Jones left the house. Jones got in his car and drove back to the office. He got there right on time to head home after his shift was over. He clocked out and headed to his house. Upon arrival he removed his clothes and dressed in something more comfortable. He then ordered dinner for himself while he watched the news. When the news was finished, a television show came on. He was enjoying the sitcom which was comical and making him laugh. Then he heard his doorbell ring. He stood up and went to get the door. It was his dinner; Chinese was what he had ordered. He grabbed the food from the delivery man, handing him a tip. He then closed the door and went to sit back down in his living area. He began removing the food boxes from the plastic bag they were in. Jones grabbed the chop sticks provided by the restaurant and dug into his meal. He was eating and laughing when his phone rang. He answered it and heard clown music on the other end. Jones asked, "Who is this? This isn't amusing and you're actually calling a detective with the police department. I'm going to track this call back and catch you!" He hung up and resumed his meal and show.

After he had enough food to fill him, he went to the restroom to relieve himself. When he got back to the living room, he realized he had missed a call from Mr. Sanders. Jones called him back but he didn't pick up so he left a voice message. Jones wondered why Mr. Sanders contacted him. He may have had some other news to share regarding this obnoxious clown. Mr. Sanders's returned his call as Jones was putting his left overs away. Jones picked up and heard Sanders's whaling, "You need to come now! Please help me, he's here in person inside my house!" The call then cut off. Joines grabbed his car keys and took off towards Sander's residence. When he finally got there, he rang the doorbell repeatedly. No one came to the door so he ran through the side, looking through the windows for activity. He observed Sanders laying on the floor and he then broke a window to go in and make a welfare check. Jones climbed through the window and ran over to where Sanders laid. He flipped him over and saw a smile over his lifeless body. He immediately called the emergency number and scanned through the dwelling to make sure there was no one there. After he had cleared the home, the paramedics and police arrived. They took the body and the officers questioned Jones. He told them, "I had spoken to this man earlier about some suspicions regarding some of the cases I'm working on. I left my card here and told him to contact me with anything new or something he forgot to mention to me. I was home enjoying my evening when he called me because he had an emergency. I then rushed over here and saw him lying on the floor unresponsive to my banging on the window after he didn't open the door. I broke the window, came in to check on him and found him dead."

Jones was released after his statement and he returned to his house. He couldn't believe Mr. Sanders- who was the only known survivor, was now gone. The night had fallen and he went to bed. He tossed and turned unable to rest so he got up and drank some night time flu medication to help him sleep. As he slept comfortably, he never realized he didn't set his alarm schedule as advised by Mr. Sanders. He began having nightmares and the medication he took to rest didn't help him wake up from them. The following morning, he was a no call no show at work.

After a few days of him not notifying the department of his absence, a unit was sent to his residence to check on him. There were no signs of activity inside his home but his car was parked outside. The officers got the green light to break in and check for his presence. They discover him dead in his bed with an enormous smile on his face. That's where the links he had been working on, dropped cold and unsolved without any other detective taking over the investigation. The clown's name was Chuckles and his background is as follows.

Chuckles grew up believing he could bring laughter into the lives of others. Since his youth, he aspired to become a clown. He attempted being the raining class clown every single year in school. His peers only made fun of him for not knowing how. Someone else always took the position he desired. His jokes were corny and his appearance was more questionable than reputable. This caused him to be bullied much of the time for trying so hard to be funny. He'd get picked on a daily basis. They'd take his lunch money and prank him harshly. One time they shoved his face inside the boy's restroom urinals. They also placed and popped fireworks under his seat on the ride back home in the school bus which caused him to shit himself. He was fed spew cake during a Christmas party. About the only audience who approved of his humor was his stuffed animals which he lined up to perform in front of.

His parents would ignore him in agreement he didn't have what it took to do comedy. His older sister too had made it clear to him he was an idiot who'd never succeed as a clown, but he didn't take no for an answer to his dreams. So, as he got older, he began purchasing custom made suits and advertised his services. He got hired quickly to entertain crowds of kids at birthday parties. The children laughed but only at him and not his act. They'd point their fingers at him and called him stupid, not funny amongst other insults. The outcome always repeated itself for him. The birthday kids would cry and complain he ruined their festivities. To which the parents would kick Chuckles out without paying him. His reputation for being a clown became tarnished with bad reviews. No one would hire him for parties and so he tried joining several circuses.

There too he was denied the opportunity after previewing his acts. He indelibly went nuts and would laugh by himself at his own jokes. One of which caused him his own death, unable to stop laughing. His family buried him along with all his suits. He then began appearing in the dreams of children and adults. First, he took over the dormant minds of the kids from the parties who laughed at him. Secondly, he gave nightmares to his past school peers. Then it was his own parents and sister as well as any other grown-ups who had humiliated him. All those who he appeared in their dreams would finally laugh at his jokes so hard that they too would die from laughter. Everyone paid by dreaming of him before their deaths. From there on, he made a home in random people's dreams where his performance caused them to laugh uncontrollably till, they died just as he did.

CHAPTER 8
BAITING SITE.

Zach had a date with some chick he met on a dating site. He was to meet up with her at her home for a casual sexual encounter. He had been masturbating to her profile pictures hoping he wouldn't ruin the moment when the time came. He did this because he was out of practice. He got out of the shower and began dressing since the appointment was right around the corner. He smothered cologne on his clothes and skin, the most expensive one he had in his possession. He wanted to impress her and even wore some of his cleanest and less used attire. He looked and smelled clean as he left his apartment.

He jumped in his car and drove off being directed by GPS to his destination. He stopped by to get gas right when he was halfway there. He filled up his tank and meanwhile grabbed a rose to hand to the women he was to meet- paying for his products. He walked to his car and placed the nozzle back in its place, then got back in his ride. He traveled some miles till his GPS stated, "Your destination is on the left."

Zach parked his vehicle across the street and down a few houses. He observed movement inside the home. He turned off his engine and proceeded to the front door. He knocked and simultaneously the door opened as he did so. He was allowed to enter the residence by a physically desirable woman. She told him to take a seat as she finished preparing their dinner. Zach sat down in her living area and gazed at her television set which was playing a flick. Soon after, the female walked over to the living area with a plate of food and a beer for him. He gladly accepted it and thanked her. She then returned to the kitchen and brought back her plate and drink. They sat next to each other and ate while watching the tv. Zach told her, "You look lovely. Snaps, I almost forgot I brought you something. Let me go grab it from my car." After placing the plate and drink over the coffee table, he darted to his vehicle to retrieve the rose he purchased.

When he came back inside her house, he handed it to her and she appreciatively said, "Thank you. It's beautiful, that's so nice of you." She placed it on top of her coffee table as they continued feasting.

As he concluded his meal, he began to feel intoxicated and unable to guide his body movements to the response of his brain activity. He found it weird and mumbled, "Did you put any peanuts in this meal? I feel a little dazed and confused. I might be having an allergic reaction."

She answered, "That's weird, I didn't use peanuts or peanut oil to prepare the food. You're probably a little nervous about being with me. Why don't you relax and sip some more of your beer?"

Zach fumbled to grasp the brew but managed to do so. He sipped on it and felt even more disorientated. He suddenly collapsed on the couch where he sat, spilling the drink on the ground. The woman sighed, picked up the can and began to pull him off the couch. She dragged him to her basement and tied him up. She then grabbed a hammer and began hitting him across the head with it. Blood gushed out of his cranium.

He wasn't coherent- lucky for him otherwise he would've been in a stage of shock by then. She mangled his face and skull, watching him gasp for air. She was able to see his throat contracting in search of oxygen as he wheezed. She continued to hit his head with her blunt object. She halted her assault once she witnessed him take his last breath. She then began to dismember his body into pieces with a saw. She had difficulty chopping up his bones since she was a bit dainty- lacking physical strength. She grabbed an electric saw and facilitated her act. Once done, she placed his body parts inside two plastic bags and took them down the street to dump them in a large commercial trash bin which belonged to a small shop. She also drove down to another neighborhood whose trash would be retrieved the next morning to dump his cell phone and wallet. She returned to her dwelling and began cleaning up all the blood and flesh which lay on the floor using acid amongst other cleaning chemicals and burned the evidence along with his clothes in her chimney.

The following day, Zach's friends, neighbors and relatives began questioning his whereabouts. They had been attempting to reach him on his cell phone but their calls would go directly to voicemail. One of his female cousins posted and blogged about his disappearance on social networks. She tried tracking his cell phone and followed its coordinates. She ended up at the waste management center outside of the city, as the truck contain-ing the device drove in. She was able to recover the phone after speaking to the site supervisor who granted her access to the area where the cell was at. She picked the device out of a pile of trash and washed it off some. From there she tried hacking through his security passwords but to her surprise, none was required. His female cousin who knew him best went through the device. As she attempted to investigate his phone, she concluded it had been factory reset. There wasn't any crucial information left which may be used to locate his last movements. She departed to gather at a restaurant to ponder and seek a solution with Zach's best friend.

All his other friends were contacted and asked if they had seen him. No one had had personal or visual interaction with him in the past three days. The police had advised her to file a missing person's report after thirty- six hours of his absence. So, they sped up their efforts in locating him since it was extremely unusual of him to disappear without trace. They had been to his apartment and nothing stuck out or appeared abnormal. So, there they were dining and discussing plots. Yuri- his female cousin who was in her mid-twenties, around the same age as he- suggested they check in with his work.

So, after they finished their food, they drove over to where he was employed. Yuri questioned his peers and supervisor at the clothing store he held a full-time job with. No one had seen him since he went on his days off, which was about three days ago. He was to have returned to work today and failed to do so. Things became more suspicious as she investigated who was last to have had contact with him. Yuri thought- I shouldn't have told the police I spoke to him yesterday. With all these people claiming to have not seen him in three days, it would've been perfect for the police to take charge. She thanked his coworkers for their cooperation and assistance, then departed the shop.

She strolled to her vehicle along with Zach's best friend- Kile. Once inside her car, she broke into tears. Kile told her, "Don't cry, we will find him alive and well. We're going to look back at this and laugh at ourselves for believing something bad happened to him." Grasping her hand between his.

Yuri replied, "I hope so but it's not like him... I can tell some-thing is off... Even as I try to remain positive, every information we come across makes me bet otherwise." Sobbing.

Kile answered, "I agree with you but I'm not losing faith that he may just have baffled us with a spontaneous new him. He had been working on himself for some time now so I'd rather head that direction than to believe my negative thoughts."

Yuri commented, "Where else can we look for him or what else can we do?" Whimpering.

Kile stated, "Let's go back to his apartment and search through his laptop. We might find a hint for our hunt there." Yuri concurred and they proceeded to his residence.

When they arrived at Zach's place, they gained entry just as before with a spare set of keys Kile had since he had resided with him in the past. Yuri walked in and went directly to his bedroom to find his computer. Kile went to take a piss right after he grabbed a water bottle from the fridge. After Kile summoned his natural duties, he went to the bedroom and found Yuri attempting to hack the laptop. She inquired, "Do you know what password he uses on this? I already tried his name and birthday."

Kile responded, "Try ZachAttack90!"

Yuri uttered, "Ok, let me try that," She imputed the password and relayed, "Nope, that didn't work either."

Kile said, "That's weird. That was his password for the longest time. I wonder why he swapped it? Try ZachAttack1990 with and without the exclamation." She did so but without victory.

Yuri received a call from her best friend Lola. She picked up and informed her, "I can't find my cousin Zach. He's gone missing and seems to have disappeared. That's why I called earlier." She began to weep.

Lola told her, "Maybe he's with his girlfriend or took a short trip somewhere to get away from the city?"

Yuri answered, "No dude, we found his cell phone by the landfill inside a dump truck and it had been reset... I spoke to him yesterday and nothing seemed out of the ordinary... We also went to his job and they hadn't seen him in days... We're in his apartment right now trying to get into his laptop and hopefully reveal something." Crying as she vented.

Lola uttered, "Don't worry Yuri, he'll be back hopefully in no time. Zach is your cousin, the one I've never met right?"

Yuri responded, "Yeah, that's the one… Thing is that this isn't like him… He's predictable and never wild and spontaneous… I have a bad feeling something happened to him!" Whimpering.

Lola told her, "No girl, don't think negatively. Don't invoke tragedy. Let me have his address so I can meet up with you and help. I'm heading out now." Yuri provided the location and they hung up afterwards.

Kile and Yuri continued searching for evidence of either him being alright or not. They were kicked off the laptop after several unsuccessful attempts so they had to wait five minutes in order to try again. Meanwhile they went through his personal belongings. There was a knock at the door. Kile walked over to check who it was anxiously expecting it was Zach. Disappointed, he shouted, "Yuri, Is, your friend some skinny chick who drives a black hybrid?"

Yuri answered, "Yes! Let her in please!" Kile unlocked the door and allowed her to enter.

Lola introduced herself and questioned, "Is Yuri here with you? Or am I at the wrong address?"

Kile replied, "She's in the back, you're at the right place. Come on in, I'll take you to her. I'm Kile by the way." As they gave each other a respectful half hug since they'd never met before.

When Lola got to Zach's room, she embraced Yuri and allowed her to vent in her arms. Yuri retorted her previous statement to her and Lola consoled her with positive reinforcement. Kile offered Lola something to drink and she responded, "Some water would be fine please, thank you."

Kile commented, "Cold or room temperature? Because he has both."

Lola uttered, "Whichever is fine." Kile then ran over to the kitchen as he heard Yuri whaling in sadness.

When Kile returned with the water bottle, he handed it to Lola and opened it for her. Lola thanked him and smirked. Yuri noticed the lockout was timely overdue and she attempted several other passwords without success. She once more locked herself out of his laptop. Kile told her, "Maybe we should take it to a computer specialist and have them unlock it. If not, we're going to be trying and trying without being able to. At least you should write down the ones you've used already so you won't reuse them."

Yuri uttered, "You're right. Let me write down the ones I've used so far. If I can't unlock it, then I'll take it to a software specialist tomorrow since it's already late."

Lola asked, "How do you two know each other?" With wandering eyes.

Yuri said, "Kile is Zach's best friend. They've known each other for decades since middle school."

Lola mentioned, "Oh, for a second I thought he was your new gentleman who you failed to inform me of."

Yuri stated, "No, I wouldn't keep secrets from you dude. You're my best friend. Now he and I dated a while back in our teens, way before we met. I don't remember if I mentioned it to you or not? But we're just friends now and nothing more, right Kile?" He nodded his head.

Lola commented, "I don't recall if you told me or not. Anyhow it doesn't matter, I'm sorry for questioning you with my doubts. Have you eaten anything? I can call in an order to your favorite restaurant if you haven't?"

Yuri answered, "We just ate not long ago. Right before we went to the shop to ask his coworkers if they had seen or heard from him." Lola said, "Oh, well that's good you guys ate. I'm kinda hungry myself so I might place an order. Would you guys like something?" Kile and Yuri kindly rejected her offer.

Kile suggested, "Why don't you just go make yourself a sandwich or find something to eat here instead of wasting your money? follow me and I'm sure you'll see something which will curve your appetite." All three headed towards the kitchen.

Kile opened up the fridge and began naming what he saw. Yuri checked through the pantry and did the same. Lola was enticed to choose some leftover lasagna and potato chips. Kile heated up the food in the microwave and Yuri served her chips in a paper plate. When the lasagna was out, Lola sat down to consume some well needed protein and carbs. Yuri and Kile watched her munch. Kile handed her a napkin after viewing some food dripping from her lip. Yuri fondled her phone in her hands. She was looking at an old picture of her and Zach at some family gathering. Lola inquired, "So what else have you two tried already? Have y'all gone to the police?"

Yuri responded, "They told me they wouldn't be able to file a missing person's report before thirty-six hours of his disappearance." Lola commented, "What? Why? That's stupid, isn't it? Just imagine if within that time frame he could be saved or something!"

Yuri stated, "I thought the same but they told me it was policies and procedures."

Lola uttered, "Policies and procedures they probably don't follow when it's one of their own I bet." She took a spoon full of lasagna in her mouth after speaking.

Kile said, "You know how things work. Can't argue with the police… What if we call them and pretend, we are Zach in danger? Maybe then they'll get involved."

Lola told him, "If they track back the phone call, they might charge you with a crime if something bad happened to Zach. How're you going to win that case even if we vouch for you?"

Kile answered, "Good point. I sure wouldn't want to get in trouble and have to fight my innocence and freedom."

Yuri mentioned, "What if we drive around looking for his car? We might find it and then locate him."

Kile told her, "It'll take us several days to commute through all the streets in the city and check everywhere possible. And what if he drove out of the city limits?"

Yuri replied, "You're right, we'd be wasting our time if we went that route. But what we could do is keep our eyes open every time we drive somewhere. I just hope he's alright." She wept again as Kile and Lola hugged her.

They decided to stay at his place and wait for him to return, at least for the night. Yuri had advised her mother of the situation and she contacted her for an update. Yuri told her, "He's not back yet. We're at his apartment waiting and hoping he'll be back soon."

Yuri's mother replied, "I'm worried about him. I hope he's ok and we hear from him soon. I'm going to go to your aunt's house and keep her company since she's panicking, imagining the worst-case scenario."

Yuri uttered, "Alright mom, let me know if y'all need anything please." They then ended their conversation.

Yuri and Lola laid in Zach's bed, still trying to gain entry to his computer. Lola got up and went to the restroom. Kile told Yuri, "I think I'm going to head out now."

Yuri inquired, "Why? Why don't you stay here with us and wait for him?"

Kile said, "Well, I don't want you two to feel uncomfortable with me around.

Maybe y'all want some privacy to lounge in?"

Yuri commented, "You don't make me feel uncomfortable one bit. I'd actually feel more secure having you around here at night. Stay, please."

Kile responded, "Ok, I'll spend the night here with you two. Let me just notify my roommate." He sent a text and received an ok immediately.

Kile slept on the floor and the girls in Zach's bed. The next morning, Yuri's phone rang and woke them up. It was her aunt asking if her son- Zach had returned. Yuri told her, "No, he didn't. We're still here waiting for him at his place."

Zach's mother uttered, "I hope he does. I'm going to go look for him right now with your mom. I'll call you if anything."

Yuri replied, "Ok, I'll be praying you find him." They then hung up.

Yuri charged the laptop which had low power. She rose from the bed and walked to the kitchen to make something for them to eat. She cracked open some eggs and dropped them over some chorizo she had sizzling in a pan. Kile joined her in the kitchen and told her, "It smells really good. Do you need some help with anything?"

Yuri answered, "Thanks. Yeah sure, if you don't mind can you serve us all a glass of orange juice, please?"

Kile stated, "No problem." He grabbed three glasses and the OJ from the fridge to pour inside each one.

Lola joined them after she washed her face in the restroom. She glanced at a picture frame hanging from the living area and grabbed it. She stared at it carefully and asked Yuri, "Is this him?"

Yuri answered, "Yes, that's Zach. He's so handsome and such a sweetheart."

Lola responded, "He looks very familiar, like I've seen him before. I just can't figure it out." Yuri replied, "Maybe you ran into him somewhere before? He enjoys hanging out at the same coffee shop you regulate. You've probably seen him there, sitting down reading a book."

Lola commented, "Maybe, small world if so."

Kile was sitting down at the kitchen table messing with Zach's laptop when he shouted, "I got it! The password was ZachAttack90's."

Yuri asked Lola to watch the food as she told Kile, "No way, let me see."

They both navigated through his computer. They checked his social media accounts which he had saved his passwords for on the remember me setting. He had been chatting with some women and friends. Yuri sent them all a message to verify he wasn't with them.

All replied he wasn't and they hadn't spoken to him since their last registered conversation. Yuri continued checking through his laptop. She found a bunch of saved files of when he was enrolled in school to receive his business administration certificate last year. He also had saved the pictures he took on his cell phone. She verified his search activity and found nothing outstanding. Kile told her, "Click that website. It's a dating app. He may have gone on a date."

Yuri scrolled through his account and discovered his last conversation was with some chick he was gonna meet up with the night he disappeared. Yuri clicked on the girl's profile picture and observed a girl who obviously wasn't real. Yuri stated, "These photos look fake, like if it's a fake profile or something. There's no way he could've fallen for this. We need to take this to the police department for evidence. Lola glanced at the pictures on the dating site. She nudged and said, "They could be real. Who knows. Anyhow, yeah, we should take this piece of evidence to the cops."

They all ate in a rush and after they did, they took off headed to the police department. There was an officer at the front desk who asked, "How may I help you?"

Yuri explained, "I came by yesterday to try and report my cousin missing. I just found this in his laptop. His last conversation was with this girl on a dating site where they had made plans to meet later that night."

The officer questioned, "How long has he been presumed astray?" Yuri replied, "Two nights ago."

The officer mentioned, "Since he's an adult, it's our policy to not file a report until the third day. What I can do is turn this over as evidence but you won't be able to get it back till the case is solved. And that would also be after thirty-six hours of not locating him."

Yuri rolled her eyes and said, "Never mind. I'll just be back tomorrow when it's officially three days and hopefully he's still alive!" They walked out of the station disappointed.

Kile told Yuri, "This really sucks. I can't believe they can't do anything till then.

What a waste of time."

Lola replied, "Fuck them. Fucking assholes! I hope they don't go through the same situation one day and have the same fucking result." They all got in Lola's ride and headed back to her place, before returning to the apartment since she needed to feed her cat.

As they drove up the street and were near Lola's house, Yuri yelled, "Wait! Stop the car!" Lola hit the brakes and observed Yuri hop out of the car.

Lola parked, got out and asked Yuri, "What happened girl? Why'd you jump out of my car like that? What's going on?"

Yuri told her, "This is Zach's car. I can't believe I found it. It's locked though. Kile, can you try and break into it?" Kile had gotten off as well and was right behind Lola.

Kile uttered, "I can try but I don't have anything to open it with. Lola, are we close to your house? Maybe you have a clothes hanger or some type of tool I can use?" Lola turned around and pointed at her house down the street and claimed, "Yeah, it's right there. I should have a clothes hanger or something you could use." They both headed to her home and searched for something as Yuri remained outside next to the car, talking to her aunt on the phone to update her of it.

Shortly after, Lola and Kile returned with a clothes hanger. Lola inquired with Yuri, "Are you sure this is his vehicle? The people who live in the house in front of it are elders, retired. What would his car be doing around my neighborhood? Also, if it isn't his car, we could get in deep shit. Plus, if it is and it has evidence of a crime, we're going to tamper with it and possibly contaminate it."

Kile laughed and answered, "You watch too many crime scenes documentaries huh? This is his ride; I recognize it by this decal I placed myself on the rear bumper." It read, "Honk for the hunk."

Kile managed to pop open the locking mechanism and enter the vehicle. Yuri and he went through it. It was clean and conspicuous. They waited for Zach's mother to arrive at their location. Meanwhile, Lola told Kile, "You're pretty good at breaking into cars, aren't ya? Did you used to or still do auto theft?"

Kile said, "No, I just learned how to from a cousin of mine who was into bad things in the past."

Lola commented, "Oh, I hope I didn't offend you with my question. I was just being nosey and not criticizing."

Kile mentioned, "No offense taken. It's ok to be curious, I probably would too."

Zach's mom arrived in Yuri's mom's car. They found a parking space behind Zach's vehicle. Zach's mom exited and walked over to her son's ride. She said, "This is it, alright. I recognize his school parking sticker which he never removed. Did you guys find anything inside?" She broke into tears and almost fainted.

Kile and Yuri's mother grabbed a hold of her. She began to feel better after some minutes. She had an extra set of keys and wanted to take the car with her but Kile informed her, "I don't think that's a good idea. It would be best if we stop touching it and looking through it let alone remove it from here. I'd say the best option is to wait till tomorrow when it's been three days and report it along with his disappearance." They all agreed and Yuri locked it back up while holding her shirt between her hands and the automobile in order to not leave any more prints.

Lola offered them all to go to her home and hangout. Zach's mother asked her, "You live nearby? You didn't see my son by any chance?"

Lola answered, "I live a few houses down the street. No, I didn't see him or even knew him personally or his car to have done or said something. I do hope he's alright and y'all get the peace y'all deserve."

They all headed to her house and she allowed them inside. Lola began hosting and offered them something to eat or drink. They all were just thirsty so she served them some beverages. They spoke about the incident at hand and had no other option but to sit and wait till the following day. After about thirty minutes or so, Yuri's mother and her sister thanked Lola for the hospitality and departed. Kile also left for his place to shower. Lola drove Yuri back to her home so she too could clean up and get some rest. Lola went back to her residence.

As soon as the sun rose the following morning, Zach's mother, Yuri and hers were at the police station filing a report. They notified the officer attending them they had located his vehicle and gave him the address. They also turned over his cell phone and laptop as evidence.

Unfortunately, the dating app conversation had been erased by the other party along with her profile. The officer generated the report and told them they'd be contacted shortly by a detective. They then headed out of the precinct and went to grab a bite at some restaurant.

Kile joined them after Yuri called him with an invitation. Lola was contacted but she didn't pick up or reply to Yuri's texts. They all were dining at a buffet which served multiple dishes from around the world. They had an extensive variety of meals to choose from for anyone with a precise taste bud. Kile walked in through the front doors as they had already sat down and began eating. He paid his fees and spotted Yuri and them at a table on the left-hand side. He strolled over towards them and once in front, he kindly greeted them all. He took a seat as the waiter went over to ask what he'd like to drink. He ordered a lemonade and then Yuri told him, "I'm gonna get up to get some more food. Why don't you accompany me so you can grab something?"

Kile responded, "Ok, I was waiting for you to do so, so I wouldn't go up there myself alone. Where's your friend Lola?"

Yuri said, "I'm sorry we didn't wait for you but we were starving all day since we went to the police department to file the report. She hasn't picked up or replied, she might be busy or still asleep."

Kile stated, "It's alright, you didn't have to wait for me. What did they tell you guys at the police station?"

Yuri told him, "They finally took our report along with his cell phone and computer. We told them where the car was and they said a detective will be calling us shortly."

Kile uttered, "Well at least they'll get to it now. Hopefully they're able to locate him and tell him we've all been worried sick about his well-being." They began to serve themselves food and then went back to take a seat and eat.

Suddenly Zach's mothers' phone rang. She picked up and heard a detective on the other end. He informed her he'd like to talk to her in person in regards to her son.

She told him she'd be over at the police station in less than an hour. She hung up the call and began getting worried. They all sped up their edible consumption process and took off to the police headquarters where the detective was at. When they arrived, they waited in the lobby after notifying the clerk of their presence. The detective met up with them and took Zach's mom back to his office. Once there he closed the door and informed her, "I have some good news and bad news mam. We have a suspect in custody who voluntarily came and confessed to their crime. With their confession we were able to locate your son's body. I regret to inform you he's not alive, I'm sorry for your loss."

Zach's mother began whaling without resistance. She let everything out and the detective offered her some tissue to wipe her tears. She took the tissue and blew her nose and continued sobbing. She asked, "How do y'all know it's my son's body y'all have found?"

The detective answered, "We were given specific details by the person responsible of where to locate his wallet and car keys.

Besides that, we ran fingerprints off of the cadaver and they came back to your son's."

She yelled in agony, "No! Not my son... Please tell me this is not happening, please!" The detective uttered, "I wish otherwise mam, but it is our duty to inform you of what we have concluded with a testimony given by the assailant and all we have discovered after."

She inquired, "Who was it? Who did this to my son?" In a demanding tone.

He replied, "At the moment we are not able to disclose such information with you ma'am. The person has requested legal representation. You will know eventually when the trials begin. They're not getting out anytime soon, I can assure you of it. Let me just get your statement since we didn't get it when your niece filed the report and have you sign some documents. Once done I'll escort you back to your relatives so you can update them."

Zach's mother's hands shook as she held the statement document and signed a few sheets regarding the case. It took her more than usual to fill out the paperwork since she was weeping inconsolably. The detective handed her copies of her statement and forms she signed. He then accompanied her back to the front.

As soon as she saw her sister and niece, she sobbed uncontrollably and within breaths relayed what she had been disclosed by the detective. They all began crying loudly, including Kile. They held each other in their arms in a group hug sort of position. Soon after, they left outside to get some fresh air. Yuri's mother asked, "Can we see his body?"

Zach's mother stated, "The detective said we may not be able to due to the nature in which it was found. He told me it would be all up to the funeral services once they take possession."

None could believe it even after they had a gut feeling. They all drove to Zach's mom's place and began to mourn Zach's departure. They also began calling some funeral services to obtain an idea of how things would work plus the cost. News spread around and people came to Zach's mother's residence to give her their condolences and support her in any form possible. Some showed up with food and drinks for everyone to share. They remained at her house till very late in the early morning when Yuri and her mother left for their home.

A few days had gone by and the service took place. It was a closed casket and all those who attended paid their respect to Zach. He was going to be remembered as the great young man he was. Kile asked Yuri, "How come Lola didn't show up?"

Yuri replied, "I hadn't even noticed she wasn't here. Matter of fact I've been so distracted by all this to remember if she ever texted back." She hadn't as she checked her phone.

Once the ceremony came to an end, they all left. Some went over to Zach's moms place to congregate, keep her company and continue to support her. Yuri went to her house to grab some things. When she was about to head back to her aunt's house, she remembered to check the mail. She found a correspondence letter from the county jail with Lola's name on it. She opened it and began reading Lola's confession to being the one who murdered Zach. Yuri was furious but kept it to herself. She never spoke to her again. About Lola and the reasons behind her crime.

Lola was a twenty-year-old female who was having difficulty establishing a romantic connection with the men she knew. She didn't have trouble attracting them but she was peculiar in her choosing. There was always something wrong with them. So, she opened an account on a dating site, believing she'd find what she was looking for there. Right away she made several conversations with guys. She began narrowing her search and eliminating those not fitting her criteria. Eventually she chose one and turned her full attention towards him. She felt a deep connection with this particular man. They exchanged numbers and started to contact each other on their cell phones.

After about a week or so, they planned out a date together. When the day came, Lola was excited yet nervous. She got ready and drove to their meeting point which was at a park. When she arrived, she called him to see where he was located since, he wasn't present at the spot. He inquired what type and color of vehicle she was in and she informed him. He told her he had a visual of her and asked her to get out of her car and close her eyes for he had a surprise. She trusted her intuition and followed his instructions. She heard a car approaching. She then felt someone nab her, forcing her inside another vehicle. She was tied up and blindfolded right before she heard a door shut and felt the car moving. Her date wasn't who he had pretended to be. Matter of fact, he had used false information to create his account as well as pictures. Lola was raped and abused by his real identity during several days of torture. He did end up releasing her out in the middle of nowhere. She never got a chance to see his face or car since she was left blindfolded and tied up.

She managed to free herself and found a dirt road which she followed. The dirt road led her to a highway where she forced a truck to stop and render aid. She filed a police report but they were unable to apprehend the man responsible for her sexual assault. He had covered his tracks upon committing his crime. She held a grudge of frustration and created an evil image of men in general.

Eventually she decided to make another account on the dating site, hoping she'd find the guy and take matters into her own hands. She didn't bump into him but found the others there disgusting as they made perverted sexual verbal advances towards her. That's when she began to hunt them down. Every single guy she lured to fornicate with became her victim. She felt she was saving the world by eliminating males. She was only temporarily alleviating her pain with the innocent.

Her conscience convinced her to turn herself in as she witnessed her friend mourn the death of her cousin Zach- who had fallen for her evil plot. Once she comprehended it was him for certain after observing the picture at his place and his vehicle near her home. Zach was her ninth homicide and the one to stop her dead in her tracks when she was found guilty of several counts and ordered to remain in custody of the state without the possibilities of parole and a term no less than three life sentences. She remains behind bars up till this day.

CHAPTER 9
DEMONIC FERTILITY.

"Good morning my essence in life. The reason behind my smile," said Lucio, as his girlfriend Bertha opened her eyes in bed.

Bertha gleamingly responded, "Good morning wonderful man. Did you get enough rest?"

Lucio answered, "I sure did. How about you, the enchanting beauty of earth?"

Bertha bashfully responded, "I did, I hadn't rested this well in quite some time to be honest. It feels relaxing to wake up beside a great man like you. One who makes me feel protected, loved and desired."

Lucio chuckled, uttering, "I share your emotions. I too feel what you described of me, but of you." He then planted a peck over her forehead and cuddled with her in bed.

The sun made its way into the bedroom through the cracks in the window blinds, dazzling over her dresser. It was Saturday and they both had an amazing date Friday evening. They had met up after work and partaken in dinner and a movie. The feast was held at an exquisitely romantic Italian joint. Their food was gourmet and delicious along with a few glasses of wine to wash it down.

The big screen unfolded a comedy skit which made them laugh on multiple occasions. They held hands and expressed their love physically to one another.

They had been seeing each other for about six months. Their first interaction occurred while Bertha and her friend were heading towards a tattoo parlor and Lucio was exiting a library. Bertha bumped into Lucio as she distractedly conversed with her pal. Lucio had several books in his arms which dropped to the ground upon impact. Bertha apologized and assisted him in regrouping them from the floor. She perceived a good vibe expelled from Lucio's aura. They made eye contact and grinned. Bertha had mentioned, "I'm really sorry I didn't notice you there. How can I make this up to you for I feel embarrassed by my clumsiness." Displaying guilt.

Lucio told her, "It's ok, don't worry about it. I'm fine, the books didn't get damaged and there's no reason to feel debt for a simple human error." Bertha was attracted to him though and only extended the conversation, hoping he'd catch on.

"No seriously, allow me to redeem myself. I'm fascinated by men who read and are as charming as you," stated Bertha.

Lucio commented, "Alright, since you insist. How about we exchange digits and grab a bite some day?"

Bertha, without hesitation, grabbed his phone and imputed hers in it then said, "You can text or call whenever you'd like to or when you get a chance to do so... So, we could agree on a place and time of course." Trying to minimize her interest in him.

Lucio answered, "Why yes of course. I'll talk to you soon. My name is Lucio by the way. What's yours?" She divulged hers and shook his hand.

Lucio uttered, "Nice meeting you in this awkward fashion Bertha. You have a magnificent day now." As he turned away and marched down the street.

Lucio took a couple of days to get back to her. He had been busy working; reading and had almost forgotten he had her number saved in his phone. When he contacted her, they settled for coffee and breakfast. She arrived punctually in a stunning outfit. They chatted as they waited for their food to be served. She was intrigued by his profound knowledge in life. His extensive vocabulary aroused her without intent. He was well educated like her. Only difference was he didn't obtain his in a classroom yet instead from life itself. He shared quotes to her from some of the greatest men to have ever walked the earth. After they feasted, they hugged and she rapidly rushed in for a kiss. He allowed her and returned the affection. Then he courteously departed from the restaurant and went on his way. She kept gazing at him as he entered his vehicle- she did the same. There was something about Lucio which turned her submissive without self-will to counter his charismatic effect.

They continued seeing each other, utilizing each opportunity to become acquainted. Then came the day she failed to resist his sexual invite. He hadn't brought it up since they met, not even slightly mentioning the word. This made her drool over him with the mystery as the main attraction. She was at his place when he began to delicately caress her. She didn't deflect her desire and allowed him to make her his. That night had been precipitating as they fornicated in his living room listening to the rain hit his window. She begged him to ejaculate inside her. When he succumbed to her request, there was thunder nearby. It somewhat turned her on how there was lightning as he came inside her. She spent the night at his place but didn't rest much since he had a tremendous sexual energy to share with her.

Following that night, they engaged in intercourse absolutely every single day. After about three weeks, she began feeling nauseous. One of her friends and also a coworker advised her to see a doctor. She set an appointment and when she attended, the doctor gave her startling news- she was expecting.

She hesitated to inform Lucio of her diagnosis. Mainly because she felt he would refuse to accept accountability. When she finally shared the news with him, he was first reluctant to believe it. Then he was displeased she had kept it from him for about a week. Afterwards his eyes glistened and reality set in. He was going to be a father which brought him cheer. They began planning things together and decided they didn't want to know the gender until the exact moment the child bloomed. They had begun purchasing baby items including a crib. Since they didn't have knowledge of the gender, they didn't obtain clothes or other necessities which were gender colored, specific. They did pile up some boxes of diapers from several sizes.

Back to the weekend in the beginning, Bertha told Lucio, "I'm craving some pancakes honey. Would you be kind enough to prepare some for us?"

Lucio answered, "That sounds delicious. Let me go check if we still have some because last time, I made some, I think we ran out."

Bertha uttered, "Don't tell me that, please. I really want some badly." As Lucio had gotten up from bed and began making his way into her kitchen.

Lucio returned and informed her, "I told you so. Why don't you get up and I'll take you to a restaurant to enjoy some instead? The other option would be for me to run to the store but I really don't want to go and then have to cook as well."

"Ok, I'll get out of bed and we'll go dine out," stated Bertha, as she rose up and began dressing along with Lucio.

Once they had suited up, they left her place and headed down the street to a small dinner. They took a seat by the window and a waiter approached them. The waiter took their orders and headed to the back to notify the cook. Bertha felt movement in her belly. She grabbed Lucio's hand and placed it over. Lucio said, "Hold on baby, the pancakes are on their way now. No need to fuss and throw a fit."

Bertha giggled and questioned, "Do you even believe he or she understands you?

That's spontaneously cute of you to hold a conversation with it though."

Lucio responded, "I'm sure it doesn't comprehend my exact intent but the sound of my voice may soothe and relax him to be more patient."

Bertha commented, "You're hilarious. It might be laughing at you right now saying, dad, you're not feeding my appetite with words. Where are those pancakes, I requested?"

Lucio pointed at the waiter and uttered, "Coming right up to be exact."

Bertha rejoiced on sight and said, "Finally baby, our food is here and you'll get to calm down."

As soon as the waiter placed the plate of pancakes in front of Bertha, she had the syrup container in hand and poured heavily over them. She dug right in as if she hadn't eaten in days. Lucio took his time dressing his sunny side up eggs with toppings. He shook some hot sauce over them and sprinkled black pepper. They were consuming their meals when Bertha suddenly spewed her intake. Some of the people felt disgusted without knowing the reason behind her actions. A priest walked over to their table and asked her, "Are you alright child of Christ? Let me help you clean up this mess." As he grabbed a handful of napkins to wipe off the floor.

Meanwhile, Lucio cleaned her face with napkins. The waiter rushed over and took her plate as Bertha apologized relaying; she was pregnant. The priest said, "Oh, how wonderful of you to be expecting my dear child. Makes sense why you regurgitated your elements. How far along are you?"

Bertha replied, "Five months and a half."

The father questioned, "So is it a male or female?"

Betha responded, "We decided not to know until it is born."

The priest turned to observe Lucio acknowledging her comment of we. The father's eyes began turning black and he convoluted, falling to the ground. The waiter had returned with a mop bucket and mop to their table. Bertha hysterically shouted,

"What's wrong with the priest Lucio? Someone please help him!" Lucio sat with a frozen gaze in his seat.

People assisted the father who laid on the ground unable to gasp for air. A crowd formed circling him. The staff called the emergency number who advised the caller to perform CPR on the father. The male waiter rushed to begin chest compressions being coached through the phone by the operator. The priest was unresponsive even after the paramedics arrived. They took the man with them into their mobile unit and departed with their sirens wailing. Bertha observed how Lucio remained unshook despite the situation which unraveled right in front of his reach. Bertha asked him, "How come you didn't help him? Are you feeling well honey?"

Lucio swallowed his food and answered, "I'm fine. There was nothing I could have done to save the priest. I also panic during commotions like this. I may seem calm and collected but inside there's a whirlpool of fear and anxiety pulling me deep."

Bertha commented, "Oh, I didn't know that about you. You did appear to be unbothered by what was happening."

Lucio told her, "I just froze, that's all. I know it might seem cruel but that's part of life. One day we're here and the next we're gone." Bertha stayed mute after his comment.

The waiter returned to their table with a new plate for Bertha. She said, "Here you go darling, I'm sorry it took long to replace but with the emergency at hand, the cook took a break."

Bertha mentioned, "Thank you so much for the trouble of making me another plate of food. I'm grateful for your kind gesture. Unfortunately, I don't think I'll be able to enjoy it without throwing up again. Would you mind wrapping it up to go?"

The waiter replied, "Don't worry hun, I understand. I have kids of my own too. Let me go get you a box and a bag so you can take it with you and eat it later when you get hungry again."

The waiter rapidly returned with a box and bag in hand. She delicately placed her pancakes in the box and bagged it. She then looked at Lucio and asked, "Was everything alright or may I help you with something else?"

Lucio had finished his meal and stated, "Everything was great besides the accident which occurred right in front of us. Here's my card to pay the bill." Handing her his debit card.

The waiter uttered, "I'm sorry about the accident but it was out of our hands. He was a regular here and a very generous kind man. I hope he's ok. Let me go check you out and bring back your receipt." She darted to the cash register to close their account.

The waiter made her way back to their table and handed Lucio the receipt and his card. Lucio signed the receipt and left her a twenty-dollar tip for her excellent service. He and Bertha stood up and walked out of the restaurant. Bertha wanted to walk a bit and get some exercise so they strolled a few blocks on foot.

Located in the downtown area, they ventured into some shops which Bertha suggested. They mainly window shopped beside a few little things Bertha acquired and an ice cream they shared. They had traveled near a catholic chapel where an unhoused man stood outside preaching gospel words from the bible. The man halted his speech and gazed over at Lucio. He then shouted, "The devil is upon us! The fight between good and evil has been declared! The blood of Christ has power and conviction upon you Satan! Glory is his name who beholds your life and casted you into the shadows!" He pointed at Lucio.

No one paid attention to him other than Lucio. He turned to see the man's eyes and caused him to depart from where he stood preaching. The man ran off in a hurry, leaving his belongings behind. Bertha requested they enter a small boutique across the street from the chapel. Lucio agreed and they walked over then inside. Bertha scanned through a few items, mainly candles. She grabbed two scented ones and proceeded towards the counter.

Lucio paid for her products and they then left the store and headed back home since her feet were swollen and in pain.

When they made it to their home, Lucio removed her shoes off and massaged each one of her feet. Bertha said, "Oh that feels so good honey. Thank you for taking care of me and our unborn child."

Lucio replied, "You're welcome my love. Would you like for me to go turn on one of your new candles?"

Bertha answered, "I'd appreciate it if you would. Especially if you're going to light it up and place it near here so I can smell it as you massage my feet. It might just be a great therapeutic experience."

Lucio got up and turned one on, placing it on the center table in the living room and told her, "There you are baby, you just lay down on the couch and enjoy this tender loving care." As he resumed massaging her feet.

Bertha smiled and said, "You're a gift from God."

A couple of weeks down the line, Bertha's family organized a baby shower for her. Friends and relatives attended the event. They served nachos with a variety of toppings to choose from. Including lettuce, tomatoes, onions, black olives, jalapenos, sour cream, guacamole, salsa both red and green, chili beans and pinto beans, grilled shredded chicken and crispy taco flavored ground beef. They also had some Texas style smoked brisket with a perfect pink ring around each slice accompanied by some potato salad. Soda pop and bottled water filled the coolers. They played games for entertainment; Lucio was short to trim the sufficient amount of toilet paper to wrap around his woman's belly. They had small prizes for the winners who participated effectively during the contests. They took a break after engaging in healthy fun. Lucio and Bertha served themselves some food and ate along with some of the guests who had just arrived.

Bertha's uncle was one of the ones sitting at the table. He was a Christian pastor and volunteered to say grace before they indulge.

As he began his prophetic speech, a drain pipe burst above them. A painting of Jesus Christ's last supper which hung in front of them fell and shattered into pieces. They all opened their eyes and looked around at each other. Water flowed downward engulfing the dining area rapidly. Bertha's cousin's husband (Jim) who were the hosts and providers of the home, ran to shut off the main valve outside. Everyone got up and darted outside to the backyard. Bertha's uncle said, "That is a first for me. I've never had a similar reaction to my gospel. Hey Jim, is your house haunted or something? Have you had any paranormal activity in the past or present?" Jim had just gotten back from shutting off the valve.

Jim uttered, "Nope, it's not haunted and we haven't had any ghost encounters either. Matter of fact we don't believe in such nonsense."

Bertha's uncle replied, "Well I'd highly suggest praying with you and your wife alone in the house one day."

Jim responded, "Sure maybe you could stick around after the baby shower. Let me go inside and help my wife clean up the spill." He ran inside the house excusing himself.

Once Jim, his wife and other volunteers dried up the leak, they headed outside as Jim contacted a plumber. They gathered in the yard to open up presents continuing the agenda. Bertha and Lucio sat together facing the crowd at a table which was filled with gifts. Bertha began reading out the to and from notes before opening each present.

She pulled out a set of both male and female clothing her sister had given them just in case. Her sister stated, "I left the receipt inside, for if you want to exchange or get a refund later when my niece or nephew arrives."

Bertha told her, "Thank you sister. Next up let's see who this one is from. From, Jim and Delilah hope you like the gift." She took out a baby crib bed set in gray color. Bertha stated, "Awe, I love this. Thank you, Lilah and Jim. Our baby will sleep comfortably with this set."

Lucio commented, "Great choice in color guys. This is a neutral nonsexual discriminatory tone." Jim winked at him.

Bertha resumed opening gifts and grabbed the following one nearest to her. It was one from her uncle, the pastor. She took it out of a gift bag and exposed a Jesus Christ cross and a bible. As she displayed the cross in her hand to the group, it imploded. It was constructed from ceramic and cut her hand. Lucio got up and held her hand in his, reviewing the injuries. He applied pressure to the wound after removing a shard of glass lodged in her skin. Delilah ran inside her home to grab her first aid kit. Everyone in the crowd was in shock. Her uncle was disturbed and believed something evil lurked near them. There was no other explanation for two similar events occurring back-to- back. He then began praying and calling on our lord and savior. Just as he did, the clear skies up above turned black. Thunder and lightning struck, then rain began to pour on the gatherers. They had to relocate themselves inside the home to continue.

Once inside, Delilah retrieved some gauzes, alcohol pads and antibacterial ointment to prep Bertha's wound. She finished up by placing a band-aid over the cut. Lucio and some of the guys ran inside with the rest of the gifts. Since Bertha's hand was in pain, she requested Lucio continue opening the presents. Lucio resumed reading out the notes and removing the items from within the boxes and bags. Just as he was on the final gift, Bertha's water broke and she began contractions. Everyone panicked and believed she was having a miscarriage since it was still a bit early for her symptoms.

Lucio rushed her to the hospital and after they filled out paperwork and provided their insurance and medical background information, the staff attended her. They performed ultrasounds to see what the issue was since she wasn't due quite yet. The doctor eventually got to her and informed her she was about to give birth. He also informed her of several abnormalities he had observed from the ultrasound. Bertha searched for Lucio to obtain comfort and support from him, but he had vanished. She inquired from the staff if they had seen him. To which they all answered no. They told her she had checked into the facility all alone without anyone accompanying her. She was in denial up until she started crowning and babies started exiting her vagina. She couldn't believe Lucio had abandoned her and was gonna lecture him when he'd return. Even if he disappeared out of fright or nervousness. Little did she know of the surprises which awaited her in the delivery room.

Bertha was unable to conceive children no matter how hard she tried. Her efforts had a tragic pattern of commitment in vain. She slept with several men in her lifetime but none were able to impregnate her. It was all she desired in life, to bear a child. Nothing else would give her the satisfaction and wholeness of emotions she yearned for. She attempted raising another woman's kids once when she established a relationship with a single father. She couldn't handle the disrespect the kids offended her by. They always reminded her she wasn't their real mother.

She had also spent most of her life studying and achieving success by obtaining various degrees. She would venture in high adrenaline activities but they too would only grant her temporary joy. All of her friends and relatives were married and had seeds of their own. This placed an enormous pressure on her to become equivalent. Not only because of her own desire but also due to sarcasm she received from them at gatherings. They'd question when she would settle down and raise a family of her own. She never shared the truth with them about trying yet failing.

She had been married in the past but her unachievable dreams brought out anger and resentment in her heart which led to divorce. So, she vowed to not remarry any other man other than the one who'd plant a seed allowing her to become a mother. Then she met Lucio who was a demon in disguise. He was able to enceinte her with thirty little evil beings. The doctors and staff at the labor and delivery department were beyond shocked. A priest was contacted to assist them with their issue at hand. This priest had no other option but to remove them and place them in an incinerator to destroy their existence on earth. One by one burned in hell.

Lucio never returned and as she laid all alone in the maternity ward, Bertha flatlined halfway through the process.

CHAPTER 10

UPON EVIL SOIL.

O mar was a man in his late twenties who worked in the city's public transportation department. He loved his job, especially helping people in need. He was very generous to the point he would help accumulate payment for those riders who didn't have enough to board his bus. He had a good soft heart and was extra kind to everyone whether he knew them or not. His route ran from downtown to the central terminal and back several times during his shift. He lived in an apartment alone for quite some time after he had graduated from high school and moved out on his own. He would get home after work and cook himself something or grab a bite on his way there. Then he would study, always learning something new, read his bible and play the guitar right before he'd fall asleep. This was his usual daily routine.

One time during one of his routes, a woman one year younger than him, boarded and sat right across him. She began asking him questions about his job. Eventually their conversation got a little personal where they began sharing relevant details of each other. They spoke about their likes and dislikes, preferences and deal breakers. By the time he traveled to her stop, she had written down her number on a piece of paper and handed it to him, since she was intrigued by their dialogue. He gladly accepted it concurring with the connection. When he got home and finished his daily rituals, he called her to resume their talk. They held that chat through the late night. He had to go to bed so he could wake up to go to work the next morning. She also had to rise up early for her job. Otherwise, they'd never hung up. Their relationship continued to grow from there, taking baby steps but never retracting.

Her name was Naomi and she worked at a senior citizen day center. Omar and her began hanging out, going on dates and spending a lot of time together. It took about a month for her to finally have the courage to inquire, "So are you gonna ask me to be your girlfriend or what?" While they sat at the cinemas about to enjoy a show.

Omar replied, "Would you... like to be my girlfriend?" Hesitantly.

Naomi uttered, "You need to ask me correctly with determination, not all shy like if you're uncertain of what you want. That's if you want to be boyfriend and girlfriend of course?"

Omar told her, "You're beginning to sound demanding which is a red flag I avoid due to previous bad experiences."

"I'm sorry, you're right I am being a bit demanding huh? Well, I'll leave it at that. I just would like to know where we stand?" Stated Naomi.

Omar responded, "We're friends for now. I do like you but I'd like to get to know more about you before I start taking you more seriously. Hope you understand."

Naomi commented, "Alright, I comprehend and will not rush you anymore into something you might not adhere to."

Omar surprised her one day at the establishment of her employment. He showed up with a bouquet of white roses and a box of her favorite chocolates. He then asked her to be his girlfriend in front of everyone present. All the seniors in the center cheered him on. Even her coworkers shouted remarks of love being present in the air. Naomi agreed to be his girlfriend as all the spectators chanted out happily in approval. So, they dated as an official couple for another six or seven months.

It was during the spring when she made an announcement to him. She was pregnant and carrying his child in her stomach. Omar leaped from the ground approximately three to four feet as happy as can be. He had feelings for her and also wanted to form a family together. He actually had an engagement ring hiding in his pockets which he plotted to pop the question later that day with. So, he instinctively got on one knee right then and asked her to be his wife. She accepted and they celebrated both that they were engaged and expecting.

Eventually they shared the news with their friends and family. Omar also began searching for a house to buy. He took a first-time homebuyer's course and got educated on the process of purchasing a home as well as other useful information he learned along the way. He then started looking around for a bank to get a preapproved loan. When he finally found the one which had the best offer and lowest interest rate, he signed and began the process. From there, he looked for a realtor. His friend recommended him one and they began talking about what he had in mind and how much he'd be willing to spend. The realtor worked with him and began showing him a few properties around his price range. Omar did all this without Naomi being aware. He wanted to surprise her. He finally picked out a house which had everything he wanted and was within his budget. He signed off the final paperwork after the haggling process. He was able to drop the price down after finding small details during the home inspection which he planned on fixing himself. He waited about a week and some days before he received the keys to the house.

The following day after receiving the keys, he picked up Naomi at their apartment since she had moved in with him. He drove her to the house and told her to accompany him for he had to speak to

147

the residents who left their wallet on his bus. She fell for the excuse and walked with him to the door. Once at the door he handed her the keys and told her, "Here open it."

Naomi asked, "How do you have the keys? Did you find them too? Even then we're not supposed to just open their door and walk into their home. Let me ring the doorbell." She hit the button.

Omar cracked up in laughter and replied, "No one's home, just open the door with the keys and we'll drop the wallet in the entrance and take off."

Naomi uttered, "You're crazy but fine, let's get this over with since I'm starving."

She inserted the keys in the slot and turned the door handle. When the door swung open, their friends and relatives were inside and shouted, "Surprise!"

Naomi was confused but entered the dwelling to greet them all. There was brand new furniture in the living room. A table filled with gifts and food freshly cooked. Naomi asked her mother, "Who's house is this and what's going on?"

Her mom responded, "Ask Omar, he'll tell you."

Naomi grabbed Omar by the arm and questioned, "What's going on and who's house is this?"

Omar handed her the keys and answered, "It's yours and ours. I just bought it, got some new furniture and planned this house warming party for us. Tomorrow I'll start relocating the rest of our stuff from the apartment here."

Naomi was weary but replied, "Are you serious or playing around?"

Omar told her, "Why would I lie about something like that? It's our new home baby. Now let's sit you down in your new dining set and serve you some food so you can relax."

He escorted her to the destination and she took a seat as he placed a plate of food in front of her. He then served himself one and sat next to her. She ate some of her food, enough to soothe her hunger and wanted to look through the house. Omar accompanied her to check out all the rooms and even the backyard. It was a single-family dwelling with three bedrooms, including the master. It had two full restrooms and a double garage. The kitchen was spacious as well as the living area which had a beautiful brick chimney. It measured approximately sixteen hundred and a half square feet. She fell in love with it immediately and composed a life in her head of what their future would look like. Naomi went to the backyard, she found it peaceful and quiet. She imagined her garden as she always dreamed of having. She then kissed Omar and told him, "Thank you honey. Thank you for getting us a home of our own. How'd you do it though is my question you little sneaky guy?"

Omar replied, "Well it was complicated to sneak around behind your back since you'd always ask me questions but this has been about a two-month process. Where I secretly took a first-time homebuyer's course, got a loan approved and checked out a few homes with a realtor. Most of which I did while at work on my breaks and some I told you I was going to the store or made-up other excuses. But don't worry, I won't be sneaking around anymore and hiding things from you."

Naomi stated, "I sure hope not. At least if it's not for something like this which will benefit us both."

Omar kissed her and reassured her, "I promise I will not sneak around behind your back for anything which will compromise our relationship." They then went back inside the house to finish eating and open up their house warming gifts.

Everyone was enjoying themselves in Omar's and Naomi's residence. They danced around and had a few drinks. The younger kids ran in and out of the house from the front and backyards-playing. They all ate and congratulated them both on their purchase. Omar felt proud to have been able to get him and his soon to be wife and child a house to live in. They then began unraveling the presents in front of everyone.

They collected a bunch of useful items which, back at the apartment where needed but didn't have the sufficient space for.

The sun began to fall behind their home and the guests started heading out one by one. The last ones to leave were their parents. They helped clean up the place and made some plates to go. They said goodbye to their son and daughter, then took off. When Omar and Naomi were finally left alone, they walked to their bedroom and laid down. They made gentle love and eventually dozed off cuddling together as their television was left turned on.

The following morning, Omar woke up early, turned off the tv and went to rent a moving truck. His brother joined to help move all of their stuff from the apartment to the house. Their first trip wasn't enough to fit everything but they had all day to accomplish the task. They drove over to the house and began taking things out of the truck and into the home. When they finished, Naomi had made breakfast and told them both to eat before their next trip. They ate in a hurry and drank a ton of water. Omar told Naomi, "I don't want you to move or pick up anything heavy ok. I'm sure you'd like to help and have all this organized before we return with the second trip but please don't hurt yourself."

Naomi said, "Alright, I promise I won't. You don't have to worry about that, ok?" They then left and hopped on the truck to head back to the apartment.

Naomi began taking things out of boxes and placing them where she felt they'd make a great fit. She then went to their bedroom, grabbed her clothes and started hanging some in the closet. She picked up the rest which went inside their dresser and nightstands and put it all away, nice and neatly. She did the same with Omar's attire, went to the restroom and started unpacking some boxes of hygiene products. Once she finished, she served herself a glass of water and took a seat to relax a bit in the living room. Afterwards she began unpacking the kitchen ware and placing it in the kitchen cabinets. She organized the whole kitchen, bedroom and living area right before Omar and his sibling returned.

Omar and his brother arrived at the front of the house with their second load. They parked on the curb and began unloading boxes, bags and items to take inside. They went in and out of the dwelling with things in their hands till they had concluded removing everything from the truck. Naomi saw they were finished and served them a cup of water. She told Omar, "I already organized the bedroom, kitchen and restroom.

We're gonna need to go to the store to get more things for the other restroom." Omar replied, "That's great babe. I'm glad you were able to help and not hurt yourself or the baby. I'm sure it makes you feel good and I'm proud of you."

Naomi uttered, "Yes honey, it did make me feel good to be able to help out and make this move much easier for you. Thank you for feeling proud of me but I'm sure it's nowhere near as proud as I feel about you."

Omar responded, "Well, on to the last trip. Almost done, just a few more things which didn't fit in the truck. You want me to grab a pizza or something on the way back?"

Naomi commented, "I'd love that if you would. I've been craving some pizza to be honest and you'd really hit the spot if you'd get one."

Omar answered, "Alright then. We'll be back shortly. Don't hurt yourself and leave my old bed and furniture alone. When I get back, I'm gonna put it in the garage and sell it some other day."

Naomi told him, "Ok babe, don't work too hard and I'll see you soon." She gave him a kiss right as he headed out the door.

Once Omar and his brother were gone, Naomi began unpacking the rest of the stuff he had taken. Their winter wear was placed in the living room closet. She also grabbed a chair and started organizing miscellaneous items on the top of that closet's shelf.

She opened up a box of picture frames and started hanging them up in the living area, some in the hallway and bedroom. She stumbled upon a box which carried hand tools and removed them, organizing them in the garage. She then found a box containing their bedsheets and comforter and took it to the room. She made the bed and also grabbed the pillows from another box and placed them in their designated location. She continued assisting in the moving process and was about done with most of the light stuff before Omar and his brother came back.

Omar and his brother got off the truck and went inside to drop off the pizza and drinks. They then started unloading the final items. Once done, Omar and his brother drove down to the truck rental company and returned the vehicle. Omar's car was parked outside and they jumped in and drove back home to finish up.

When they returned to the house, they found Naomi sitting down eating pizza and noticed she had really fixed everything pretty well. Omar and his brother took a seat and Naomi got up to serve them food. They ate and then they began moving his old furniture into the garage. There were only a few things left in the living room which Omar could move on his own so his brother departed their residence. Right after Omar and Naomi thanked him dearly for his volunteering service.

Omar locked the door behind him after walking his brother out to his car. He then continued moving things where they went. Naomi was in the kitchen washing dishes and when she finished, she swept and mopped. Omar concluded arranging his old stuff in the garage and asked Naomi, "Do you need any help with anything? I want to jump in the shower."

Naomi answered, "Not at all honey. You go ahead and shower while I finish cleaning up here. I'm almost done and then I'll sweep and mop the living room to call it a day. Oh, by the way, I put all your clothes in the dresser and nightstand how you had it before. I also hung up your clothes in the closet in case you wanted to wear any of it."

Omar commented, "Thanks babe for putting away my clothes. Are all the things I need to wash up in the shower?"

Naomi responded, "Yes babe, just not the towels. They are in the closet in the hallway."

Omar told her, "Ok honey. I'm gonna shower now. Shout if you need anything." As he walked over to their bedroom to grab his clothes and a clean towel.

Everything seemed fine. The move went well and the house was coming alive. Naomi was sweeping and mopping while admiring the way their home looked. She was delighted with a grin on her face. She swept twice and grabbed the dustpan with a handle which Omar had gotten her to avoid not bending down. She picked up the dirt and then tossed it in the trash. She then put the broom and dustpan away and got the mop and mop bucket. She turned on the hot water in the kitchen sink and filled the bucket up after pouring some chemicals. She started mopping the whole house. She did this twice as well. When she was about to finish, Omar had gotten out of the shower and told her, "Let me help you finish so you can shower too if you want."

Naomi replied, "It's ok babe. I'm almost done anyhow. I'll wash up soon as I'm completely done here. You just relax since I know you carried a bunch of heavy things down those stairs in the apartments today."

Omar said, "Alright then, just don't say I never tried to help. I'll be laying down in the bedroom for a bit. Then I'll come get the tv and take it in there so I can connect it, program it and the DVD player as well. Then after we both shower and rest a little, we can drive down to the store to buy some things for the other restroom and anything else we really need."

"Sounds good honey. I'll be over there in no time to grab my clothes to shower." Stated Naomi as Omar strolled towards their bedroom.

About twenty minutes or so later, Naomi walked out of the restroom fresh and clean. She found Omar asleep in the bed and silently grabbed some of her socks to slip over her feet from her nightstand. She then pulled them up to her legs and slid back her sandals on. She walked out of the room and closed the door so Omar wouldn't hear her getting ready. She connected the hair dryer and started drying her hair. When she finished, she straightened it and curled the ends. She then plucked her eyebrows and did her nails. By the time she concluded her glamorous routine, Omar had woken up and opened the door to their room. He gazed at her while squinting his eyes since he had just woken up. He then asked her, "Are you ready to go to the store now babe?"

Naomi answered, "I am, are you? You were asleep like a baby after a couple of spanks down the cranky cut road." Smiling.

Omar started laughing and said, "Where'd you get that metaphor from? Have you been reading my mom's journal or something?"

Naomi laughed and uttered, "I'm going to ask your mother where exactly to land my hand on you to make you comply."

Omar responded, "Who said anything about a hand? You'd have to use the belt like she did. Otherwise, I'd interpret it as a tease." They both were cracking up.

Naomi grabbed her purse as they headed out of the house and drove down to the store. She had made a list before she knew she'd be relocated into a new house and that's the list they began to stock on. When they passed by the restroom aisle, they stopped and grabbed things to make the other restroom not look abandoned. They continued placing items from their list inside the cart. Eventually Naomi went through the list one more time to make sure she had everything on there before proceeding to checkout. As they formed a line at the register, an older woman recognized Omar from his route and told him, "Hi Omar, what are you doing around this side of town? I've never ran into you before at this store."

Omar greeted her, "Hello Mrs. Sullivan, how're you doing? Let me introduce you to my fiance and soon to be mother of my child. Noami, this is Mrs. Sullivan." They shook hands.

Mrs. Sullivan told Naomi, "You're very beautiful. Congratulations on your pregnancy and engagement. You picked the best young man I've come across. Omar here is such a sweetheart."

Naomi replied, "Thank you very much Mrs. Sullivan. I know I did that's why I had to secure him for myself, I'm just kidding. "Smiling.

Mrs. Sullivan chuckled and inquired, "So do you two live nearby?"

Omar uttered, "We just moved into our own home a few blocks from here."

Mrs. Sullivan said, "That's great news. I too live a few blocks away. What street do you two reside on?"

"Lawson St.," Commented Omar.

"Lawson street? You two need to be very careful in that neighborhood," responded Mrs. Sullivan.

Naomi questioned, "Why's that mam, are there high rates of crimes committed in that area or gang activity?"

Mrs. Sullivan answered, "No dear, nothing like that. There's a house which everyone knows…" An important call came in which she had been waiting for and apologized as she took it.

Omar and Naomi began placing their items in their cart after being bagged and accounted for. They then paid the balance and said goodbye to Mrs. Sullivan who was still on her call. She waved at them with a smirk. Omar and Naomi walked out of the store and over to his car. He opened the truck and they began placing the bags inside. Once done, Omar grabbed the cart and put it in the cart return. He then hopped in the driver's side and turned on the vehicle. Naomi said, "I wonder what Mrs. Sullivan meant by being careful in our new neighborhood if it's not due to gangs or crime?"

Omar told her, "Me too but I'm sure it's probably something which occurred back in her days and no longer exists. You know how some old folks could be sometimes still living in the past."

Naomi replied, "Yeah, you're right. I mean we haven't seen anything strange or dangerous around our home to consider a hazard."

Omar uttered, "Yeah, let's just forget she said anything and remain positive." Naomi nodded her head in agreement as they drove back home.

When they arrived back at their residence, they took everything out of the trunk and unpacked it inside. They put every single item away and Naomi took the things to the restroom to decorate it. Omar went to the room to set up the television set. Once they both had finished, they met up in the bedroom. Naomi walked in with some snacks and asked if they could watch a flick. Omar accepted and they laid in bed eating chips, popcorn and soda pop observing a movie. They hung out until the movie finished and they cleaned up the bed to fall asleep.

They continued living some of the best moments together in their own home as the weeks rolled. Naomi began feeling a bit weak and developed chronic headaches which caused her to renounce her job. Omar had it all covered since he had just received a raise and planned his home purchase well. So, he didn't mind that she stayed home and rested. Naomi spent most of her days in bed unable to find the will to get up and do things. Her headaches intensified and she didn't feel healthy. Omar had to be cooking for them and feeding her in bed. He even set up an appointment with her doctor so she could be diagnosed and treated. Omar continued caring for her and their unborn child. He was a good man who prayed for even the most wicked of bad people on earth. It did take a toll on him but he knew sooner or later she would feel better.

Naomi continued to deteriorate mentally and physically. She had even gone to her medical appointment and the doctor didn't find anything wrong with her though. What he did recommend was to change her prenatal vitamins and try a more expensive brand hoping she'd feel better soon. But she didn't, as the weeks marched in, she felt worse and worse- losing weight in the process. She became somewhat anemic and worried Omar. She began telling him, "I've been seeing horrible things in my sleep and hearing voices. I think I'm being spiritually attacked by the enemy himself."

Omar consoled her saying, "Let me pray for you and our baby. Don't you worry or give in to any dark war against you. You're a child of Christ and the enemy is not welcomed in this home, body and soul." He then began praying and reading from the bible.

The words of wisdom helped Naomi fall asleep and get some rest. Omar continued praying and reading the bible as he held her hand in his, sitting next to her. When she woke up, he had prepared chicken soup for her. He took her a bowl to the room and fed her as she laid in bed. She consumed some and began spewing her intake. Omar removed the food away from her just in case it would make her nauseous seeing it. He cleaned her up and removed the blankets off the bed. He tossed them in the washer. He returned to their bedroom and gave her a drink high in electrolytes. She drank and said she felt better. He bathed her in bed with towels and water. Omar grew more and more concerned with her symptoms each day. He took her to the hospital several times but they too said she seemed fine after conducting multiple studies. No one fetched an answer to why she felt ill.

Her mother had been spending the day with her while Omar went to work. She would care for Naomi and do her chores around the house to help Omar not get sick as well from all the stress. She observed Naomi acting strange and murmuring tongues in her sleep. She notified Omar of it when he got back from work. They collaborated together to call in a priest to the house with all the abnormalities. When the priest arrived, he refused to help because he felt an immense evil power too great for him to battle. He gave them a number to call and Omar kept calling it without an answer or a call back.

The days came without luck. It had been about three months since she fell ill and no one could save her. Then one day as Omar slept, he woke up and found her outside in the backyard digging the ground up. She seemed zoned out as if she was sleep walking. He grabbed her and returned her to bed. Things became eerie and there was nothing Omar could do or anyone else who could help. Her family would go and visit her. They would pray in groups but nothing changed. Her mother wanted to make her a baby shower and thought if she'd tell her she may cheer up. Naomi didn't bother to display any sort of interest in a baby shower. Omar came back from work that day and found her mother crying in the living room. He asked her, "What happened, is she ok?"

She turned to see him displaying a gash on her cheek and said, "She attacked me for no reason. I don't know what's wrong with her. I was only praying for her when it happened. She was asleep, just woke up and attacked my face."

Omar asked her, "Are you serious she did that? She hasn't attacked me before.

That's odd and alarming."

Her mother stated, "Yes, anyhow, I'm leaving for the day, call me if you need anything."

"Alright, thank you very much for all your help and I'm extremely sorry this happened," mentioned Omar, as she departed the dwelling.

Omar went to their bedroom and found Naomi asleep. He didn't want to disturb her and pondered if it would be a good idea to rest beside her tonight after being informed, she had become violent. He began reading his bible in a soft pitch for her to hear as she slept but not loud enough to wake her up. He continued reading all through the night. He didn't even cook or eat anything that evening as he took care of the woman he loved. He eventually fell asleep and in the middle of the night, he heard sounds in the kitchen. He opened his eyes and discovered Naomi had gotten up out of bed. He rose and walked towards the kitchen to see what she was doing. As he drew closer, he observed her with a knife in hand and began stabbing her stomach with it. He ran to halt her and took the knife away. She spoke in tongues to him. He saw she was bleeding profusely and dial 911. When the paramedics arrived, they called the police just in case the incident arose from a domestic dispute. The police interviewed Omar at the hospital as he waited to hear any news about Naomi and their unborn child. He cleared his name with the law and since she had been acting erratically, they closed the file and left. Omar had called in to work that he wouldn't be able to go since he was in the hospital with his fiance.

The doctor eventually went to the waiting area and called out his name. Omar jumped up from the couch and said, "That's me, Is everything alright with my fiance and unborn child?"

The doctor stated, "I have some very bad news sir. Due to the piercing of the sharp object, your unborn child sustained an injury and was pronounced dead upon arrival. Your fiance was treated and her wounds were suited but we're going to be placing her on emergency detention due to the nature of the incident. She'll have to be psychologically evaluated before being allowed to be released back home. So, in the meantime, I'd suggest you see her and say goodbye to her since you won't be allowed to be around her once a security officer is assigned to her." Omar broke out in tears and walked with the doctor to see Naomi.

He arrived and observed her in a gurney tied down to it in a room they had moved her to, following the operation. Omar asked her, "Why did you do this to our unborn child Naomi?" While sobbing.

She didn't reply since she was heavily sedated. She had become combative during the procedure. Omar left once the security personnel arrived. He went home alone and even called his boss back to let him know he was going into work after all since he didn't want to think about what had happened.

He showed up a bit drowsy, unable to sleep but kept his mind off of the current situation. He made it through the day and went back to an empty home at the end of his shift.

Naomi was interviewed by a phycologist at the hospital and diagnosed not mentally sane to be released. She was administered into a psychiatric facility where she remained for a few weeks. She eventually gained her sanity and realized what she had done. She wept inconsolably. They ended up releasing her back to Omar and he drove her home. She begged him to not take her back home again since she felt guilty for killing their fetus. He pulled the car to the side and looked at her saying, "I'm glad you've regained consciousness of what you did. I forgive you for it. If you don't want to go home then where do I take you?"

Naomi replied, "I'm sorry for what I've done. I'm ashamed of it and will have to live with it the rest of my life. I don't feel I did it in my senses and I believe something in our house was the cause of my actions. That's why I don't want to go back there. I felt fine before living there and then something came onto me and my mind where I became a prisoner against my will." While sobbing.

Omar told her, "I don't feel the same way about our home. The home I've been working for to pay. I can't force you to come with me so tell me where it is you'd like for me to drop you off at."

Naomi uttered, "Take me to my mom's please." Still crying.

Omar kept quiet and pulled back into traffic. He made his way towards her mother's house. Naomi was scared and she didn't want to lose him but she knew something was wrong with that house which he or anyone else didn't agree with.

When they got to her mother's house, Naomi tried kissing and hugging him but he refused and got out of the car. He then walked over to the passenger's side and opened the door for her to exit. She began whimpering and got out as he got back in his car. She walked to her mother's front steps and rang the doorbell. Her mother opened the door and let her inside. Omar observed she was accepted and drove off. He had been contemplating on leaving her for her act. Her not wanting to go home with him only reassured him it was the best thing to do. He drove down to a bar and grill since he had gotten off of work hungry and instead of eating, went to pick her up.

When Omar got to the location, he exited his vehicle and walked inside. He took a seat at the bar, ordered himself a cheeseburger with fries and a beer. He fixed his eyes on a tv monitor and began watching sports. When his meal and drink were placed in front of him, he enjoyed them both. He ended up sticking around at the bar having more drinks. He left late, a bit intoxicated but made it home safely.

As he attempted to open the door he felt like crying. He held it in and went inside. Once he got to his room, he kicked off his boots and removed his uniform. He then laid in bed as the room spun around a little. He fell asleep and as he rested, he had nightmares. In those dormant visions, he saw witches, murderers, rapists and very evil people chasing him. They yelled profanities to him and claimed his soul belonged to them. During the middle of the night, he woke up startled dripping in sweat from the nightmares. He looked around and saw it was around four in the morning so he fell back to rest.

When he arose the next morning at the sound of his alarm, he felt ill. He ran towards the restroom and threw up. He then jumped in the shower and got ready to head to work. He performed exceptionally as usual maneuvering his bus through the city streets without issue. When he clocked out, he darted to his house.

He began cooking himself some food and watched television. He then started hearing voices in his head telling him to commit atrocities. He shook his dome and picked up his bible to read. The voices continued no matter how hard he tried paying no attention to them. He started feeling sick and went to lay down. As he rested, he had nightmares again. This continued for a few weeks where he got worse every day as his health declined for no apparent reason. It got to the point he stopped showing up for work and didn't answer anyone's calls. He fell off the map.

Naomi had been attempting to reach him to chat. She worried for him so she asked her mother to drive her over to his house. When she got there, she didn't want to enter but had to. She walked through the front door and over to their room. She swung the door open and witnessed Omar asleep, covered in sweat and pale. He had lost some weight and didn't look healthy. Naomi shook him awake and told him, "You need to get out of this house honey. Have you seen what conditions you are in? This house is now attacking you. Come on, get up, let's go." She tried picking him up but he was still too heavy for her.

She was about to go call her mother for help when Omar jumped up and began assaulting her. He strangled her by the neck and hit her violently in the face. His eyes had turned black as if they had no signs of life in them. He heard her wheezing for air yet didn't let loose of his choke. He ended up killing her. He released his grip and saw her body plummet to the floor. The voices then instructed him to go hang himself. Omar walked to the garage and grabbed some rope. He tied himself up and let the chair under him fall. Just as he was passing out, he heard Naomi's mothers voice screaming for help. She tried lifting him up but he was gone.

Naomi's mom found her in their bedroom dead and called the police. They went over to the residence and blocked it off as a crime scene. No one was allowed to enter. Naomi's parents and Omar's got together to mourn their deaths. Nobody had a clue as to why things had occurred that way. Until a few years later when news reports spoke of what lied beneath the foundation of the house.

The property on 3352 Lawson St. had been on the market for quite some time. Most of the people in town were well aware of its poor conditions as well as the history left behind. It was constructed in 1956 under a mass production of a major development company. Its first owners were a couple of newlyweds who wanted to start a family together. Within the first year of their residency, there were problems. As if a curse had taken over their relationship and exchanged love for turmoil. The man eventually killed his wife after several months of unending conflict amongst them. He shot her on the head with a thirty-eight-caliber pistol. He then turned the firearm on himself. She was carrying their three-month-old fetus inside her. Once the police department released the property back to the bank concluding their investigation, it was cleaned up and placed back into the market.

The year was 1958 when the second owners moved in. They were a small family of three. The father, mother and their two-year-old child. During their first week of living in the house, chaos sprouted in the marriage. Approximately two months later, the mother murdered her son and husband as they both slept by asphyxiation. She then slid her carotid artery and bled to death sitting on the kitchen table. Once again, the dwelling was for sale.

In 1960 a family of four got the keys of their first home hoping to start a new life in the city they had relocated for work. Within the first month, scuffles rose and escalated to domestic violence. On the sixth month, give or take- the father drowned his two kids in the bathtub after decapitating his spouse. He hung himself in the garage from a wooden beam of the structural support of the home. Their bodies were discovered a few days later when their friends and relatives notified the police, they had not had any contact with them and were worried for their safety. A welfare check was conducted by local authorities who found a macabre crime scene which left some traumatized. The process continued, the house was cleaned up and relisted on the market. This time it took longer to find a buyer.

In 1965, a man in his mid-thirties signed off on the mortgage and moved in with his fiance who had recently accepted his proposal. They had been described as a happy young couple by neighbors. Something which took everyone by surprise one evening as they heard two gunshots coming from the house minutes apart. The police were dispatched and they found two bodies with no signs of life. The woman laid in bed covered in a white bed sheet which had a pool of blood under it. The man was lying on the ground face down. It seemed he had ended her life and took a seat at the edge of the bed before shooting himself with the same handgun which remained clinched to his right hand.

Similar scenarios commenced in the years of 1967, 1970, 1973, 1978, 1981, 1983, 1986, 1990, 1994, 1999, 2002, 2005, 2007, 2010, 2013, 2015, 2017, 2020 and now in 2024 with Omar and Naomi.

This home seemed to lure couples in and destroy their love, bringing hatred and confusion till death parted them. It sucked the joy out of those who called it home. Somehow entering their mind and controlling their emotions. Making them feel despair which caused depression and a false sense of emptiness. It robbed the faith of even the strongest of believers. Turning them into heartless creatures who practiced and engaged in evil deeds. Fabricating lies in their brains until they cooperated with the voices committing homicide and suicide.

The structure itself was constructed over a satanic burial ground where many bodies were placed to rest centuries before the house was built above. Those wicked spirits were the ones responsible for the atrocities. Eventually the house was demolished and the land was excavated, determined to be uninhabited. The area was marked condemned by the city and gated so no one else would become a victim after the remains were taken by the church and properly disposed of.

CHAPTER 11

THE GILA KILLA.

Jacob, Walter and his girlfriend Susie were on their way to their summer short vacation. Their plans were hiking The Gila trails, rafting the river in an inflatable raft and fishing at Lake Robert's. They had booked a nice spot somewhat near the famous cave dwellings. On their way from Las Cruces, they stopped at a little restaurant near I10 to grab some burritos for their trip. Jacob got a refried bean and cheese. Walter picked a picadillo with beans and Susie grabbed a red chili with no beans. They got back in Jake's crossover SUV and hopped back on I10 heading westbound.

Jacob was driving and eating his burrito as Walter and Susie sat in the rear seats eating theirs. Jacob began swerving after spilling some hot beans on his leg. Walter told him, "Jake, slow down bud! Pull over if you're gonna be distracted eating and driving. I'd like to make it to and back in one piece."

Jacob replied, "Walt, let me do the driving and breath to remain calm. I've got this, done it a thousand times before without issue. It's just that some beans fell on my leg and burned me, that's all." As he cleaned up his leg with napkins.

Walter uttered, "I'm about to finish mine so if you want to pull over, I can drive as you eat? I'll be fine with it."

Jacob responded, "I'm good bro, trust me, relax. I already covered the burrito up where it had a small leak and I'm eating it carefully as I drive. I don't want to waste any more time. You were supposed to pick me up at eight and because your truck didn't want to start, we're running a little late to check in."

Walter stated, "It was out of my hands that my truck didn't want to start up this morning. I've been keeping up with its maintenance but who knows what's wrong with it? Good thing is it happened at home and not where we're headed. Out there I'm sure it's quite the task to find a mechanic who won't charge an arm and a leg for just diagnostics. As far as running late for check in, it isn't that big of a deal. As long as we do check in and not die on the road there, the host won't mind, I'm sure."

Jake said, "Yeah, you're right about it being better it happened outside your home than in The Gila. I'm not speeding or doing anything erratically for you to be so concerned with my navigation capabilities. Just sit back and chill with your girl. Let me raise the radio station so y'all can feel more comfortable." He hit the control button on his steering wheel and the music played at a higher volume in order to halt their discussion.

Jacob managed to finish his burrito without causing a deadly accident on the road. Susie ate hers and began kissing Walter as a melancholic song aired over the vehicle speakers. It was a song they had danced to during their prom a few years back. Jake observed them in his rearview mirror and smiled. He didn't believe in love since had had his heart broken too many times for hope's sake. But he did enjoy seeing others who did and didn't have his same luck. He fixed his gaze back on the road and continued towards their destination. Jake observed his exit and drove off of I10 towards the 25. They were getting closer to their destination. His radio began losing signal as he drove through the outskirts of Deming. He then tried his bluetooth but had poor signal as well. He tuned into a usb drive he had filled with a variety of music and it saved the monotony of the trip. Guns and Roses- Patience, was the first song in his collection. They continued driving through an isolated highway which they had traveled before when they camped out in the Gila on multiple instances. Jake lowered the volume and asked Walter, "Hey bro, do you remember that time we camped out and there was a pack of skunks near our tents? Then your dog -Ruger- woke us up in the middle of the night because he killed one right before he got sprayed?"

Walter answered, "Yeah! That was a cool trip man! The following morning, I had to shower him in the cold waters of the creak next to the Grapevine campground. We partied that night like there was no tomorrow since you had just broken up with your ex. Do you remember you burnt the steaks that evening because you had been drinking heavily and dancing around the fire like a neanderthal?"

Jake replied, "Ha, ha, ha! Yeah man! Those steaks ended up being more like beef jerky. Hopefully we have a great time as we've always had and one more for the book of good memories." They bumped fists to that.

Susie hadn't heard the story so she asked Walter for an update. Walter began sharing the fond memory circulating through his mind. Jacob began driving uphill through sharp turns and dips. He observed how Susie was laughing at the recap Walter divulged. He too chuckled at the manner his friend described the occurrences. Susie grabbed a water bottle from the back and Jake asked her if she could hand him one as well. She gave him the first one off her hands and got another for her consumption. Walter didn't really like to drink much water. He would hydrate with soda pop, kool aid, juices and beer. So, he popped open a can of cola. Susie asked Walter, "How far is the place you booked?"

Walter answered, "Maybe about another forty to forty-five minutes. It is past the dwellings and we just drove by the rangers' office. So yeah, I'd say more or less. Why do you need to use the restroom?"

Susie replied, "Oh, no I don't. I'd just like to get off and stretch my legs some. Been cramped up back here for some hours already and I'm starting to feel claustrophobic."

Walter stated, "We're almost there baby. If you feel you can't hold in your anxiety levels, feel free to communicate and I'll ask Jake to pull over."

Susie uttered, "No It's alright. If we're almost there, I can wait and keep calm enough to not have a mental breakdown. Let me just place my legs over yours and that should help in the meantime." She loosened her seatbelt and maneuvered her legs over his.

Jake began signing a jam with a funny vocal pitch. Walter and Susie giggled in the back. At first it was entertaining to hear him sing but then they merged their voices and all three were repeatedly shouting out the lyrics to the song together. It was a good distraction for Susie's disorder.

All of a sudden, some black colored truck with super dark tinted windows almost pushed them off a cliff as it swung wide on a curve. Their hairs erected on the back of their necks followed with goosebumps. They almost defecated themselves. Jake said, "Damn! Whoa! That was a close call man. I felt my heart pop out of my chest. Imagine if we'd be driving downhill knowing we weren't gonna make it? What a fucked-up way to die."

Susie uttered, "What an asshole that person driving such a big truck with no consciousness of its size."

Walter replied, "Fucking dick! Yeah, it would be a bad way to go man. Watching everything moving rapidly without any control to stop the vehicle before it crashes into something and we all propel forth to our deaths. Imagine dying while taking a shit though? That would be pretty sick too. To have the EMT's wipe you before placing you on their gurney. And still have to pull up your pants and all."

Jake started laughing and responded, "Yeah that would be messed up bro. But imagine dying at sea after running out of oxygen? Unable to take that much needed breath to save your life. The pressure buildup from being deep underwater. That too would be a harsh reality to accept. Or any form of drowning."

Walter commented, "Damn! That does sound pretty cruel, man. But imagine…." Susie interrupted them and shouted, "Enough with the worst ways to die guys!

It's creeping me out since we just survived a close encounter. I feel we're jinxing ourselves speaking of death while we're out here to have a good time. Let's focus on remaining positive and not allow negative thoughts to depict our experience." Walter and Jake giggled as they stared at each other through the rearview mirror.

Walter told Susie, "We usually have odd conversations with each other while on road trips or camping. Didn't think you'd be offended by it." Jake nodded his head in accordance.

Susie said, "I'm not offended at all. It's just that I was still scared about the situation and you guys were like whatever, soon after discussing deaths." The guys chuckled.

Walter told her, "Sorry babe, I didn't think it would be a sensitive subject for you. Anyhow, hey Jake, are we getting our nails painted at the salon next week?" Jake burst in laughter catching on to the sarcasm.

Susie smiled and stated, "You're such a dick Walt. Like the driver of that truck, careless. But you're funny and at the most random time say the most awkward things. You know that's why I love you. It's your spontaneous dialogue which sets you apart from the rest." She planted a kiss on his lips which had a grin on them already.

Just before getting to their destination, they stopped at Lake Robert's to get some fresh air and stretch. They gazed at some men fishing out of a boat some yards away.

After about five minutes of taking in the scenery, they jumped back in Jake's ride and continued forward. As they were almost there, Susie began complaining she had to utilize the ladies room. Walter advised Jacob and Jacob said, "There's not a restroom nearby but I'll stop at Grapevine. It should be coming up so just hold it a bit longer."

Susie replied, "Ok, just don't crash or make sudden movements that may break my concentration."

Jake uttered, "Sudden movements like this, you mean?" As he pretended to make a sharp turn off a hill.

Walter stepped in and told Jake, "Chill bro, If you piss her off, I'm the one who's gonna have to deal with her. It only be fair if I take it out on you afterwards and I know you hate creepy crawling bugs."

Jacob responded, "Sorry guys, I got a little carried away with excitement since we're getting closer." The sign that read Grape-vine was in sight. Jacob drove down the entrance and over to the restroom. He hit the brakes and parked, running out to take a piss himself. Susie got out and opened the door to the porta John. She then yelled out, "Walter, there are bugs in here! It's pretty filthy and there's no toilet paper!"

Walter grabbed a roll of paper from their cargo and opened the restroom door saying, "Babe, calm down. It could be worse and there'd be no restroom whatsoever. Let me kill these bugs for you and make sure they don't land or do anything while you relieve yourself. Oh, and here are some wipes I got from my bag so you can clean the seat and feel less grossed out."

Susie cleaned the seat and sat uttering, "Thanks babe, for making me feel secured in this primitive restroom. Kill that one right there please." Pointing at a spider.

Walter smacked the arachnid and told her, "Primitive? You call this primitive? This is sophisticated to be exact. Primitive would be squatting behind a tree or bush and having to wipe with leaves. Having no soap or water to wash your hands."

Susie questioned, "So where's the soap and water to wash my hands?" As she finished and cleaned herself.

"The soap is in my bag and the water is in the creek," replied Walter with a smirk on his face.

Susie and he exited the booth and walked over to the vehicle so Walt could hand her the soap. Walter opened his bag, placed the wipes back and retrieved the soap. He then walked with her towards the creek. As they got closer, she said, "Wow! This is gorgeous. I've never been this close to mother nature's enchanting wonders. I love it. Ah! Is that a frog?"

Walter told her, "It sure is. No need to be frightened by some defenseless frog honey. I hope you get used to the wildlife out here or I'm gonna eventually get irritated by your screams. Now wash your hands so we can get going please."

Susie uttered, "Ok, is this the campground y'all were talking about on the way over here? Where Jake burnt some beef and your dog killed a skunk?" As she dipped her hands into the creek to wash them.

Walter commented, "As a matter of fact it is. This place brings back some fun memories. I love this campground. This is my favorite campground so far that I've stayed at."

Susie said, "Ok, I'm done washing my hands now. It does look really nice. I'm sure I'd like it myself if I'd camp here one day."

They both went back to the vehicle and got in. Jake was sitting in the driver's seat waiting for them. Once they buckled up, Jacob began driving out of the campground and back on the road. They drove over a bridge and continued their route.

A few minutes later, they passed by the dwellings and then began to see small houses that offered relaxing hot tubs. Eventually they made it to the rental property they had booked for the weekend. Jake parked on the driveway and got out. Walter and Susie did the same. Walter walked up to the front door and entered a pin on an automated key box. He retrieved the keys to the home and they opened the door. They all headed inside the residence and looked around the place. There was a note on the television stand in the living area. It was written by the host- Herbert- who greeted them on their stay as well as provided some helpful numbers to include his. They then walked outside to the vehicle and began taking their luggage out. Walter and Susie would be sharing a room and Jake would have his all to himself. They began taking their things to their sleeping quarters. When they were done, Susie suggested they hike the cliff dwellings. So, they closed up the place and drove over to the location.

Once they got to the dwellings, they checked in and paid a small fee. Then they began their short hike. As they crossed the bridge over the creek, Susie stopped to see the Trout swimming under them. Susie was excited since she had never been there. The guys had visited the dwellings several times in the past but they were intrigued by Susie's first experience. They continued to hike the trail. She was mesmerized by the scenery and when they got to the top, where the dwellings were, she was speechless. They explored the dwellings and Susie felt appreciative of the conditions in which the natives had built and lived in their community. She was like a child searching her gaze at the rooms the dwellings exposed. She visualized natives living there in the past and what their lives were like. After they had been there a while, they began heading down. Susie thanked Walter for taking her on such a journey.

When they made it back to the SUV, they boarded and drove back to the home. As soon as they pulled up, they spotted a deer walking towards the backyard. Susie questioned, "Can we go pet it?"

Walter answered, "I don't think that's a good idea babe. The animals out here are wild and may attack. Also, you'd make them lose the fear of humans, making them susceptible to being easily hunted or harmed."

"Ok, I agree with what you mentioned," divulged Susie.

They reentered the house and Walter grabbed some steaks he had already marinated to grill. He and Jake popped some brews and headed outside to start cooking.

Jacob and Walter turned on the gas grill. Susie was in the bedroom, her and Walter would be crashing out at. She was going through her things to grab her sandals and remove her tennis shoes. She found them and took off her foot wear to slip her feet into her more comfortable gear. Once she had her sandals on, she went outside with the guys.

As Susie strolled outside to the backyard, she observed Walter placing steaks over the grill and Jake wrapping up potatoes in foil paper. She then glanced at the wilderness behind them. It was marvelous, such a pretty sight for her to enjoy. She took a seat by the swimming pool and leaned her gaze at the forest surrounding them. Walter had placed a foil sheet on the grill over one of the corners. He started placing pre-cut slices of squash, onions and asparagus which he had soaked in olive oil and sprinkled with seasoning. The food began cooking and Susie got a whiff of it. Her stomach began growling for intake so she got up and asked, "Is it almost ready? It smells delicious."

Walter told her, "Give me about ten minutes or so. Unless you want your meat rare and your veggies fresh." Susie replied, "Ok, I can wait ten minutes. In the meantime, I'll gulp down a bottle of water." She went back sightseeing out of the lounge chair. Jake had finished placing the potatoes to be baked over the flames across the grill. Walter continued to keep his eye on the food in order to make sure it didn't burn and become beef jerky as the one Jake had messed up some years back. Walter asked Jake, "Hey bro, can you hand me another beer please? And bring out the steak seasoning I left on top of the kitchen counter right next to the fridge?" Jake headed inside to obtain what was requested.

Walter called out Susie's name so she could turn around, blew her a kiss then said, "You look so beautiful out here in the forest like a native Goddess of the earth. Not that you're not beautiful anywhere else other than here but the scenery behind you makes you appear spectacular."

Susie uttered, "Awe, you're such a romantic man babe. You too look like a king of the jungle out here and I can't wait for you to roar over my nude body later on tonight." Winking as she finished.

Jacob came out from the house with a beer and the seasoning in hand. He handed the seasoning to Walter along with the beer. Walter took it from his hands and popped the beer open. He then began sprinkling the steaks with the dry seasoning. As soon as he sprinkled some, he turned the steaks over to the other side and repeated his course of action. After seasoning all the meat, he began removing them and placing them in a container with a lid. He began removing the veggies off the grill as well. Once he concluded the removal of the steaks and vegetables, he poked the potatoes to see if they were almost ready. They didn't quite slip off the knife he used so he left them a bit longer and opened a pack of franks to grill in the meantime. He and Jake started conversing about their childhood memories. Susie was overhearing them as she stared in a peaceful bliss over the forest. She had captured a hawk flying over them in her view and followed it.

A few moments later, the food was all done and they gathered at a patio table with chairs to dig in. Susie served herself a ribeye, some veggies, a potato and two winnies. She also grabbed a soda pop from a cooler where the waters and drinks were located. Walter served himself a ribeye and a half with three franks, veggies and a potato. Jake had the same as Walter. They feasted in the tranquility of the atmosphere which surpassed that of the city they were accustomed to after smothering their baked potatoes with butter, salt and pepper. Once they finished, they tossed their empty paper plates in the trash and changed out into some swim wear to dip in the pool.

Walter dove in as Susie was already inside. Jake was the last one and when he exited the house, he sprinted towards the edge and jumped in. Walter got out and pulled the cooler closer to them so he could grab another beer after disposing of an empty bottle. He then dove back inside and when he emerged on the surface, he popped the bottle open. Sussy told him, "That's a nice trick babe. What do you call it? Dive and pop?" Giggling afterwards.

Walter stated, "I call it the swim and win and it's precisely the fountain of youth." He swam up to her and they began making out as Jake laughed.

They remained in the pool for some time and got out right before the sun set completely over them. As they headed inside the home, they left a trail of puddles of water behind. Walter and Sussy grabbed some clean clothes and jumped in the shower. Jacob did the same but, in the shower, located in the hallway of the residence, near his room.

As Jake lathered his body with soap, he heard a noise coming from the side of the house. He opened the window and looked around. There was a censored light which had turned on. He spotted a racoon looking up at him and Jake shouted, "Hey there trash panda buddy! Why don't you stop scaring visitors around here and mind your own business. Better not be heading towards the trash bin in the backyard to make a mess! I'll find you and kick you right under your tail where the squirrels feed." The racoon walked off before he even finished his reprimand.

When they all had freshened up, they congregated in the living area to watch television. Walter and Jacob continued sipping brews. Susie was drinking water. They started observing a horror film which was recorded in the woods similar to the forest they were at. Susie began getting scared and looked around the windows to make sure no one was spying on them. There was a suspenseful scene where the murderer chased some broad. Once the bad guy caught up to her, he began slicing her face. Susie closed her eyes and then became terrified when she heard a loud bang outside. Jake jumped out of the couch and ran over to the backdoor. He peeked and then opened it. He shouted, "I told you little buddy not to come mess up this trash can!" He tossed his beer bottle which shattered on the ground, at the raccoon and took the trash bin inside- informing them it was only a trash panda scavenging.

Susie felt at ease after acknowledging it was just an animal out there and not some killer. She began feeling drowsy halfway through the movie and informed Walter. They both notified Jake they were headed off to bed and he replied, "Alright guys, have a good night. I'm gonna finish up this flick and then probably have me a smoke outside just in case y'all hear me." They gave him a thumbs up and walked towards their bedroom.

When they got to the room, Susie shut the door and locked it. She then began undressing and when in her birthday suit, pranced over to Walter who was removing his clothing articles while sitting at the edge of the bed. Susie got close to him and rubbed her soft body over his. He felt her warmth and grabbed her by the waist, pulling her in closer. He then began to kiss and suck on her breasts. They seduced each other until they connected their private parts and became one. Their intercourse lasted about thirty minutes in which they both came twice. They then laid next to each other, cuddling and closed their eyes. They were so tired neither of them heard Jake go outside to smoke before going to bed himself.

The next morning, Walter opened his eyes and saw Susie laying over his arm. He kissed her with a smile of delight in his visage. Susie felt his lips and woke up herself. They both said good morning to each other and began getting dressed. Susie told Walter, "I think I'm gonna take a shower before we head out."

Walter stated, "Alright babe, sounds good. I'm gonna go see if Jake is awake while you clean up."

Walter closed the bedroom door behind him as he left the room. He strolled over to the other side of the home and found Jake's bedroom open. He peeked in to see if he was asleep. To his surprise, Jake wasn't in bed and the bed was made which threw him off a little because Jacob wasn't the type of guy to make his bed needless to say one that wasn't his. So, Walter left the room and searched for him throughout the residence. He didn't find him anywhere so he went outside to check. Outside in the front yard, his vehicle was still parked. Walter shouted Jake's name but didn't get a reply. He then shut the door and headed towards the backyard. Walter gazed around the yard but didn't find his pal. He yelled out his name with no response. He looked inside the pool hoping to not find his drunk buddy's body floating in it. It was a relief for him not to. Walter wondered where he might have gone. He went back to the house and as he passed by the table they had eaten at, he witnessed Jake's beer bottle half empty. Another clue to be suspicious, something might have happened to Jake. He never left a beer bottle half empty. Once again, he shouted his name but didn't hear his friend's voice call back. He headed inside to inform Susie. When he told her she asked, "What if he went for a morning run or a hike on his own?"

Walter replied, "No babe, this guy isn't a morning person whatsoever. Besides, he made his bed and left his beer half empty outside. That's not like him to do. I know him very well to know he wouldn't make his bed nor leave a beer half empty. I have a strange feeling something happened to him babe."

Susie finished washing up and uttered, "Let me get dressed and we'll go search for him. Don't worry, I'm sure we'll probably find him out there passed out drunk sleeping with the raccoon from last night." She grabbed her towel and began drying her body and then started getting dressed.

They both went searching relentlessly throughout the property for Jacob. Yelling out his name loud enough for him to hear if he'd be within half a mile radius or so. Susie asked Walter, "Have you tried calling his phone?"

Walter answered, "There's no signal out here but let me try and give him a ring." He took out his cell phone and dialed Jake's number.

The atmosphere was silent enough for them to hear a ring tone at a distance. They made their way down a hill behind the backyard property line. As they got closer, Walter had to dial Jake's number again since his phone had stopped ringing. When it started ringing once more, they found it under some brush. Jacob was nowhere in sight though. Walter told Susie, "This is strange, babe. Why would his cell phone be out here alone? Where the hell can Jake be?" He shouted out his name several times but received no response.

Susie continued scanning through the brush and found Jake's car keys stating, "Look, I located his keys a few feet away from the cell phone. You think he may have been out here drunk and fell off the hill?"

Walter replied, "Damn! Hopefully not but let's continue walking down to make sure he's not down there in need of help." They hiked down the hill. Once they made it to the bottom of the hill, there was no sight of Jacob. They walked around to make sure as they shouted out his name. Walter then told Susie, "We need to go back up and drive down to the ranger's office to let them know. I hope they're able to locate him alive and well."

Susie uttered, "Ok, let's do that and I too pray we find him." They made their way uphill slowly since it was a steep hike up.

When they finally got back to the property, they locked the residence and jumped in Jake's vehicle. They buckled up and turned it on. Walter placed the transmission in drive and traveled over to the ranger's office at the cave dwellings site.

When they arrived, they found a parking spot and exited the vehicle. Walter found a ranger inside the small museum and office at the entrance of the trail. He approached a female in uniform and began narrating his friend's disappearance to her. The ranger radioed over to headquarters the situation at hand. Headquarters advised her to take a full description of the missing visitor. She inquired with Walter for Jake's last known details. She began to jot down what Walter and Susie divulged. She then called over to headquarters relaying the information.

The rangers now scattered throughout the wide forest looking for Jacob. They also stopped with locals to advise them of the current situation and ask if they had seen anyone fitting the description. No one had any information to assist them in their search. Walter and Susie had met up with the supervising ranger who attempted to calm them down with positive reinforcement. The ranger advised them, "It's not out of the ordinary to have people venture far from their campgrounds and get lost. We always find them though. Our success rate is superb and we've recovered everyone gone astray whether alive or not. So, keep your faith strong and your eyes wide open. Here's my business card so y'all can contact me directly with any new information or for an update. My name is on the card in case y'all forget." He then left the dwellings area in his truck to find Jake.

Walter and Susie got back in Jacob's ride and drove to the rental home. When they arrived, there still wasn't any sign of Jake returning. Walter jumped in the shower as Susie cooked up some breakfast. So far, their plans to do some more group hiking were on hold since Jacob was missing. Susie grabbed a carton of eggs from the fridge. Walter and Jacob had planned out their trip effectively, taking enough food to last them their entire stay. She grabbed a pan and sprayed some olive oil from an aerosol can. She turned on the range and placed the pan on top. Once the pan had begun to simmer, she cracked open two eggs and let them cook sunny side up. She also grabbed some of the franks left over from last night's dinner and put them in a plate to microwave. She brewed some coffee for her and Walter as she flipped the eggs over. Once the eggs had cooked, she placed them on a plate and added two winnies next to them. She then cracked open another two eggs and scrambled them in the pan. The sunny side up ones were for her and the scrambled ones were for Walter. She continued cooking her eggs and when done, she placed them in the plate she used to microwave the franks which had one left for her. She set the plates on the kitchen diner and grabbed two mugs to fill up with coffee. After pouring the dark brew into the mugs, she added creamer and sugar to both cups and sat them over the table where the food was located.

Walter got out of the shower and was dressed. He strolled over to the kitchen and heard Susie tell him, "Sit down to eat babe. I made you breakfast and also a cup of coffee."

Walter replied, "Thanks honey. Which is mine and which is yours?"

Susie stated, "The scrambled ones are yours since I know you don't like your eggs sunny side up. I also added two scoops of creamer and one of sugar to your preference."

Walter commented, "Yup, you sure do know me huh? Thank you again for this meal and drink babe." As he took a seat in front of the plate with the scrambled eggs.

After they summoned breakfast, Walter decided to contact the host of the property to see if he had heard from Jake by mere chance. He dialed the number from the landline so he wouldn't experience any interruptions. Herbert- the owner- picked up on the third ring and said, "Hello." Walter uttered, "Hey Herbert, this is Walter over at your rental. I'm sorry to bug you but I was wondering if there was a miracle my pal Jacob contacted you either this morning or late last night?"

"Oh, hey Walter. Hope y'all are enjoying the place and making great memories. No, I haven't heard from your friend Jacob. Is everything alright down there?" Questioned Herbert.

Walter replied, "Ah man, well to be honest with you, he has gone missing overnight. We haven't been able to locate him this morning and have already filled a missing person's report with the rangers."

Herbert uttered, "Oh my, that's not good to hear. What was he wearing if you don't mind me asking? I was just about to head to the store to grab some things. If you share a description, I may know what to look for." Walter gave him a detailed summary of Jake's appearance and they hung up.

Susie inquired, "What did he tell you? Has he seen or heard from Jacob?"

Walter confirmed, "No, he hasn't but he said he was heading to the store and would keep an eye out for him."

"Oh," mentioned Susie.

They remained at the rental property for the reminder of the day, hoping Jake would return. Their agenda of hiking some trails was discouraged due to the circumstance they faced of having their friend disappear. They both became concerned for Jacob's whereabouts. They attempted to go about their day as normal as could be. They fixed their attention to the television set and watched some movies, distracting themselves some. Every now and then, Walter looked out of the window to see if he spotted Jake but he didn't. Walter felt a perpetual void and unresolved anxiety not having his bud around. As the hours of the day rolled, they got hungry so Walter grabbed some of the ingredients he took to make sandwiches from the fridge. Susie assisted him in preparing some bologna, ham and cheese sandwiches for them both. They took a seat at the table, grabbed some sodas and chips to top off their easy meal. As they ate, there was a loud ruckus coming from the backyard. Walter pounced up from his chair and addressed the commotion. He opened the door and found no one or nothing around.

What he did came into view was the head of a dead raccoon sitting over the table outside. Susie asked, "Is everything alright babe? What was that noise?"

Walter shut the door and told her, "Yeah honey. It wasn't Jake that's for sure. Just some raccoon messing with the table outside." He actually believed the head of the animal was left behind by a predator who nabbed the raccoon.

They resumed their meals as they watched the film on tv from the kitchen table. When they finished, they tossed their paper plates and washed the dishes they left from the day before and the utensils they used to make the sandwiches. Once they concluded their small chore, they nestled back on the couch to continue watching television. The previous movie had ended so they started another one.

The moon peeked as the night fell. There wasn't any news regarding Jake's wellbeing. Walter had contacted both Herbert and the ranger via landline. Both informed him they hadn't located Jacob. It wasn't what Walter expected to hear but it was the honest brutal truth.

As they glanced at the screen in front of them, Walter recalled Jacob had a firearm in his vehicle, tucked in the glove box. He got up and walked outside to the SUV. He hit the fob keys unlock button and opened the passenger side door. He took a seat inside and opened the glove box. There was a bunch of old paperwork so he began removing it out of his way. Underneath all the documents, there was a forty-caliber pistol. Walter grabbed it out of the box and slightly pulled the slide back to see if it had a round chambered. He then removed the magazine to review if it was topped off to its maximum capacity. The gun was loaded and the magazine was maxed out. Walter laid the gun next to him and inserted all the paperwork back into the glove box. When he finished, he took the firearm and headed back inside. Susie had fallen asleep during the film and opened her eyes back up at the sound of Walter locking the door. She asked him, "Are you ok babe? Did Jake come back already?"

Walter turned around to speak to her uttering, "Everything is still the same. No signs of Jake anywhere. I remembered he had a gun in his ride so I went to grab it. We don't know what's going on and it's best we arm ourselves in case there's foul play and the possibility of being targeted by someone or something. I don't believe in the sasquatch myth but our current situation makes me wonder about the probabilities with an open mind."

Susie replied, "You're right, good thing you remembered he had a gun and now you have it just in case. I think I'm gonna call it a night and head off to bed. I'm drained with drowsiness and can't keep my eyes open. Are you gonna come sleep with me?"

Walter responded, "Ok, get some rest. Hope you sleep well. I'm going to stay up a little longer. Can't sleep right now with my mind racing. I'll try not to stir you up when I go to the room to rest."

Susie stated, "Ok honey, have a good night. See you in the morning unless you wake me up in the middle of the night with good news that Jacob is back."

Walter said, "Hopefully I do. Goodnight baby, I love you."

"I love you too," answered Susie as she walked to the bedroom.

Walter sat back on the couch and finished the film on tv. Right as it ended, he began feeling tired so he shut the set off and was walking back towards the room. Just as he held his hand over the knob, he heard some noises outside. He let go of the doorknob and checked what it was.

As he stepped outside the front yard, Jake's car alarm began to sound. Walter had the keys in his hand and turned it off. He didn't observe anything out of the ordinary. Then suddenly he felt someone grab him from behind. He believed it might be a bear and tried to retrieve the gun from his waist. As he nudged his arms down, he felt the handgrip of the gun. Whatever had constricted around his torso had enough strength to pick him up and carry him away from where he stood. As he attempted to grasp the firearm, it fell from his grip. Suddenly, Susie must have heard the commotion outside and woke up. She peeked through the door and saw someone taking Walter. She yelled, "Leave him alone!" And ran towards them.

Walter told her, "Stay back babe! Run back inside and call the rangers! Save yourself!"

Susie ignored his advice and as she closed in on them, she spotted the gun on the floor. She picked it up and pointed at them. She shot the firearm, striking Walter on the shoulder as she attempted to shoot the assailant on the head. Walter shouted in pain and told her to grab the keys which had fallen out of his pockets and to take off. He tried loosening the embrace around him but wasn't able to. He couldn't even see who or what was taking him away against his will since it was dark. Susie ran to get the keys from the ground and picked them up. She aimed once more and fired another round. This time, she was able to hit the person dressed in camouflage attire who she observed forcibly hauling Walter away. The person dropped Walter from his grasp and ran into the darkness. Just before slicing his neck with a sharp knife. Susie fired one more time into the dark forest around the area the person was last seen. She sprinted towards Walter who laid on the floor choking on his blood. She kneeled and asked him, "Babe! What happened? Oh my God! You're bleeding pretty bad!" She tried picking him up but he was too heavy.

Walter, between breaths, told her, "Leave me here... go get help... Drive to the rangers... tell them what happened... Come back for me." Blood gushed out of his wound with every heartbeat.

Susie replied, "No! I can't leave you here like this." As she attempted to raise him up.

Walter retorted, "Go! Listen to me!"

"Ok!" She stated as she grabbed the keys, jumped inside the SUV and sped to the ranger's station.

When Susie made it to the ranger's station, she rapidly got out of the vehicle shouting for help as she ran inside. She rushed to the front desk and found a ranger asleep sitting down in a chair. The ranger rose up and asked, "What's going on?"

Susie informed him of the situation and he told her to stay there as he ran out to his unit and took off towards the incident site. Susie was crying and didn't feel safe in the office so she got back in the SUV and drove back to the rental property. When she got there, the ranger held her back from getting closer to Walter since he had died. The ranger had called for backup and when they arrived, they wanted Susie's declaration as to what had happened. She described everything in detail to them as they wrote her statement. Eventually they told her to drive back home after an ambulance picked up Walter's corpse and transported it to the morgue. Susie didn't want to drive alone and they didn't allow her to go inside the house since it was under investigation. She contacted her older brother who drove out there to pick her up at the ranger's station.

She left with her sibling back home unable to cease her sobbing. She now had to inform both Walter's and Jake's families of what had happened to them. Jake never was found and neither was the culprit of Walter's death. Susie never returned to the Gila in her life. She did explain in detail the time she spent there to those who asked. As to who and what had really occurred over there goes as follows.

A breathtaking backyard scenery attracted tenants to this getaway home. Amenities on point, scattered all throughout the property. Two bedrooms, four beds, a porch to fix one's eyes at the wildlife surrounding the area. A swimming pool with a maximum depth of ten feet and a hot tub to soak and relax in, were amongst many features offered. Located in the hills of a mountain top, in a secluded spot in the Gila National Forest. A perfect rental for those who wanted to escape the city and experience nature's wonderful beauty.

The cons- it was nearly impossible to obtain satellite signal for reception. The police department was almost an hour away. Medical facilities were around the distance of an hour and a half from saving your life in an emergency. There weren't any shopping centers or malls within a reasonable commute. Restaurants too were a long drive from the property. Even fuel service stations weren't a short ride away. Yet, it had no bad reviews from any of the past guests. And at a bargain competing with some less welcoming places, you couldn't go wrong.

Herbert- the owner- was an abbot hunter who loved to follow prey. He had taxidermy trophies hung inside the residence. No one knew he had succumbed to his dark side though, as he played off being normal. He had sustained a traumatic experience a few years back. His whole family had been butchered by some random asshole who viewed them as an easy mark. They were out on vacation during a fall trip. Herbert left to get something from the store unaware they had been targeted. Upon his return, he discovered his entire family, both daughter and son, including his wife annihilated. There wasn't anything he could do and the case veered cold soon after without the capture or incarceration of the responsible party.

Eventually he began doing the same at his rental property. None of the guests foresaw they'd never leave the residence they booked to have a good time. Herbert would stalk them from a far with the scope on his thirty ought six. Watching their every move in his camouflage hunting tent. Once he'd spot an opportunity, he'd slip in and out of the home with ease- cautiously elusive as a ninja assassin. No one would even suspect him as a culprit with his established track record of being generous, kind, humble and caring. Plus, he had experienced a similar tragic event with his own family not long ago. Then again, there wasn't anyone on his tail since nobody had made a report or escaped his wrath. He'd move the bodies out into the open forest to feed the carnivores, making it seem as if that was the reality. He covered his tracks and cleaned up all evidence which may lead back to him. He was skilled at his craft to the point more visitors checked in rather than those who checked out.

Herbert was selective of his prey though. He only hunted young men and women who had no kids back home or with them. Only he understood his reasons for picking in such a form. The few missing persons who last stayed at his house were all concluded to have left or been killed by bears, wolves or mountain lions. Herbert was never caught and remains at large out there in the woods he roamed in. One more reason to be wary of the rental properties one will book for their getaway. Or paranoid to run into him out in the open fields where he has the upper hand of experience and familiarity plus his big blacked out truck. The Gila Killa is one of the myths circulating in the tales the locals told and spread around the surrounding cities.

CHAPTER 12
ANNA'S KARMA.

D aniel had gotten home from work late and tired but he had a date with his wife. So, he gathered his reserved energy as he walked into his residence. As soon as he passed by the kitchen, he observed a pile of dirty dishes in the sink. He began to wash them to include his own from his lunch. His two oldest step kids were in their rooms and his wife was somewhere in the house. The other three young children were with their grandparents- sleeping over for the weekend. Daniel finished washing dishes and checked the fridge to see if there was anything to snack on. There wasn't much other than some saltine crackers in the pantry. He chewed on a few as he made his way towards his bedroom. Upon entering his room, he viewed his wife lying in bed scrolling through her phone. She didn't realize he was home and Daniel startled her as he greeted her, "Hi honey, I'm home."

Anna answered, "Oh shit! You scared me, Danny. I didn't realize you were back already. I lost track of time on the internet."

Daniel stated, "I can imagine how staying at home you forget what time it is.

Anyhow, I'm going to take a shower and get dressed for our date." Anna inquired, "What date Danny? We have a date today?"

Daniel replied, "Don't tell me you forgot our anniversary?" As he hugged her and handed her a bouquet of roses.

Anna responded, "I'm just kidding. Of course not. How could I forget this special day out of all the things in the world? Thank you for the roses, they're beautiful." She rose up out of bed and began getting her clothes ready.

Daniel questioned, "You haven't gotten ready? Or why're you getting your clothes too?"

Anna commented, "I was waiting for you to get home so we could shower together and then get ready to head out."

Daniel said, "Oh, ok well I'm jumping in the shower now." As she set her phone down to charge and followed him to the restroom.

Moments later, they had both washed up and got dressed. Tonight, they had reservations at a fancy restaurant uptown. From there they would go dance a bit at a nightclub a few blocks from the restaurant. Once they both looked presentable, they said goodbye to the oldest kids and headed out the door. They got in Daniel's truck. Daniel leaned in for a kiss which Anna didn't see since she was back on her phone. He landed one on her cheek instead of her lips either way. He then cranked the engine up and departed their neighborhood. During the trip, Daniel didn't get one word out of his spouse. She had her vision affixed to her handheld device.

When they got to the restaurant, there was a valet waiting for them at the front of the establishment. Daniel got out and notified Anna they had arrived since she was so distracted with her cell. She exited the truck and the valet took over. They made their way through the front doors. There was a host behind a booth who asked them if they had reservations. Daniel informed him they did and shared his name for confirmation. The host replied, "Alright Sir, we have you and another guest checked in for seven o' clock. We're a little busy today as you can see so, please take a seat in the waiting lobby so we can clear a table for you. It shouldn't take long before your waiter comes to get you." Daniel sat down in the waiting area.

Anna told Daniel, "I'm going to use the ladies' room meanwhile they seat us.

I've been holding it the whole ride here."

Daniel said, "Ok, I'll send you a text if we get seated before you're finished." She smiled as she turned around and marched towards the restroom.

A couple of minutes later, a waiter came up to Daniel and called his name. When Daniel verified it was him, the waiter asked him to accompany him to his table. Daniel let the employee lead the way. When they got to the table, Daniel took a seat. The waiter asked, "Can I get you something to drink while your other guest arrives?" Handing him two menus.

Daniel uttered, "I'll take the coldest beer in the fridge."

The waiter responded, "Got it, I'll have that coming right up." He then walked towards the bar to get the alcoholic beverage.

Daniel sent Anna a text specifying more or less where they were seated. He then glanced at the menu and began scanning through the many entries. The waiter returned with a cold beer and handed it to Daniel. He then inquired, "Are you ready to order an appetizer or something sir? I noticed your companion isn't here yet, would you rather wait till they show up?"

Daniel said, "She's in the restroom right now. I'll wait till she comes out and check in with her to see what she'd like to have."

The waiter replied, "Sounds good sir. I'll make my way back here in a few minutes." He then walked off to check on his other customer tables.

Daniel glanced at his watch, noticing she had been gone sometime and hadn't replied to his text. He'd be worried had they just started dating but this was nothing unusual for her to do, so he just sat there viewing the menu and sipping on his brew. After about another five minutes, Anna called him and received directions to his location. She hung up the call as soon as she had visual. She kissed him as she got to the table and took a seat stating, "I'm sorry if I took a little longer than usual. There was a line. Did you already order something?"

Daniel commented, "It's ok, no I didn't other than this beer. Look at the menu and see if you crave any of the appetizers first before you make your decision on your dinner, please." Anna opened up her menu and observed the starters.

When the waiter circled back to their table, Anna asked for their sampler appetizer and a beer as well. The waiter looked at Daniel with remorse and then headed to the back to get the order going. Daniel asked Anna, "Did you see the look he gave me after you ordered?" She put her phone down and gazed at Daniel.

"No Danny, I'm sure he didn't mean anything by it though," uttered Anna.

Daniel stated, "He looked at me with pity as if he felt bad for me for some reason."

"I think you're jumping to conclusions Danny. Why don't you ask him when he comes back instead?" Said Anna.

Daniel uttered, "Nah, you're probably right. I'll just leave it at that. Now if he gives me that look again, I'll confront him then."

They both were discussing what to choose off the menu in order to make their decision. When the waiter returned, he left them salads and soups meanwhile they made up their minds. He didn't give Daniel any reason to question his stare this time. He then walked off and came back right away with complimentary fresh hot bread and butter right before he left to attend other customers.

Around five minutes or so went by when Daniel observed the waiter headed to their table with their appetizer. He set the sampler tray in front of them both and handed them small dishes to utilize. Daniel thanked him, grabbed his cloth napkin from the table and unwrapped it to get the silverware from inside. He placed the napkin over his legs and began selecting a little bit of the five samples as well as bread as he ate his salad and soup. Anna did the same after she put her phone down. They placed their main entre orders with the waiter as they munched. The waiter then rushed back to hand the chef their orders. Anna looked around the palace to see who else was there who she may recognize. She then turned back to her phone and ate from her dish. Daniel kept looking at her eyes. They glisten to him with the most magnificent sparkle. He was deeply in love with her. He recalled how she played hard to get at first. Now look at her ten years later filling in the role of his wife. He smiled remembering all the fun times and fond memories they had created throughout the years.

The waiter swung by with their main antres. He set a round table across from them and began serving their dishes individually. They both looked appealing to their appetite. The waiter asked them, "Is there anything else I can get y'all?" They both requested another round of beers. Daniel told Anna, "I hope you enjoy this moment as I am darling. To many more anniversaries to come!" Raising his beer bottle and cheering with her.

Anna replied, "I'm so glad you're in my life Danny. Not only have you stepped up to raise my children but also to be my companion. So yes, to many more to come!" At the sound of clinking glass bottles.

They feasted on their meals and shared some of their own with each other to receive an opinion. They both were content with their food and liked each other's savory taste as well. The waiter walked over to them to make sure they didn't require anything else as he set two beers down on the table. Daniel informed him they were fine for now so the waiter turned around and went on his way. Anna finished about three fourths of her plate and was full. Daniel concluded his meal, leaving only crumbs behind. He then signaled to the waiter to get her a box to go and bring him the check.

When the waiter returned with the box and check, Daniel handed him his debit card. The waiter rushed over to the cash register to charge the card. Momentarily, the waiter returned with his card and handed it back to him along with the receipt. Daniel left a generous tip and signed the receipt. Anna had already boxed her leftovers. They then got up from their chairs and headed out the front door. As they walked by the front counter, Daniel noticed two men sitting at the bar looking up at his wife- staring. He felt pride that she was with him and ignored them. They stepped outside and the valet went to get their vehicle. Daniel's silver truck swung around the parking lot and stopped right in front of them. Daniel handed the valet a tip and opened the door for his spouse. She got in, he walked over to the driver's side and hopped inside. From there they took off to go dance at a nightclub a few blocks away.

When they arrived, they parked across the street. Daniel helped Anna exit his truck since it was a bit elevated for her short stature. He locked it up and they crossed the street. They got to the entrance of the club and paid a fee as well as presented their ID's. Once inside, they found a table and sat down. A waiter came over to ask if they desired anything to drink. Daniel ordered a bucket of beers. Anna was on her phone again and suddenly told Daniel she had to use the restroom. She got up and walked away. The waiter arrived with the bucket and Daniel gave him his card so he could keep his tab open. There was a group of three attractive females sitting next to their table. One of the women kept staring at Daniel. She got up and approached him uttering, "Hi, looks like they left you alone. Would you care to spin me round on the dance floor?"

Daniel gazed at her uninterested turning away rapidly and stated, "No thanks, I'm married and my wife will be back shortly."

The woman was surprised yet offended, she rolled her eyes saying, "Whatever!" And walked back to her table.

Daniel looked at the time and determined Anna had been gone approximately fifteen minutes. He turned around to see a live band which was playing on stage. He heard the woman he turned down attempting to belittle him with insults but he ignored her. When the band had finished a song, Daniel observed his spouse heading his way back from the restroom as he clapped. He smiled at her since she had a smirk on her lips. She walked up to him and stretched her arms wanting to go dance. He got up from his seat and followed her to the dance floor after she french kissed him. The band started playing another song in their repertoire as they warmed up with their moves. Soon after, they had everyone's attention since they made good dance partners. Daniel spun her around and allowed her to feel special becoming the center of attraction. Every woman at the club felt envious that they weren't dancing and those who were also, that their partner didn't dance as well as Daniel. Even the lady who Daniel turned down had a sour look on her face.

They both danced the night away taking minute breaks here and there to drink their beers. Daniel was mesmerized; he still felt such a connection to his wife after ten years of marriage. She was happy he took her out to dance since it was her favorite pastime. It was around eleven or so when Anna told Daniel, "My feet are killing me, Danny. I don't think I can dance anymore. I probably won't be able to walk to the truck either." Whimpering and staggering back to the table.

Daniel uttered, "That's the problem, sometimes you women buy shoes because they look cute without taking into consideration, they may not be suitable to dance comfortably without getting tired or blisters. But don't worry honey, if you don't want to dance anymore it's alright. And if you can't walk back to the truck, I'll carry you over there myself."

Anna smiled and told him, "Thanks, Danny, you're the best man who could've walked into my life to rescue me." She kissed him and they sat down to finish the beers they had left in the bucket.

After concluding their alcoholic beverages, Anna requested they'd go home and call it a night. Daniel concurred and called the waiter over to close his tab and bring him back his plastic currency along with the receipt. The waiter returned snappy and handed him both as well as a pen to sign the bill. Daniel jotted down his John Hancock and left a decent tip for the waiter. They then departed from the club.

Anna was stumbling out of the front door leaning on Daniel. Not only because she was a bit tipsy but also because of her strained feet. Daniel helped her cross the street and opened his truck. He picked her up and sat her in the passenger seat. He then shut the door and walked around to enter his side. When he jumped inside his truck, he viewed his wife removing her shoes off her feet and complaining they hurt pretty bad. He told her, "I'll fix you a warm bath to soak them in when we get home." She grinned as he took off, directed to their residence.

When they made it back safely to their dwelling, Daniel helped her exit the truck and carried her inside the house. He set her down to insert the keys in the key slot in order to gain access. Once he had opened the door, he picked her up again and carried her all the way to their bedroom. He laid her down in their bed and went to the restroom to get the bathtub ready for her. As Daniel had the water running, he spread some bath salts inside. He stopped the water and went over to get Anna. Her son Freddy was there in their room asking her if they had brought him anything to eat. She looked at Daniel and said, "Would you be the best father in the world and order them a pizza please?"

Daniel commented, "Sure, but first come with me so you can soak those feet before you wake up feeling worse tomorrow." She went right behind him to the restroom.

Anna sat on the edge of the tub and placed her feet inside. She felt an instant relief from her ache. Daniel grabbed his cell phone and dialed the nearest pizza joint. He ordered two large pizzas with pepperoni, ham, bacon and jalapenos. The employee advised him it would take about forty-five minutes to arrive and they hung up.

Daniel walked back into the restroom to check on his spouse. Anna informed him she had begun to feel a little hangover. Daniel told her, "I already ordered pizzas, now let me go grab a beer and bring it to you so you won't feel sick anymore." She thanked him as he proceeded to the kitchen to get her a brew.

Moments later, Daniel returned with a cold beer for her. He opened it and handed it to her. She started sipping on it and kicking her feet inside the tub. He had made her feel as best as possible. He remained with her in the restroom conversing about different topics. Then the doorbell rang after about forty minutes- it was the food delivery. Daniel rushed to the door and signed the receipt taking possession of the pizza boxes. He closed the door and sat the pizzas on the kitchen table. He then yelled out to his step kids, "Guys, the food is here, come and eat!"

Daniel heard the kids cheer up and run to the kitchen as he returned to the restroom with his wife. Once there, he asked her if she wanted him to bring her a slice to which she turned down saying, "Not right now Danny but thank you for offering. This feels good. My feet don't ache anymore and my headache went away. You're really such a wonderful man Danny." They started smooching.

Eventually Anna drained the water out of the tub and dried her feet. She placed her slippers over her feet and walked towards the kitchen to grab a slice of pizza with Daniel by her side. Daniel ate two as the kids had finished theirs and went back to their rooms. Anna and Daniel walked back to their room and laid down after indulging in a late snack. Daniel tried to get freaky with her but she turned him down saying, "I'm sleepy Danny and my headache creeped back up."

Daniel asked, "How about a blow job at least?"

Anna answered, "You know I don't do that." And turned around.

Daniel stated, "It's ok, don't worry. Hopefully you're able to sleep if not let me know so I can get you something for your headache. Good night, babe." He gave her a kiss on the back of her neck since she had her back towards him then fell asleep.

The following day, Daniel and Anna were awakened by Freddy and Nicky. Nicky asked her mother if she and Freddy could go to the mall. Nicky was older than Freddy by a year and some months. Daniel asked them, "Who's gonna pick you up and drop you off?" As he cracked his eyes open.

Nicky answered, "I was hoping you would."

Daniel inquired, "And what're you going to do at the mall if you two don't have money?"

Nicky responded, "Well, I was wondering if you could give us each one hundred dollars to spend? Our friends are on their way there and we plan on hanging out with them."

Daniel uttered, "You don't think it's rude to make plans involving someone and their money without even asking first?"

Anna butted in and told Daniel, "Stop being mean to my kids Danny. Why can't you support their decision and let them have fun?"

Daniel looked at Anna who seemed upset and said, "I'm not trying to be mean to them. I'm only trying to teach them a valuable lesson in life about respecting others. Anyhow, I guess I can give you two one hundred for both and drop you off. Are you guys ready?"

They both replied, "Yes! Thanks Danny,"

Daniel got up out of bed and got dressed. He brushed his teeth and headed out the house with his step kids. They all jumped inside his truck and he drove them to the mall. Once there, he dropped them off and handed Nicky a one-hundred-dollar bill. He also informed her to call him when they're ready to head back home. From there, he received a call from Anna who requested he'd go get some breakfast for them since she had no intentions on cooking. Daniel drove towards this small place which served pozole on the weekends and grabbed a big cup. He then headed back home without making any more stops.

When Daniel arrived at the house, he shouted Anna's name to let her know he was back with the food she requested. Anna came running and took a seat asking him, "Can you grab me a plate and serve me some orange juice?"

Daniel uttered, "Sure my love but what will I get out of being kind to you today?" Anna questioned, "What do you want from me Danny?"

Daniel responded, "It's been about a week since we last had sex and we have the house all to ourselves now."

Anna told him, "Is that all you want from me? Just sex and more sex like I'm some kind of toy for your pleasure? Hand me my bowl and drink before I get pissed off about your bad behavior and attempts of manipulation."

Daniel grabbed two bowls and placed them on the table. He then served her some orange juice and took a seat next to her. She served herself some pozole adding toppings after and grabbed some bolillos. Daniel was about to pour the remaining pozole in his bowl but decided not to since he'd have more dishes to wash. He added toppings to the cup and ate from it- using the plastic spoons provided. He left the topic of intercourse alone not wanting to offend Anna any longer. When Anna finished her food, she got up and left her dirty dish in the sink. From there she went back to the room to be on her phone. Daniel finished his and dumped the styrofoam cup in the trash. He then began washing the dishes in the sink. Concluding that, he swept and mopped. Afterwards, he washed his clothes and cleaned up the restroom and took out the trash. Once he finished all his chores, he took a shower which was interrupted by the teens who were ready to get picked up. He hurried up not washing correctly as he'd like to. Daniel jumped out of the shower and dried himself up. He quickly put on some deodorant and gargled some mouthwash. He then hurried up to his room and got dressed. He told Anna he was going to go pick up the kids at the mall and darted out of the home. He got in his truck and flew over to the mall.

When he arrived, he drove around looking for his step kids who were nowhere to be found. He called Nicky on her cell phone and when she answered, she informed him they were still inside shopping. He had to wait for them in the parking lot for about twenty minutes.

Finally, he spotted them both walking out of the mall. They got in the truck and he raced back home. When they arrived, his step kids didn't even thank him for picking them up from the mall. It seemed as if no one in the house cared for what he did. They didn't appreciate his generosity or kindness. He had no respect in the dwelling he'd pay for to have peace of mind. Yet he didn't want to call it quits since he believed one day they'd appreciate all he did, including Anna.

Later on, that day, Anna asked him if they could go to the movies. Daniel agreed and all four took off. They arrived early to the viewing so Daniel and the kids formed a line at the concession stand to get popcorn and drinks. Anna left them since she had to use the restroom, just before telling Daniel she wanted a cola and taking her ticket from him. Daniel and his step kids were next in line and once the customers in front of them got attended, they walked up to the counter to place their order. The employee served them two large popcorn and four drinks. He coughed up the money to pay for the snacks. They then strolled over to the check in counter and handed the attendant their tickets. The attendant told them, "You'll be in theater number ten straight down to your right- hand side. Enjoy the show."

Daniel uttered, "Thank you very much." Then he and the kids proceeded towards their destined theater.

Once they walked into the theater, they searched for their seats and sat down. There were previews on the big screen. Daniel silenced his phone and placed it on top of his lap. He and the kids began chuckling about a hilarious commercial which aired. They ate their popcorn and sipped on their drinks.

Anna showed up just before the movie started. The lights had already dimed and she had a hard time finding them. She took a seat next to Daniel and kissed him. Daniel handed her drink. She thanked him for it and looked at the screen. The movie started and her phone went off. She received a notification and glimpsed at her phone then put it away. Daniel told her she should silence it and she told him she did just before she placed it back in her pocket. They then enjoyed the film together without any more interruptions.

When the movie ended, Daniel took them all to get an ice cream before heading back home. Once they got back to the house, the kids ran to their rooms and locked themselves up. Anna and Daniel went to theirs to undress. As they removed their clothes and got into something more comfortable, Anna asked Daniel to eat her out. Daniel had been deprived of sex so he didn't refuse the opportunity. He laid her down and spread her legs. He began kissing her pelvic area before putting his mouth over her private. When he started licking her vagina, Anna curved her back and became submissive to him. After she came several times, she allowed him to fuck her. Daniel nutted right away since he hadn't had any in some time experiencing the downfall of semen retention. She didn't say much about it since she had several orgasms already. They both rested in bed closing their eyes and dreamed off into the night.

The next morning, Anna woke up Daniel to go pick up her other three kids from her parent's home. Daniel felt like sleeping in since he woke up early every day for work. He had become sleep deprived with work and family. He shut his eyes stating, "Just five more minutes and I'll go get them."

Anna shook him immediately and said, "Come on Danny! My parents are heading out to some appointments and won't be able to take the kids with them."

Daniel uttered, "Ok, I'm up. How about we go to church today after I get back with the kids?" He began putting on his clothes.

Anna replied, "No, I don't think the kids want to go to church. Why don't you take us out to the zoo and eat instead?"

Daniel responded, "They're never going to want to go to church but if we make it a custom, they'll have no other choice. I really think we should go to church and maybe afterwards the zoo."

Anna commented, "It's not right to try and force my children to attend church Danny. They're just kids. I'm sure your parents made you go to church and you didn't like it so why put my kids through that?"

Daniel uttered, "I didn't like it but now as I'm older, I'm thankful they did. I now understand the importance of knowing and believing in our God." He then went into the restroom to wash his face and teeth.

Anna stated, "No Danny, no church today. I'd rather stay home so my children won't be upset." She got on her phone as Daniel finished getting ready.

Daniel mentioned, "Well, we'll see what happens when I get back. I'll ask them during the drive to see if they want to go to church or not." He then made his way out of the house.

When he got to his in-laws, they had left the kids outside and taken off to their appointments. Daniel saw the kids' faces saddened for being abandoned. He felt like calling up Anna's parents and complaining but he instead grabbed the kids and took them in his truck. He sat them all in their booster chairs and asked them if they were alright. The oldest of them said, "Grama and grandpa left us outside because you took too long." He was four years old.

Daniel replied, "I was just notified I had to pick you guys up. Rudely awaken to the orders or your mom. It's not my fault there is a lack of communication in our home. So, accept my apology for being the one to take the heat from the hot potato being tossed around… Would you guys like to go to church today? You'll get to play with other little kids and eat some food."

Mikey, the four-year-old replied, "Yeah! I want to go to church and play. I'm also hungry. Grama didn't make us breakfast."

Daniel uttered, "Great, I'll let your mom know you guys want to go to church. Your grandparents probably didn't have time to feed you guys. But don't worry, let's pull in here and get you some food." Turning into a restaurant with a drive thru.

Daniel called Anna and asked her if she, Freddy or Nicky wanted something. He then read the menu to the kids in order to see what they wanted. They advised him of their choices and he placed an order for them through the intercom. He then proceeded to the first window to pay. Afterwards, he drove to the second window to obtain the food. He glanced through the bags and made sure everything he ordered was present. Once he was satisfied that all was there, he took off and headed home.

Upon arrival at their residence, he observed Freddy outside talking to someone on his phone. Freddy walked up to his truck and grabbed his food. Daniel assisted his little step kids exit his truck. They all entered the house and Danile sat them at the table to eat. Anna came out of their room and said hello to her children, asking them how they had spent their weekend at her parent's home. She also grabbed her food and ate. Nicky said she'd eat later on because she wasn't quite hungry at the moment. Daniel sat down with the kids and Anna to feast. He informed Anna he had brought up going to church with the kids and they wanted to attend. Anna told her kids, "You guys would rather go to church than the zoo?"

Mikey replied, "I didn't know we could go to the zoo. I want to go to the zoo instead of church."

Anna looked at Daniel with a winner's face and said, "You see, they want to go to the zoo instead of church." She had won the debate.

When Daniel concluded his meal, he jumped in the shower to get ready to take them to the zoo. Anna waited for him to get out before she showered herself. In the meantime, she bathed the little ones and instructed Freddy and Nicky to shower in the other restroom. When they all were ready to head out, they did just that.

When they got to the zoo, they found a parking space and walked over to the entrance. Daniel paid and they displayed their tickets at the entrance doors. They began walking through the zoo. The youngest ones were excited to see the animals. Daniel was reading the general knowledge posters of each animal to the children, educating them of the species name, natural habitat location and their diet intake. Freddy and Nicky just tagged along with Anna, showing very little enthusiasm for being there. After a few hours of strolling through the zoo, they had viewed every single animal there and even enjoyed some shows. The kids were hungry again and so was Daniel and Anna. They left the zoo and got back in Daniel's truck. He asked them what they had in mind to eat. Something he had forgotten to remind himself not to do, due to the confusion it stirred with everyone's different opinions. They all mentioned distinct restaurants so he picked three of the ones mentioned and had them vote for the top one. They came to a mutual conclusion and that's where he drove to.

They parked the truck after arriving at the restaurant. They went inside and sat down after ordering at the counter. The little ones went to go play in the playground. Freddy and Nicky were on their phones and so was Anna who said, "I need to go to the restroom. I'll be back, can you watch my purse, Nicky?" Nicky shrugged in compliance as her mother departed their sight.

Moments after, Daniel received the order at the table from one of the employees who brought it to them. He asked Freddy to go get his little brothers from the playground. When they came, they all grabbed their food and ate. Anna eventually returned from the restroom and sat with them to eat her meal. One of the employees there looked at Daniel who caught him staring at him. The young man gazed at Anna and back at him then turned away and went towards the back of the employee area. Daniel thought it was awkward but he continued to eat his food. When they all finished eating, Daniel asked the kids if they wanted to go play at the park so he could walk off his meal. They all agreed so they threw their trash in the bin and exited the establishment.

When they arrived at a park down the street from their house, the kids found some of their classmates and hung out. The little ones made new friends in the playground. Daniel took a seat on a bench and Anna told him she had to use the restroom. Daniel observed the children meanwhile Anna utilized the ladies' room. Daniel saw how the kids were having fun interacting with others their age. He had to wait till Anna returned to watch over her kids so he could go walk around the park. After about ten minutes, she showed up to the bench and sat down. Daniel told her he was going to walk off his food. He stood up and began strolling the perimeter surrounding the area. As he completed his third time around, Anna waved at him that she wanted to go home. Daniel made his way over to her as she gathered the kids. They then drove back home and called it a day.

Monday came long and Daniel went to work, Freddy and Nicky to school and Anna stayed home with the little ones. The same occurred on Tuesday and Wednesday. Nothing out of the ordinary took place. Then came Thursday and after Daniel got back home from work, he and Anna left to have dinner at a restaurant. It was her idea to do so since she believed they needed more alone bonding for the sake of their marriage as she verbally expressed so. Daniel went with the flow.

When they showed up at the restaurant of her choice, they took a seat in a booth. Anna looked over her menu and so did Daniel. A waiter came around to ask for their drinks and they advised him of their choice. While the waiter was there taking their order for a starter, Anna got a phone notification and told Daniel she had to use the restroom. Daniel comprehended her dialogue and continued to order some cheese dip and chips to open up their appetite. Daniel sat there at the booth waiting for Anna to return and for the waiter to bring him his beverage and appetizer. He was starving since he had only eaten a sandwich at work which he made himself in the morning.

Finally, the waiter returned with his drink, cheese dip and chips. Daniel told the waiter to return later on since his wife wasn't present to order their main dish. The waiter politely accepted and departed the booth. Daniel was drinking and eating wondering what was taking Anna so long to get back. He observed a female employee walking to the women's restrooms with a cleaning cart. He figured then Anna would return and they'd be able to order their dinner.

The employee came out of the restroom screaming for help. She seemed disturbed as if she had found someone dead inside. Daniel jumped out of his seat and ran to the entrance of the bathroom. There was a group of spectators there already with shocked looks in their eyes. Daniel peaked inside and saw Anna laying on the ground. The following is a summary and explanation of the last scene.

Anna had been married a decade to her first husband ever-Daniel. She was lucky to have landed herself a good man who looked out for her children and her. Her five kids were products of different donors, none of which accepted accountability. Yet her history lingered around her present like a bad odor on shit. She had been promiscuous, sexually free in the past and just couldn't shake it out of her system. She would cheat on Daniel who was unaware of her true nature. She had the nerve to meet up with total strangers using a dating application on her phone. She was lured to the mystery and sin of engaging in intercourse inside public restrooms. Usually while out on dates together. She'd sign into her app and check in to her current location. Then review if there were other users nearby and request to meet up in the bathroom.

There she would do just about anything Danial was denied. Oral, annal and even threesomes with two men at once. It was mostly quickies and she'd return to her man promptly so as to not raise suspicion. She did this often, even at bars, parks, movies and just about anywhere her significant other would take her out to. She had the audacity to kiss him after giving head to other men. This made her feel powerful and indestructibly important.

Once they'd make it back home, she'd ask him to eat her out while another man's semen leaked from inside her vaginal cavity. She had gotten her tubes tied after her fifth baby so it wasn't like she feared getting pregnant to spoil her selfish pleasures. Her husband didn't have the same experience she did. Therefore, she'd manage to fool him by concealing her true self being- as an imposter. She wanted to live two lives. One to enjoy the perks of being married and the other to fill her emotional emptiness by whoring around.

Eventually her secretive reclusive lifestyle caught up to her. She met up with some guy at the restaurant restroom. The man who waited for her inside had distinctive plans and was not interested in fornicating. He had vengeance on his mind. After she attempted to sneak him inside one of the stalls to have sex, he removed a rope from his pocket and strangled her to death. At first, she thought he was just being kinky and didn't put up a fight, until it was too late.

Nobody witnessed the occurrence and he was able to escape without capture. He knew she was married and had a grudge against cheating wives. One of the employee's found Anna lying on the floor as she entered to clean up the sanitarium. She immediately dialed 911 and yelled for help, that's when Daniel became aware of the situation. He rushed over and encountered disbelief that Anna was dead. While a crowd gathered around the entrance to the restroom, he overheard several men talking about his wife and the things she would do behind his back. It infuriated him but he kept quiet at the moment holding his spouse in his arms shocked with dismay.

After she was laid to rest, he found out from friends and relatives they too had had their way with her. They confirmed she was a whore and comforted him with, "It's good she will no longer be around to disrespect you."

He felt betrayed and belittled. He went through her phone and discovered what she hid from his knowledge. It disgusted him to come across what she was doing behind his back. He learned a valuable lesson in life.

After grieving and healing from his unfortunate circumstance, he eventually moved on and abandoned her kids since they weren't his to begin with. They had begun to act up without their mother's presence, both at school and home. The youngest were turned over to child protective services because no one assumed responsibility for them.

Her family was similar to her- cold hearted and maliciously selfish. The oldest two- Nicky and Freddy- became heavy drug users lost in addiction. They'd offer sexual services in order to obtain their daily fix. They lived out in the streets and had no dignified employment. Anna never believed in Karma till it introduced itself right before it took her soul for an unpaid debt.

CHAPTER 13

THE HUNT.

James was outside Cody's home waiting for him to come out. They were headed on another adventure. This time it was a weekend hunting trip in Sierra Blanca. James was listening to some music as he waited for his pal to exit his residence. Cody came out and began putting his things inside James' Jeep Gladiator after shaking his hand. James asked him, "Were you jacking off or something bro? Sure, took a long time to come out. Plus, your hand felt wet, ha ha!"

Cody answered, "Yeah bro, I was beating my beast thinking or your sister." Laughing loudly.

James replied, "That's as close as you'll ever get to her anyhow you fuck- o. Make sure you don't forget the MRE's and your weapons along with ammo. I'm not going to lend you mine like last time you forgot yours, dick head." Chuckling.

Cody uttered, "I've got the MRE's right here and I won't forget my rifle this time. I learned my lesson that time you speak of when you kept nagging and complaining about me mistreating yours, you fruit cake." Giggling.

Cody then headed back inside his dwelling to retrieve his firearms and ammo. He also grabbed his backpack, which he almost forgot as he was leaving his house. He then walked out and locked the doors. He ran to James' vehicle and threw his stuff in the back as he got in the passenger seat. James told him, "Buckle up and let's go fuck up some deer you little queer." Laughing as he began to drive.

Cody responded, "Not with your discounted prize scope you won't. Plus, that shaky hand you've got from masturbating too often won't allow you to zero in on an elephant should it be standing right in front of you." Chuckling.

James said, "Whatever bro, you're the one who missed the perfect shot last time and allowed a nice doe to get away. You can't shoot for shit with that freaking cockeye that only targets dicks." Bursting in laughter.

Cody uttered, "Man shut up, and stop somewhere to grab breakfast and coffee." Cody hadn't had his coffee yet and his brain wasn't functioning as sufficient as

James'. He had been out roasted without the roasted grounds in his system. James pulled into a drive thru which was open early. The sun wasn't even out yet since they wanted to get out there before it did. James ordered himself a breakfast biscuit with an orange juice and Cody got an egg sandwich with a large coffee. Once they paid and obtained their food, James veered into the highway. Cody had the bags in his hands since James was the pilot. Cody handed James his biscuit and his orange juice. James started munching his food as he drove. Cody started off with his coffee since he couldn't live without some. Cody asked James, "You sure you saw a herd of deer out there when you were driving back from Odessa?"

James said, "I'm not kidding man, it looked like almost one hundred deer out there requiring some population control."

Cody told him, "I sure hope so. Otherwise, we're going to have to hunt whatever is out there, whether it be rattlesnakes, doves, quail or even jackrabbits in order to not use the backup MRE's."

James replied, "No need to be negative right now. I'm telling you I saw a shit ton of deer. All we have to do is once we get out there if we don't see them, we find and follow their tracks. For sure they're out there though, waiting to become steaks and taxidermy trophies." They both giggled.

James continued driving past Fabens, then Tornillo. It took almost an hour from there to get to Sierra Blanca. Just before the checkpoint, they exited the highway and got on a dirt road. Cody hadn't finished all his coffee and as the Gladiator hopped on the bumpy road, it splashed on his pants. Cody was a little upset at himself so he chugged his coffee before it spilled some more. James continued driving through a dirt road picking up dust, till he finally found a good spot to park. They both got out of the vehicle and grabbed their stuff. James said, "They should be out here bro. Look at those tracks on the ground and the trail of shit. Let's pack up our gear and follow the trail." He then locked his ride after they had all their equipment on them.

They began to walk in the silent desert scenery. The sun peaked in the distance as they trekked through. Cody asked James, "You think we could take a break now? We've been hiking for about an hour and I'd like to get some water out of my bag."

James said, "Well why didn't you say anything? I don't read minds bro. Let's chill under that shade over there." Pointing at a cool area under a ledge from the mountains.

They made their way under the shade and began to remove their gear off their backs to get their water out. Both were sweating already with their backpacks fully loaded, their rifles and sidearms adding to the weight. They laid down on the ground and relaxed as they observed the sunrise. James was gazing at the sun when he looked over at where Cody laid. He told Cody, "Oh shit! Don't move bro. Don't twitch and don't breathe." He got up and snuck towards him.

Cody was petrified as he inquired in a low tone, "What is it man? You're fucking scaring me bro. Is it a fucking rattlesnake?"

James reached behind him and grabbed something. He shouted, "I've got it!" As he pulled something towards him, Cody jumped up shaken.

He had the shedded skin of a western diamondback in his hands. Cody told him, "You're a fucking asshole man. I was fucking constricting my butthole as tight as I could expecting a rattlesnake to start rattling its tail."

James uttered, "Well it could have been one. Just look at the size of this skin bro." As he laughed and examined the remains.

Cody snatched it from his hands and threw it on the ground-fuming, "Don't be playing with me like that bro. I almost shit myself." He was bothered.

James uttered, "It looked like it was a snake behind you bro. I thought it was. I didn't mean to scare or prank you. Anyhow, we should keep moving since we're not here for snakes."

They both grabbed their gear and swung their backpacks over their shoulders. Once they had their things secured, they continued trekking through the desert. As they came to an open space, James noticed something shiny in the distance. He made his way over to it to verify what it was. As he got closer, he realized it was a balloon which had made its way there and got stuck on some tumbleweeds. "It's a baby girl," read the balloon. Cody heard a noise and hushed James. They both turned around to see what it was. It sounded similar to a beast growling. Cody asked James, "What the hell was that bro?"

James answered, "A mountain lion." As he scanned his vision over the horizon to see if he could spot it.

Cody replied, "Damn, it sounds pretty pissed off man. Maybe we should fire a warning shot to let it know we're out here so it won't come near us."

James replied, "That'll spook our deer's as well bro. Not a good idea since we're hunting and not fishing. Come on, let's keep going. There's a really nice area a few hundred yards in front of us which we can use to camp out at. Right on the edge of that mountain."

They both trekked forward towards where his finger had directed them.

When they finally made it to the area James had mentioned, they took off all of their gear and set up their camp. It was obvious the spot had been previously used. There were remnants of a previous camp with a burnt-out fire and trash all around. James uttered, "See, the locals must use this area to hunt deer. Why else would they camp at this spot?" As he began unpacking his tent from his backpack.

They both set up their tents and placed their extra stuff inside to lighten their backpacks. James sat up on a boulder and Cody sat on a little tiny fold up chair he had recently purchased online. They stared through binoculars at the vast land in front of them. Cody shouted, "Holy shit! You're absolutely right bro. There's a massive rangale of deer at nine o' clock about two miles out." Pointing at their direction.

James turned his binoculars towards the parcel and said, "I told you I wasn't lying. Man, I can barely see them out there to even distinguish does from bucks."

Cody replied, "I know dude. We need some more expensive binoculars for that." James told Cody, "I'm guessing they travel in during the night over to where I parked and then head off that way as the sun starts to rise. Which means, if we camp, here, we'll be able to shoot them tomorrow morning as they're either headed towards here or headed back."

They both continued keeping their eyes on the prize as the deer walked further into the distance where they weren't able to be seen anymore. Cody removed a bottle of vodka from his backpack and took a swig straight from the bottle. He offered James some and James took a sip. It was a bit chilly out there that morning so the alcohol helped warm them up a bit. James got up from the boulder and walked towards the bottom of the mountain they were on. He needed to take a pee so he turned his back to his pal and poured fluids out, striking the rock formation in front of him. Cody grabbed a stone from the ground and threw it at James' back. James had finished his necessities and turned around to see his friend. James told Cody, "You freaking faggot. I bet you threw that rock at me so I could turn around and display my cock at you huh?"

Cody replied, "Not really, but had you been your sister, it would be a different story. I'd probably be right under you as you crotch down and drink your urine."

James uttered, "You're fucking sick bro. I can't picture that happening to begin with but why would you drink my sister's pee?"

Cody responded, "She's beautiful bro. Good thing she doesn't look like you otherwise I'd either not find her attractive or want to fuck you instead ha, ha!"

James stated, "If only you'd see the massive stinky shits she drops from her rectum. I had to unclog the toilet more than once after she used it. And you're gay for saying you'd fuck me. I'd cut your dick off and shove it up your ass before you'd get close enough to do so." Holding a serious stare at him as he got closer.

Cody answered, "I'm not gay. I'm just kidding about that bro. Does she really take mad shits though? I'm starting to get turned on by your story. I think I've found the love of my life." Giggling.

James said, "She does, you demented fuck." With a smile on his face.

They both continued conversing in order to not be bored. As the sun rose over them, James went inside his tent to hide from it. Cody stayed out there, staring at the area and sipping on vodka. He spotted some movement nearby and got up from his chair. He went to investigate, moving sneakily towards the commotion. As he got closer, he observed a baby cottontail bunny. Cody thought it looked cute. He continued glancing at the bunny who was eating some of the vegetation. Then the bunny noticed his presence and darted inside a hole in the mountains. Cody went back to his chair and took a seat. He found some shade and moved over towards it since the sun began to burn a bit. He heard James snoring and decided to get him back from earlier.

He grabbed a long twig and quietly unzipped his tent's entrance. He then stuck his hand in and began caressing James' face with the twig. James swiped it off his face and stopped snoring. He then fell back to sleep again. Cody was chuckling as quietly as he could. He gently rubbed the twig over James' face again. This time, James woke up and smacked the twig away from him. He looked at Cody and told him, "For a second there, I thought it was your little dick and you were trying to sodomize me. Why don't you take a nap as well since it's going to be a long day?"

Cody replied, "I'm not sleepy. Had my coffee already, and I wouldn't dare to rub my cock on your face. You might take a bite of it." Laughing.

James uttered, "Then don't go to sleep but let me get some z's dipshit. Go away Cody and zip my tent back up."

Cody removed his arm from inside the tent and zipped it back up. He walked away to his tent and went inside. He laid down on his sleeping bag and removed a book from his backpack. Good thing he took his novel so he could entertain himself as they killed time. So, Cody drifted away into his reading material. As he read ten pages through his book, he heard some noise outside. He placed a bookmarker inside his novel and closed it. He got up and unzipped his tent to check. As he gazed outside, he observed James standing at the edge of the cliff they had set up at. James was looking through his binoculars once more to see if he could spot any deer. He didn't see any so he turned around and saw Cody hanging halfway out of his tent glancing at him and said, "Hey bro, I'm a little hungry how about you?"

Cody answered, "Yeah, me too. You want to go see if we find anything or would you rather eat an MRE?"

James uttered, "Let's go for a hike and see if we find anything before, we use one of our emergency reserved foods."

Cody agreed so he exited his tent and grabbed his backpack. James strapped his pack as well and they both began hiking up the mountains in hopes they'd run into some edible critters. They were jumping over boulders and slightly rock climbing through the terrain. They took a small break to rest a little and hydrate. Then Cody remembered about the cottontail he witnessed grassing earlier and mentioned it to James. James uttered, "Really bro? You seriously let it get away and didn't bring it up till now? Tell you what, let's keep searching and if we don't find anything, we'll try and get it when we're down there."

Cody replied, "Sorry bro. It totally dawned on me since I began reading a book in my tent afterwards but yeah, let's keep searching."

They threw their backpacks over their backs and tightened them up to continue moving. Once again, they were hiking and rock climbing up to the top of the mountain. As they almost got to the top, James observed a mouse hiding behind a boulder. He inserted his arm in the crevice and trapped it in his hand. He pulled it out and glanced at it. He said, "Well, this is more like a snack but if we get a cottontail then it'll be a decent feast till, we drop a deer." He then snapped its head off and placed it inside a zip lock bag he had in his pocket, then secured it to his backpack.

They made it to the top and took a break. James retrieved his binoculars from his bag and looked over to the horizon. He was hoping to spot the deer but they had not begun to make their way back towards them. They had also vanished from the last spot they had seen them at. He put his binoculars away and took out the mouse. He skinned and gutted it using his pocket knife. There wasn't much left of the little furry creature once he did. He knew they'd better find something else or they were going to be starving and would have to eat some of the MRE's. There was hardly anything up there they could hunt. Cody looked at the side of the cliff they were on and spotted an eagle's nest. It had eggs inside. He informed James of his findings. James got up and took a look.

He then commented, "Thing is, eagles are a protected species bro. So, we'd be in a whole lot of trouble if a game warden was to watch or catch us taking the eggs."

Cody replied, "Look around bro. There's no one out here but us. Let's just take them and cook them up along with the mouse." James scanned their surroundings, then agreed.

Cody reached over to the nest with James' help. He grabbed the eggs and handed them over to James to safekeep. Once he had both of the eggs, he secured his feet on the boulder they stood on. James placed the eggs in his chest pocket to make sure they wouldn't get crushed. Both of them began making their way down to their campsite.

As they crawled back down, Cody slip and almost fell over a cliff. He was holding on for dear life with his feet dangling over an approximately two hundred feet drop. His hands grasped on to some crevices in the rocks. James grabbed him from the end of his backpack and pulled him back up. Cody was relieved his friend had saved him from falling over. James inquired, "What happened buddy? How'd you end up there if you were right behind me?"

Cody said, "That's what I get for being nosy. I was looking over the edge to see if I'd see any critters we could use for lunch. Thanks for saving me, James. I don't know what I'd do had you not been there to help me up."

James replied, "Be careful man. Keep following me and don't venture on your own again. You're welcome, bro, you know you can count on me." They then continued climbing and crawling back down to their campsite.

When they arrived at their camp, James removed his back-pack and placed it inside his tent. He then grabbed his foldable pan and gathered some shrub, twigs and wood. He ignited a fire and began to chop up the mouse. Once he had cut it up into pieces, he placed it in the pan to cook. When the meat turned brown, he cracked the eggs and mixed it all up. He continued cooking until it was ready. He then divided the meal in two and served Cody his share in a small bowl. He ate the rest out of the pan. The cottontail was safe for now. They enjoyed their meals and joked around about previous scenarios they both recalled. As they giggled at past events, they heard the mountain lion hissing. Cody felt goosebumps crawling up his skin. They froze their gaze at each other in silence. Cody uttered, "Bro that mountain lion sounds ferocious. Hopefully it doesn't come over here at night and tries to eat us."

James answered, "If that thing comes close to us whether we're asleep or not, it better be ready to fight for its life. I'll fill it up with lead and eat it too." Laughing out loud Cody joined in laughing as well.

They finished their meals and Cody had to take a dump. He grabbed his toilet paper and wipes from his tent and ran down to the bottom of the mountain to find a spot. He located a boulder that stuck out just long enough for him to rest his back on it as he squatted with his pants down. James had grabbed his binoculars in the meantime to see if he could spot the deer. Once again, they were out of range. Cody was finishing up when he felt something fall on his back. He turned around and jumped up thinking it was a tarantula. He smeared poop on himself in the process. Turns out James had tossed the fur from the mouse at him. James was bursting in laughter as his pal threw a fit. He began shouting at James, "You mother fucker! I've got shit all over my hands because you startled me! Fuck! You're an asshole!"

James was still laughing and replied, "That's what you get for playing with me as I slept earlier. What did you think it was by the way?"

Cody was wiping his hands with the wipes and responded, "I thought it was a tarantula or something. I noticed it was furry and since it's shredded out of its original form, it appeared like a tarantula to me."

James was cracking up as Cody finished and walked back towards him. Cody, grabbed some hand sanitizer from his backpack and washed his hands as best he could. They kept the blaze-they initiated to cook- going, feeding it wood from time to time. They also began consuming vodka and got hammered accordingly. They partied all evening, singing and dancing. Cody almost fell inside the fire as he pranced around it. James played some music from a saved playlist he had on his cell phone. He wasn't too worried to discharge his mobile apparatus since he had a charging station on him and a car charger in his vehicle. Cody took out a joint he had stashed in his belongings. He lit it up and they both got high. The sun began to set over the horizon as they continued their festivity. When they got hungry, they opened up some MRE's and ate. Once again, the young cottontail survived being eaten. Both were wasted and began feeling lethargic after eating all the contents in the MRE's. They headed inside their tents disregarding the reason behind their trip and fell asleep.

As they rose the following day, both had headaches and dehydration as symptoms of their hangovers. Cody was first to exit his tent in broad daylight. He shook James' tent and told him, "Hey bro, the sun is out and I think we missed our shot at getting a deer."

James answered, "Ugh, Fuck! That sucks and more because I feel like shit." He got up and opened his tent to exit.

Cody had taken some electrolyte packs to add to their water just in case. He handed one to James and they both drank a cure to their ailments. James looked over the horizon with his binoculars and observed the bevy of deer heading off to where they had seen them disappear the previous morning. He shouted, "Fuck! Damn it! We lost our opportunity to take a buck down man."

Cody replied, "Well, we still have one more shot tomorrow morning or later tonight. So, let's not worry so much about it right now. The good thing is we know their direction of travel and we're located inside of it." James kept quiet since he was upset. They weren't hungry whatsoever since the MRE's had filled them up for days.

So, they continued to hydrate. Cody saw their camp fire was close to turning off so he began placing twigs and wood they had gathered the day before to get it up again. The blaze sparked right back up and he began making himself a coffee. James took a seat on a boulder and watched his friend boil water then open a pack of instant coffee and pour it into a cup he filled up with water. Cody looked at James and told him, "Lighten up man. We're going to take down a nice buck and take it home with us before Sunday afternoon. You want some coffee to elevate your spirit?"

James uttered, "Yeah, hopefully we do. Nah man, you know I don't like coffee or any kind of upper that'll trigger my anxiety out of control."

"Alright, suit yourself," stated Cody.

After Cody drank his coffee, he had a burst of energy and asked James, "Hey, do you want to go explore these mountains with me? I feel like going for a hike and see what I find."

James commented, "Sure, beats staying here reflecting on not catching a deer."

They both grabbed their packs and marched out in a different direction than the day before. They began walking along the edge of the mountain at the bottom. Cody spotted something ahead and signaled James. They both froze and waited for something to pop out of the bush in front of them. They couldn't tell what was in there since all the wildlife camouflage to the surroundings. Then out of nowhere a jack rabbit hopped out and darted away from them before they could draw their weapons and shoot it. They both were surprised and laughed about it. They then continued walking to see what else they'd discover. About ten minutes after running into the jack rabbit, they took a break to hydrate and get out of the sun. Cody took a seat on the ground where a cliff provided shade for them and so did James. James was gazing out into the open field in front of them and Cody was staring at some round plants on the ground.

They were peyote and Cody informed James of it stating, "Look bro. Is that what I think it is?" He then removed two of them off the ground. Cody retrieved his pocket knife and began peeling off the exterior lining. He then chopped the rest up into pieces and bagged it. James inquired, "What're you going to do with them?"

Cody uttered, "I'm going to brew tea at our campsite and drink it bro. What else am I supposed to do with it?" Chuckling.

They then stood up and continued walking around. As they trekked through the bottom of the mountain still, they came across some cactus fruit. They began cutting off prickly pears and shaving off the spines around them. They knew they'd hydrate with them so they began consuming the fruit. After they replenished their fluids, they continued walking around. Eventually they made their way back to the camp since they had been out strolling for a few hours without really finding anything to hunt.

When they made it back to the camp, Cody retrieved the bag out and began boiling more water for the mystical tea. He filled up the pot with water and placed more wood in the fire. He then inserted the peyote and added some rohypnol he had in his pockets. James was glancing through his binoculars to see if he spotted any deer while Cody added the extra ingredient to the concoction. Once it came to a boil, he served himself a cup and one for James. James was hesitant to participate in drinking the magical tea. He said, "I don't want some bro. I'm good and would much rather be alert to get the deer when they make their way back here later on than miss my chance again."

Cody replied, "Don't be a wuss man. We're not going to be under the influence for that long. It'll only take a few hours to wear off and then we'll be back in no time."

James questioned, "Are you sure bro? Have you ever even taken some before to know what you're talking about?"

Cody responded, "Trust me bro, I'm sure. I had some a while back when I went camping with Sam. It was a pretty cool trip.

It wore off after a few hours and we were back to feeling even better than before we took it." Sam was their other friend who couldn't make it out with them on this trip. James mentioned, "I'd rather not take it. Sucks Sam wasn't able to come out since his wife didn't let him." They both laughed.

Cody said, "You're begging to act like Sam yourself bro. All scared to drink some tea with me." James answered, "Alright, hand me that cup then since you insist. If I get sick or go on a bad trip it's your fault." He took the cup avoiding becoming the stereotype of a pussy. After they drank the peyote tea, James asked Cody, "How long is it going to take before it kicks in?"

Cody replied, "About an hour or so and then we'll be hallucinating like two mother fuckers." He didn't mention he had spiked the tea with another substance though.

After close to an hour had gone by, they both began retching and spewing- feeling sick. James told Cody, "I feel like shit again bro. I shouldn't have listened to you." As he vomited on the ground.

Cody said, "It's normal to throw up and feel like shit. It'll go away and we will begin tripping balls. Just chill and drink some water to not dehydrate." They both began to sip water.

Within the following minutes after throwing up, they began to hallucinate. James was tripping out at the tents and Cody started tripping on the fire he sat in front of. They were both enjoying their trips until it took a turn for the worse. Somehow the mixture of drugs they had ingested made them hallucinate that the other was a monster. James yelled out, "Get the fuck away from me you ugly fucking creature." Pointing his gun at Cody.

Cody shouted, "Who the fuck are you and where is my boy, James?"

Cody punched James in the face and ran off into the desert. Away from the monster he perceived James to be. James was hiding in his tent from Cody. Their trip didn't turn out to be as satisfying as expected. James began sobbing and crawled into a fetal position. Cody was out in the middle of nowhere digging a hole with his bare hands to hide in. He was desperate to elude the monster he made of James.

After some time had gone by, Cody returned to the camp and looked for his pal. James was still inside his tent. Cody grabbed his weapons from inside his, and searched for the monster. James heard noise outside his tent and began shooting his firearm. Cody managed to escape his death as a bullet flew within inches from his head. He then ran back into the desert. James exited his tent and saw the monster departing. He took a few more shots at his friend. Cody fell to the ground after listening to the gun shots buzzing over his cranial hair. He then turned his weapon at James and fired back. Both allies had turned nemesis and engaged in a gun battle. Ducking and taking pod shots at each other, they spent the evening.

Their trip didn't wear off and actually increased their paranoia within time. They rose and started shooting at each other once more. Both had run for cover experimenting with psychedelic warfare. They were experiencing a deep panic, wondering how the monster was going to assault them. Unable to calm down, they decided to fight the monster and started shooting at each other again. They never got to hunt deer and they never returned home. What was to come, baffled everyone they knew once they found out.

Evidently, they both sustained life-threatening injuries from the gun battle. Cody lost his life instantly as he took a round to his head. James was able to walk towards I10 with his wounds. He was bleeding to death though. By the time someone stopped to render aid, he had lost his life in the asphalt heading eastbound.

When their family and friends became aware of the tragic news, they were in disbelief. Cody and James had been best friends for decades and that wasn't their first hunting trip together. Cody's body had to be located though and when it was, search and rescue teams tracked his cell phone to get to it. As they closed into the location, they witnessed a partially eaten corpse which a mountain lion had been feasting on. The deer and the cottontail survived being shot at as the two hunters rather hunted each other.

CHAPTER 14
THE CENOTAPH.

Dilan was on the phone texting his girlfriend Beth. He had been trying to meet up with her after they got out of school. His plot was to go to the cemetery which was conveniently located on their route home. Beth feared going anywhere near cemeteries unless for funeral services so she continued rejecting his offer. Dilan texted her, "Come on baby. You have nothing to be afraid of while you're with me. I'll guard you with my own life." He looked up as his teacher, who grabbed his attention and placed his phone down.

Beth replied, "It's not that I don't believe you but I'm petrified of cemeteries. I guess I've seen too many horror movies and feel as if the corpses are going to come out from the ground and chase us."

Dilan waited until his teacher turned away and texted back, "Babe, that only happens in Hollywood. Zombies don't exist and if they did, I'd stab them in the brain and save you from any harm." He sent it right before his professor observed him back on his phone and not paying attention to class.

Beth responded, "Why do you insist on taking me to the cemetery? Sounds suspicious to begin with and the fact that you're pushy about it makes me wonder what you're up to."

Dilan answered, "Suspicious? What do you mean? I just want to show you something there. Just forget about it then. You're acting like you don't trust me after we've been dating for some months now. Trust should be the least of my worries."

Beth wrote back, "I'm sorry, please don't be mad. I do trust you and to show you I do; I'll go see what you want to show me. I love you babe."

Dilan was being monitored so he waited to reply, then when he got the chance, he texted, "I'm not mad. I was a little disappointed but since you agreed, I can chill and look forward to it now." He sent the text as his teacher got on his ass about using his phone in class again. Dilan stopped texting Beth after he announced to her that his instructor had scolded him. When class was dismissed, he met up with her in the hallway. Dilan told her, "My teacher wanted to take my phone away. So, I had to tell him it was my mom texting me something important."

Beth asked, "And did he believe you?"

Dilan said, "Great question but he sure didn't contest my excuse." He giggled and wrapped his arm around her neck to begin walking out of the building together.

As they exited the back door, one of Dilan's friends bumped into them and told Dilan, "Hey bro, did you hear Bryan and Paul are going to fight right now at the park?"

Dilan uttered, "No I didn't. Are you headed that way?" His pal stated, "Yeah, let's go bro."

Dilan looked at Beth and she seemed excited to see the fight so they all three made their way to the park. When they arrived, they noticed Bryan waiting for Paul to show up. He was shadowboxing, getting warmed up for combat. Dilan went up to him and asked, "Where's Paul at bro?"

Bryan uttered, "He's probably hiding in the restrooms, scared to get these hands landed on his face." He chuckled afterwards.

The crowd which gathered to view the battle began dissipating since Paul never showed up. Beth and Dilan said goodbye to everyone present and walked away. They made their way outside of the campus grounds and saw Paul driving away in his mom's van. Dilan inquired, "Is that Paul in his mommy's van? What a punk. I don't know why they were going to fight but if he agreed and didn't show up, he's a coward."

Beth replied, "It sure is him. That's funny how we were all waiting for him and he was waiting for his mother to pick him up instead!"

They both laughed and continued to make fun of Paul as they strolled towards the cemetery. When they finally walked through the front gates, Beth commented, "I'm getting the creeps now. Are you sure it's safe?"

Dilan uttered, "Yes baby, don't worry just follow me and you'll be fine."

They continued going in further until they were in front of a mausoleum. Dilan opened the door and told her to enter with him. She responded, "What's in there? I don't have a good feeling about this Dilan."

Dilan hugged her and said, "Baby, as long as you're with me you don't have to worry about anything or anyone hurting you." He then grabbed her hand and walked her inside.

Once inside, he began to kiss her and she forgot about her fears. He slowly moved his hands onto her buttock. He noticed she didn't flinch or remove his hands from it so he made his way up to her cleavage. Once again, she allowed him to place his hands comfortably over her breasts. At that point, he shoved his hands inside and began fondling her nipples. Beth became aroused and from there he undressed her and went inside of her. They engaged in sexual activities for about twenty minutes before she told him, "Ok, let's go now because my mom is probably worried for me!"

Dilan cooperated with her request and they got dressed. Once they had their clothes back on, they heard a strange noise and some of the fixtures inside fell to the ground. They rushed to exit the cenotaph feeling creeped out. As they jogged out of the cemetery, Beth noticed Dilan's shadow not following his exact movements. She disregarded it at first, believing she was hallucinating probably because she was out of breath. They proceeded out of the cemetery and Beth once more observed Dilan's shadow out of proportion. She informed Dilan and when he looked downward at it, he jumped up believing someone was behind him. He scanned his vision all around- spooked- yet there was no one around them both. He looked at the silhouette behaving inappropriate with his bodily functions. It appeared it was slow to follow his moves and had its own maneuvers. He was in disbelief as they both stared at it. Dilan told Beth, "What the hell is going on with my shadow? Did we enter a time portal and I slowed down time or something?"

Beth answered, "I'm telling you. That's weird. At first, I thought I was tripping, thinking I was seeing things but now I know I'm not and you're seeing the same thing I'm seeing."

Dilan moved around looking at it and uttered, "This is really strange Beth." He ran a little and saw the shadow following him some seconds behind- hesitantly.

Beth replied, "What's going on with your shadow Dilan? Why's it doing that?"

Dilan stated, "I don't know. Let's just ignore it and keep walking." They strolled along gazing at the silhouette periodically.

His shadow continued to slack a few seconds with the present time. Dilan was no longer worried about it and now was intrigued. He had Beth film a video of him and his silhouette. She went ahead and recorded him on her cell phone. He asked her to send him the video as they came to the front of her house. Beth's mother was looking through the window as Dilan kissed Beth. She walked through her front gates and as soon as Beth entered, her mother told her, "I thought I warned you about those little boys? Don't fall in love or he'll break your heart. I'd ask why you're late but it's obvious to me now... Come sit down and eat."

Beth remained mute while being lectured by her guardian. She took a seat at the kitchen table and ate. As she consumed her feast, she texted Dilan the video and engaged in a sexual conversation recapping their previous physical interactions.

Dilan received the video and posted it on his social platforms. He demonstrated to his siblings the new trick he had supposedly taught his silhouette. His brothers were mesmerized as to how it was possible. Dilan failed to inform them he himself was unaware. He instead took advantage of the situation by humering his siblings. Afterwards, his mother went to the living area to see what was going on since they were being loud laughing at the crazy shadow not keeping up with Dilan's movement. His mother inquired, "What's going on? Why're you guys shouting and laughing so hard?" One of Dilan's younger brothers replied, "Look mom! Look at Dilan's shadow.

Pay close attention to what it does." She fixed her gaze at Dilan's silhouette.

As soon as she witnessed the awkward activity, she jumped and ran away. She grabbed her bible from her bedroom and returned to the living room. She started praying and telling her kids to do the same. Dilan thought it was a bit overboard but he kneeled down with the rest of his household and talked to God. His mother then opened her bible and began reading passages from it. Dilan looked at his phone's notifications and realized his video had begun going viral. He put his device away upon his mother's instructions. She read and prayed holy words believing there was an evil spirit hovering around her eldest son. By the time she had concluded her calling on the Lord, Dilan's silhouette had resumed its original function. Dilan and his siblings were in awe, surprised their mother had assessed the disturbance and cast away a demonic entity. Their mother prayed once more thanking God he had addressed the issue and taken care of it. Dilan then thanked her and walked away towards his room as he texted Beth.

Beth could not conceive his shadow had returned to its normal status. She asked for him to send her a video, which he did. She then questioned, "So what was it? That's strange and even more so now that it's gone and why or how?"

Dilan replied, "My mom had my brothers and I praying in the living room. Next thing I know, my shadow wasn't disproportionate any longer. What's even crazier is that I uploaded the video online and it's gone viral. I also received a message from several people who claim the same thing happened to them or someone they knew after visiting the cemetery. None of which gave me a concrete or definite answer as to why or how, to respond to yours." She called him instead and he answered.

Beth uttered, "I did see that it's got around ten thousand views and counting already within an hour of posting it. What else did those people tell you?"

Dilan stated, "Well one girl told me she and her friends were at the cemetery when she entered a mausoleum and that's when she noticed the shadow. I told her the same thing happened to me. She mentioned that ever since that occurred, she has been seeing paranormal activity as if the silhouette opened a realm with the unliving."

Beth commented, "So you'll be able to converse with ghosts shortly?"

Dilan uttered while chuckling, "I never said that. Matter of fact she never answered that question either. The others just mentioned they too had a similar experience but they might just be like liars or attention seekers."

Beth divulged, "You need to be careful babe. Hopefully nothing bad happens and it was just a glitch in the system."

They carried their conversation and eventually changed the topic. Beth was worried she may conceive a child from their sexual conduct. Dilan advised her, "Don't worry, I pulled out on time so you should be fine. I really don't see why you would be against having my kid but I'll take it as you just don't want to be pregnant period."

Beth replied, "Imagine I do? My mom would kill me and then things would get complicated for us. And what if the baby is born cursed by whatever spirit was in the mausoleum?"

Dilan uttered, "Nonsense baby, I didn't cum inside you. You're not going to become a mother from today, I promise. So don't even worry yourself thinking you will. As far as the spirit or demon, whatever it was, it's gone." They continued talking until right before they had to go to bed.

Bryan, Dilan's friend, was fascinated by the dark side of things. When he encountered Dilan in school the next day, he had a bunch of questions for him regarding the video he had posted. Bryan asked, "How'd you edit the video to make it seem as if your shadow had a life of its own?"

Dilan answered, "I didn't edit it. Something strange happened after I visited a cenotaph yesterday."

Bryan questioned, "Where at?"

Dilan responded to all his inquiries and Bryan wanted to go to the mausoleum after school. Dilan advised him not to but he disobeyed rebelliously.

When school was out, Bryan went to the cemetery on his own. He searched for the mausoleum. He tried entering one which was on the opposite side. It was secured with a chain and lock then a deadbolt as added security. Bryan tried kicking it open but it was useless. He then heard some voices at a distance. He hid behind the mausoleum. As he crouched down observing who else was there, he noticed a caretaker walking around singing music he was listening to on his earbuds. The man was going around picking up trash and cleaning the tombs up. Bryan gazed at a cenotaph behind the man. It appeared more like the one Dilan described to him. Once he saw the man walking away, he headed over to the mausoleum. When he got to it, he turned around to make sure the caretaker wasn't around. The coast was clear so he entered the cenotaph.

As he stepped foot inside the mausoleum, he felt an energy within. Bryan called upon it to make itself present. The entity scratched the walls behind him and shut the door. Bryan began to perspire, feeling impacted by his finding. Bryan asked the spirit to communicate with him. He said, "What is your name and why're you here?"

He waited a few seconds, then observed the entity writing on the ground clearing up accumulated dust and leaving words behind. The entity wrote, "None of your business."

Bryan chuckled and replied, "Why're you being rude? Are you a woman or just act like one?" A small dust storm arose inside the mausoleum, making Bryan cover up his face and nose.

When the dust settled, Bryan stated, "Hey man! I'm not here with bad intentions. I'd like to figure out who you are and what you want. My friend was here yesterday and I believe you followed him to his home. I'd like to know why and how? Also why did you return here?" The room got chilly and silent as the entity refused to respond to the inquiries.

Bryan waited but heard nothing so he asked, "Can you talk to me please?"

All of a sudden, the cenotaph door opened and light shined in. It was the caretaker who was there to find out what was going on. He shouted, "What the hell are you doing here kid? Get your ass out of here and don't come back!" Bryan took off running as the caretaker continued, "I'm sick and tired of you little punks coming here to jack off and trash the place. Find a new hobby!" As Bryan darted out of there, he turned around and noticed he wasn't being followed.

He stopped and yelled back, "Fuck you, old man! Stop molesting little kids, you pervert. I'll be back to take a dump all over the grave stones!"

The man replied, "What did you say you little turd?" As he gave chase towards Bryan."

Bryan started running again. He made it to the front gates and made a sharp left. He flew down the street and into a residential area. He sped right by a man who was watering his grass. The man yelled at him to get off his lawn. Bryan was running so fast that he didn't hear the man. He continued sprinting towards his home. He had to run across his high school football field. He jumped over the fence and made his way to the other side of the field. Bryan was already on the opposite side and climbed over the fence. When his feet landed on the ground, he was already tired from running. He crouched down to supply his lungs with oxygen. As he gasped for air, he observed a shadow coming towards him. He got up believing it was the caretaker and continued sprinting all the way to his home.

When he made it to the safety of his house, Bryan ran in through the back door. His mother shouted at him, "Why're you running in her like you just saw a ghost? I hope you're not out there getting into trouble again!"

Bryan halted his pursuit and replied, "I wouldn't run from a ghost. I'm also not in any kind of trouble mom." He inhaled air and continued, "I just felt like running home to get some exercise."

His mother told him, "Are you hungry? I made food. Grab a plate and serve yourself if you are. I'm heading off to work now."

Bryan grabbed a plate from the cabinets and served himself. He also got a fork, napkin and a cup then served himself food and a drink. He took a seat at the kitchen table and began eating. Just as he took his second spoon full, he looked down at his shadow which had displayed its own character. Bryan shook his head in disbelief. He was ecstatic that the entity followed him home just as his pal Dilan. Bryan asked the silhouette, "I'm glad you came. I see you're a shadow figure. Let me grab something for you to communicate with me." He grasped a pen and paper then set it next to him.

He then asked, "Why did you follow me and is there something you want or need?" He placed some food in his mouth as he saw the pen and paper make contact.

The pen dropped on top of the paper signaling the spirit had finished writing. He had jotted, "I want your body and soul."

Bryan uttered, "You want to possess my body? What for? How will you be able to anyhow even if I'd be willing to?"

The pen moved and began writing, "I need someone's body to live. I was condemned by God out of heaven and made a deal with the devil." Bryan chuckled.

After the pen fell again, Bryan stated, "Why would you make a deal with the devil? Don't you know he doesn't play fair? Why weren't you allowed into heaven?"

The pen began moving over the sheet of paper writing, "God did not forgive me for my sins. The devil tricked me on the deal but I'm going to outsmart him by entering your body, as soon as I know how."

Bryan started laughing out loud and replied, "You can't outsmart the devil. All you can do is ask God to keep him at bay. I'd like to help you out but I have a ton of homework to catch up on. So, if you don't mind, let me finish it before you possess my body." He then began filming the silhouette, writing its response on paper.

The shadow wrote, "I'm not going to be stuck in this realm I'm in so I will outsmart the devil. You'd have to come back to my cenotaph before the end of the day. Otherwise, I'll vanish back to where you found me."

Bryan got up from his chair, saying, "You're crazy. I'm not going back there. I told you I have a bunch of work to do." He posted the video online, placed his dirty dishes in the sink and went to his room to start his work.

The entity followed him and made his presence known as Bryan opened up his school books and read through his assignment- flipping the pages. He ignored the silhouette and got busy. His phone began blowing up with activity on his social network. His video started receiving many likes and comments. He glanced through his notifications and put his device down. As he got back to his work, he witnessed the shadow disappear. Bryan thought about going to the mausoleum but he really didn't want the entity to possess his body. He instead finished his homework and contacted Dilan afterwards.

He informed Dilan, "Bro, I went to the cenotaph and the spirit followed me back home. Did you check out the video I posted? It was communicating with me."

Dilan replied, "You never listen huh Bryan? I don't think it's a friendly ghost to be honest. Let me check out your video."

Bryan relayed, "You know I like ghosts and paranormal activity bro. I couldn't refuse to experience some for myself. It was freaking cool man. I actually had a conversion with it."

Dilan started watching the video and commented, "That's wild, man. It was writing to you and answering your questions. But to be frank. Dude, do me a favor and don't go back there please. I need to get ready right now. I have a date with Beth but I beg you to not go back there. I'll send you a text later on."

Bryan uttered, "Bro, you go ahead and go on your date without worrying about me. I'll be fine no matter what daring decision I make. Have fun and use a condom." They ended their conversation.

Bryan began replying back to people who had commented on his post. He was beyond belief of the publicity his post generated and the actual reason behind it. He had come into close contact with an entity, something he had been hoping for. He signed on to another of his accounts and posted the video with a comment on top which read, "Have a conversation with a ghost- check hashtag running out of ideas for my bucket list lol."

Immediately his post began grabbing other people's attention. Bryan was having a blast reading what the viewers wrote. He eventually got bored of replying to some of his new followers and decided to go back to the cemetery. He contacted his other friend Leo to see if he'd be willing to accompany him. Leo agreed and they were to meet up over at Leo's residence since it was a few blocks from the cemetery. Bryan exited his home through the back door, leaving the front one locked.

Approximately fifteen minutes later, Bryan was walking up to Leo's house. Leo was outside waiting for him dressed in black attire. He crept up on Bryan and startled him. Bryan swung around and said, "What the fuck bro? You scared the living crap out of me."

Leo laughed and replied, "Dude, you should've seen the look on your face. I do believe you almost shit yourself." Bursting in laughter.

Bryan stated, "I wasn't expecting that. Only reason why I got scared was the element of surprise you utilized… Are you ready or what?"

Leo uttered, "Ha! It worked though… Yeah, let's just stop by the convenience store on our way there. I need to grab a few things." Bryan agreed and they made their way down to the store.

As they strolled to the store, Bryan advised Leo he would wait for him outside. Leo responded, "Alright, I shouldn't take long." He entered the establishment as Bryan sat on a bus stop right in front of the store.

Bryan got on his cell phone and observed how there were more likes and comments on his videos. He began writing back to some. He was interrupted by a text from Dilan who wrote, "Hey bro, hope you didn't go back to the cemetery. Someone messaged me on my video about the high risk of coming into contact with that particular ghost who's lost in this world unable to transition to its destination. I sent them a link to your video and they should be contacting you soon. Stay safe brother and I'll see you tomorrow at school."

Bryan texted back, "Ok Dill, thanks. I'm home right now and not going back there, don't worry. See you tomorrow."

As soon as he sent the text, Leo barged out of the store with the clerk on his tail.

He shouted, "Run!" Bryan got up and ran with him.

They ran a few blocks down and Leo stopped. Bryan asked him, "Why're we running man? What did you do and why's the man chasing you?"

Leo explained, "I stole a beer. He saw me through the mirror and when I was paying for a candy bar, he asked for my ID. I then asked why he needed to see my ID and he told me he saw me hide the beer in my waist. That's when I took off."

Bryan commented, "Why the hell are you doing beer runs man? That wasn't the purpose of this outing. Damn it, Leo! I hope he didn't recognize me because he gets along very well with my mother and might tell her." Suddenly they heard sirens in the distance, believing the cops were called out- they took off to Leo's home.

As they swung around Leo's front gate, Bryan stopped and told him, "I'm going home bro. I'm not going to get caught with your stupid ass at your house." Leo looked at him, walked inside his house drinking his beer as Bryan ran off towards his residence. When Bryan arrived back at his dwelling, He was upset his plans were ruined.

As much as he desired to return, he felt the police were looking for him and Leo. So, he stayed home and watched tv. He got back on his phone and saw he had a message from some paranormal group. He opened it and began reading what was a warning. He was informed of the threat such an entity derived. The creator of the group was the one contacting him. He wanted the address and exact location of the mausoleum so he could address the situation with his expertise. He did specify clearly to not return to the cenotaph for his own safety. Bryan ignored the message and didn't reply. He instead notified Dilan via text, that he was a snitch. Bryan continued watching television until it was bedtime. He fell asleep in his room after locking both doors since his mother would get home from work in the middle of the night and had her own keys.

During his rest, he had nightmares of the ghost possessing his body. He tossed and turned until he was woken up by his mom who had just gotten back from work and noticed he was having trouble during his sleep. Bryan thanked his mom and went back to sleep without further issues.

The following day Bryan woke up late for school and didn't shower. He immediately rose from his bed and got dressed. He managed to brush his teeth and ran towards his first period classroom. Dilan had been blowing up his phone since Leo had told him they had attempted to go to the cemetery and almost did, had he not gotten chased by the store employee.

Bryan got to his class and as he opened the door- disturbing the lecture- all his peers turned around and gazed at him. The teacher told him, "Glad you could make it to class but since you're late, go to the office and get a tardy slip."

Bryan walked out of class and directed his path to the attendance office. When he came around the hallway corner, he ran into Dilan. Dilan greeted him and uttered, "Bro, did you get the message from those people? Stay away from that place man. I know how you're crazy stubborn but it's for your own good."

Bryan replied, "Look Dill, I did get a message from some paranormal group but who's to say they really are professionals and know what they're talking about?

Anyhow, I'll talk to you later because I need to get a tardy slip otherwise the prof won't allow me into class." They shook hands and parted ways.

After Bryan got a tardy slip, he went back to class and was allowed entry. His phone kept ringing and he had to silence it so his teacher wouldn't get more irritated at him. He was being contacted through video chat by the paranormal creator who insisted on speaking to him. Bryan really had no intentions on communicating with this person or his group. He had little faith in their services and reputation. Then he got a notification from Dilan who requested he'd talk to the guy to educate himself on the type of spirit they were dealing with. Bryan wrote back, "Sure thing bro. I'll contact him when I get out of class. Just tell him to stop bugging before I get in trouble and have my phone confiscated."

Dilan replied, "Alright, I'll let him know but please talk to him and don't go back to the cemetery until you do." Bryan liked his text after reading it and placed his device back in his pocket.

Bryan continued going to all of his classes and the paranormal individual stopped contacting him eventually. It was until after he got out of school that the person called him again. Bryan noticed his call when he looked at his phone to check the time. When the call ended, he blocked the caller on his device and exited the campus building. He was beginning to feel frustrated and harassed by the paranormal so-called expert. He observed Dilan walking across from him with Beth as he got to the last step of a stairwell leading to the structure's entrance. Bryan knew he was going to pressure him to talk to the individual he refused to speak to. So, he ducked behind the school's sign and monitored until Dilan and his girlfriend had left.

Once they were no longer around, he proceeded to his house. His video had reached a higher volume of viewers than Dilan's. As he traversed through the surrounding neighborhoods, he was reacting and replying to comments his footage received. Having his gaze preoccupied, he failed to notice Paul and some of his friends were following him. When he least expected it, they ambushed him from behind. He fell to the ground and got in a fetal position.

Paul and his accomplices launched a violent attack on Bryan. After a few seconds of beating him, they fled the scene. The moment Bryan looked up, they were long gone and he was left wondering who had assaulted him. He rose to his feet almost unscathed. He sustained some bruises and flesh wounds to his body but his face remained intact due to him crawling into a ball. He continued making his way home as he brushed off some dust and grass which adhered to his clothing.

When he made it to his residence, his mother greeted and fed him. Once done eating his supper, he retracted himself from the dining area and relocated to his room. He shut his door and called Dilan. He informed Dilan about his physical incident. Dilan told him, "It was probably Paul, don't you think? Who else has a grudge against you?" Bryan replied, "If only I knew what others truly think of me, I'd answer that question. Unfortunately, not everyone who pretends to be an ally is one... Keep your ears open to see if anyone boasts about what I just shared with you and let me know if you come across valuable news."

Dilan replied, "Sure thing bro. I'm sure right now you're having difficulty distinguishing friend from foe but I assure you I'm on your side. Which brings me to asking if you've spoken to the." He didn't conclude his sentence when he heard Bryan disconnect.

Bryan waited for his mother to notify him she was departing to her employment. Once she left the dwelling, he walked out through the back door and headed to the cemetery. He wanted to converse with the entity again. Out of curiosity and to fulfill his personal agenda due to his fascination with the unknown. He guarded himself from his surroundings, preventing another attack.

When he got to the cemetery, the front gate was closed. He jumped over it and proceeded to the cenotaph. Once at the mausoleum, he entered and flicked a lighter he had in his pockets to see. He began attempting to talk to the spirit who dwelled there. At first, he received no response.

Just as he was going to give up and leave, the entity began writing on the floor, separating the dust from the concrete surface. Bryan bent down and flicked his lighter to read. As he read, he felt a burst of energy surfing through his body. Eventually the ghost stopped communicating and he returned home. He fell asleep as soon as he scarfed down some leftovers.

The next day at school. Dilan approached him and notified him he had overheard Paul discussing the ambush with another classmate. Bryan seemed uninterested as if he had become another person overnight. Dilan tried asking him if something was wrong but Bryan didn't answer. He just continued moving along to his next course.

Over the next days, weeks and months to come, those who knew Brayn claimed and argued he wasn't himself anymore. As if the spark in his eyes was blown out and he didn't have any more will power. Even his own mother unrecognized him. What had happened to him remained a mystery to all. Had the beating he received changed him? Or was there another motive behind his new character?

The paranormal team eventually drove into town to study the active site Dilan had provided the coordinates for. When they began testing their devices and equipment, they had no activity to report. As if it was all a hoax set up by Dilan. The lead in the study contacted Dilan and asked, "Are you sure the videos were real and this exact location was where you and your friend made contact with this entity?"

Dilan uttered, "Yeah, why?"

"Because my team and I are at the mausoleum right now and we have zero activity. None of our gadgets are picking up any type of frequency or energy," stated the lead investigator.

Dilan responded, "Well that's weird. Let me meet up with you all and see what's going on." He ended the call and rushed over there.

Upon arrival at the cemetery, Dilan made contact with the group and assured them they were at the correct location. They all wondered what was going on. If the entity had dispersed or crossed into another realm. After several more attempts, they took off disappointed with the outcome. Dilan returned to his house and contacted Bryan. He inquired if he knew anything about the ghost. Bryan told him he didn't.

What in reality occurred was as summarized. The soul who made its final home in the cenotaph never was allowed into heaven or hell. It was condemned to dwell on earth forever. During its lifespan, the man was rude and evil to everyone he knew or came into contact. Even those what seemed to be good deeds on his behalf were configured to his benefit. He was a bitter person with no other objective than selfishness due to the displeasure he had for humanity. His cold heart had no emotions of empathy. To the extent no one attended his funeral services. He had no friends and his family had disowned him since he was in his teens.

Once he died and was judged by God, he was deprived of eternal life in heaven. Satan granted him the power to pursue those who entered his mausoleum and attempt to possess their bodies. Lucifer ruse the man when he bargained with him. It was a one- way deal, if he managed to take over a human body- he'd be allowed to live their life as a second opportunity. If he failed, his soul became Lucifer's property to do as he wished. That's why he'd follow unsuspecting visitors becoming their shadow. A silhouette which they thought was theirs and flabbergasted them as to why it would act unaccordingly.

Satan only fooled him into believing the contract which he didn't intend on abiding by. The man's soul had to overtake a body before the day ended otherwise it would return to its cenotaph unable to wander in the dark as an entity. It relentlessly attempted to possess a human form in order to live once more and when dead, be allowed in either heaven or hell. This lost soul's faith was to act on a hopeless promise, the same ones he made during his life. Yet he figured it out and outsmarted the devil. The unspoken rule was, he had to ask the person for permission to possess its body. That was what it wrote on the ground and Bryan agreed to. Answering both mysteries as to why Bryan acted unlike himself and why the paranormal team wasn't able to detect the entity in the cenotaph. It had possessed Bryan and no one suspected it.

CHAPTER 15
WRITER'S BLOCK.

"Mr. Jewel, how are you doing today? This is Tamy, your publisher. I'm glad I was able to get a hold of you. It's been quite some time since you had submitted any new works. I was going through the contract and we need one more story from you before the month ends. Will you be able to turn something in today?" Inquired Tamy.

Joseph Jewel answered, "Hi Tamy, I know it's been a while since I produced another novel. I've been struggling with personal issues. I don't have anything to turn in to you. I am currently working on one but haven't finished it yet."

Tamy replied, "Why don't you send in what you have so far? Let me take a look at it and if you need assistance from our ghostwriter department, we can facilitate a discounted price for the services."

Joseph uttered, "That's the thing, I don't want to give more of my percentage to anyone else. I appreciate your offer, Tamy. I will turn in what I have by the end of the month."

"Alright Mr. Jewel. Hopefully you do stay within the time frame as indicated in our contract. I'll be expecting your next big hit by the end of the month. Thank you very much for answering my call and hope you have a great day." She hung up after Joseph wished her the same.

Joseph Jewel was actually having writer's block. He had been perturbed by his success and felt he had to outdo his last best seller. He was facing problems in his marriage and household. His wife and children had become leeches who just wanted to spend his hard-earned money as if it grew on trees. He had spoken to them as a group and told them they needed to slow their roll. They didn't listen to his advice and continued racking up debt by purchasing unneeded luxury items. So, Mr. Jewel not only faced his own burdens but also the ones his family had compiled on his behalf. His wife wanted for him to spend more time with her. She would insist they needed more dates to keep up with their marriage. As much as Joseph adhered to her requests, she failed to reciprocate. He was frustratedly trying to explain to everyone at home how he needed to work on his story in peace without any distractions. His wife felt he was being hostile, selfish and didn't care for her any longer. Right that moment she told him, "You're neglecting me for your work again Joseph. I feel you prioritize your work more than you do me."

Joseph divulged, "My work is what makes you enjoy your fine dining and all the things you buy. I've been blunt about your spendings and you selfishly contest me. How do you expect to continue living the way you do if I were to stop writing and focus solemnly on you? I bet the second I stop generating income, you'll leave me. It seems you're becoming not only demanding and ungrateful but also interested in what I provide."

Mrs. Jewel stated, "How dare you call me demanding, ungrateful and interested. I've been by your side when you had nothing to offer but that beat up car and a cheesy apartment you called home. And frankly, I wouldn't mind going back to those days since you paid more attention to me then than you do now. All the materialistic things you've showered me with are a cry for help. I'd rather have you than them."

Joseph argued, "Beat up car and cheesy apartment huh? That was me then, I've worked my ass off to be where I'm at now. I haven't seen you do anything for yourself other than wait with your hand out to see what rains from my generosity. As if I have what I have just because it fell from the sky. I don't see you complaining about your shoe collection, your over piled closet. Your fancy sports car, your limitless credit card and everything else that has to do with money. You see it as materialistic but it cost me my time, my energy and my imagination. Now if you're going to continue arguing about our life, then make your own without me and let me live in peace." He turned around and walked away towards his office.

As he took a seat behind his desk, he heard the front door shut. His wife and kids had left to do some more shopping. He ignored everything and opened up his laptop to concentrate on his work. He was on the first chapter of his soon to be finished masterpiece. Joseph resumed where he had last left off. After a few sentences, he had to stop writing since his argument was influencing his work.

He didn't want to make his characters argumentative nor negative. He stopped writing, swinging his chair around and staring at the panoramic view from his window as he placed his hands behind his head. He reminisced on the days his wife brought up nostalgically. When he had that beat up car and apartment. Even though back then he didn't have his current wealth, he was happy and at peace. He wished he could turn back the hands of time just as everyone else who was displeased with their present moment. He questioned what his future would look like. If his family would stop spending excessively. If his wife would stop nagging and if he would continue with his successful career as an author. The inquiries consumed his emotions and he was unable to continue working. After approximately thirty minutes, he gave up and shut his computer off.

Joseph headed towards the kitchen to see what he could eat and drink. Scavenging through his refrigerator, he found some leftover spaghetti. He served himself some and a glass of grape juice. He heated up his food and waited for the microwave to ring. When his meal was ready, he sat down in the living room to watch tv as he ate. He searched for a horror movie in hopes it would inspire him to get back to work. As he flipped through the channels, he inserted his fork full of food in his mouth. He entertained his eyes on an old flick enjoying his meal and drink. When he concluded his feast, he went to the garage after placing his dirty dishes in the sink. He walked towards the back of his garage where he had some of his things organized. He reached towards the back of some boxes labeled "My collection of books." When he drew back his hand from behind the box, he had a pack of smokes. Everyone believed he had quit cold turkey as he had mentioned to them. Yet he had relapsed with this last story twisted and tangled in his head. Since his family wasn't home yet he took advantage and smoked in the backyard.

The first drag made him feel light headed. He felt glittery but relaxed at the same time. He took a seat in his patio set and inhaled the toxic fumes. Just as he took his last drag, he heard his wife's car drive in their driveway. His camera systems also alerted him there was movement at the front of his home. He put out his cigarette and tossed it over to his neighbor's backyard. He waited a bit to allow the fresh air to conceal the odor on his clothing. Once he heard shouting coming from inside his house, he entered and saw his kids running around with new toys. His wife was on her cell phone bragging to someone about what she had just purchased. Joseph avoided them all and headed towards his office in order to pretend he was busy. One of his kids busted in through the door evading his brother's playful attack. Joseph told him, "Hide under my desk so your brother won't find you."

His son ran underneath his desk just in time before his older sibling stood by the door looking for him. The boy asked Joseph, "Have you seen Mat? Did he come in here to hide? As he stood his ground with an airsoft rifle.

Joseph uttered, "No, I haven't seen him since you guys came back from the store.

What're you two playing?"

Joseph the third replied, "We're playing robots and humans. I'm the robot and Mat is the human who I'm going to terminate."

Joseph senior stated, "Is there just one robot and one human left in all existence?"

Jr. responded, "Yes, Mat and his army defeated the rest of the robots with an atomic blast which also killed the rest of their group."

Senior commented, "Sounds interesting, can I play too? I can be the robot creator and the second to last human alive to stop the war between you two."

Jr. said, "I guess but the creator was eliminated a while back and it wouldn't fit the story to bring him back from the dead. Anyhow, I'm going to look for that human and destroy him before he destroys me." He ran away in search of his younger brother.

When he departed, Joseph told his youngest, "Your brother left so the coast is clear. What else did you guys buy at the store?"

Mat answered, "Mom got us some new sneakers for school. She also got a bunch of stuff for herself and for the house." He came up from under the desk and continued, "Well I've got to go and kill the robot before it gets me dad." He took off as Joseph watched with a smile on his face.

Joseph was content that his two sons were having fun and enjoying life. He felt proud they had an imagination like his and hopefully one of them would follow his path and write later on in their lives. He got on his laptop and started writing a little. He finished the paragraph he left at and began a new one, still on chapter one. As he regained some of his imagination and proceeded with his story, his wife walked into his office and continued arguing with him. She told him, "There you are. For a second, I thought you had abandoned us. Hey, I'm talking to you. Can you get off your computer and focus on me for a second?"

Joseph finished his sentence and glanced up to her eyes stating, "Why would I abandon you guys? And it's quite rude you interrupt me as I write. I'd compare it to interrupting someone who's talking."

His wife uttered, "Anyhow, I brought some fried chicken in case you're hungry. And also, I was wondering if you could contact the insurance company because someone scratched my car in the parking lot."

"Thanks, but I just ate not long ago. I heated up some leftover spaghetti. How bad is the scratch and how come you don't call the insurance to make a claim? You should have done that as soon as you noticed the damage," commented Joseph.

His wife replied, "You mean to tell me I waited in line to get food just so you could tell me you're not going to eat? And I just noticed it when we got back home as we were taking out the stuff we got."

"Is it really my fault you didn't communicate with me? Isn't that why you have a cell phone? To call and let me know or ask me what I'd like to eat? I'm tied up here with this story. I had just gotten a burst of imagination and you ruined it. Call the insurance company and let them know what happened," divulged Joseph.

His wife told him, "I guess I'll leave you alone so you can write your story then. I'll call the insurance company after I'm done with the things I have to do first." She walked away.

Joseph fixed his eyes on the screen in front of him and reread what he had written. He felt satisfied and continued writing. He was only able to finish the paragraph he was on before he lost interest after his imagination and motivation faded. His kids were being loud also which didn't allow him to concentrate. He saved his work and took his kids out to play in the backyard. They played until the sun went down.

When they went back inside, Joseph heated up a plate of fried chicken and served his kids one too since they said they were hungry. His wife walked in on their meal and told him, "Good thing you haven't neglected your kids yet." In a negative burlesque tone.

Joseph said, "Why don't you go get ready so we can go out tonight? I don't want you to continue feeling left out. I can use a little getaway to distract myself in order to clear my mind."

His wife replied, "Are you serious? Or are you being sarcastic?"

Joseph uttered, "Dead serious. Go get ready while we eat in peace." She almost ran up to their bed room to get ready as he and his boys concluded their meals.

When Joseph and his sons wrapped up their diner, Joseph headed towards his room and got in the shower. He knew it would take his wife around two hours to be set. So, he had sufficient time to lounge after his shower. When he exited the glass doors, he observed his wife standing in front of the bathroom mirror doing her hair and makeup. Joseph dried himself, slipped into his briefs and went to their bedroom to lay down for a bit. He told his wife to wake him up if he fell asleep.

Joseph was deep in his sleep dreaming he had finished his story and had major success with it. His wife woke him up and told him, "I'm ready now. Are you going to take long to get dressed?"

Joseph stretched out and yawned. He looked at his wife up and down and told her, "Wow, you look stunning. Are you the same woman who's been on my ass to take her out?" As he stood up out of bed and started getting dressed.

It only took him around ten minutes to be ready. After brushing his teeth, he asked his wife, "Is the babysitter on her way?"

His wife answered, "She should be here any minute now. She said it was good I called her since she had nothing to do today and is in need of some money."

Joseph replied, "Well I'm glad it works out for all of us. Hopefully the kids don't give her a hard time like the last." They both went down stairs to wait for her to arrive.

It took the nanny around thirty minutes to show up. As soon as her car pulled into the driveway, Mat said, "Mom, is she going to take care of us again? Last time she kept yelling at us for playing like we always do."

Joseph responded, "Yes, she's going to take care of you two while we go out. Now I want you both on your best behavior and not stir up any trouble with her. If while we're out there, I receive a complaint or when we return, both of you will be in serious trouble." The doorbell rang and his wife let her in.

The babysitter was greeted and welcomed inside the home. Joseph reminded his kids once again to behave or he was going to discipline them once he'd get back. He handed the sitter half of her pay and told her he would give her the rest when they'd return. He and his wife exited the residence and hopped into his truck. From there they drove down to a restaurant where they were regulars and didn't need to make reservations. The owner had befriended Joseph as one of his truest fans.

After being welcomed by the host and walked to their table, they took a seat and their waiter came by to take their orders. He asked, "Mr. and Mrs. Jewel, will you be having the usual tonight?"

Mrs. Jewel replied, "I will, how about you honey?"

Joseph uttered, "I feel like having a steak tonight instead of the grilled chicken I love. Also, I want a beer. For starters, let me get the fondue."

The waiter stated, "Right away Mr. Jewel. I'll be back with your beer, same one as before?" Joseph nodded his head and the waiter departed their presence to get their orders going.

Moments later, the waiter returned to their table with his beer, the fondue and Mrs. Jewel's soda which she always ordered. Joseph was venting to his wife about his emotions. How he felt pressured to turn in something by the end of the month and how her and the kids were stressing him some. She said, "You've written three-hundred- page stories in four weeks amongst the same atmosphere. I don't see how we're an issue to your process or progress."

Joseph stated, "The stress of not turning in a story on time and having to return some of the money the publishers advanced me. Then you all have been spending like it's never going to run out. Being home with you complaining I'm neglecting you and the kids running around wild is more than enough."

Mrs. Jewel uttered, "Blame it on us right. Why don't you just sip your beer and eat your cheese. Let me enjoy this night out without the kids bugging me."

Joseph commented, "I'll let you enjoy this night but I'm going to go stay the rest of the month at the cabin so I can get this work done."

Mrs. Jewel was upset and replied, "Well don't let me stop you and hopefully you do finish your story. Otherwise, you'll see how it wasn't us distracting you and only your thoughts and pressure."

Joseph didn't counter her statement and just relaxed as he ate his fondue and drank his beer. Their food came out fast and they both began to eat. It was obvious their marriage had lost the spark it once had. His wife wanted to compensate for the lack of romance with dates and shopping. Mainly because she would get frustrated of watching out for the boys and had nothing else to do with her life. Joseph felt she had become a gold digger but kept his opinion to himself. There was a lack of communication between them both. That needed conversation of what's really going on and how they could work together hadn't been brought up. Holding it off was only separating them further away and creating distance between them.

After they finished their meal, they headed over to a nightclub where Mrs. Jewel loved to dance to the music they played. They danced the night away like two distant strangers who just embraced for public display. When the night was over, they drove back home.

Upon arrival at their dwelling, Joseph inquired with the babysitter how his kids behaved. She didn't have any complaints this time so he handed her the rest of her payment and dismissed her. He then walked to his kid's bedroom and observed them both asleep. He gave each one a kiss on the forehead and tucked them in. He then walked over to his bedroom and found his wife lying in bed. She had gotten home a bit tipsy and tired so as soon as she entered their home, she went straight to their room. She undressed and jumped into bed without waiting up for Joseph. He removed his clothes and crawled into bed slowly, to not wake her up.

The next day, Joseph arose early. He began gathering his things to head out. His kids were still out and his wife woke up to the noises he caused while packing. She asked him, "You weren't kidding huh? You're really going to spend the rest of the month at your cabin."

Joseph answered, "I have no other choice unless I want to owe them and lose all I've worked hard for." As he finished packing his clothes and headed to the restroom to grab his hygiene products and articles.

Once he had everything required for his trip, he kissed his wife and told her, "When I return, we will continue working on our marriage and family. I hope you're fine for the next few weeks alone with the kids. Please don't be upset and take it out on them. I will stay in touch; I love you and will miss you." He then gave her another kiss and a hug before going to his kid's room to kiss them too without waking them up.

Once he said his goodbyes, Joseph placed his luggage in his truck and got in himself. He drove slowly off his driveway, observing his wife looking at him through the window. He waved at her before turning his wheels on to the street. He proceeded forward towards his destination.

On his way there, he stopped at a fast-food restaurant and ordered breakfast through the drive thru. After receiving his food, he got back on the road and ate cautiously as he maneuvered his vehicle. The cabin was around two and a half hours away from his home. He had to make a stop at the local grocery store in the small town where it was located. In order to grab something to eat and not have to leave the cabin so he could use his time effectively. He kept that in mind as he turned his music up loud in his truck to enjoy his drive.

Some hours had gone by and he had just made it into town. He drove to the store and parked. He exited his truck and headed inside. He got a shopping cart at the entrance and began going through the isles obtaining things from a list he had created on his cell phone. Once his list had vanished after erasing what he already had gotten, he made his way to the checkout. As he stood behind some older lady who had plenty of things still in her cart, he recalled he was going to grab a bottle of whiskey. He ran towards the alcohol section leaving his cart back in line. He scanned through the varieties of whisky and picked one out then sprinted back in line. The lady was about to pay when he returned. When she got her receipt, she pushed her cart out of the store. Joseph was next and began placing his items on the conveyor belt. He received his grand total and swiped his card. He then headed back to his truck with all his merchandise. He put all the bags inside and returned the cart to the store. He then got inside his truck and departed.

A few minutes later, he had made it to the cabin. He drove up the driveway and shut his truck off. He texted his wife he had arrived safely. He then got out and walked to the front door. He opened it with his keys and went back to his truck to begin taking all his things in. After about ten minutes, he had finished bringing everything out of the truck and into the cabin. He started organizing his produce and placed what needed to be refrigerated inside the refrigerator. Concluding that task, he went to his bedroom and began organizing his clothes in the closet and dresser. Afterwards, he organized his hygiene articles in the restroom. When he had done that, he grabbed his laptop and laid down in bed to start writing.

It seemed the trip and the getaway had helped because he was working without issue. He finished the chapter he had been stuck on and started the next. He felt excited and proud he was finally able to concentrate on his novel. It wasn't even midday and he had already concluded another chapter. He sure was on a good streak so he continued working. He occupied his time writing plenty before the sun had gone down. He finished chapter three and was almost half way through chapter four. He was happy but began feeling hungry so he saved his work and shut his computer off. He grabbed his keys and left the cabin to go get something to eat.

Joseph drove over to this restaurant which offered tasty meals at a reasonable price. He went inside and took a seat at the bar so he wouldn't have to wait for a table to empty before getting called. The bartender approached him and handed him a menu at his request. Joseph glanced through the menu and found they were serving their special still. It was a ginormous burger with grade a beef. Topped with nacho cheese, chili beans, bacon, mushrooms, and jalapenos. He waved at the bartender and pointed at his pick. He also asked for a whiskey with soda. The bartender took his menu and went to notify the cook of his selection. She then came back to the bar and served him his drink. She handed it to him and continued attending other guests at the bar. Joseph turned around to look at the people at the place. He sipped on his drink with a smile on his face. He replied to his wife's text and to his oldest son who had sent him a voice message. He turned around to face the bartender and looked up above her. There was a TV monitor which aired a baseball game. He fixed his attention on the game and waited for his burger to be served.

Five minutes went by when he observed the waiter walking towards him with his burger and fries. She placed the plate in front of him and he dug in right away. His taste buds shouted out of joy due to the magnificent flavor of his burger. He took his time after the first three fast bites in order to savor his meal. The bartender came back to him and asked, "Is everything fine? Do you need anything else?"

Joseph replied, "I couldn't ask for a better burger or service. I'm good just like this, thank you for checking in on me."

She uttered, "You're welcome. You look familiar but I know I haven't seen you around here for sure."

Joseph inquired, "Do you like to read horror stories?" as he looked at her and took another bite of his burger.

She smiled and responded, "I actually do. I'm currently reading one called Midnight Terror, but I don't see why you'd answer my question with another question." Then it clicked as she saw him smiling. She continued, "Oh my gosh. You're Joseph Jewel the author of that book and all of my other favorites. I can't believe it. What're you doing out here though? Can I take a picture with you and get my book signed?"

Joseph giggled and commented, "It's me. I'm getting away from the city to concentrate on my next novel. I'll be here for the remainder of the month focusing on work. Go ahead and take your photo and bring that book so I can sign it." She jumped with joy after snapping a shot of him eating his burger while she stretched in to view on the left-hand side of the picture.

She then went to grab her book from the employee's lounge. When she ran back, she handed it to him and he dedicated it to her thanking her for her great service. She was overwhelmed since she was a dear fan of his work and now, she had a book of his autographed with her name on it. She thanked him for the autograph and was called over by another customer to close his tab. Joseph took advantage and finished eating his burger and fries. When she returned, she asked him if he wanted to hang out after she got off work. Joseph said, "As much as I'd love to Blossom, I'm a married man and it wouldn't be correct if I would. I really appreciate the offer and the service but I must go now." He handed her two twenty-dollar bills and told her, "Keep the change. Also, I'd greatly appreciate it if you wouldn't tell anyone I'll be here this month so I could have my privacy without any distractions please."

She uttered, "Thanks but I can't accept your twenty-dollar tip. Here take this twenty back." He pushed it back towards her.

Joseph divulged, "Keep it, you've earned it."

She replied, "Thank you Mr. Jewel and don't worry, I won't let anyone know you're in town."

He then strolled away and out the front door. He got in his truck and went back to the cabin. As soon as he entered his home, he got back to work and had himself a few more drinks. He was exhausted by ten at night. He had made it to chapter five feeling a little drunk and tired. He saved his work and went to bed. During his rest he had nightmares about his story. He first began having visions of the main character haunting him. He then dreamed the character had erased his story off his computer and was unable to rewrite it again.

When he woke up around five in the morning, he was sweaty and felt his body temperature high within his bedsheets. He flipped them off of him and laid in bed looking at the ceiling attempting to recollect his nightmare scenes. He eventually got up and out of bed. He walked to the kitchen to make himself a cup of instant coffee. As he sipped on his drink, he made his way back to the bedroom to open up his laptop and proofread what he had written. His cup fell and spilled, splashing some on his computer and the rest on the floor. He immediately went to grab some napkins and cleaned up his laptop. He then soaked up the rest off the floor. He threw the drenched towels in the trash and got the mop and bucket. He prepped the bucket with chemicals and hot water from the bathroom shower. Joseph moped the floor and as it dried, he got some more napkins and sprayed them with a surface antibacterial chemical. He scrubbed the exterior of his computer with the napkins and was thankful the interior wasn't affected. He then turned on his laptop and made himself another cup of coffee. He was extremely careful this time around as he sat at his desk and began to read his work. He couldn't fathom what had happened. One of his chapters was missing and the others had a slightly different outline than the one he had inputted. He checked through his other files to make sure he was reading the correct one. He realized it was the right story but the wrong words. Puzzled, he pondered if someone had messed with his work. Yet no one was there with him or had access to his cabin. So, he believed he had woken up and sleep walked- well more like sleep wrote. He started editing his work and when he finished, he rewrote the missing chapter. Joseph went on the rest of the day writing until his hunger wouldn't allow him to concentrate. He didn't feel like cooking so he took a quick shower and got dressed. Once he was ready, he left his cabin and got in his truck.

Joseph drove over to a small barbeque shack which had the best brisket in town. He got out of his vehicle and went inside. He ordered some Brisket, potato salad and macaroni. He received his plate and he paid for it along with a large soft drink. He then walked over to an empty table and took a seat. He dug into his meal and glanced at the few people doing the same. He utilized his spare time and called his wife. She was at home taking care of the kids. They had just gotten back from shopping, she had informed. Joseph spoke to his boys one by one and they both told him they missed him around the house. He advised them he did too but that he'd be back in no time if he continued with the same progress. Eventually they hung up since they were going to eat supper. Joseph had himself a smoke outside the shack after his nourishment and then hopped back in his truck after putting it out. He drove back to the cabin.

When he entered the place, he found nothing unusual but as he sat down to write some more, he realized his computer was not where he had left it at. He searched for it and found it on top of the kitchen table. He scratched his head wondering who had gone in while he was out. He checked the back door and double checked the front door to make sure they locked correctly. They did, so he went to verify all the windows were shut and locked. They all were secured and there was no other possible entry point someone could've used to come in while he wasn't there. He concluded he had accidentally moved it himself before departing and since he was hungry, he didn't remember. Anyhow, he thought as he sat back down to continue writing. He had a successful working day and got another chapter done. He thought he'd be able to finish the story on time if he kept the same pace.

As he turned off his computer, he brushed his teeth and hit the sack. He tossed and turned for about an hour, unable to find a comfortable side. He got up and went to the medicine cabinet, reminding himself he had some melatonin there. He took one and went back to bed. Once again experiencing horrific night visions.

Joseph woke up soaked in perspiration gasping for air. The main character of his novel had been choking him in his sleep. He immediately sat up after opening his eyes- breathing oxygen. He stared outside his window and observed a moose walking past his view. He got up out of bed and made himself a cup of coffee. He then took a seat at his desk to proofread his work. After turning on his device, he clicked on a file. His story popped up and he scrolled all the way to the bottom. He then scrolled upward to where chapter six began. That specific chapter was missing. He went through the ending of chapter five and didn't find anything wrong with it. He was a bit upset since he knew he had concluded another chapter and it was now missing just like the previous one the day before. Joseph recalled most of what he had jotted down so he rewrote the entire chapter. From there he continued writing up until he was done with chapter eight. He started feeling hangry and so he paused his work and got ready to grab a bite. He departed his cabin after dressing himself and cleaning up. He got in his truck and took off back into town.

Joseph showed up outside a Mexican restaurant and locked his truck with his key fob as he walked inside the establishment. He went straight towards the back and took a seat at an empty table. There was only an older couple present beside the employees at the place. When the waiter greeted him, he requested a soft drink along with chips and salsa as he continued to glance through the menu. His waiter went to go grab his requests. She returned shortly with his soft drink, chips and salsa. She then asked, "Are you ready to order Sir?"

Joseph looked at her and replied, "Yes, let me get the flautas with everything." The waiter uttered, "Got it, anything else you'd like or need?"

Joseph commented, "No, thank you. Just that."

The waiter stated, "Ok, I'll have that food coming right out. Enjoy the chips and salsa and let me know if there's anything I could help you with." As she turned around and took the ticket to the cook so he could begin preparing the meal.

Joseph gazed outside through the window and observed Blossom walking to her job at the bar and grill. He stood up and sprinted outside to approach her. He shouted out her name and she turned around and waved at him. He crossed the road and asked her, "Did you tell anyone or have you been snooping around my place?"

Blossom made a confused facial gesture and replied, "Excuse me? I don't understand what you're talking about Mr. Jewel. I have not said a word about your visit or even know where you're staying."

Joseph said, "Well I believe someone has been messing with my story. I haven't caught them in the act but they keep erasing chapters and changing the scenes."

Blossom stated, "I'm sorry to hear that Mr. Jewel but I assure you it isn't me or has anything to do with me either."

Joseph told her, "Alright, we'll let it be known I'm armed and will fire upon trespassers." She nodded her head in fear of his threats and walked confusedly to her place of employment.

Joseph headed back to the restaurant where he was at and found the waiter waiting for him with his food at his table. She inquired, "I thought you had done a prank on me for a bit till I saw you coming back inside."

Joseph uttered, "I'm sorry, just want to grab something from my truck." He took a seat and began indulging on his plate.

When he finished eating, he paid and handed the waiter a tip. He then walked out and jumped in his truck. On his way back to the cabin, he stopped at a local gun store to get some ammo for his shotgun back in the cabin. He made his purchase and drove to his home.

When he got back to the cabin, his computer hadn't been tampered with. He grabbed his shotgun from a secret compartment in the wall and loaded it up. He then took a seat back at his desk and continued writing. He wrote well into the night and got another chapter done before falling asleep. He had nightmares again and woke up in the middle of the night. He grabbed his shotgun and cleared all the rooms in his cabin, believing there was an intruder. He then tried going back to sleep.

After about an hour of tossing and turning in bed, he got up figuring he wouldn't be able to sleep more. He made himself a cup of coffee and got back to work. Someone had erased his last chapter again. He was pissed and went outside to see if he could spot footprints on the ground. There weren't any prints and so he called a security equipment distributor and ordered some outdoor cameras. When he hung up, he got back to rewriting the ninth chapter.

After finishing it, there was a knock outside. It was the camera installers. He showed them where he wanted the cameras located and allowed them to get to work as he got back to his. He finished another chapter when the men informed him, they were done. He thanked them as they left. That's when he began getting hungry so he took off to get something to eat.

When he returned from eating, he observed his laptop had been moved. He connected into the cameras and saw no one had come in during his absence. He searched throughout the cabin to see if anything else was misplaced. Nothing else had been tampered with so he got back to writing and wrote another chapter. He got sleepy but he wanted to remain awake during the night to see if he would catch whoever was messing with him. He spent all night watching tv and writing a bit more. At daybreak he couldn't stay up any longer so he fell asleep.

When he woke up, he found his last chapter missing on his lap top which he had left turned on next to his bed. He couldn't conceive what was going on. The same exact cycle continued within the next few weeks. He was almost done with the story but had gone mad and unable to finish. He had become paranoid and developed Insomnia. He also had been drinking a lot of alcohol to try and cope with his incapacity. What follows summarizes the remainder of the story.

Joseph Jewel the world-renowned author who had written countless horror stories. Had an arsenal of diabolical tales at his fans' reach, circulating online and at top notch book retailers. The one he had been currently working on was the first to boggle him. He had experienced writers block mid chapter one. Something he wasn't accustomed to. Stress, fear and anxiety lingered around his career. His publisher pressured him continuously to turn in his next best seller, close to being in violation with his contract by the end of the month. Discouraged, he didn't inform them he was having difficulty jotting down the nonexistent scenes occurring in his mind. He went back and forth for weeks, rewriting and restarting the entire novel. He even got away from his permanent residence and secluded himself in his cabin out in the middle of nowhere to try and concentrate, which he did. Yet something else was going on. Every morning he'd find a chapter missing and things misplaced.

He began drinking excessively to cope with his high cortisol levels. He continued writing what he could off the top of his head. He gave it all he had in the midst of sabotaging his career and reputation. As he wrote his tale, he felt he was going insane. Every time, he proofread what he had previously written, it didn't make sense and troubled him as if someone had messed with his story. He couldn't recall if he had written what was there. The awkward situation persisted for about a few weeks like dejavu. He developed insomnia from the pressure of turning in something to his publisher so they'd let him live in peace and locating the culprit responsible for erasing and editing his work.

One day as he returned home for the holidays, he stopped at a bookstore. He began glancing through some of the novels along the lines of the genre he worked on. He hoped to find something to inspire his progress. He flipped through the pages of one which had caught his attention. One of his fans startled him as she approached him for an autograph. Joseph gladly took the book from her hands. As he was about to sign it, he noticed it was the story he was currently stuck on. He shook his head in disbelief and asked her, "Where did you get this from?" She answered, "Right over there in the newly released best sellers." Pointing at a huge shelf with more of his books.

Joseph signed her book and headed to the stand to grab himself a copy of his novel. He opened it and gazed through the pages. He could not conceive his story was complete and out in the market. He became delusional, running out of the store with his book in hand. He ran to his vehicle and got in. He called his publisher to inquire what the hell was going on. His publisher informed him his book sales were increasing day by day with his new best seller. Joseph hung up on her in disarray. Unable to accept what seemed false to him, he lost his sanity. He assured everyone he knew he hadn't finished such a story. Something no one believed since the actual book stated otherwise.

Evidently, he was enrolled against his will to the looney ward. There he spoke to himself arguing who had written the book. He blended in with the crowd who divulged with themselves most of the day. His career came to a halt with his last novel which had outsold all his previous titles. People who had heard of his current situation and location, flooded the stores to buy his story. They felt something in it was worth reading to figure out why he had lost his mind. The blessings from the sales were not enjoyed by him. His family gained his guardianship rights in court for his incompetence and incapacity to make his own decisions. They spent all his money within a year and filed for bankruptcy. He remained institutionalized at the ward arguing with himself who had finished his story since he hadn't. He also never turned in what he had to have ghostwriters pick up where he had left.

What occurred was, at some point a group of satan worshipers entered his cabin while left unattended. They began summoning spirits and made a connection to them in his bedroom. There was a lost soul in his cabin he was unaware of. As he began writing, the jokester soul began messing with Joseph and his story. It fed on the energy Joseph released from his stress. The novel itself was based on a writer who had writer's block and encountered a demon who haunted him, not allowing him to find the imagination to continue writing his story. Creepy enough, the same entity completed the novel for Mr. Jewel and turned it in ahead of time. Unfortunately for Mr. Jewel, he was unaware of what went on to realize why and how things actually occurred.

CHAPTER 16
DEADLY DELIVERY.

A delivery was registered on Nick's application. He had been parked outside a fast-food chain restaurant waiting for such an instance. He was getting familiar with his new vehicle and messing with the dashboard functions. As soon as the order was made available, he accepted it and drove a few feet to obtain it. He showed the employee at the register his phone and she scanned a code then asked him to drive to the pick-up window. Nick obeyed and when he arrived at the pick-up window, the attendant handed him a bag and a drink. He opened the bag to make sure there weren't any items missing. Once he cleared any diversions, he drove towards his drop off location as indicated on his application.

As he maneuvered his automobile- some car cut him off, causing the drink to spill on the floor. Nick honked at the vehicle, lowering his window down, shouting obscenities and flipping the other conductor. The other motorist felt threatened but was a coward in a hurry so he ignored Nick and sped out of traffic. Nick pulled over into a parking lot and got the drink from the floor mat. He grabbed some napkins from his car and soaked them up. He wiped down as much as he could with what he had and then got back in the driver's seat. He proceeded towards his drop off point. He was a bit annoyed by the other driver who caused him to dirty his vehicle. All the way to the delivery address, he fussed as if speaking to the motorist who cut him off. He imitated punches in the air as if striking him as well. All part of his venting and defusing method.

When he arrived at the client's residence, he parked across the street and observed the home, the neighbors and all his surroundings. He lasted about five minutes in his car, scoping out the area. Something didn't feel right to him since there was vast activity. So, he drove over to the front drive way of the delivery address. He got out of the car and walked up to the front door. He rang the doorbell and placed the bag of food on top of a chair on the porch. He took his phone out and took a still image to prove he delivered the items requested. He then ran back to his vehicle, got in and went back to the area he was previously at.

As he returned to the parking lot outside a shopping center where there were five restaurants, he grabbed a t- shirt from the trunk of his vehicle and finished wiping off the spill on his passenger floor mat. Just as he concluded the task, he received another order confirmation and accepted it, leaving the shirt on the ground. He drove to the establishment where the order must be collected. This particular location required the drivers to enter and pick up in person instead of driving through the drive thru. Nick parked his vehicle in front of the pickup spaces marked with signs and walked inside since he was well aware of the protocol. He checked in with the employee at the register and displayed his phone's screen to her. She scanned the code and handed him the order. Nick obtained it and headed back to his car to drop it off to the client. He jumped inside his vehicle and traveled to the coordinates on his mobile app.

Upon arrival, he parked across the street and scanned the area. The neighborhood seemed quiet and pleasant. He gazed at the address and scouted for cameras along the property. There weren't any video recording devices present. Nick got out of his car and walked up to the front door. He peeked through the window and saw no one in the living room. He walked around the home looking through the windows. He observed a single female in her forties all alone in her bedroom. He opened the bag and added a powder to the food. He walked back to the front door and knocked, took a picture of the order sitting on the ground next to the door then hid behind some bushes. When the woman opened the door, she glanced around and found the bag sitting in front of her. She leaned over and picked it up. She turned around and walked back into her home. Nick quickly and silently came out of the bushes and placed a piece of cardboard wrapped in tape over her door latch. She didn't notice her door was unsecure. Nick observed her take a seat in the living area and opened her bag of food. She set everything in front of her on top of a coffee table. She then began eating her meal. Midway through her feast, she collapsed on her side. Nick took the opportunity to enter her dwelling. He shut the door behind him as he observed the woman lying on the couch on her side unresponsive. She had foam coming out of her mouth and her eyes remained wide open. Nick took her pulse and confirmed she was dead. He then went through her refrigerator and made himself a sandwich.

When he concluded his meal, he removed the order ticket from the delivery bag- placing it in his pocket and disposing of the bag in the trash can. He also grabbed her phone and opened it with her face recognition and erased her order and application. He walked through her home looking for items of value. He gathered some jewelry and dollar bills which were in her purse. He placed every-thing in a plastic bag and made his way out of the home. As he exited- cautiously- he removed his rubber gloves and placed them in his pockets. He ran to his car and jumped in. He turned on the ignition and darted out of the area. He headed back to the shop-ping center for one more order before calling it a successful night.

As Nick got back to the shopping center, there were police units hurling past him in the opposite direction. He presumed they were headed to the woman's residence. As he pulled into the parking lot, he received another order notification. He accepted it and got the merchandise from one of the restaurants. The delivery address was on his way back to his habitat so it worked out for him. He traveled over to the drop off point and delivered the goods. He took a picture and uploaded it to the system after confirming he had completed his delivery. He then got back in his car and headed to his home.

As he entered his dwelling, he was greeted by his dog who was ecstatic to see him. He jumped up on him and licked his face. Nick played with him a little and fed him. He then removed his clothing and washed it in the sink since he felt he smelled like fryer grease from all the deliveries. He dressed in his pajamas and took a seat in front of his computer to log into his social media sites. Nick began scrolling through his news feeds and his dog laid in the hotel bed looking at him. Nick turned on his bluetooth speaker and played some of his favorite music. It must have been a little loud because he heard banging on the wall coming from the room next to his. Nick banged back but didn't lower the volume. He instead continued scrolling through his sites. His dog started barking at the sound of more banging on the wall. Nick decided to put on his head phones instead so the police wouldn't be called to his room. As his music played loud through his headphones, he searched for information on nearby towns and cities. Eventually he felt tired and turned off all his electrical devices. He and his dog fell asleep in bed.

The following morning, Nick woke up at the sound of his dog barking at some chattering outside their room. They were staying at one of the cheapest hotels they could find. So, there was drug and prostitution present. Nick overheard a woman yelping as a man insulted her. Their conversation went mute all of a sudden.

Nick grabbed his phone and saw it was only four in the morning. He put his phone down and fell back to sleep.

A few hours later, he woke up again and this time it was six thirty. He got out of bed and jumped in the shower. When he finished, he got dressed, brushed his teeth and started putting his things inside his car. When he concluded packing up, he grabbed his dog and they headed towards their next stop.

His dog rode shotgun and stuck his head out of the window the whole ride. Nick took a small detour to get something to eat. He stopped at some spot which had a drive thru and ordered some egg burritos one for him and one for his dog. They parked around the corner in order to eat. As they indulged in their nourishment, his dog started barking at some pigeons who were outside gathering, eating something from the ground. Nick told his dog, "Don't pay any attention to the bird's buddy. You eat your food and let them eat theirs." Pointing at the egg in front of his nose.

His dog seemed to have understood. It stopped barking and went back to eating his sustenance. When they finished, Nick tossed out the little he left for the birds. He then got back on the road and continued their journey. His dog looked happy as he let the wind hit his face. Nick had a smile on his visage because of it.

After some minutes, they arrived at some run-down hotel. Nick left his dog in the car and went to check in a room. Inside the lobby there was what appeared to be a female junkie. She kept staring at Nick as he paid for a room. When he received his room card, the woman asked him, "Hey honey, do you need some company? I can keep you cozy if you do?"

Nick looked at her and said, "No thanks, I'd rather not. I have my German shepherd with me for that." He turned around and walked away as the woman replied, "I'll be around in case you change your mind, handsome."

Nick strolled outside the office and went over to his car. He saw some guys congregating near his car, agitating his dog. He froze his steps and turned on the vehicle with the remote fob key. His dog lowered the window and jumped out to chase the men. They all scattered like flies in different directions. He got a kick out of it as he observed the actions first hand.

After a few minutes, his dog returned to him. By then Nick was taking out his belongings out of the car and transporting them to his room. He and his dog made their way up the stairs to room number forty-two. He opened the door and his dog ran in there to clear it out in case someone or something was there. Nick looked around as he placed his things by the bed. The bed itself had some old comforters and it smelled like cigarette smoke. The tv was old but it worked as he found out when he turned it on. Nick went to shut the door as one of the guys who his dog chased ran by. Good thing his dog didn't see him, otherwise he would have stirred trouble for them both. Nick observed how the walls were tarnished. It seemed like what once were white walls had transformed to a cream pigmentation. There were also stains visible which appeared to be blood on the walls and comforter. When he sat on the bed, it squeaked like it was worn out and needed to be replaced. He didn't mind though; he had grown up in poverty with his abusive father. Sleeping on the floor was how he got by during his youth. He checked into his employment application and saw an order available. He took it and left the room with his dog there taking care of his things, should someone break in. Nick turned on his GPS and headed a few blocks down to pick up.

When he got there, there was a short line of customers at the drive thru. He was the third one waiting to be attended. The vehicle in front of him had loud rap music on and it appeared to be three young hispanic men aboard it. Nick avoided eye contact with them since he knew how aggressive they could be. He had been picked on almost all his life in school by hispanics and blacks. The guy in the back seat turned around and saw Nick hiding his face. Then the line moved some and they were next to be served.

As they received their order, the passenger threw something at the attendant. Their car took off and got out of there. Nick was next and drove up. He saw a young female attendant covered in ketchup. She told him, "Those guys just threw ketchup at me! Can you believe it?" She looked embarrassed and upset.

Nick replied, "Why did they do that? Did you tell them something?"

She uttered, "No, I handed them their order and they just threw it at me for no reason! Well actually the one who threw it at me is my ex."

Nick stated, "Well you must have broken his heart or something." She was wiping off the stains on her shirt as she handed him the order without verifying his application.

Nick checked to make sure it was all there and stated, "Thanks, hope you feel better after a while and they don't come back to bother you anymore." She smiled and thanked him as he drove off.

He then made his way to the delivery address on his map. Upon his arrival he parked around the corner. He got out and walked to the front door. He rang the doorbell and took a photo. He then got back in his vehicle and drove back to the hotel, hoping he'd get another delivery notification on his way back, so he could make some extra cash. The universe conspired to grant him not only one more delivery, but five. He went ahead and made all five before the sun set and afterwards, he took a break heading to his hotel room.

His dog was happy to see him. He had defecated on the floor and the room reeked awful yet masking the cigarette aroma. Nick cleaned it up and tossed it in a plastic bag. On his way to throw it in the trash can outside, he ran into the group of guys again. They stared at him in a conflicting demeanor since they didn't recognize him from around the area. He saw them staring and kept his head down to not seem as a threat to them. He got rid of the bag and walked back to his room avoiding eye contact with those guys at all cost. Even though he was a serial killer, he was a coward who hid behind his actions. Which is why he would rather poison his victims than get his hands dirty. He got to his room and opened the door rapidly and shut it even faster. He gazed at his dog and told him, "Your friends are out there again. They said hello." His dog bent its head sideways as if confused.

Nick got on his lap top and checked his email. He was awaiting a response from his previous employer in order to obtain a copy of his w2. He had been waiting for a reply for weeks already. The company had not written back to him or sent him the documents he required. He shut his computer off and laid in bed. He turned on the television set and began watching rerun Cops episodes.

Next thing he knew, he was deep in sleep, envisioning the people he had murdered. Nick woke up to his dog licking his face. He opened his eyes and observed the television was still on. He looked at his cell phone and realized he had slept for about two hours.

He got up out of bed and fixed his dog some food, serving it to him straight out of the can. He then brushed his teeth and left outside to go look for any deliveries. He got in his car, logged into his app and drove down the street where there were plenty of restaurants.

He was about to look for parking when he received a notification of an order in process. He accepted it and drove to the restaurant to pick it up. He veered his vehicle through the drive thru and stopped at the service window. The attendant opened the window, scanned his phone and told him, "Can you do me a favor and park at space number one please?" Nick nodded and cooperated with the request.

He pulled into the spot and placed his transmission in park. He hoped they didn't take long because he wanted to make as much money as he could. Five minutes had gone by as he waited patiently. He got on his phone and started watching videos to entertain himself. Suddenly there was a knock at his window which startled him. He looked up, noticing it was an employee standing outside with the order in hand. Nick lowered his window and received the bags. He thanked the young man and drove to the destination for drop off.

When he got to the neighborhood, he noticed some kids playing in a park. There weren't any adults present monitoring them, but kids weren't on his radar. He was searching for the address since his service was malfunctioning and said he had arrived at his destination yet he hadn't. He drove slowly to the address and when he was right in front of it, passed it and parked two homes further down. He waited and looked around for activity. When he felt there wasn't anyone around, he got out of his car and walked cautiously to the residence. He peeked through the window and witnessed a young man in his late twenties sitting down watching tv. Nick then walked along the side of the house to see if anyone else was present at the dwelling. He went all the way around and spotted no one else inside the house besides the young man. The dog in the neighbor's yard started barking so he held still without making a sound. He then sprinkled the food with a powdery substance. The dog stopped barking and Nick placed the bags on the ground then rang the doorbell after taking a photo and uploading it. He hid behind the pillars of the front porch. The young man got up from the couch and walked over to the front door. He glanced through the window on the door and opened it. He looked around and then got a notification on his phone informing him his food had been delivered. He turned his eyes downwards and spotted the bags. He picked them up and turned around heading inside.

Just as he did, Nick tampered with his door. Nick witnessed the guy sit back down and begin to eat. The guy began to choke and ran to the back of his home. Nick opened the front door and went inside. As he searched for the guy, he heard water running from inside the restroom. Nick opened the door believing the fellow was out. The guy was rinsing his mouth under the sink and saw Nick through the mirror. He turned around and began assaulting Nick. Nick tried running away but the guy knocked him down. They scuffled on the ground and then the guy got up to his feet. He started kicking Nick in the ribs. Nick grabbed the guy's leg and pulled it towards him. The young man fell to the ground, hitting his head on a table. He began bleeding profusely. Nick got up frightened and took off. On his way through the living room, he spotted the guy's phone and took it. Nick ran to his car and jumped in. He turned it on and got the hell out of there before the guy came out of his home to write down his plates.

Nick couldn't believe his mistake. He had adrenaline pumping through his body still even after driving a few blocks away from the delivery site as he removed his mask. He thought to himself that he messed up. He believed the guy was going to call the cops and they'd be out looking for him soon. He tossed the guy's phone out the window and drove back over it to run it over. He then removed his rubber gloves and placed them in his pocket. He began to panic in negative thought. Nick decided to go back to the room and get the hell out of dodge. He failed to know the guy dropped dead as he ran after him.

When he got to the hotel, he ran up the stairs ignoring the guys who were outside hanging around selling narcotics. He got to his room and opened it. He went inside and shut the door behind him. He began grabbing his things and took them down to his car. When he finished packing, he went back for his dog. As he and his dog made it to the vehicle, the guys started yelling things to him. One of them said, "Hey man! Your dog chased us earlier today motherfucker! Did you let him out of your car?"

Another stated, "That's right! Fuck you and your dog. I'm strapped now! Let that fucking dog come near me again and it'll be the last time you take him for a walk alive, pussy!" The other guys laughed as they saw Nick frantically retreating.

Nick put his dog in the car and got in the driver seat. He turned it on and took off as the guys chased him down. They threw rocks at his car. One of them fired a shot in the air to scare him off. Nick ducked after hearing the shot and stepped on the accelerator. The town was hot, crawling with police and criminals all around. It had been a good idea to get out of there for them both. Nick got on the highway and headed north.

When he had left town, he pulled over into a gas station to fuel and to use his GPS. He headed inside after paying at the pump and began fueling. Once inside, he ran towards the restroom to get rid of some urine overload. After finishing, he grabbed some snacks and paid for them at the register. There was a drunk man behind him holding a quart size glass bottle of malt liquor in his hands. The man shouted, "Come on! I'm going to pop this bottle open and start drinking here. I'll probably be done before you ring up this kid!" He chuckled afterwards and Nick turned around to observe him.

The man inquired, "What're you looking at cupcakes? Hurry up and pay so I can get the hell out of here and drink my beer." Nick felt threatened so he handed the clerk a twenty-dollar bill and left without getting his change.

He ran out of the store and by the time he got to his car, the pump had stopped. He removed the nozzle and placed it back in its place. He then got inside his car and drove away. He had set his GPS to the next town and followed directions to another hotel. As he departed the station, he saw the drunk walking around the corner consuming his alcohol. Nick continued driving and traveled all the way to his next location within thirty minutes or less. When he showed up to the hotel, it looked much better than the other one. There weren't any drug dealers hanging out in the parking lot or sex workers. He parked next to the office and got out. He walked inside the reception area and was greeted by the night shift employee. The worker questioned, "Are you looking for a one bed or two bedroom? Smoking or nonsmoking?"

Nick replied, "I need a one-bedroom nonsmoker. The last one I stayed at smelled like an older woman had just smoked a whole carton before I got there." The guy giggled at his remark. The employee went through his computer database and told him, "I've got one available for sixty bucks right now. It's one of the best and cleanest ones we have to be honest. Usually, I save it for families who check in late at night but I doubt anyone will come tonight."

Nick responded, "Thanks for your generosity, I'll take it. Here is my credit card." Handing him his plastic currency.

The receptionist asked, "Oh, you don't have any dogs with you right? We don't allow dogs in that room."

Nick stated, "I don't, beside myself woof, woof!" He chuckled as the employee looked at him weird.

The attendant took his card and swiped it. He then gave him a receipt and an access card. Nick departed the office and went back to his car. He drove closer to the room's location and parked. He then began getting his things out of the vehicle and transported them to the room. He took his dog next- secretly- so nobody would see him and file a complaint. He locked himself inside the room and saw it was just as the employee had described. He turned on the television and observed a movie which was airing. He and his dog started munching on the snacks he had purchased at the gas station. He told his k9, "You can't bark here, ok? You're not supposed to be in here. No woof, woof, ok?" His dog growled.

They stayed up pretty late finishing the flick which had just begun as they tuned in. When it was over, he and his dog crashed out with the monitor on. During the night, he woke up choking his dog since he was having nightmares. He hadn't been diagnosed with PTSD and his childhood traumas continued to surface unwillingly. All that his father had put him through was still present within him. He released his grasp after realizing what was going on. His dog was panting as they went back to bed after he apologized.

The next day, Nick's dog was slobbering all over his face, guarding him as he slept. Nick woke up covered in saliva. He told his dog, "Boy, what the hell is wrong with you? You slobbered all over me." He got up and went to wash up.

When he got out of the shower, he fed his dog and got dressed. He wanted to go get himself something to eat and familiarize himself with the small town.

He made his way to some spot that had a sign up offering the best burritos in town. He had to be consciously frugal with the low cash he had. He drove up their drive thru and got himself a bean and cheese and another of barbacoa with a soda pop to wash it down. After paying and receiving his order, he drove across the street to the public library. He parked his car and began grubbing. He noticed the library employees getting off their vehicles and walking in to begin their day. He hadn't read much in quite some time, so he decided to kill some time after nourishing and find himself a novel to entertain his dome with.

He got out of his car and strolled right into the library. The lovely ladies greeted him as he walked through the front door. He said hello to them and continued making his way around the place. He found some interesting books on psychology and glanced through each one. One of the employees came up to him and asked, "Did you find the book you were looking for? I could assist you if you need help."

Nick replied, "I don't really know what I'm looking for other than to kill some time." He smiled at the woman as he stared into her eyes.

She uttered, "Well killing time is better than killing people, right?" With a smirk on her face.

Nick cracked up and said, "You're funny! Why would you say something like that?" She responded, "Well usually those who read a lot of psychology books are mass murderers. You kinda fit the stereotype too. Young, brittle, caucasian and lonely... I'm just kidding. I actually love to read books about murder." She giggled.

Nick laughed with her and told her, "What if you're correct about your assumption and I'm going to kill you next?"

She stated, "In that case, write down my number and I'll wait for you at home after work all alone and vulnerable." Giggling seductively.

Nick wrote down her phone number. She excused herself and got back to work. He took a seat and began to read the book he had in his hands. He read through the first couple of pages really fast. He had almost forgotten how fast he read. He felt a stare and looked towards his left. He saw the female who gave him her number gazing at him with a smile on her face. He caught her stare and winked at her. She winked back and dropped a book she had in her hands which she was putting back in its assigned location. Nick chuckled and put his eyes back on the book to continue reading. He read about halfway through it and put it back. He then left the library to head back to his room. As he got in his vehicle, he spotted the girl looking at him through the front door. He waved at her as he drove off. She waved back and blew him a kiss.

Nick went ahead and turned on his mobile application for deliveries. As soon as he did, he had some orders pending pickup. He accepted two at once since they were from the same location and near the same drop off point. He drove to the restaurant and retrieved the orders. He then transported the merchandise to the customers. After delivering the food, he went back to his room to check on his dog.

When he got back to the hotel, the manager was outside his room about to open it. He had received a complaint from another guest that he heard a dog barking inside. The guest informed he knocked and waited for someone to open the door but no one was there other than the dog. Nick rushed up the stairs and asked the manager, "What's going on? I'm staying in this room. Why're you trying to go in?" His dog was barking inside.

The manager stated, "I'm the manager of this hotel and I received a complaint of a dog left unattended. Not only is that a violation to the contract for staying in our rooms but a safety and possibly a legal issue." He removed the key from the doorknob since he felt the dog would attack him should he enter.

Nick replied, "I'm sorry sir, but I don't have anywhere to go. I don't have a home of my own and I've been traveling and working as a food delivery guy. Please forgive me and my dog. I promise we won't make a mess and I'll hold myself responsible for anything that occurs in this room."

The manager inquired, "Is the dog trained? Is he tied up and is he in good health?"

Nick uttered, "He is trained. He's not tied up but he's well behaved. He is as healthy as could be."

The manager questioned, "How long do you plan on staying here? I mean, I love dogs myself, that's why I rushed over here as soon as I was informed. If you're not going to stay here long then I could allow you and your dog to stay but only if you promise you won't leave a mess and clean up all the dog hairs."

Nick responded, "Maybe one more day. Like I said, we've been traveling from town to town. I promise and give you my word I will not trash the room and clean up after us."

The manager asked, "Does he have water?" Nick answered, "Yes he does and he ate earlier."

The manager commented, "Alright, I'm going to allow this but don't forget to clean up and not leave a mess or any foul odors."

Nick stated, "You've got my word sir. I will uphold my promise to you and thank you for allowing this to slide." They shook hands.

The manager told him, "I sure hope you do or I'll make sure you won't be allowed in any of our other hotels anywhere in the states. Or any of our other merged company locations." He then departed as Nick nodded his head and gave a thumbs up in accordance.

Nick waited for the man to leave and then he opened the door to his room. His dog jumped up on him and wanted to run outside to see who he was speaking to. Nick shut the door and didn't let him out. Nick told his dog, "Boy you have no idea how lucky we are. We almost got kicked out because of you. You need to be quiet when I'm not here." He pet him and went to use the restroom since his nerves were agitated.

When he came out of the restroom, his dog was there waiting for him- sitting down. Nick petted him again and decided to take a break since his stomach didn't feel so good. Last thing he wanted was to have to use the restroom in an emergency while out on a delivery.

He laid in bed and turned on the television. He flipped through the channels and found the news sharing information to the public of one of his victims. He watched it with a smile on his face. The reporter stated the police had no leads and were asking for the public's help to locate whoever committed the crime. Nick felt powerful as he had never felt his entire life under the tyranny of his father's rage. He had escaped his father's wrath when he fell ill and passed away. They lived in a trailer but it hadn't been paid off. When he died, the bank kicked Nick out into the streets and repossessed the mobile home. He then wandered the streets for years until he found a job. He picked his life back up. He even got himself a car and a place to stay. Yet the remnants of his traumas caught up to him and he eventually lost his employment along with his car and apartment. From there, he hit the streets again. Right before he started killing people to cope with his frustrations of the world. When the news broadcast ended, he took a nap waiting for his stomach to feel better.

When he woke up, it was already getting dark. He had slept through half the day. He got up and took a dump. Afterwards he headed back to the streets to make deliveries and find someone to pray upon. He left his room and locked it up. He walked down the stairs and got in his vehicle.

Moments later he was waiting at the parking lots again to get some orders in. As he waited, the girl from the library had gotten off work and spotted his car. She drove over towards him and startled him by honking. Nick jumped up and looked at the other vehicle about to get triggered. He then noticed it was a woman inside and realized it was the girl from the library. She drove and parked her car next to his, facing him. She asked, "What're you doing over here weirdo? Why haven't you called or texted me?" with a smile on her face.

Nick uttered, "I'm waiting for a customer to order food on the app in order to make some change. I haven't texted or called you because I knew you'd still be at work."

She said, "Oh, why don't you follow me home and forget about deliveries for the rest of the night?"

Nick thought about it and answered, "Ok, lead the way." She drove away and he followed her to her apartment.

When they got to her place, they both got out of their vehicles and walked to her home. She opened it and allowed him inside. She then closed the door and asked him, "What if I was the serial killer they're talking about in the news and you just walked into my trap?"

Nick answered, "What if it's the other way around and you're my next victim?"

She giggled and replied, "It would kinda turn me on. Are you thirsty, want something to drink?"

Nick uttered, "Sure, what you got?"

She walked to her fridge, opened it and said, "I've got kool aid, orange juice, a beer that's like a year old and some milk."

Nick responded, "I'll just have some water."

She closed the fridge and served him some water from her dispenser. She handed him the cup and told him, "You're awfully handsome. Do you have a girlfriend or wife?"

Nick drank and then commented, "Nope, neither but thank you. You're good looking yourself." She blushed.

They kept on talking for almost an hour before she got touchy and so did he. They made their way from her living area to her bedroom where they fucked for hours. When they took a break from sex, Nick admitted to her he was the serial murderer. She didn't believe him so he asked her to accompany him to one of his killings. They both got dressed and took off in his ride. He told her not to worry because he wasn't going to kill her, unless she'd rat on him. She promised not to.

They headed towards the restaurants and he got a delivery. He picked it up and drove to drop it off. When he got to the address, he parked across the street and explained to her what he was doing just as he had done in all his other crimes. She was intrigued and excited at the same time. After clearing the neighborhood and the house for cameras, he told her to get off with him. She did and they both walked over to the house. He showed her how he'd check to see who was inside. Once he verified it was an older man all alone, he went to the front door and rang the doorbell after showing her how he would poison the food. They both hid and observed the man open the door. He grabbed his delivery and walked back in. That's when Nick stuck the piece of cardboard in the door. They then waited for the man to stop breathing as they watched from outside as he ate his food. Nick told her, "It's time, he just dropped dead."

They headed inside and he asked her to help him look for valuables. He took the man's phone and removed the order ticket from the bag. He then placed them in his pocket. They found some things of value and left the house.

She was full of adrenaline. She felt powerful herself and informed him as they drove away. She had become his accomplice and would now be charged with the crime if he'd get caught. He let her know of it. She said she wanted to go with him wherever he went. They skipped town that night, together with his dog.

They went on to a few other towns where they murdered more people. No one had stopped them yet. She learned the tricks and even committed her very own crime. They pawned all the things they had gotten from the last few victims.

Then one day, they got into an argument over who would kill the next person. Nick strangled her to death after they both murdered a woman in her home. He left the girl there and took some cash in hand. When the police investigated the murder, they believed the girl was the one killing and she had finally been stopped. They didn't know that Nick was still out there, hunting for vulnerable customers.

What was supposed to be a fail proof system for both customers and employees, became compromised. A bright individual with malice intentions manipulated the network the delivery company had established for safety. The information on their database was never reported stolen after the real employee had been murdered. The driver's license, insurance, vehicle information and including the bank account to where the monetary deposit was designated to were in the hands of a serial murderer. Nick had killed and disappeared the person whose identity he was utilizing to commit his crimes- the real Nick. The victim had no friends or relatives who questioned his whereabouts or to recommend a welfare check. The perpetrator knew this by going through the deceased's phone and finding no contacts registered other than his employer, bank and grandma's numbers. This facilitated Nick's purpose without raising flags as he continued on his macabre course.

He needed money to survive so he delivered food for customers using the deceased's identity. He would hop from town to town after killing someone as he pretended to be a delivery driver. After marking his potential victim and going through with it, he'd ransack their residence and take any valuables including money. His prey never imagined such a catastrophe as they made business with a reputable company to deliver their goods. He made sure to erase their transactions to include their order from their phones before fleeing the scene. So, when their deaths were investigated, there wasn't any evidence he was there or clues to tail him by.

He was clever enough to search for cameras along his unsuspecting victim's properties before making his move. Only those without cameras would he target. Before finalizing his delivery, he'd park down the street and observe the client's homes. He scooped out the neighborhood also in order for his scheme to work. He only hunted people at night during dark hours to not have witnesses see him clearly in the vicinity. During the day he'd act accordingly so that customers would leave him good reviews. As well as during the night with people he'd eliminate from being his potential marks.

After a few close encounters where he fought some of his victims, Nick took a break from killing. This was after murdering his accomplice. For a few weeks he lived off of what he had stolen and made a few deliveries so as to not raise suspicion. He had pawned and sold most of the valuables he had obtained from the homes of his prey. He kept a low profile at every hotel he checked into.

There were news reports circulating of a possible serial killer on the prowl. They were missing crucial information to really alert the public correctly. He boasted to himself how slick his crimes were and how the police had not apprehended him yet. As cocky as he felt, it had only been mere luck assisting him in the success of his atrocities. It's been said he went back to murdering but no one has come into contact with him. He hasn't been identified nor the public has been advised of his characteristics. So, he's still out there delivering someone's last meal. Lurking and resembling a delivery driver for one of the most reputable food delivery companies. Take precautions to not be next, for he won't discriminate against genders.

CHAPTER 17
THE CURSED TREASURE.

They were ready to head out into the sea. Five friends who were experienced scuba divers, had been waiting for this day to come since the beginning of the year when they made plans for it. Rumor had it, there was a shipwreck out in the bermuda triangle which hid a treasure with enough value to retire off of. They had secured all their diving gear in a boat they rented for the day. When all were on board the vessel, they released the mooring line and departed the marina as joyfully as could be.

They were somewhat terrified they may never return from their expedition as many ships and aircraft had gone astray near the location of their destination. Yet the treasure that awaited them was worth the gamble. Apparently one of them had come across an old map in his great grandfather's attic. His great grand dad was an explorer and scuba diver himself. He had shared countless tales to him as a child of all his adventures but never one where he had found the treasure in the map he displayed numerous times with confidence. The exact map he had found in his grandfather's belongings as he cleared out the attic before placing his property up for sale. He had passed away a few years back and was now with his great grandfather.

They were excited, staring into the vast sea all around them as they had been moving over the water for twenty minutes or so. They looked back at the beach where they had traveled from. There were waves which hit their boat, not allowing it to coast steadily. A pod of orcas swam past them, two jumped in mid air. They were chasing a pod of dolphins. The guys were gazing at the activity taking place under their vessel. There were also seagulls flying over them- close to their boat- looking for unattended food to steal.

After about one hour and a half of commuting, they got to the exact coordinates of the shipwreck. They threw the anchor off and began suiting up into their gear, inspecting it as they did so. All five of them had smirks on their faces. Once ready, they dove into the waters. They dived to the seafloor and began searching for evidence of a wreck. As they looked, they came across a coral reef which housed several types of species of fish not found elsewhere in the world. They observed multiple schools of fish and their colorful skins swimming away from them. There was an array of enchanting life down there for them to gaze upon.

Then one of the guys signaled the others. He had found the ship submerged at the sea bed. It had been partially covered up in sand. As they got closer, they witnessed the elegant decor all around it. It looked old, nothing new whatsoever. They admired the artistic structure undetectable to the untrained eye as they swam along its side. Life had formed around it since it had been there for a long period of time. It was covered in a carpet of algae, corals and other invertebrates. Colonized by large schools of fish who called the wreck home. They took pictures and video with waterproof cameras. One of the men found an opening, leading inside into a chamber. They discussed whether to go in or not with hand gestures. They all agreed to enter and so they did.

As soon as they entered the main chamber, it was pitch dark. One of them saw something moving as he withdrew his waterproof flashlight and turned it on. But there was nothing visible which resembled the dark figure he observed moving rapidly across the chamber as he lit up the area. His pals turned their flashlights on as well. They illuminated all around them as they witnessed first hand what an old ship looked like from inside. They were intrigued with the decor; everything had been intricately designed and now hidden under algae. From the tables, chairs to even the wooden floors and ceiling. They were in awe at the sight their eyes gazed upon.

Soon they began finding relics as they hunted for the treasure. One of the guys located a gold vase stuck between a crevice on the floor. He immediately informed his friends and removed the algae attached to it. They all swam over to him to study the object. They had smiles on their faces, knowing very well they had discovered their first gold piece. They knew they were onto something spectacular which would make them all rich. So, they continued their quest for gold. They started turning things over inside the vessel. Hoping they'd find gold underneath each item they flipped over.

Ben- the guy whose grandfather had the map- felt something touch his leg. He flinched and turned his flashlight to see what it was. He scanned the area but found nothing out of the ordinary. He was shocked since he knew something had clearly touched his leg. He positively concluded it must have been a fish in order to not deter himself from the adventure. He continued looking through things hoping he'd be the one to track the treasure while eliminating the thought of what had just occurred. He remained positive in their quest.

Suddenly, one of his buds swam over towards him. He had located another piece of gold. It was a thick gold chain with a huge ruby pendant. Ben was thrilled with his friends finding. The rest of the guys swam over to see what was going on. They were all amazed at the size of the necklace and pendant. Right then and there, everyone felt confident they'd find more as long as they didn't stop searching. So, they continued looking for more treasures and possibly the biggest load ever recorded in history.

Ben swam inside a room, hoping he'd find the treasure there. He began scavenging through the room's contents. Turning things over and looking between things which were affixed to the boat. There was an old wooden bed in the middle of the room- bolted to the ground. Ben crept under it and spotted something shiny just a hair from his arms reach. He stretched out his arm attempting to retrieve the object but wasn't able to. He then looked for something he could utilize to reach the item under the bed. Scanning his vision all around the room, he spotted a wooden pole. He grabbed it and went under the bed once more to try and get what was trapped under there. When he looked under the bed again, the shiny object was gone and there was a dark figure replacing it. Ben squinted his eyes and rubbed his face mask, attempting to make out the figure. He thought it was one of his pals playing a joke on him at first. He stuck out his middle finger and giggled. Then out of nowhere, the dark figure took him under the bed with lighting speed. Prior to his nabbing, the last thing he saw was some red eyes opening up and staring at him. None of his comrades had realized he was gone as they searched for clues of the hidden treasure.

One of his buddies found a big chest. He had dived in through a large hole, leading all the way down to the bottom of the ship. More than likely the reason behind it's decommission. The chest was secured with an old cast iron lock and he was unable to open it. He tried prying it open but there wasn't much leverage underwater to do so. He knew he had to surface up to their boat and open it there. He signaled to one of his friends with his flashlight, who swam over to his location. They both carried it out of the room where it stood. They all met up at the opening where they had accessed through. One of them conducted a headcount and realized Ben was missing. He signaled to his friends to take the chest up and he and the other guy would search for Ben before heading back up themselves. The two who had the chest made their way out of the wreck. The other two split up and searched for Ben.

One of the guys swam towards the back of the ship and the other towards the front. Lionel was searching for Ben near the room he went missing at the front. He heard and felt the ship shake. He stopped and glanced around to see if he could spot the motive. When he turned around, he saw something moving and heading inside the room where Ben had disappeared. Lionel swam inside the room, hoping it was Ben. He had a smirk on his face eager to inform Ben they had found the treasure. Lionel entered the room which was pitch dark. He scanned his flashlight all around but Ben was nowhere to be found. He then began imagining images of what had happened before the vessel was submerged. He observed the boat intact as it was previously found before the wreck. Pirates were running in and out of the rooms in distress. They appeared to be under attack. Then the images eluded him and reality returned. He went back to searching for Ben. As he swam past a closet, the door opened up on its own. He turned around to see what was inside and vanished as something yanked him in. The dark figure had taken him too.

The other guy who was searching also, went from room to room. He too was excited to tell Ben they had secured the treasure chest. He exited the chow hall and swam towards the back of the boat. He looked at his oxygen tank gauge and noticed he had seventy percent left. He entered another room and saw a dark figure sporadically moving towards him. He shut the door and swam away rapidly full of adrenaline and freight.

The other two who had taken up the chest to the boat, had just surfaced above the water level. One of them got on the boat and grabbed a rope to tie the treasure with so they both could pull it upward as the other remained in the water holding it so it wouldn't drop back to the sea bed. The one on the vessel tossed the line over and the one in the water began to tie the chest with it. Once he had managed to tie the treasure, he climbed on board the boat. Just as he got on, a gray white splashed out of the water, missing him by a few seconds. The hair on the back of his neck erected as he realized how close he had come to becoming the shark's meal. After removing their gear, they began pulling up the chest. It took them all their effort and strength combined to get it inside the vessel. Once it was on the boat, they didn't find anything to pry it open with. Eventually they gave up, knowing they'd have to return to land in order to find something to break in with. They realized their crew hadn't surfaced and they had been out of the water for approximately ten minutes. Don informed Peter, "I'm going to head back down to look for the others. I'm confused as to why they haven't come up yet."

Peter said, "Let's just leave them out here and leave with the treasure. We'll split it in half between us."

Don replied, "Are you crazy? Betray our friends like that and not care to leave them behind without anything to fend for themselves? You saw how that gray white tried to eat me and you want to abandon them with it nearby? No way. Matter of fact, thanks for sharing your intentions. I'll be taking the boat keys with me so you won't leave without us." He grabbed the keys and started dressing back into his scuba gear.

Don sat on the edge of the boat looking at Peter trying to mess with the chest still. He knew he had to find the others and get back up there faster than Peter would find a way to double cross them. He jumped in the water and swam down to the wreck. As he descended, he followed the anchor cable downward to the wreck. He was almost halfway there when a whirlpool caught him by surprise and pulled him down. He was stuck in the current which hurled him uncontrollably for about three minutes. Then as the whirlpool seemed to be losing strength, the dark figure nabbed him. He attempted to swim upward but the figure yanked him the opposite direction. He was taken back to the shipwreck by the dark figure who didn't seem to want them leaving. The dark figure stabbed him with a golden sword while submerging him back to the wreck. He died instantly as he bled out.

His blood attracted sharks to the location. There were about five great whites swimming around the vessel. They followed the blood scent and began fighting each other. They found Don's body and shred it to pieces as they feasted on it. The blood trail they created, lured in more sharks. The shipwreck was now surrounded by sharks in search of more edibles. Peter was up on the boat attempting everything possible to crack the chest open. He was arguing with himself since he had cut his hand while lodging a knife in the keyhole to the lock. He shouted, "Fuck! I fucking cut myself. I have to find a way to open this and take some things for myself. I can't allow the others to receive a fair share when I was the one who found this in the first place. Fuck them! What have they ever done for me?" He scattered throughout the vessel in search of the first aid kit.

He was able to locate the first aid kit and opened it. He retrieved some alcohol and gauzes to clean and cover his wound. As he wrapped up his hand, he felt the boat jolting. A shark had slammed into the vessel as it ran from a much larger one trying to bite it. Peter grabbed a hold of the steering wheel to not lose his balance and fall overboard. He saw the shark swimming around the boat. He uttered, "I hope you ate Don! You're not going to eat me for sure! Stupid shark!" He then made his way back to the historical safe.

Louie, the last guy down at the shipwreck who remained alive, had found the entrance to the wreck. He was still swimming away from the dark figure who chased him. As he got to the opening and exited halfway outward, he spotted a great white swimming around. He quickly grabbed a hold of the edge of the hole and paused. He looked back to see if the figure was still pursuing him. It had disappeared and was nowhere to be found. He was terrified, not only was the dark figure around but there were sharks surrounding the site. He was trapped from both angles. He peeked outside and continued to observe several sharks swimming around. He began praying, "Dear heavenly father who art in heaven, please allow me to be safe and get out of this one in one piece. May you deflect whatever that is following me in this boat and deter the sharks so I could make an escape back to the boat. I also pray that all my friends are well and alive, for I've lost contact with them. Please forgive me for all of my sins which I repent and regret. Thank you for all you've done in my life. I place all my faith in you and know you will allow me to get back home safely." He then opened his eyes and saw the sharks weren't there anymore.

Peter was still on the boat trying to open the treasure chest. He had found a fire extinguisher inside the vessel and was colliding it over the lock. He turned around and observed the shark's fin creeping out of the water. He yelled out, "Leave me alone motherfucker! Go find someone else to fuck with! I'm going to shoot your ass with the emergency flare gun aboard if you keep circling the boat!"

He returned his attention back to the lock. He hit it hard and the fire extinguisher busted open, expelling its contents all over him. He lost his balance and fell over to the water. He rapidly swam up to the vessel's edge and grabbed a hold of the side. He turned behind and saw the shark's fin approaching. He immediately began pulling himself up aboard. The shark closed in with its mouth wide open, displaying its razor-sharp teeth. Just when the shark was about to rip him apart, he managed to climb back to the boat. He turned around to look at the shark and screamed out, "I fucking told you; you weren't getting me! Ha, ha, you fucking ginormous Meat-eating fish! Fuck you and all your kind! Kiss my ass mother fucker!" As he tossed the empty fire extinguisher at the great white.

Louie believed this was his final shot to get back to the boat. He turned around and observed the figure reappear and heading his way. He swam out of the ship and headed upward following the anchor cable. Adrenaline was racing through his body. He felt like turning back to see if the figure was chasing him still but was scared to do so. He continued swimming upwards in a hurry. He saw a shark up above him but it seemed to be preoccupied with something else to notice him. When he finally made it up, he climbed up the boat without the shark realizing so. He saw Peter trying to open the chest. He told him, "Boy am I glad to see you. Where's Don? I couldn't find Ben and lost sight of Ed.

There was this dark figure in the ship chasing me. I wonder if it got Ben and Ed?" Peter answered, "Don dove back in and said he was going back for you all. He hasn't resurfaced. What is this figure you're mentioning to me?"

Louie stated, "I don't know what it was but it looked scary and chased me like it wanted to kill me or something. I wonder if it got a hold of Ed and Ben. Are you sure they haven't come up here?"

Peter replied, "I don't believe in ghosts, spirits, monsters or supernatural entities. So as much as I'd like to believe your story I can't. But yeah, besides Don, no one else has returned up here. I've been trying to crack this thing open. That fucking shark circling the boat almost ate me earlier. I fell overboard after I popped open the fire extinguisher on the lock. You sure you didn't run into Don and maybe he told you something?"

Louie uttered, "That's crazy bro. I was glad the shark didn't get me. No, I didn't see Don at all down there or on my way back up. How long had he gone back down before I came up?"

Peter commented, "Yeah, crazy. He had left maybe about ten minutes or so before you got here. I don't know, maybe the shark got him? Anyhow, what do you say we get out of here and head back to the marina?"

Louie exclaimed, "Negative brother, we need to wait for the others to come back.

We can't just take off and leave them. Are the keys here still anyhow?"

Peter responded, "I'm having a panic attack due to the shark man. I want to get the hell out of here and never return. We already found what we came for. I don't think the others are alive. Don took the keys with him though, and said he didn't trust me here alone with the chest."

Louie said, "That's strange, man. He said he didn't trust you alone and took the keys? How're we supposed to get back now?"

Peter replied, "Beats the fuck out of me. I think I could hot wire the ignition. If I've done it to cars before I'm sure it shouldn't be that hard to do on this. I just haven't tried it yet, been busy with this chest. Maybe you should go back down there and try to locate the guys while I tamper with the ignition?"

Louie stated, "It would be pointless to head back there to search for them. I have a feeling the figure got them or like you said, maybe a shark did. All I know is I'm not leaving this vessel anymore. I'd say it's your turn but I'm not pressuring you because of the dangers lurking in the water."

Peter uttered, "Well then why don't you try and open the treasure while I mess with the ignition? In the meantime, hopefully the others come back." Louie agreed and walked to the chest to try and unsecure it as Peter tampered with the ignition, as he thanked God for allowing him to survive through his encounters.

Peter began removing the steering shaft cover and exposing the electrical wires. He grabbed the knife he used to attempt opening the safe with and began splicing the wires. Louie was observing the chest and figuring out how to open it. He searched around the vessel to locate something he could use as a tool. He began lightly tapping the padlock with the corner of a cooler he had carried along with him in the voyage. He believed if he did so, eventually the lock would open gradually. He looked over at the shark still circling the vessel and told Peter, "I see why you're scared of this relentless man eater. It's still swimming around us, hoping one of us falls into the water to be his diner."

Peter replied, "Why don't you plunge into the water and find out for sure?" Sarcastically speaking.

Louie uttered, "Nope, I'm good where I'm at right now. Maybe you should swim with it and find out how heartwarming it really is. For all we know, it probably just wants a hug?" Chuckling afterwards.

Peter responded, "Well you're more affectionate than I am to go give it a hug, don't you think? I mean, as much as I'd like to test your theory, I'd rather not. I didn't come all the way out here to be eaten by a great white." He suddenly got the boat running.

Peter was proud he had managed to intertwine the ignition wires and gotten the vessel up and running. Just as he began to hit the throttle, the engine sputtered and shut off. He then threw a fit exclaiming, "Fuck man! Come on fucking boat. I don't have the keys to open sesame for you or the chest. I'm only trying my best with what I have." With frustration in his voice as he went back to messing with the wires.

Louie asked him, "Does it have enough gas?"

Peter answered, "Yes it does. I think I may have caused a short circuit with the wires but I'm going to keep messing with them. Did you get that treasure chest open already?"

Louie replied, "Bro, you seriously believe we have the proper tool to crack this safe open? There's nothing in this boat that'll help open it up. We need to get back on land and get a hold of a grinder, torch or a sledge hammer." He had halted his effort in opening it and looked underwater, hoping he'd spot their friends swimming up.

Peter commented, "Yup, that's exactly what we need to open that thing. Can you come over here and give me a hand?"

Louie said, "Sure, what can I help you with?" As he walked over to the captain's chair.

Peter divulged, "You see these two wires I'm holding? I need you to keep them together as I hit the throttle and make this thing turn on."

Louie responded, "Ok, hopefully it works and the boat turns on.

In the meantime, I wish the others would surface." Peter got the engine turning again and leaped in joy. He handed Louie a roll of tape he found in the first aid kit and told him, "Grab this tape and wrap the wires so they don't come loose."

Louie grabbed the tape and began wrapping the wires as he questioned Peter, "Are you leaving the others behind? Maybe we should toss the life jackets over at least in case they do return? I could write a message and leave the flare gun attached to one of the floating devices."

Peter uttered, "I don't want to leave without them but I also don't want to be out here longer. I think that's a great idea bro. Go ahead and write that message and toss the life jackets over."

Peter left the engine running so he wouldn't have to mess with it again. He observed Louie writing notes on the life jackets and tie the flare gun on one. He then helped him toss the jackets over into the sea. When they had finished, Louie spun around to look at his pal who had a different plot in mind. He pushed Louie over into the water. Louie fell in the water and saw the shark swinging by. He swam up and when he surfaced, he shouted, "What the hell is wrong with you man? Why'd you toss me overboard with the shark?"

Peter stated, "I'm claiming the treasurer all to myself! I found it and don't want to share it with any of you all!"

Louie tossed a life jacket near the shark to grab its attention as he swam towards the vessel and replied, "I could care less about the treasure bro. Help me get back up and take me with you." He grabbed a hold of the boat and was unable to see what Peter was doing.

Peter had hit the throttle and the vessel began to move. He didn't care to help Louie up. Just as he was about to pick up speed, the boat stopped abruptly. He had forgotten to reel back in the anchor. He was sent flying over and plunged into the water.

He grabbed the shark's interest and it swam towards him. The shark began circling him right before it attacked.

Louie was still holding on to the boat and climbed over. When he made it safe back inside the vessel, he looked over at the water filled with blood from the shark attacking Peter. The scene was gory so he turned around to preserve his state of mind. The engine had turned off but he wasn't even thinking of that at the moment. He was in shock at why his friend had pushed him overboard and was about to abandon him. He felt redeemed and merciful he was still alive. Although Peter had been consumed by the shark and the rest of his friends had not returned, he breathed still. He began praying and looked over into the water. He noticed more sharks in the area and knew he'd have to be very careful to not fall over. When he concluded his faithful approach, he stood up and began pulling up the anchor with a motorized pulley system. He then went under the steering shaft and messed with the cables himself. After the anchor resettled in its place, he managed to turn the engine on again. He was thankful to be well. He hit the throttle and started making his way back. He hadn't navigated much when the boat was ripped apart in half. He fell into the water and before any of the sharks got a hold of him, the dark figure had nabbed him. Louie observed the treasurer chest falling down back to the ship wreck as the dark figure sliced his belly open with its majestic sword. The sharks began tearing his flesh apart after he bled into the sea. The dark figure vanished back into the wreck. What it wanted was the treasurer not to leave its sight.

All five men went missing and after not reporting back to the marina with the rental boat, the owner of the vessel went out to look for them. He searched tirelessly but didn't locate any sign of them the following day. He notified the coast guard of the occurrence and suspected the guys had disappeared and were probably in danger. When the coast guard made contact with the man, they searched for the boat and the occupants but came back empty handed. They weren't able to find a trace of the vessel but did locate the life jackets with the message and flare gun. They never sealed the case after not locating any survivors or the boat.

The dark figure who killed the group of friends was the spirit of a pirate. This particular pirate and his men had attacked a kingdom centuries ago. They stole the king's gold and murdered him along the way. This gold treasure had been fought over in numerous battles throughout history. Every single person who obtained it in their possession, died. As if the treasure was cursed.

When the pirates made it back to their ship, they pulled the chest up and set sail. They embarked the seas heading back to their island. Halfway to their destination, a storm changed their course. Lightning struck their boat setting the middle on fire. That caused a massive hole and their vessel to sink. When they submerged underwater, all of the pirates died. The captain pirate held on firmly to the steering wheel as his ship sank to the bottom of the sea. He was a greedy pirate and had left a violent reputation for he and his men. They had murdered hundreds in their lifetime for one thing or another. His greed was what propelled his soul to not allow anyone to remove his stolen treasure from the shipwreck. A story Ben's great grandfather knew very well yet failed to advise Ben of.

CHAPTER 18
THE KILT.

Alex loved to shop at the thrift stores. There wasn't anything as fascinating to him as looking at articles which had belonged to somebody else. They had a story to tell and he dwelled on each piece he acquired. Imagining and fabricating his own conclusions. He was frugal when it came to things he purchased. A character he developed at an early age due in part because he came from a low-income family who scraped by feeding eight on the great depression era meals.

Some of his friends and relatives criticized him since he was able to afford new merchandise without the need to buy used things. He had also convinced some to follow his strategy and save up as much currency for retirement or to make large investments or purchases. He had plenty of funds in his bank accounts and stashed in his home. He also had made several investments throughout his life. He owned three homes, two which he rented and two businesses all which brought in revenue.

So, there he was at the thrift store glancing through goods on display. He was currently gazing at the books. He had an extensive collection of novels in his library and read them all more than once. A passion he also developed as a kid who had no means to escape reality with cheap entertainment other than reading stories. He loved a good tale, especially those which depicted a life from rags to riches. He also admired autobiographies with similar plots. He grabbed a few books after reading the back cover and being enticed by the compendium, placing them in his cart and moved along.

He stopped at the movies section and began going through the DVD's. He also enjoyed collecting old flicks which he grew up watching. He carried a list in his cell phone of those titles not in his possession. He hadn't been to this particular store in about a month and they had restocked new items from the last time he was there. He found a disc on his list and added it to his cart. He continued searching through the selection of used films. Spending about fifteen minutes there before continuing elsewhere. After scanning through DVD's, he headed over to the men's clothing aisles. The weather at his city had been nippy so he searched for a sweater. Flipping through the large outerwear, he found himself a cozy one. He placed it inside his cart and continued looking through the rest. As he inspected another one- which seemed more adequate for his style- he picked up the one he had in the cart. While comparing them side to side, he realized the one he previously got had a permanent stain and placed it back on the racks.

Alex spent about an hour and a half at the second-hand store before proceeding to the checkout aisle. As he stood in line waiting for the register to clear up from customers in front of him, he recalled he wanted an extra quilt. The one he had been sleeping with needed to be cleaned and was beginning to tear, becoming flimsy after being washed often. He left the line and darted to the comforter section.

When he was in front of the bedsheets, he started shopping for one. There were plenty of them out on display since the weather outside was their marketing tool for a quick sale. He had a king size comforter in his hands and was inspecting its quality. The first issue was its color and then the material it was composed of. It was manufactured entirely of polyester as identified on the label. The material itself was enough to put it back and continue searching since he was allergic to polyester. Eventually he found a quilt. It was the exact size he required and a color he could work with- being gray. It was made of cotton and seemed old yet in great shape. He began wondering how many people had slept in it during the course of its existence. He caught himself needlessly dwelling on the quilt's history and snapped out of it. He placed it in his cart and headed back in line to pay.

When he strolled back in line, there was only one individual in front of him. She was a senior citizen who required help. Alex volunteered and assisted her with scanning her pickings. The woman was technologically illiterate so Alex guided her through the process. When she finally received her receipt, she thanked him and walked off. Alex began scanning his items and bagged them. He paid, pulled off his receipt and headed to his vehicle.

From there he decided to go to his friend's home. His pal lived approximately five minutes away from the thrift shop. Before heading over there, he made a stop at the bank. He wasn't there to make any transactions or deposits though. He went to grab some free coffee. He served two cups, one for him and one for his pal. The manager and tellers already knew him and didn't bother since he was a customer. He greeted the employees by name and departed the facility. He got back in his car and traveled down the street to his buddy's pad.

When he arrived at his friend's residence, he parked in his driveway since there was room for two vehicles and he only had one. He got out of his ride and walked to the front door. He rang the doorbell and waited patiently for his bud to let him in. Xavier opened the door and greeted Alex with, "What's up thrift hunter. Got us some free caffeine from the bank again? Come in, hope you're not here for a free meal. It seems as if you smell me cooking or something. You always show up at the exact time." He chuckled.

Alex entered and stated, "I did get us some free coffee but then again it isn't. I had to open an account at the bank for it. What're you cooking? I'm hungry and was debating whether to stop by my moms, knowing she probably made some frozen burritos or come see the chef in action." They walked towards the kitchen after Xavier locked up his front door.

Xavier replied, "You're lucky I actually like you enough to feed you bro. I don't even feed the one night stands I catch at night... I'm making some molletes with a sunny side up eggs over them. With a red chipotle salsa and muenster cheese to top them off."

Alex's mouth watered and uttered, "Damn! That does sound more delicious than what my mom is probably eating right now." Laughing afterwards.

Xavier commented, "That's the difference between me and your mom. I really love you and your mom only loves you for mother's day." followed by laughter from both.

Alex responded, "You're right, that's about the only time I see her smile. When I take her out to eat with coupons and give her something I bought at the thrift shop." Giggling.

Xavier handed Alex a plate as he sat at the kitchen table. He then served himself one and sat across from him. They both ate their food and drank their coffee. Alex began shouting out, "Hey boy! This salsa is hot. Where'd you get the peppers from, hell?" Getting up to grab a water bottle.

Xavier told him, "I sure did. It's really good though, isn't it?"

Alex sat back down and answered, "I got a hint of roasted chipotle, onions, garlic, tomatoes and cilantro but just a hint since its main ingredient is flames from satan himself with a dash of dragon's cough."

Xavier said, "It's free though," Laughing out loud then continued, "Don't complain and eat your food chicken turd. Sometimes when you're out being a cheapskate, you can't ask for gold without even putting in coal."

Alex continued eating his food uttering, "Maybe you made it hot on purpose knowing I was coming over. You probably don't want me eating up all your food with my stingy ass huh?"

Xavier mentioned, "How'd you know? On top of saving money on used merchandise you mean to tell me you read minds?" Chuckling.

Alex stated, "As much as it appeals to be able to read minds, I wouldn't want to. I can only imagine reading yours and the deception I'd obtain from doing so." Smiling afterwards.

Xavier replied, "If you would be able to read minds, you'd know I'm thinking how fortunate you'd be if they served food at the thrift stores. Second hand food acquired from donations. I'm sure then you'd stop being my friend and coming by."

Alex uttered, "You're funny bro. You actually believe I only come to eat your food and if not, I'd stop being your friend and visit? I also come to use your Wi-Fi." Laughing out loud.

Xavier told him, "Yeah, I wouldn't doubt it when the benefits stop so would your visits. Anyhow, what did you get at the store today Mr. Second hand hunter?"

Alex answered, "Found me a couple books, a DVD, a sweater and a quilt." Xavier responded, "Well bring that DVD over here so we could watch it."

Alex had finished eating and since his pal requested to see the DVD, he went outside to his car to grab it. He returned to his buddy's house and popped the disc inside his DVD player. They both sat down to watch the film. Xavier was between observing the flick and texting some of his girls. He had no plans on settling down-ever and kept his options open but never his heart.

During the movie, Xavier got up and made popcorn. One of the females he spoke to wanted to go over but he let her know he was busy. When the popcorn was ready, he removed it from the microwave and served it in a bowl. He then went to sit back down to watch the film. Alex grabbed some popcorn and continued enjoying the flick he had once seen as a child, sitting outside a movie drive-in since he had no cash to enter. That was the first memory that arose in his mind. How he gazed outside the drive-in, sitting on top of a tree to get a good view of it along with his older brothers who were the ones to teach him how to watch films for free. He sure had come a long way from his indigent childhood. He shared the story of when he first watched the movie to his friend. Xavier told him, "That's crazy bro, but you've succeeded and don't have to be frugal anymore. But I get it, sometimes we grow up but don't grow out of old habits. I've got my own to be honest so I can't judge you."

Alex smiled and returned his gaze at the movie as he consumed popcorn. His friend went back to texting another chick as he glanced at the film every now and then. Alex felt nostalgic and couldn't contain his happiness. He recalled how the little things in his childhood made him happy and they still had that effect on him. He wasn't one to ask for more and was content with minimum. He didn't climb trees to see big screen films anymore though. It had been many years ago but still made him smile instead of complaining as he remembered his past.

When the movie ended, Alex said bye to his pal who was getting ready for some girl to go over. He ate the last of the popcorn in the bowl and headed outside. Xavier told him, "Thanks for swinging by bro. The movie was cool. I hadn't seen it before. They sure don't make them like they used to anymore. Take care now and see you some other time." He shut the door after Alex shook his hand and left.

Alex got in his car and received a call from one of the tenants residing in one of his rental properties. She was informing him that her sink had broken. She claimed it was leaking and her water bill might be high if he didn't fix it. Alex told her he'd be there shortly to check it out. He knew exactly what she was talking about and made a quick stop at the hardware store to buy a gasket. That was his next destination after driving out of his pal's drive way.

When he got to the hardware store, he exited his vehicle and walked towards the entrance. Outside the store, some kids had set up a hot chocolate stand to sell for a non- profit organization. Their posters said their team needed to raise money for new equipment and to cover their travel expenses. Alex approached the stand and asked one of the kids if he could have a free sample in order to know if he'd like it or not. The kid served him half a cup and handed it to him. Alex walked off without buying anything from them.

He went inside the hardware store and walked straight towards the plumbing aisles. He went through the merchandise on a wall where they had replacement parts and found the gasket he needed. He then headed towards the checkout and paid for the part. He grabbed his receipt and walked outside. Normally he wouldn't buy things he didn't need but the kids made him feel bad he didn't help and so he went to purchase a cup of hot chocolate from them. When he received his cup, he thanked them and so did they. He walked back to his vehicle and went inside. He placed the hot chocolate in his center console and the bag with the gasket on the passenger's seat. He then headed to his rental property.

When he arrived at the home, he exited the car with an empty cup. The hot chocolate was delicious and he drank it during the drive. He took down the cup to toss in the woman's trash can. He opened his trunk and retrieved his tool bag. He then walked up to the house. He knocked on the window and a few seconds later, she opened the door and allowed him entry. He greeted her and made his way to the restroom. When he got there, he threw away the cup in the trash and got to work. He shut the water valve under the sink and dismantled the faucet. He removed it and replaced the gasket. He tossed the old one which was torn and obviously the problem. He then reassembled the faucet back how it was and turned the water back on. He opened the faucet and witnessed everything back to normal- problem solved.

He then headed back to the living area to inform the tenant he had fixed the issue. She thanked him and he walked out of the house and back inside his car. After telling her, "You're welcome, ma'am. Good thing is I know a thing or two on how to fix things from growing up poor. That way I save money on calling a plumber to do what I could do myself."

Alex drove to his residence afterwards. He made a quick stop at the library to pick up a free copy of today's newspaper. He grabbed it and went back to his car. The library was down the street from his dwelling. He got home in no time and as he entered his front door, he was spooked by his girlfriend who surprised him with an unexpected visit. She was hiding behind the couch and jumped up from behind it as Alex walked by to place his purchases on the kitchen table. Alex swung at her not knowing what scared him. He missed her by inches as she laughed at him. She then ran into his arms and embraced him. She told him, "I missed you sweety. What did you do all morning long? I've been here for about an hour or so."

Alex answered, "I went to the thrift shop and got these things here. Then I went to the bank and stopped at Xaviers. Had breakfast with him and watched a movie. Then I had to go fix a faucet at my rental property. I just finished that not long ago and got the paper before I came home. What about you, what have you done all day?"

His gal- Marisol uttered, "I woke up late and missed my job interview. Then I showered, got ready and came over here to surprise you but you weren't home. I came in through the back since I know your door doesn't lock and have been waiting here patiently for your arrival. I was going to call you but figured you wouldn't take long to get back. Let me help you put away your things." She grabbed the bags and removed the contents inside.

Alex inquired, "And you didn't make something to eat while you waited? Not even coffee?"

Marisol uttered, "I ate one of your yogurts and a banana. I was about to make a pot of coffee when I heard your car pull in. I can still make it for us since I know you probably need a refill to re-energize by this time."

Alex replied, "Ok, make some meanwhile I put all this stuff where it goes." He took his items from her arms and walked towards the back of his house with them.

When he got back, he hugged Marisol from behind and kissed the back of her neck. She loved it when he did that and turned around to kiss him back. They smooched until the coffee was ready. She poured him a cup and then herself. They sipped their hot drink sitting down at his table as he read the newspaper and she glanced at the back of it. When he concluded the paper did not have any vital information, he put it down over the table. Marisol was staring at him and he knew what her facial expressions read. He got up and took her to his room. They had sexual intercourse for roughly half an hour and then laid in his bed- naked watching television. Alex took a nap after observing a soap opera she tuned in to.

When Alex woke up, Marisol had reorganized his things, washed his sweater and quilt and cleaned up his place a little. He thought she had left but she was in the kitchen washing dishes as he rose out of bed. He realized so when he walked out of his bedroom and found her there. He helped her rinse the ones she had left. She asked him, "Did you rest well baby?"

Alex answered, "Yes, I did darling. What time is it? I think I might have overslept."

Marisol laughed and uttered, "It's three thirty. You slept for about an hour and a half. So, I cleaned up for you baby."

Alex uttered, "Damn, felt like I slept till five. Thanks darling, you didn't have to. You're so attentive and I love that about you."

He kissed her as they finished putting away the clean dishes and cleaning the sink.

Marisol blushed and replied, "I love you baby. Are you hungry? I can make you something to eat?"

Alex told her, "I'm a bit hungry. How about we cook something together?"

Marisol agreed and they began looking through his refrigerator and pantry to see what they could make. He had some steaks, pasta, alfredo sauce, bread and vegetables to make a salad. They began making steak alfredo, toasted bread with butter and garlic powder. Alex took the meat out and placed it in the sink under lukewarm water to defrost. Marisol grabbed a pot and filled it up with water to boil the pasta. She set the pot of water over the stove top and added the linguini. When the steaks defrosted enough for him to separate apart, they both began chopping them up into pieces. Alex then grabbed a skillet and set it on the stove. He turned on the pilot on medium setting and added some olive oil. When the skillet heated up, he threw the beef inside. He then grabbed some steak seasoning and slightly smothered the steak with it. The pasta had boiled. Alex grabbed a string then tossed it on his kitchen cabinets to see if it would stick. It did so he turned off the pot and placed it aside. Marisol was toasting four slices of bread at a time in the toaster and chopping up the salad. Alex let the beef cook thoroughly since Marisol didn't like hers rare. As the steaks cooked, Alex grabbed the pot of pasta and drained the water out. After doing so, he placed it back over the stove. When the meat was ready, he added the alfredo sauce and mixed it all up adding italian seasoning to it. Once it boiled, he added it to the pot with the pasta and mixed it up. He then grabbed two plates and served equal amounts. He covered the pot and walked to the table with the plates in hand. He set them down and Marisol served salad on each, placing the bread with butter and garlic powder in front of them. Alex served them a glass of red wine and handed Marisol hers. They both took a seat and dug in after a thankful prayer. Marisol said, "I love this idea. I've never had steak alfredo with the bread and salad, oh my gosh, delicious. Where'd you learn this from?"

Alex answered, "It did come out very good huh? I learned it on my own after having it at some Italian restaurant once. Your salad came out great and so did the bread."

Marisol replied, "Thanks but it's your credit not mine. I just followed your instructions." Alex uttered, "Well you followed them correctly." They continued feasting.

When they finished, they put the leftovers in tupperware and washed the skillet, pot, glasses and utensils they used. Alex asked her if she wanted to watch a movie and she agreed. They took a seat in his living area and he turned on his tv set. He searched through his apps and found one which aired new ones. He flipped through them and located one they both hadn't seen and knew they'd enjoy. He paid to watch the film using his remote control. Marisol got comfortable putting her head on his shoulder and her feet over his legs. They went silent when the flick started.

During the middle of the show, Marisol got up to make some popcorn. She sat back down in her previous position with a bowl of cooked kernels. She raised the bowl in front of Alex to see if he wanted some but he refused since he had some earlier at Xavier's. He did though interrupt her comfort to grab a drink. While he served himself a beverage, Marisol asked him if he could pour her one as well and hand her the hot sauce. Alex was managing everything as he glanced back at the screen to not miss the scenes. When he finished, he walked back to the couch and sat down. Marisol took the hot sauce from him along with her drink. She placed her beverage on top of a coffee table next to the couch and shook the hot sauce bottle over her popcorn. She then placed the hot sauce next to her drink and got comfy once more. They continued enjoying the film until it ended.

When the movie finished, Marisol headed to her home. Alax had a rule at his that no female was allowed to sleep over. He didn't want any female objects left behind as well. His ideal relationship was for them to live separately and not together. He had several bad experiences and derived a new relationship formula which best suited him. Before she left, she gave him a kiss and a hug. She thanked him for dinner and the movie. She also told him she'd be back the following day. She walked away, headed towards her automobile which she parked down the street to scare him.

Alex shut the front door to his place and locked it. He went to his bedroom and got on his computer to check on the status of his financial investments on the stock market. When he caught up on his earnings and losses, he shut his computer off and went to his restroom. He brushed his teeth, washed his face and hands. Afterwards, he went to his bedroom and removed his clothing. He placed his pants back in the closet and took a whiff out of his shirt. It smelled a bit fresh still so he placed it back in his dresser. He tried saving money every day, one way or another. Reusing his clothing was something he learned growing up. He then laid in bed and turned off all his lights and his heater on, since the temperatures were going to drop overnight. Alex shut his eyes after covering himself up with his newly washed quilt and thanked God for a great day and all of his blessings. He then fell asleep as he heard the neighborhood dogs barking.

The following day, Alex arose to the sound of sirens in his neighborhood. There was a heavy presence of law enforcement a few houses down from his. He looked out of his window and observed the SWAT team suiting up to serve a search warrant. A uniformed official came up to his front door and knocked. Alex went to go open up and see what was going on. When he swung the door open, the officer introduced himself and advised him, "Sir, we're serving a search warrant down the street. Please remain inside your home until we resolve the issue for your own safety."

Alex inquired, "What's going on officer? Is everything alright? Am I in danger?"

The officer answered, "I can't share any details with you. Just stay inside and don't come out especially to interfere with our situation." The officer turned around and walked off to advise the next-door neighbor the same.

Alex shut his door and made himself a pot of coffee as he stared out his window being nosey. He witnessed the SWAT team enter the home after dispersing flash grenades. His whole street was closed up by the police and they weren't allowing anyone in or out. His phone rang and he answered it. It was Marisol on the other end asking him why his neighborhood was locked down. Alex informed her, "I don't know darling. The SWAT team just broke down the door to my neighbor's house across the street and they barged in. Some police officer came and told me not to go outside for my own safety. That's all I know so far."

Marisol questioned, "Are you hiding under your bed or staring out the window being nosey?" She chuckled.

Alex uttered, "I'm not hiding. I am watching out from my window to see what is going on though."

Marisol said, "I knew it. Take video footage of what's going on so I can at least see for myself."

Alex replied, "And how am I supposed to do that while speaking to you on the phone?"

Marisol stated, "You're right. Well, I'm right around the corner being blocked off by the police from going to your house. I was going to scare you awake but I'm sure the cops beat me to it, huh?"

Alex responded, "Why do you like to startle me? Yes, they beat you to it. They woke me up with all the commotion they had going on a few minutes ago."

Marisol told him, "I like scaring you because of your reactions. I should record you so you'll see for yourself and maybe upload the content to the internet so you could become an instant celebrity."

Alex commented, "You better not record me and post the videos online. Oh my, they just escorted the neighbor in handcuffs outside. They should be clearing the scene soon. I'll let them know to search your car for drugs and pat search you as well." He laughed.

About ten minutes after the apprehension of his neighbor, the police opened the street back up and allowed Marisol to drive to his home. When she pulled into his driveway, Alex was standing by his front door. Marisol parked and got out with a bag in hand. She walked up to the front door and Alex let her in. He greeted her with a kiss and embraced her in his arms. She closed the door behind her and they walked to his kitchen. Marisol opened up the bag she had brought and handed him a breakfast burger with tater tots and a coffee. She retrieved the same for herself out of the bag and they sat down to eat. Marisol asked, "So did you find out why they arrested your neighbor?" After Alex thanked her for breakfast.

Alex answered, "Nope, I sure didn't. Must have been a serious crime he committed since the SWAT came for him."

Marisol replied, "I wonder what he did. Your neighborhood is peaceful enough to leave valuables outside and not have them stolen. I can't believe what just happened."

Alex sipped his coffee and uttered, "I know. I've been living here for years and this is the first time I see the police out here arresting someone."

Marisol stated, "Did you like your food? I woke up craving it and thought I'd come and bring you some so we could eat together as we are now. It's occurring just as it did in my head when the thought surfaced."

Alex commented, "Yes, it's very tasty darling. Thank you for thinking of me and wishing to spend this moment together." He leaned over to kiss her.

After they wrapped up their first meals of the day, Alex jumped in the shower. As he washed up, his friend Xavier called him. Alex had his phone connected to a speaker where he was listening to music. Alex had the speaker answer the call. Xavier shouted, "Hey bro! Are you coming over today to eat my food again? Because I'm not going to be in. I spent the night over at some girls place and probably gonna stay here again as well."

Alex replied, "That's cool man. No worries brother, Marisol is actually here and brought breakfast. I too will probably be spending the entire day with her."

Xavier uttered, "Oh, nice. Tell her I said hi. Well see you some other day bro." "Will do, alright, see you," said Alex as they hung up the call and he continued to shower.

When Alex concluded his shower, he got dressed. He and his girl left his place and went to watch a movie at the cinemas. They spent the whole day together enjoying each other's company. After the movies, they went to the mall to walk around and build an appetite. Marisol loved to shop so before they had lunch, she had several bags in her hands of new things she had purchased. Alex had built patience in his past to not fuss about her shopping addiction. When they began feeling hungry, they both decided to go to the cafeteria at the mall to grab a bite.

When they got to the cafeteria, there were many options to choose from. Alex took charge since he knew Marisol was indecisive. He pulled her hand to follow him towards a chinese restaurant. They placed their order with a young lady who greeted them and asked if they needed assistance. Alex paid and they both grabbed their cups and filled them up at the beverage dispenser. From there, they picked an empty table and took a seat as they waited for their food to be ready. Marisol was looking through her purchases already thinking of returning a few. It was something common for her to do. Over spend and regret it afterwards then return items to not fall behind on her cost of living. The young lady behind the counter walked over towards their table with their meals. She removed them off of a tray she used to transport them and placed them in front of them. She then asked, "Is there anything else I can get for you all?"

Alex replied, "No, thank you very much."

The young woman uttered, "Let me know if there is then and enjoy your food." As she walked away.

Marisol and Alex dug into their plates and devoured their sustenance. Marisol took a break from scarfing her feast and Asked Alex, "You think after we finish eating, we can go return some of the things I got?"

Alex froze as he was about to stuff his mouth and stated, "Did you overspend again?"

Marisol commented, "You know me very well and I did. I always tell myself not to, but get lost in the moment and do it anyway."

Alex shook his head and said, "Yeah, no problem. Even though I warned you as usual you still managed to go against your own advice and mine." He continued eating his food, foreseeing this moment which didn't upset him one bit.

When they were done, they threw their plates and cups in the trash. She grabbed her bags and they both headed back to the stores to return some items. They proceeded to each store to get her money back.

When they finished, they strolled out of the mall and headed to his vehicle. They got in his car and drove back to his place. On their way to his home, Marisol thanked him for not getting upset at her for not listening and having to put up with her bad choices. He let her know he loved her and supported her even with her flaws. She leaned over and kissed him.

When they got back to his place, they exited the automobile and entered his residence. As soon as they did, she rushed him. She kissed him and grabbed his crotch then directed him towards his room. When they got to his bedroom, she threw him on top of his bed and removed his clothes. She took hers off as well and then went down on him. She called him daddy every single time she popped his shaft out of her oral cavity.

Alex's body was found unresponsive as he was believed to be alive. The whole day he had envisioned was fabricated through the last of his cerebral functions and stored memory. After he purchased those items at the thrift store, he fell asleep with his newly washed quilt and never woke up. He didn't realize this since he was a positive individual who thrived from negative instances.

The quilt he had purchased had been cursed by several witches from medieval times. It had been gifted to many kings in order to overthrow their power. This quilt had taken many lives before. Its curse was never broken since nobody knew of it. It had survived through many years and made its way to the second-hand store after its last owner passed away.

The quilt would wrap the person around comfortably keeping them warm during the night. Once the individual was resting, it would wrap around the person's face and asphyxiate them. Making it seem as they suddenly died in their sleep. Who in their right mind would suspect a quilt possessed the power of killing someone? The unfathomable conclusion was never annotated or taken into consideration.

After Alex's funeral, his family and friends cleared up his belongings from his home. His mother was next of kin and she sold his property and took over his two businesses. The remainder of his personal belongings were donated to thrift stores. The quilt made its way back to the second-hand retailer where it had come from. It still hangs on a rack waiting to be taken home to repeat the process.

CHAPTER 19
THE END OF THE WORLD.

World war three had commenced. Nation versus nation, kingdom against kingdom. There were many casualties across the lands as armies faced armies. Leading to far greater deaths than ever recorded in history, from both military and civilians. It came out of nowhere following political disagreements fueled by pride. People who were against the battle rebelled and began their own civil war- fighting their governments. They attempted to overthrow their leaders, attacking military installations as well as federal buildings. In a last-minute decision to gain control, one of the leading countries launched the first nuclear bomb. Their desperate action began a chain of events which left devastation all over the globe. Other countries returned fire with their own nukes. Most of the inhabitants were wiped out. What once was a beautiful place to live, became an apocalyptic scene.

Groups of militants gathered and continued fighting each other for control. During the nuclear strikes, the temple in Jerusalem was destroyed. Soon after its prophetic confirmation, there were earthquakes, tsunamis, tornados, volcanic eruptions and great storms which swept the earth. Famine arose from all this turmoil. The survivors of men's battles and mother nature's fury, forged for food. Nourishment was scarce and had become another reason to fight over, amongst the clans of survivors. The terrain they resided on looked like hell. Fire, smoke and ashes had replaced grass, dirt and asphalt. The sun hadn't been seen in months from all the pollution of the bombings. satellites' fell from the sky and there was no form of communication. All internet, television and radio stations were inoperable. Besides several groups who transmitted to each other via CB radios. There was a cloud of smoke lingering over the land hindering sunrays. Giant demons fell from the sky standing at around thirty feet tall. This was the beginning of armageddon.

A mountain of fire hit the sea and turned it to blood. A third of the sea creatures were wiped out. A third of the ships were destroyed as its wave of impact stretched across the water and made it to the land. It left a huge crater which sucked up just about all the water from the sea. The aftermath of such a catastrophic event, eliminated another large number of human beings and creatures.

One of the groups pressing forward was led by a man known as Jud. His group of survivors numbered nineteen. They lived underneath in a bunker, hidden from the destruction above. They had built an elaborate community. There was a water well right in the middle of their bunker which kept them hydrated. Some of the only suitable water to consume since it came from deep within the ground and had no access to the contaminants outside. They also had grown edible plants which required minimal sunlight and water. They had several animals and bred them for food. An arsenal of weaponry was near the entrance to their bunker, ready to be picked up and used for defense. A large stash of canned and dry goods was their treasure. Most of which they had scavenged above ground. In order to head up to forge, they had to use gas masks or oxygen tanks they had retrieved from a store which was partially destroyed. They also had to suit up in hazmat gear or anti-radioactive bodysuits. Something they'd only do when they had no other option. They rarely got involved with combat. Their priority was survival and peace.

Jud and his group or as he called them, "Family," were reproducing. There were eight women and had already bred a pair of homo-sapiens within a few years since they merged and hid from the chaos up above. Three children were part of their clan and two infants of which accounted for their nineteen members. Jud had taken charge of the gang since he was the rightful owner of the bunker. He met some of the members while scavenging for food. Three women he saved from a group of rebels who were about to rape them. A few others stumbled to the bunker and knocked for help. His brother and ex-wife were with him when all hell broke loose and took refuge underground by his side. He was a retired special unit service man. He had been trained on how to survive and fight by the government. He also served in several wars and special operations while enlisted. His resume spoke for itself and his expertise and experience in the matter, made it clear he was the leader.

They were in the safety of the bunker preparing a meal in the middle of the day. Everyone had a smile on their face since they had grown tight over the time they had spent with each other. They coexisted together for approximately two and a half years. The women were attending the plants and animals as Jud and his brother cooked up some meat from a rat infestation, they had taken care of. The children played, running around pretending they were shooting each other. Then out of nowhere, they all went mute. Their surroundings began to shake violently. Debris fell from the ceiling. Someone had detonated a grenade outside near or right over their bunker. They heard gunfire and a loud thud at the metallic vault chamber door in the entrance. Jud hushed everyone and said, "Everyone stay calm and get ready. I'm going to check who's out there." He ran up a flight of stairs leading to the entrance, grabbed an AR and checked through the peephole. His brother checked through a periscope.

Jud observed a wounded rebel sitting on top of the vault door. He also glanced at several militants fighting for control including giant demons. He stayed there watching, then saw three uniformed men execute the one sitting on top of the door ordered by a demon. He looked down and witnessed some of his family standing worriedly under the stairs. He gave them a hand signal to be quiet and stay put. Jud returned his view to the peephole and observed the men depart the area. They had not noticed the door to the bunker or weren't interested in it. Once they had left the area, Jud called his brother over and they both suited up to head outside.

They opened the door and creeped out to make sure there was no one around. Another man looking through the periscope cleared any danger. They exited the bunker and began retrieving all the weapons and ammunition from the casualties left behind. After picking up everything they went to get, they headed back to the bunkers entrance. There was a wounded rebel still clinging to life. He asked Jud, "Can you help me?"

Jud laid eyes on him and saw he was bleeding pretty bad, then replied, "We can't.

We don't have medical staff to attend to your wounds... Sorry man."

Jud's brother - Kain- stated, "We can't leave him out here to die alone. Let's take him with us and see what we can do." Jud was cautious and pondered a bit.

Jud uttered, "Fine, but you're going to tend to him. He'll be your responsibility." Kain responded, "I'll take care of him. Help me pick him up."

Both men carried the injured rebel and took him inside their bunker. As soon as they went in, they shut the vault door back up. They frisked the rebel to make sure he had no weapons on him. Some of the others assisted them to carry the rebel to one of the free beds they had. Jud went back to cooking while his brother stayed with the newcomer.

The women grabbed the weapons and ammunition and placed them with the rest. Kain began treating the man's wounds. He removed his shirt off of him and saw he had been shot in the torso, shoulder and back. He asked one of the females to grab him some water and boil it. He then left the guy laying down as he retrieved a bottle of alcohol they had in the back by the treasure of food. Kain returned rapidly and began cleaning up the man's gunshot wounds. As he washed the blood off with soap and water, he felt to see if he could feel any lodged rounds. He felt some and had one of the females grab him some pliers they had in a tool set. When she brought them back, he ran the tip through a candle flame and inserted them through the man's injuries under his flesh.

Kain began removing bullet fragments from the man's body. He had taken out two and couldn't get the one in his shoulder out. Afterwards, Kain sewed him back and spilled alcohol over the skin sutures. He then handed the guy some pain medication and let him rest.

Jud concluded his rat soup and the group began to feast. Kain served his new friend a bowl. He handed it to him and the rebel ate some before going back to sleep. As they all ate, the children curiously surrounded the rebel as he healed with rest. Their mothers told them to leave the man alone and eat their food. The militant was safe now and lucky to be alive. Jud and Kain sat across each other at their large table. Jud asked Kain, "Did you ask him who those men were? Why did they kill his friends and what did they want from them?"

Kain commented, "No, he hardly had any energy to let me treat him. He seems bad but I hope he makes it through the night."

Jud responded, "Yeah, as long as he doesn't try to take over the family or hurt any of us. Otherwise, he definitely won't make it out of here alive." They continued eating their soup.

Everyone finished feasting and the woman began washing dishes. The guys were corresponding to another group over the radio. They also were fixing a few apparatuses they had found and thought may be useful. The kids began some of their lessons. One of the men in the clan was a teacher and had several books he'd educate the adolescents with. Some of the other guys in the gang were bringing up water from the well and confining it into jugs for later use. The rebel was still out. Kain sat next to him taking his pulse off his wrist and covering him up with a blanket.

Jud was cleaning up the weapons they picked up from the other rebels who died in the gun battle. He glanced at his brother caring for the man and hoped the guy would appreciate his dedication if he survived his injuries. One of the mothers of the infant's breast fed her child, as she laid in her bed reading a novel. The only teen in their group was sweeping the debris that fell from the ceiling after the shock waves from the explosions. Jud's ex walked up to him and asked, "You think it was a good idea to bring that wounded man in here?"

Jud stared at her and replied, "No, but Kain wanted to rescue him and he's responsible for anything which happens."

Cristina, his ex-uttered, "What if he has diseases, we have not come across yet and contaminates us all? Or if he's just out to infiltrate us before turning us over to his squad?"

Jud told her, "Look! I'm no longer married to you to have to listen to all your preoccupations. Go ask Kain about him and get under his skin, not mine."

He got up and headed to the restroom leaving her surprised with his response. The men on the CB radio informed Jud's men that another group of survivors had reported large military armies around the area. They claimed the armies were searching for survivors and groups of rebels. Nobody knew exactly what their motive was. Jud had one of the men inquire to the other group if they had any more information regarding the military presence. The guy went ahead and questioned the responding party over the radio. The answer remained unknown. All they transmitted was that the military were heavily armored and in convoys of thirty men and several demons. There was another group of survivors who claimed they had witnessed a battalion of around two hundred men, patrolling the remnants of the town. They then ended their transmission to reserve the power to their radio units. Jud and his family used solar powered units and had a few generators to provide their bunker with energy. But there wasn't much sunlight to power the solar panels or fuel to run the generators all day long.

Class ended for the children and they played some more before they had to go to bed. The wounded rebel was still asleep. Everyone was picking up the place. The females washed clothes and hung them across a wire line to dry up. Jud avoided Cristina at all costs. She had been bugging him for days already being bossy and nosey- questioning his decisions. Had he been heartless, he would have already expelled her from the bunker. He and Kain were doing inventory on their treasure of canned and dry goods as well as an extensive selection of books. Once they all finished their chores, they went to bed. The kids giggled as everyone shut their eyes. Jud turned off the power and Cristina ignited some candles to not remain in total darkness. They all then fell asleep for the night.

During the middle of the night, the rebel woke up whaling. He was having visions of what he faced up in the new world. He woke up everyone with his shouting. The infants helped scare everyone out of their sleep as they began to cry out too. Jud and Kain ran up to the newcomer and began asking him what was wrong. The guy began saying, "You guys are lucky to be down here safely. Up there in the new world, there's nothing but war. I'm sorry I woke everyone up. It's the traumas I've lived through that seep into my dreams at night."

Jud told the man, "The good thing is you're safe with us now. We are aware of the lifestyle survivors are faced with out there."

The rebel replied, "Thanks again for helping me out. I don't know how to thank you enough for saving me from my death."

Kain inquired, "What's your name brother?" The militant uttered, "Cole."

Kain responded, "Well Cole, you're very welcome but tell us, who were those men after you and your group? And what did they want from you all?"

The man stated, "Those are his men. some people pleasing hero who surfaced out of the shadows and has been establishing peace amongst nations and rebel forces. He and his men have been reconstructing the holy temple in jerusalem. They have been taking prisoners from many of the rebels and survivors. Those who oppose joining him are killed. He is also accompanied and defended by demons." Jud asked, "Have you seen this character? Would you be able to describe him for us?"

Cole commented, "No, I've never seen him not even in pictures. All I know is that those who are aware of him have been calling him the antichrist. That's why my team and I were fighting his men. Thing is, his army is well equipped with weapons and roam in larger numbers than any group of survivors. They attacked our neighboring campgrounds during the night. My team and I ran off but they tracked us down. I don't know if any of my brothers are alive. All the ones in my team are dead outside your bunker." He groaned out of pain as he tried to stand up. Jud told him, "Don't try and get up man. You're going to hurt yourself more." He held him down.

Cole said, "I just thought I'd take off now and start burying my brothers before some wild beast eats them."

Kain uttered, "Nonsense man, you're welcome here as long as you come in peace. You'd have to make a full recovery before going back out there to bury your friends." Kain and Jud looked at each other then, Jud told the man, "Go back to sleep brother. You need all the rest you can get."

The infants' mothers had breastfed them and the rest of the clan had gone back to sleep already. Jud fathered one of the babies and Kain the other. The rebel closed his eyes back up after Kain handed him some pain medication. Jud and Kain went to kiss their kid's goodnight and laid in their beds afterwards. What the newcomer had informed them of lingered in their heads as they dozed off.

The following day, the group arose to the sound of tanks and heavy trucks driving over their bunker. Jud jumped out of his bed and ran to the cliche of weapons. Kain and the other men followed. Cole was still asleep. The children and woman got up and ran towards the back of the bunker where there was an emergency shelter. The females who didn't have kids also joined the men and armed themselves. Kain observed up above through the periscope. He informed them all that there were military troops up above investigating the dead rebels. Kain said, "They're going through their pockets and looking at their patches probably to identify them. There's like fifty of them all armed up to their necks. They've got tanks and trucks. The demons are feasting on the deceased."

Jud hushed everyone and uttered, "We need to be as quiet as could be. We don't want to let them know we're down here. They've got enough firepower to burst our door open and take us all."

Kain commented, "They haven't discovered our bunker yet. They seem to be moving on." They heard the convoy of vehicles proceeding on their rounds.

Jud asked Kain, "Are they gone out of sight?"

Kain answered, "Affirmative. They've moved on westward." He then got off the periscope and went to notify the women the coast was clear.

Jud stated, "I'm glad they didn't discover our bunker. Also, that we picked up the weapons of the deceased rebels before they did. Kain, get on the radio and warn the other groups that there's a convoy out there right now and may head their way." Kain ran towards the CB radio and reporter over what Jud ordered him to do then described first-hand what he saw through the periscope.

The other groups thanked him for relaying the information to them. They said they'd be on high alert. Kain went to grab his child from his mother so she could bathe. Jud and two others gathered eggs from the chickens to begin preparing breakfast for them all. Meanwhile Jud and the other guys cracked open the eggs over a large skillet, Jud asked one of them, "Hey Isaiah, you grew up with religious parent's, right?"

Isaiah answered, "Yes, I attended church every Sunday and studied the bible because of my parents' upbringings.

"Jud replied, "That's great you did. You know, the rebel we took in was telling Kain and I last night of this antichrist who's formed an army. He has been helping make peace with nations and rebels. He also began to reconstruct the temple in jerusalem. What do you think about that?"

Isaiah began recalling the scriptures of the bible to address the question. He advised Jud of the coincidence and how relevant this person in question's actions correlate with what is written in the bible. He began educating Jud on what he knew off of reading the bible. Jud paid close attention to what Isaiah told him as they continued cooking. It was somewhat of a refresher course for Jud since he had read the bible once himself. He did believe in God though, yet didn't go to church. Even the other guy helping them, listened to their conversation. That's when Jud realized they were living through prophetic times which had been warned in the bible. Mathew 16:3 states, "You know how to interpret the appearance of the sky but you cannot interpret the signs of the times," uttered Isaiah.

Jud was intrigued by what he was relearning with Isaiah. It was now all making sense. They finished preparing breakfast and began serving the group. Once they all had some food on their plate, they took a seat and Jud asked Isaiah to bless their meal. Everyone remained silenced as Isaiah began praying. Once he said amen, they all repeated those words and began to consume their first meal of the day. Jud appointed Isaiah, minister of the clan. He asked him to begin reading and teaching them about the word of Christ. Isaiah gladly accepted his new role and title. Jud regretted not listening to him when he joined the group. Isaiah had warned them about what was happening. He had an inclination of the turmoil being part of biblical manifestations. It was then that Jud recalled listening to a voice speaking to him about God and warning him of what was to come. A voice he ignored believing it was a figment of his imagination.

After they finished their meals, they all sat down in front of Isaiah as he began to read them scriptures from the bible. They had a few bibles in hand and some of the adults read along what Isaiah uttered. Just as Isaiah came to a closing statement, their CB radio had chatter. Jud interrupted the mass and ran to hear what was going on. On the other end of the radio frequency, one of the other groups sounded to be in distress. The person transmitting shouted, "They've come to take us! The army has infiltrated our bunker and killed those uncooperative with their orders! Oh my God, what is this?

A man on a horse is fighting them back and destroying them!" The transmission then cut off.

Kain was next to Jud and asked, "Did he just say a man on a horse was fighting the army?"

Jud answered, "I heard the same thing. How is a horse still around after all the bombings, is what I'm wondering."

Isaiah butted in and said, "He could be witnessing the four horsemen that God sent during the apocalypse. He may be talking about the fourth one which is death."

Jud questioned, "So what shall we do?" Staring at Isaiah for an answer.

Isaiah replied, "We need to turn ourselves to Christ. Believe in him and his resurrection. We need to ask him for forgiveness of our sins as we seek him and his word. We need to stop sinning as we learn his way and let him be king on earth as he is in heaven. Other than that, we can't do much but continue praying. He's in control of everything and we must not contest his power."

Kain stated, "We should go help the group which is being attacked." He was about to take off but Jud grabbed him by his shirt and commented, "No, we need to remain here together and pray for them! If we go, we might not return. It's too risky for us to even step foot outside while the army is out there waiting to shoot us down." One of the other men was attempting to get a hold of the group which called in but they didn't respond.

Jud asked Isaiah to continue his sermon. He asked that they all pray for the group which was under attack. Isaiah began preaching off of the top of his head. The entire bunker quieted down and listened to Isaiah speak. They held each other's hands forming a circle and prayed for their neighbors. Then they heard someone on the radio say, "It's a miracle! The horsemen saved us from the army. We have been spared from death by the man on the pale horse. Thank you, God!"

Kain went to speak to the person on the radio, to ask him more about their occurrence. Jud asked Isaiah for clarification on the matter. Isaiah told Jud, "The fourth horseman on a pale horse is death." He then fell to his knees and began to pray.

Jud did the same and gave thanks to God for saving the other group of survivors. Kain came back and bowed to his knees as well. The entire group copied their leaders and they all kneeled down to pray and give thanks. They prayed for victory for their neighbors. They gave thanks for them being spared from the rapture. Their group had begun becoming true followers of Christ.

The rebel woke up screaming and Jud got up to see what was going on with him. Kain checked his temperature and realized he had a fever. He was in a lot of pain. Kain handed him some medication to soothe his pain and bring down his body temperature. The rebel was trembling but uttered, "The horseman is out there again. He's fighting the army of demons all alone. I've seen him defeat an entire platoon of around one hundred men. Then I heard a voice telling me to turn to God. I looked around but didn't see anyone. I felt I was going crazy so I dropped to my knees and prayed. I believe in God and I see what we're living through is the apocalypse." He then fainted without warning.

Kain tried waking him up but he was out cold. Jud began fanning air towards him. Cristina ran over with a rag damped in cold water and began running it over his head. They had the kids turn around to not see them remove the man's clothing. They picked him up and took him to a bath where they placed him inside to cool down his temperature. Kain remained by the man's side as he held his head above water so he wouldn't drown. Jud asked Isaiah to pray for Cole. They all joined in prayer for his condition to improve. When his fever declined, they took him out of the bath, dried and clothed him then placed him back on the bed.

Up above them and their safety was another war. I am's army was going around hunting and murdering christians. He had already eliminated around a thousand men and women who followed Christ. This was a religious genocide. I am, had written his own bible and was attempting to overthrow the old testament or any other form of religious belief so he could push his onto the people. He was trying to erase Christ and or any other type of God as he manipulated everyone to believe he was God himself. His men had strict orders to also burn any other form of religious books or articles they'd come across. So, there was blood shed in high quantities all around the world. His power reached every corner and crack in the land where men dwelled. All hell had broken loose as he rained his wrath upon the innocent. Fire filled the grounds and smoke continued to cover the day. The roads had been doused in red once more. Word had spread throughout the groups of survivors about the inequities lived by the forsaken.

All around the globe, people were being forced to follow I am. Against their will, morals and beliefs. He had some great plan to rule the earth but it required violence to convince them all. The peace he had promised was only temporary. Only lasting until he unveiled his true purpose and identity. He and his men lived in a castle far from the destruction they had created. But even then, the sunlight wouldn't shine upon them. Their community was filled with sinners who didn't repent. They'd engage in orgy worship rituals with the demons, and just about any other form of satanic activities. They'd rape and torture some of their captives who didn't renounce Christ. Forcing them to praise I am as God almighty of the wicked and evil and the new lord of the earth. His men and followers were marked with the mark of the beast. On their foreheads they wore a broadening scorched on their flesh like cattle. They'd hear voices to turn away from sin but blocked them out and continued on their dark paths. Fights would erupt amongst them and the demons constantly.

Later that day, Cole's fever returned. Everyone in the bunker tried helping. They put him in a cold bath. There was no ice to make it colder. They gave him medicine and fed him soup. His body began to shut down in the middle of their efforts to cancel his fever. Isaiah was present praying for him. Kain felt overwhelmed since he was caring for him. He felt responsible that Cole wasn't getting any better. Jud noticed his brother's slanted look and told him, "You've tried your best. Given the conditions in which we found him and the lack of medical equipment we have. There isn't much more you or anyone here can do."

Kain replied, "I thought I'd be able to save him. I've failed at my own expectations." He held Cole's hand in his as he began seeing Cole's pigmentation turn pale.

Jud told Kain, "It's not your fault brother. Don't take it personally and let it get to your head. His time has come beyond our control, it's God's will."

Cole took his last breath unable to heal from his wounds. He had gotten an infection from his internal bleeding and succumbed to his injuries sustained in battle. Everyone there mourned for a man they knew little of. A person who had recently joined their group through unfortunate events. They held silence as Jud requested Isaiah pray for Cole's departure. After a small service was held in his honor and name, Jud dressed him back up in the military clothing he wore when they found him. They knew it was best to not keep his soon to decompose body there. Kain and Jud carried Cole's corpse back up to where they located him. They opened the hatch door and walked to where he once was. They then laid him down on the ground, next to a bible he carried on him yet they didn't see nor did the army find. Kain picked up the bible and placed it under Cole's armas which they had crossed over his chest out of respect. Jud and Kain paid their farewell to Cole and went back to their bunker. They secured the hatch door and returned to see everyone's eyes teary. It was a sad moment for all.

It took the group time to get back on track but when they did, they were back to their routine. Jud and the men began to cook and the women cleaned up the home and washed linens. The kids played around the bunker until Kain took out some board games and taught them how to play dominos. He kept them well entertained up until it was lunch time. Then they all congregated and gave thanks to God for their meal. They consumed their feast in harmony with smiles on their faces. As they wrapped up their feast, they heard rumbles above them. Kain ran to see what was going on through the periscope. As he did so, there was a loud bang.

The military had located their bunker and exploded the door open. A few women ran towards the back to hide. Everyone else had geared up for battle. Jud and his people fired upon anyone peeking through the door. They held their ground for some time. Then someone tossed a hand grenade into the bunker. When it detonated, it took out two females and one man who were at the bottom of the stairwell shooting upwards. Everyone else hit the floor and covered their heads with their arms. The army men entered and took over the bunker. They Shot and killed Isaiah after seeing he carried a bible in his hands. They then burned the bible. They disarmed Jud and his family at gunpoint. A figure walked down the stairs ordering his men to ransack the place. They began destroying everything and carrying out the canned and dry goods. They found the rest of the bibles and burned them too. The commanding officer questioned, "Who's in charge of this group of scavengers?"

Jud looked at him and stated, "I am."

The officer replied, "He sure is," with a smirk on his face as he shot Jud in the head as the demons laughed and ate from the dead.

Kain jumped up fighting his way towards his brother's body. He had tears in his eyes as he held Jud in his arms. He looked up at the commanding officer and shouted, "Why'd you kill my brother? I'm going to kill you and all your men in return if you don't kill me too." He placed his brother down and jumped up.

As the officer viewed Kain about to attack him, he shot him in the head as well. He then uttered, "You didn't have to warn me twice of your intentions. Problem solved." He looked at his men holding all of the group hostage and asked, "Who else here is a believer of Christ?"

Everyone in the group admitted their faith and the officer ordered his men to shoot them all. They located the females with the infants and took them up to the officer. He asked them if they too believed in Christ. One said she did and the other denied her faith. The officer shot the one who didn't renounce her Christianity. He ordered his men to take the children and the only female left and burn the place down after taking all the food with them. The demons had devoured all the dead corpses.

When they were all out of the bunker, they set bombs inside and detonated them. The strong bunker collapsed from within and even the entrance sealed off after the implosion. The officer and his army took the children and the woman with them. They headed back to the castle where their leader lived.

Along their journey there, they all heard voices telling them to turn away from sin and follow Christ. The demons taunted the woman. It wasn't something out of the ordinary to listen to those voices but for some reason this time they were louder. Some of the army men in desperation cut out their ears. The commanding officer kept ignoring the voices, blocking them off with thoughts of evil.

When they got to the castle, the woman's child was snatched away from her. The infants were handed over to I am. The woman was tortured and raped in a dark dungeon where other prisoners were chained. The place felt like hell. It was hot since there was no ventilation. Everyone there screamed from pain and fear. The women regretted dishonoring her faith. She thought death would have been a better outcome than where she was now but it was too late to retract her testament.

I am was pleased to receive the children. He hadn't seen any babies in many years. Most children born in the apocalypse had not made it since they faced harsh times of famine. I am began listening to the voices warning him again. They got louder and louder so he cut his ears off too and fell to the ground in agony yet with a smile on his face. Little did he know what was to follow.

An army of Christians came and waged war on his men who were unaware. They crept up on them all as they indulged in alcohol and partying. When I am found out there were intruders, he ran with the kids to a spaceship he had for such a case. His plan was still in effect. He boarded the ship with the kids and turned the engine on. He saw through the windows that his men were losing the war. He began flying his ship away from the castle. Its power maxed out and went airborne. He then looked down and observed the horseman decapitating all his men and demons. I am dropped the last nuclear bomb over his castle and shot away on his ship. The ship trembled from the wave of impact. He thought he was getting away from it all but he never imagined what came next.

The horseman flew above the mushroom cloud and followed the ship. He then landed on top of it as it soared up the sky. The horseman broke through the window and grabbed I am. He was tossed back down to where his castle once stood. The horseman took the children and disappeared into the heavens. That was the end of I am's reign.

I am had planned to overtake what was left of the world and dominate it by making everyone think he was God. He also had a backup plan for when things didn't turn out the way he expected. That's why he was happy to see the children. A male and female which he was going to raise with his religion. He was hoping to begin life with those kids as he abandoned his castle. He was headed to another planet with them. He never saw it coming though even after plotting his back up.

All life occurred between the gap of the 483 prophetic years and the last seven had been forgotten. After the evidence of the crucifixion and resurrection. Then the destruction of the temple and the dispersion of the jewish people. The holocaust had proven Ezikiel's words to be true. Many rose as false prophets and then came I am as the antichrist. Proving the testament correct. During the tribulation, all Christians who were executed laid their bodies without life upon dirt. Their spirits continued with their purpose. Those were the voices everyone heard. They were warning everyone ahead of time just as they did before the apocalypse. God granted them that authority on earth. After the elimination of I am, God took those spirits to heaven and granted them eternal life. This was the end of the seventh year and those who didn't listen to the spirits were left in the burning hell on earth.

The first period was of death and destruction which the world had never seen before with tribulation. During the millennium,

God granted peace on earth for a thousand years. He also granted eternity for those who accepted him as their lord and savior. Those who refused, were forsaken to hell on earth. There was no one left as all mankind was wiped out. This is what he meant by creating peace on earth due to the extinction of mankind from destroying it any further. For a thousand years mother nature felt peace before life emerged once more.

THE END.